Fate Rode the Wind

An American Story of Hope and Fortitude

LARRY D. QUICK

iUniverse LLC
Bloomington

FATE RODE THE WIND
AN AMERICAN STORY OF HOPE AND FORTITUDE

iUniverse books may be ordered through booksellers or by contacting:

iUniverse
1663 Liberty Drive
Bloomington, IN 47403
www.iuniverse.com
1-800-Authors (1-800-288-4677)

ISBN: 978-1-4917-3226-7 (sc)
ISBN: 978-1-4917-3225-0 (hc)
ISBN: 978-1-4917-3224-3 (e)

Library of Congress Control Number: 2014906961

Printed in the United States of America.

iUniverse rev. date: 04/28/2014

Dedication: I dedicate this book to my parents, Lilbern and Gladys Quick for their unconditional love, support and all the understanding they gave me to explore the world and to reach my dreams.

Acknowledgements: I thank my wife, Peggy Georgalis Quick for her patience, wise criticisms and superb editing. This book could never have been completed without her encouragement. And to my daughter, Lara Markelle Moody. I appreciate the precious time she spent sifting through the story's contents.

June 1941
The New Pony

Midmorning on a humid Saturday in the early summer of nineteen-forty-one, two young boys, one nine and the other four, wrestled in the broad swath of grass in the front yard of a large, white farmhouse that sat at the end of a long gravel lane a quarter mile north of a small, Midwestern farming community. It was a windless day that enabled sound to carry over long distances, and as the two played, they would stop from time to time, stand up and look out across the cow pasture fronting the house when one or the other of them would detect a vehicle traveling from town on the one-way, concrete-slab highway. From their behavior, one might easily discern that while playing, they were really outside anxiously waiting for someone to arrive.

"Dad, Mom," the older of the two, grass stained and sweaty, finally shouted up at the kitchen window high above them where their mother was working at the sink washing dishes. "I think he's coming. There's a truck coming from town that's pulling a horse trailer behind it," he exclaimed loudly and ran back out to the edge of the yard to watch the truck draw closer.

"It's them…it really is them, isn't it?" the excited younger boy asked his brother hoping to get some assurance from him. "I hope it's them," he mumbled to himself when his brother didn't respond right away.

Their mother's voice could be heard through the window yelling into the rear rooms, "Ethan! Marianne! Your brothers think they see a truck coming out of town that's bringin' the pony." Her announcement was instantly followed with squeals of excitement from her thirteen-year-old daughter, Marianne, who came rushing through the house, out the back entrance and banged the screen open; she ran wildly into the yard and focused her eyes on the distant truck pulling a horse trailer. She fought to contain her excitement once she realized that she was seeing what she had been envisioning for several days.

By the time the slow moving truck turned into the farm's long driveway, all six members of the family had gathered in front of the milk cooling shed at the end of the sidewalk. As they watched, the battered, old, 1936 International Harvester truck rattled and lumbered up the long gravel driveway. Printed on the door in bold, white letters was JAY CARTWRIGHT AND SON across the top line and underneath, ATWOOD, ILL in light blue. Riding behind in the dust was an unpainted, two-wheeled, horse trailer that softly swayed through the shallow pot-holes. The mother and kids watched in anticipation to see what kind of pony their father had bought at the sale barn a few days earlier. Several times they had quizzed him and each time he had not offered any information except to tell them that it was a fairly large, white pony with big brown spots. The old truck clattered around the two narrow curves by the garden, pulled up and stopped a few feet away from them in the large circular turnaround for vehicles.

Standing at the front of the family group was Marianne, a petite, brown-haired girl, dressed in white, short, puffy-sleeved dress with a bit of embroidery around the neck and hemmed with a flounce just above the knees. Around the small waist of the dress was a wide band of rose-colored fabric, tied in a loose bow off to the side. Marianne had been trying it on to see if last year's dress still fit when she heard the call from her mother. The very feminine, thirteen-year-old was the pride of her father. She was the main reason he purchased the pony which he had managed to buy only with careful planning and a shrewd bid at the sale barn. Initially he felt guilty about the purchase because it had been a long time since he had bought anything other than the necessities for farming; however, the pony was an early gift for his daughter's birthday and with the family's finances steadily improving, he decided on a spur-of-the-moment to frivolously purchase the pony that had caught his eye.

Dressed in his soiled work bibs and long-sleeved denim shirt, their grey-haired, fair-complexioned, thirty-eight-year old father slouched behind his small cluster of children while their dark-haired mother stood stiffly beside him in her brightly patterned, hand-sewn print dress.

The children rushed over to see more of the pony than just the top of his head, eyes and ears which were partially visible through the wooden slats of the trailer while their father walked around to the driver's side of the truck to greet Mr. Cartwright, who was delivering the pony from the man who had put it up for auction.

"Jay," their father acknowledged Mr. Cartwright who was already stepping down off the running board.

"Mornin, Milburn. It looks to me like your kids are happy with the pony," Jay commented, smiling, eyeing the kids gathered around the trailer eagerly trying to peek in through the slatted sides. "Maybe we oughta let the back gate down and get that little horse out before they start climbin' over the top or dismantlin' my trailer!" he laughed.

The younger boys jumped around in anticipation but Marianne, although in a more reserved way, was the most thrilled with the idea of having a pony and in time she would claim it as hers, which no one would ever dare dispute. She was very fond of the two horses already on the farm and when she had a free moment, she would go to the barn to curry and brush their coats and manes. While she worked, she often carried on conversations and shared secrets with them as if they understood every word she was saying. Horses were some of her best friends and she especially loved feeling their strength when riding on their bare backs. Maude, the biggest, was a large, dark-brown draft horse which, because of her size, the kids only rode out of necessity. Buddy, the other horse, was a Morgan, a smaller breed they used for a variety of purposes around the farm, and the one the kids enjoyed riding the most.

Shifting their feet and moving around to the back, the children maneuvered to get a clear view of the pony as Jay worked to lower the back gate. Marianne, standing slightly to the side, felt the new pony would add to her activities while on the other hand, her father was hopeful the pony might give both of his oldest kids a healthy distraction to keep them settled, maybe not forever but at least for the immediate future. He had recently noticed some restiveness in their behaviors, not unlike what he had felt at their age before he ran off from home. Marianne, he hoped would see the pony as an animal she could lavish with affection and continue to be satisfied with her life on the farm. What her father could not foresee was that although the pony actually would give Marianne something she desired, a welcome opportunity for a little freedom, he didn't foresee that his wife's relentless demands and expectations on her daughter would gradually create more tension between the two of them.

"Stand back!" Mr. Cartwright ordered cheerfully, working with the crossbar that held the back gate up. "I need to lower this thing so you can see your new friend. Look out now! Go on…stand back! We don't want someone ending up with a knot on their head now, do we?" he said, chattering away, teasing as he worked.

The tailgate, once lowered, acted as a ramp. Jay backed the pony out of the trailer as the children bunched excitedly around their father who waited with one hand extended in case he needed to soothe and settle the pony. He had a proud look on his face while his wife of sixteen years pursed her lips in mild disappointment thinking the pony was a waste of hard-earned money and suspected it was somehow going to be a catalyst for unwanted change; just the opposite result her husband expected.

Mr. Cartwright stepped up into the trailer. "Careful boy," he said, patted the pony on the rump and squeezed past him to the front. After untying him, Mr. Cartwright backed the pony down the ramp. "He's all yours, Milburn," he said and handed the bridle over. "Hope you kids have fun and take good care of him," Jay exclaimed, but they were so focused on the pony which was snorting, pawing the gravel and nervously shaking his mane that they didn't hear a word he said.

What Milburn saw on his daughter's face compelled him to hand the pony's bridle to her. "Here, you hold onto him!" her father commanded and she snatched it happily away.

"What are you kids going to name him?" Mr. Cartwright asked pleasantly, stepping down to the ground to lift the tailgate.

Marianne lowered her head as if to study her feet, wrinkled her forehead in thought and then quickly looked up, "Rocky," she answered before anyone else had a chance to offer other suggestions. She glanced around to see if anyone objected and then led him into the yard with her two younger brothers, Leon and Jonathan walking along beside, stroking and patting the sturdy animal.

"I'll get the saddle and his blanket out of the truck and then you kids will be all set," Jay yelled after them and climbed up into the truck's bed.

"Go grab the saddle when Jay hands it down, Ethan," his father directed.

"Okay, Dad!" he said and rushed over to help just as Jay swung the saddle over the side.

Getting ready to leave, Jay checked the trailer one last time. "I can't thank you enough for doin' me the favor of pickin' the horse up on such short notice," Milburn replied. "Tomorrow's Marianne's birthday and I wanted her to have something she'd like," he stated and then added as a correction. "The pony's really for all the kids but I was mainly thinkin' of her!"

"It wasn't no problem for me and more than happy to do it!"

Always fair in his dealings, Milburn asked, "Do I still owe you anythin'?"

"Nothin' more," Jay stated flatly. "You and me both know the seller pays for haulin'. It's been all taken care of. I just wish I had more time to hang around and watch your kids enjoy their new pony but I've got other animals to haul today," Jay stated, slid into the cab, slammed the heavy cab door closed behind him, hung his left arm over the window sill and looked around. "You know," he said and paused, "my kids are all grown up and have flown the nest. I really miss the company of youngsters," he said contemplatively just before he turned over the starter on the truck. He watched briefly out the right side window as the children worked to get their new pony saddled. The starter ground and the engine coughed into life. Jay turned back one last time to Milburn standing in the gravel close by and said, "You're one very lucky man!"

"Thanks again and have a good day," Milburn replied, rapped his knuckles lightly on the outside of the truck door and stepped back out of the way.

"You too," Jay replied, roughly engaged the gears of the truck, winced at the sound, pulled slowly around the circular drive and drove off down the long lane. He smiled at himself in the rearview mirror and felt good about the part he had played in Milburn's purchase of the pony. He glanced into the side mirror and saw the family gathered around the yard. *I think Milburn made a real wise decision buying that pony,* he thought as he recalled what Milburn had expressed about keeping his kids grounded; however, no one could predict the consequences of the father's good intentions.

CHAPTER TWO

The First Ride

"I want to ride him first," Marianne, holding the bridle stated as Ethan cinched up the saddle and she got in position to mount up. The anticipation of riding the pony first was such a strong enticement that it was on the verge of causing a bitter confrontation. The two older siblings eyed each other to see who would back down first. "Please," Marianne pleaded calmly, although it wasn't in her nature to beg, she thought it best because if she insisted, she would probably lose. "Please!" she repeated. Her brother slowly stepped back even though his posture showed he wanted to win. She looked at him with a forced smile. "Please," she said the third time.

He eyed her briefly and very reluctantly shuffled aside. "OK, but only go for a short ride!"

Taking the saddle horn in her left hand, Marianne put her foot in the stirrup and swung smoothly up into the new saddle. She tucked the hem of her dress under her legs to keep it in place, clicked her tongue, tapped the pony lightly with her heels and rode out of the yard, down to end the lane towards the highway where her widowed grandmother's small house stood facing the highway.

Gloria, Marianne's mother, looked down the driveway at her daughter sitting straight, head held high like Joan-of-Arc, riding off into a new adventure. "When Marianne gets back I want you to tell her she still has to finish cleaning the cabinets," their mother informed her husband and three sons. "There's work to do and I don't have time to stand around here," she said to convey guilt on them for the frivolous purchase.

From a young age, Gloria had been faced with family responsibilities that gave her little time to pursue her own interests and it left a lasting impression on her. She was the third of six children to Edward and Minnie Marshfield. From the first day they were married, her parents had struggled to make ends meet and as long as they lived their short lives, it had never changed.

The entire Marshfield clan had a history of tough times and it had infected Gloria like a virus, leaving her prone to insecurities. Seeking employment during a difficult period, her uncle Jim moved to Louisiana to help farm three hundred acres of rice land which the town physician, old Doc Jones, had bought at a low price for speculation sometime back in the early twenties.

Edward, Gloria's father, had not done very well either. Before moving the family to Atwood just before the great depression, where he worked on town maintenance sweeping sidewalks and changing light bulbs in street lights, he had been a farm laborer for several years in Shumway, a village that was little more than a spot in the road just north of Effingham, Illinois.

Out of necessity, Gloria always had responsibilities greater than many people her age; however, she learned that a good work ethic helped acquire a steady job, which in turn brought stability and respect. She helped around the house every day and also worked in town as a domestic for an old couple, and because she had a natural talent for music, she learned to play their organ and could play many songs, especially church songs by ear.

In elementary school she liked composition and enjoyed writing, especially poetry, but she found little time to do her studies because of the family situation, although, she did manage to finish eighth grade. She developed a concept, as people of her status, situation, place and period of time often did that she grew up in, that physical work would give one security while education was secondary for survival. It was this belief that she carried into her married life and it manifested itself into the pattern she used in raising her children.

As if life was not already grim, when she was thirteen both her parents developed tuberculosis and their illness imposed severe restrictions on her. Emma, her older sister, got married; Jessie, the older brother, got a job. This left Gloria with the worry and responsibility of taking care of her sick parents, looking after three younger siblings and doing many of the household chores.

Although many people might get mired down in all that responsibility, she found enough free time to occasionally be out with her friends. On one short excursion from the house, when she was approaching her sixteenth birthday, she met Milburn, the son of a successful farmer. After only one or two dates, they fell in love. It seemed like destiny. One year later and just before her seventeenth birthday they got married in front of the local Justice of the Peace. Two years later the great depression started and by then her union with Milburn had moved her up the social ladder and towards a life of stability.

Milburn watched his wife walk toward the house and pause in front of the flowers blooming in the small plot of tilled soil by their back door. He knew he was an average looking man and it made him proud to have a dark haired, attractive wife that he felt loved him unconditionally.

Turning his attention back to his children he said, "When you're tired of messin' with Rocky, be sure to put him in the stall with the other horses and give him some grain and water."

"Sure," Ethan acknowledged. "Is it okay if I get Buddy out and go for a ride?" he asked, knowing that his father needed his help and was surprised with the answer.

"Do anythin' you want, but if you're gonna ride him maybe you should feed him a few extra oats to keep him happy," his father replied. "And num num num," he mumbled with his unique but infrequent stutter, "you kids can enjoy youselves today and tomorrow afternoon after church but on Monday you'll have to get back to work. There's lots that need to get done around here and I need your help," he stated and walked off towards one of the outbuildings.

Looking down the empty lane, Ethan tried to see some sign of his sister. "I think I'll go look for her," he said and ran for the barn, leaving his bothers wrestling and rolling around on the ground.

"Get off me," Jonathan said when he saw his older brother disappear around a shed. "Where's he going?" he asked, jumped up and ran after Ethan with Leon following close behind.

Down at the end of the lane Marianne rode Rocky over the shallow ditch, across the backyard of her grandmother's house next to the highway and around to the front porch where the fair-skinned, white-haired, plump little grandmother sat on an old, wooden, rocking chair peeling potatoes; a yellow kitten lay curled up asleep at the grandmother's feet. Her first cousin Donald, a tall, big boned, dark haired and handsome seventeen-year-old was busily washing his car in the shade of several oak trees next to the horse tank across the driveway. Donald and his sister, Anna Lee, were wards of their grandmother since typhoid fever had taken their parents eleven years earlier.

Donald saw Marianne ride around the back corner of the house while in the process of throwing a bucket of water over the hood of his nineteen-thirty-four black Chevrolet. "Hi, cousin," he yelled and paused for a moment as he drew more water from the well.

"Hi," she shouted back and waved her arm high in the air.

"Hi, Grandma," Marianne chirped happily and reined in Rocky to a halt next to the porch where her grandmother sat.

"Well, hello," she answered. "What're you up to?"

"Oh," Marianne said, "I thought I'd come by and show you my new pony. Yesterday you said to me that you'd like to see him sometime."

Her grandmother, Susan studied him closely. "His color is sure nice and he's a sturdy lookin' thing, ain't he?" she observed, stopped her chore of peeling potatoes and dropped her paring knife into the bottom of the metal bowl.

"I think so," Marianne said and patted him on the neck affectionately. Rocky tossed his head.

"I like his white coat and big brown spots. And look at them unusual eyes," her grandmother commented. "Each one's a different color, ain't they?"

"Uh huh!" Marianne remarked, reached out and patted Rocky's neck affectionately again.

"I'll just bet you're gonna have all kinda fun ridin' around on him," her grandmother predicted and added with a twinkle in her eyes. "I suppose from now on you're just gonna be as free as a breeze!"

"Maybe," she answered, but in the back of her mind Marianne pictured that her mother probably was not going to be too thrilled with the idea of her wanting to have free time to spend with a pony. The thought made her suddenly realize that she shouldn't be lingering. "I promised Mom I wouldn't be gone very long. Maybe I should be moving along!" she explained.

"Well sweetie, I'm sure glad you thought of me!"

"I thought it'd make you happy," Marianne remarked, shifted her weight in the saddle and took a firmer grip of the reins. "You're actually the first person I've shown him to."

Still studying the pony, her grandmother asked, "Did you name him yet?"

"It's Rocky!" Marianne exclaimed through a wide smile.

Her grandmother peered at the pony over the top rims of her glasses. "That's a cute name, but why in the world did you pick it?" she asked, expecting an obvious answer.

"I can't really explain why," Marianne admitted nonchalantly, surprising her grandmother. "After Mr. Cartwright delivered him, he asked me what I was going to call him; Rocky just sort of jumped into my head and I blurted it out before I had thought about it very much. I wasn't really thinking of him as being a rocking horse or anything like that and now I realize most people are gonna think that's what I meant. It'll probably sound dumb to them!"

"Well…I think you made a good choice," her grandmother said in support of her decision. "Besides," she continued, "the name Rocky could mean he's kind of lumpy or maybe even a little unsteady."

Her grandmother's analysis caused her to giggle.

"I'd better get going if I'm going to finish my ride in time to help my mother. She'll be getting dinner ready shortly and I want to go around the woods before I go back," she said and tapped Rocky lightly with her heels and made a slight clicking sound between her teeth and tongue. "I love you, Grandma!"

"If you come by later my fresh bread will be out of the oven?" she said, trying to entice one of her favorite grandchildren to return for a longer visit.

"It sounds tempting!" Marianne answered. "I just don't think I'll have time," she added.

Her grandmother picked up her paring knife and a new potato. "I love you Marianne and I hope you enjoy the new pony!" she added.

"Love you too, Grandma!" She answered and rode off.

Running a big, soapy sponge across the long hood of his shiny, black car, Donald looked up as Marianne went slowly passed. "Would you like to have some fun by helping me finish washing my car?" he offered teasingly and held a big sponge up toward her at his arm's length.

"Only if you agree to let me drive it into town tonight so that I can pick up some friends and ride around," she joked back. "You'll just have to teach me to drive first!"

"That sounds like a good bargain," he laughed, "but you'll need to wait for another Saturday night because I have a date this evening."

"Some other time then," she tittered.

"Let me know!" he grinned.

"I will!" she replied and rode happily off.

After feeding and saddling Buddy, Ethan led him through the cavernous sliding doors of the barn into the large, grassy area in front. "I'm going to go find Sis," he said to his younger brothers, adjusted his feet in the stirrups, leaned back in the saddle and held the horse's reins tight. "After I find her, we'll probably ride across the section on the dirt lane," he said. "We may not make it back for dinner because we could go even farther. Listen to me carefully! If Mom asks where we've gone, just tell her you don't know and that way you won't be hassled to come looking for us!" Ethan loosened Buddy's reins and prodded the horse with a soft kick of his heels to get him moving. "We'll give you two rides when we get back," he told them, hoping to pacify his brothers with their obvious disappointment.

Twenty minutes later the two younger children were still playing outside the barn and throwing rocks at a fence post when they heard their mother calling them in to dinner. They ran to the house and tussled over who would get through the door first. Jonathan, the larger of the two won and they were still animated and sparring as they walked into the kitchen. They noticed their mother looked somewhat agitated.

"Stop it right now!" she demanded. "That's enough! You both need to go get washed up before your dad comes in. "I'm sure he'll be here any minute now and the food's ready to go on the table."

CHAPTER THREE

Late for Supper

"Where's that brother and sister of yours?" their mother inquired of the dusty, play-worn young boys. "I told them to be here on time!" she added irritably.

They shrugged their shoulders, mumbled something indecipherable under their breaths, gave narrow glances at each other and rolled their eyes when she turned away.

"So you don't know where they are?" she asked.

Jonathan muttered as Leon turned his head away.

"What did you say?" she asked.

"N...n...nothing," Jonathan said in a low whisper. He knew his mother wanted him to give a straight answer and prayed she wouldn't quiz him further after what Ethan had explained.

"Then I guess you don't know where they are or how soon they'll be back!" she prodded.

"No, I...I don't and I don't know where they went!" Jonathan lied unemotionally. He knew it was good to act as ignorant as possible. "Marianne was already gone when Ethan left. He said he was going to look for her and nothing else! That's all I know!"

Taking the clue from his brother, Leon shrugged his shoulders.

Their mother bent over, lowered the heavy oven door and lifted out a very appetizing meatloaf that was surrounded with steaming onions and carrots. The boys felt a surge of hunger under their belts knowing the meatloaf would be accompanied with mashed potatoes, brown gravy, fresh green beans and home-canned corn, coffee for their father and cold milk for them. They didn't suspect that she also planned to make a wilted lettuce salad or that she had a blackberry cobbler for dessert.

"I really, really don't know where they went," Jonathan continued to mumble to himself uncomfortably as he eyed the steaming meatloaf his mother was transferring onto a large ceramic platter. "I really don't!" he said emphatically. If his mother suspected that he was aware his sister and brother were riding down the old lane behind the woods, she'd order him to go tell them to get back to the house. He could picture himself running over there while his father, mother, and little brother dug into some of his favorite food. If he were ordered to go looking, the mashed potatoes and gravy might only be lukewarm or cold when he finally got to eat his portion.

Out of habit, a nervous Leon shoved his hands deep down into his pockets and felt for his lucky rock hoping it would protect him from having to answer questions. He hadn't acquired the technique of keeping a straight face which his brothers and sister had learned from experience. He wasn't sure he could play dumb without his mother seeing the truth on his face.

"Well, they better get back here shortly if they wanna eat because once I put the dishes away, I don't want them making a mess," she stated. Neither boy could understand why their mother thought it would make any difference to them whether Ethan or Marianne came in on time or not; however, neither one of them ever wanted to break their mother's rule because leftovers and snacks were rarely found in her kitchen. "Go wash up!" she instructed. "Your dad'll be comin' in any time now," she reminded them, and the two boys ran to comply. They glanced at each other and twisted their faces knowingly, sensing the drama that would play out later and hurried to get the dirt off their hands and faces.

"When you're done, Jonathan, you need to get a bucket of water from the well for your dad to wash up with and then get another one for me to do my dishes."

As he walked toward the house from the implement shed, Milburn thought of all the improvements he had made over the last five years and how lucky he had been to get the mortgage for doing the work. Having done a lot of hard physical work during that time left him feeling proud of his accomplishments. All those sore muscles and long days of the last few years had definitely shown abundant rewards. He started contemplating other improvements he wanted to make. *Maybe today would be a good time to share some of these plans with my wife and family,* he reasoned. The pony he had purchased for the kids was a reward in a small way to demonstrate that he had money in the bank and to indicate that he had finally risen above barely scraping by. The purchase of the pony had the additional effect of encouraging him to be bold in his planning.

Midway to the house, he looked out across the surrounding fields and felt pride in what he saw and then, as he walked up the sidewalk to the house, he paused, looked out through the large open woods and saw two distant figures on horseback. His stomach churned when he realized that the riders were his two oldest children and that they didn't appear to be heading home for lunch. Maybe the pony hadn't been such a good idea as he contemplated the consequences of what he had done; the pony might accelerate the behavior that he had wanted to slowdown in them.

When he was only sixteen he had run off from home for six months and worked as a shoeshine boy in Detroit, Michigan. He tried remembering why he had done such a crazy thing but he could only credit his behavior as an act of either trying to escape from farm life and maybe youthful rebellion. None of his friends had done anything similar. He recently witnessed some early indications of independence in his oldest son and he knew that Marianne might soon also. *Hadn't my wife fallen in love with me when she was only fifteen?* Somehow, deep down, he had hoped at the time of the pony's purchase that it was going to have a positive effect on them by giving them a distraction and plant their feet on the ground with the personal responsibility of ownership. *I hope it'll work out like I planned without too much turmoil*, he thought to himself. *God forbid if I've done the wrong thing!*

The well that stood off to the side of the front door beckoned Milburn with a promise of cool water, where he could quench his thirst and wash some of the dirt from his face, neck and hands before going inside to do a better job at the sink with warm water off the stove.

"Jonathan, your dad's at the back door and I want you to go out to the ice box and chip off some small pieces for our water glasses," his mother instructed.

"Okay," he said and hustled off to the big wooden ice box.

"Careful with that ice pick," she cautioned. "And, Leon, you can go get the butter."

"It's really blazin' hot out there," their father stated, walking in heavily, looking tired, his shirt blotched with perspiration and his fair complexion brightened into a ruddy glow.

"When you boys are done, you need to sit down at the table. We're not waiting on Ethan and Marianne! Dinner's ready and just as soon as your dad finishes washing up, we're gonna eat!" their perturbed mother grumbled. The two boys knew why. Their father didn't comment.

The boys waited impatiently at the table for their father to wash the deep grime from his arms, hands and neck. They could see he relished getting the dirt off and always made a ritual out of it. He was almost always spontaneous, creative and liked to experiment with things but they had noticed he was very predictable in his method of washing up for meals. They smiled at each other as he splashed water on his face three times, wetted a wash cloth and washed around his neck with his right hand. The right ear always came next. The left ear followed. Next he rinsed out the rag and dabbed around his eyes. His hands came last, with a good lathering which he rinsed off vigorously in the wash pan that he had placed down in the sink. Finally, he dried off with the big towel that hung on a hook by the sink.

Jonathan elbowed his brother lightly in the ribs and snickered softly. Leon, embarrassed, held an index finger to his lips for his brother to be quiet.

Their father hung the big towel up, turned around, gave the boys a big smile and stuck his thumbs under the shoulder straps of his bibbed overalls to adjust their fit before he pulled the head chair out from the table, sat down, took a deep breath and gave a long sigh as his body started to relax. "Don't lean back in your chair, Jonathan; it's hard on the new linoleum floor," his father instructed, unaware that the boys had been entertained with his every move.

A little embarrassed, Jonathan took on a meek look, hung his head down slightly, rocked forward and put all four legs of his chair flat against the floor.

"I'm really starving," Milburn commented as his wife placed the dishes of food on the table. His tired eyes brightened. "Boy, oh boy, meatloaf! Sure looks good, don't it, boys?"

Leon eyed the mound of steaming savory meat. "Could I have the end slice?" he pleaded.

Distracted with her duties and upset with the continued absence of her two oldest children, their mother didn't seem to hear Leon's questions. "Do any of you have any idea where Ethan and Marianne went?" she asked sternly. "They don't seem to care how much work I have to do around here," she lamented. "You all know I like everyone here when I put the food on the table. I always have other work to get done when we finish eating. I swear, if they're not here by the time we finish, they'll just have to wait until supper to eat anything!"

"Hand me a slice of that meatloaf, will ya," Leon asked, ignoring his mother's anger, overwhelmed by the feast spread across the table top. He licked his lips, raised his eyebrows and leaned well forward in his chair to get a closer look. "Gimme that end slice, pleeeease," he pleaded, eyeing the firm rounded end piece with a crunchy skirt around the bottom edge.

"Here, have some green beans!" his brother slid a bowl towards him.

"Wait for your mom to sit down," their father ordered. "You're not gonna starve!"

Shortly their plates were full. The only disturbance for the next several minutes were their utensils clinking and some barnyard sounds carried in on the warm breeze through the open, screened windows.

"You know, I have some ideas for makin' this place more livable," their father said abruptly, breaking the calm and looked at his wife. "There's some big things that just need doin' around here and I've decided we can do them now bein' that the farm's startin' to make us more money. I reckon by plannin' right, we can get most of the stuff I'm thinkin' about finished in two or three years."

"You mean to tell me you're thinkin' of takin' on more debt and do more projects now that we feel less pinched for money and are enjoying the results of our labor," his wife responded. The expression on her face reflected her anxiety over his announcement. Just at the time she was starting to feel financially secure, she found her husband was going to suggest new projects. "What in the world are you plannin' to do?" she asked, holding her fork in front of her mouth.

"Nu num num," he stuttered, seeing his wife's reaction. "Well, I've been seriously thinkin' about this house of ours and how it needs to be made much more livable. We both know that you and the kids freeze every winter," he said. "A furnace would make the house and our lives healthier and a whole lot more comfortable. I don't think the money is goin' to be as big of a problem as the work that it'll take me to get it done," he added and proceeded to explain. "I'm goin' to need to jack up the house and dig a basement, set forms, pour concrete and some other stuff. Electricity is also on my mind, as well as few other improvements around here."

"How can we afford all that?" she asked, concentrating mainly on the financial risks.

Seeing his wife nervously stabbing at her food, Milburn proceeded to carefully lay out his plans in hopes she would understand his rationale and be more comfortable and less intimidated with them. "I know these improvements will make your life a lot more comfortable. I don't think the cost will be as high as you're imagining since I can do a lot of the work myself. We can get the electricity sometime in the future when we get more money ahead. If things keep goin' the way they are, I really don't see money being a poblem," he explained, to get her to see the true practicality of his proposals. "The REA is runnin' electric lines across the rural areas of Illinois and I heard people talkin' at the drug store, discussin' how the government has already started puttin' lines out into the country over around Tuscola. All the other farmers I've talked to are happy the Roosevelt administration has got this thing goin'. I think that by the time they bring it out from Atwood and string it along our highway, hopefully within the next few months, we'll be able to afford the poles and lines to bring it back up here to the house."

His wife didn't respond.

After a long pause, he asked, "Don't you think that it would be nice to have electricity?"

"Yes, of course!" she answered. "And havin' a warm house would be nice too. But why a basement?" she inquired and searched her mind to comprehend her husband's proposals. Before he could answer, a wispy smile darted across her face, indicating some acceptance.

"Because," he said, "we can't have a gravity furnace without someplace to put it!"

Gloria toyed with her fork. "I'm not totally against the idea. I'm thinking of all the things I could do down there, like my laundry and have a place to put my canned goods and other things!"

He looked at her, started to push his chair away from the table and stopped. "Oh, and one other thing!" he added, planning to interject an additional plan. "And what's that?" his wife interrupted

"I'll need to tear off the summer kitchen before jacking up the house. It'll have to go!"

"What?" she blurted, caught off guard by the extent of the work involved. The true scope of her husband's grand plans suddenly dawned on her.

"Well, the sad fact is that I'll need to tear off the old summer kitchen before we can get started! There's no way to put a basement under the house with that old room stuck out there."

"Oh, no! Oh, no!" she stammered. Even though she had hardly ever used the outdated room since they had purchased the farm. Getting rid of it had never entered her mind.

"Why would you want to keep it? We've hardly used it and once the house is raised I'll have place to build a nice enclosed landin' and put steps down to the basement."

"I just don't know, Milburn," she added nervously, although her statement showed that she was slowly ridding herself of some anxiety and was reluctantly beginning to accept her husband's proposals because he wasn't a man who changed his mind after he had thought a problem through.

Seeing the gradual shift in her position, he added, "I think my plans will work. For one thing, I'm plannin' to get most of the wood for the framing from tearin' down the outbuildings, the ones I don't have any use for any more. I was gonna do that anyway," he emphasized, "so why waste the material, I'm thinkin'! Also, by getting' rid of them buildings, we should be able to lower our taxes a little."

Gradually he convinced her that the work he wanted to do over the next two or three years would make her life a lot more comfortable without putting them into financial jeopardy and he knew the issue wouldn't be completely over until all the work was done and the bills paid.

When the two boys had finished eating, their parents' tense conversation seemed to have nearly ended also. Their small world was swinging back into a comfortable balance. They looked at each other. Jonathan nodded for his brother to follow him and started leaning sideways to get off his chair. "Can we be excused?" he asked guardedly in the quiet atmosphere where moments before their father had laid out a broad plan to improve the house and had caused an uncomfortable tension at the table. Episodes of this nature were mostly foreign to them. When neither parent gave him an answer, Jonathan sat half-in and half-out of his chair and waited.

"When will you start?" his wife asked.

"I'm not sure," he admitted. Most things can wait until spring," he said, making her feel better because at least he wasn't rushing headlong down a slippery, difficult path. "However, I do know I'll need to remove the summer room before this winter…anyway; as you know, we won't miss it because we don't use it for much," he said, reiterating his previous argument. He nudged his plate away, pushed his chair back and said, "I need to get back to work...I've a lot to do yet today. I know the improvements are gonna be a good thing for you. I suspect they'll be good for all of us. I know you're goin' to feel better about what I've planned if you'd just consider what we have to gain. You know our lives could be made a lot more comfortable."

Gloria stared into her husband's face. "You've just got to promise me one thing: you won't get us too deep into debt."

"I think we'll be fine," he stated, and contemplated for a moment, forming an answer that would further help to calm his wife's fears. "Just trust me that I wouldn't have given a second thought to any of this otherwise!" One thing everyone knew about her husband was that he never lied. His ready answer made the last bit of tension fade from her face.

"Can weee…" Jonathan started to be excused again and got cut off by his mother just as his father stood up.

"Sure, you can get up and help me clear the table off. And, Jonathan," she said sharply, to emphasize the importance she placed on the command, "after that, before you go runnin off, you can shake these kitchen rugs!"

Jonathan slid his chair back heavily. "Come on, Leon, let's get started," he said and picked up his plate.

"Well, them kids have missed dinner. For the life of me, I don't know why they'd want to be late," the two boys heard their mother say while they hustled around the table cautiously clearing the table of the dirty dishes.

CHAPTER FOUR

A Race and No Winner

"Wait up, Marianne," Ethan shouted as they approached the little wooden bridge that spanned the meandering stream behind Mossberger's thick stand of woods where the air was blocked from any light breeze, making it very hot, humid and uncomfortable. "Where are you going?" he asked, riding up beside her.

"Nowhere!" Marianne replied and reined Rocky to a halt in the soft dirt of the lane. "I was just riding and enjoying being alone," she informed him. The ever present deerflies buzzed her head in fast circles, forcing her to swat them vigorously away with the back of her hand. Sweat glistened across her cheeks and the top of her nose. "It's well past the time we should've gone back," she announced, clucked her tongue and reined Rocky around. "I hope you know we've missed lunch and Mom's going to be really upset!"

"Yeah, you're right!" he said, acting unconcerned. "But you know what?"

"What?"

"I know that I'm not in any hurry to go hear her complain," Ethan stated.

"We've gotta go back sometime," Marianne interjected. "Staying away longer will only make things worse for us." She understood there would likely be repercussions with the possibility of some bitter words being exchanged. She knew her mother loved her but often seemed to resent the fact that Marianne had fewer responsibilities than she had when she was Marianne's age. Taking the liberty of riding off just before dinner was not a responsible action. It broke a couple of very important rules, and she understood the consequences. Growing up, doing what she and Ethan were doing was something her mother might have contemplated but would never have acted on. Even so, Marianne did not quite understand why her mother put tighter limits on her freedom than many of her girl friends' mothers put on them. She felt that since she was having an easier and more comfortable life than her mother, she was resentful and gave Marianne arbitrary restrictions that stifled her independence.

If her mother had looked carefully at thirteen-year-old Marianne, she would have seen a normal young teenager who was starting to feel a little rebellious like many her age but Gloria's background narrowed her reasoning. Maybe if her own young life had been different, she would understand that giving her daughter a little more freedom could make them closer. Life wasn't presenting many opportunities for that to happen and the new pony would deepen their conflict. Marianne would gradually and unintentionally attempt to use Rocky as a springboard to avoid being under her mother's thumb.

"Why don't we switch horses? You can ride Buddy and I'll ride Rocky," Ethan suggested, and leaned forward against the pummel of his saddle while the horses stood side by side, tails switching away at the hoard of bugs buzzing around.

"Okay, but only if you can catch me before I get to the other end of the timber," Marianne said, challenging her brother. She laughed and swiftly tapped Rocky lightly with her heels, slapped the reins on the side of his neck and yelled, "HeeYAAAAA!" Her little steed laid back he's ears and sprang forward, throwing clods of dirt high in the air.

Although her brother got blindsided with her sudden action and was already several yards away before he could react, Ethan figured he had a good chance of winning this impromptu race. He was on a larger and faster horse.

"Catch me if you can," she hollered back, pulled her arms in tight against her ribs, leaned into the rushing air and encouraged the pony to go faster even as the hem of her dress started flying up.

"Eeyah!Yah!" Ethan yelled to Buddy, slapped the reins from side to side across Buddy's neck and kicked his flanks to make him respond to the challenge. Buddy liked to race. He responded to his rider's encouragement and took off with such effort that Ethan felt that he could have been dismounted if he hadn't anticipated the power of Buddy's strength. As Buddy lengthened his stride, Ethan stood up in the stirrups and leaned into the wind. The length of the timber wasn't long but it gave him enough time to pass Marianne within the last few yards of the east edge of Mossberger's thick woods.

"Whoa!" Marianne commanded, leaned back in the stirrups and pulled up sharply on Rocky's reins. "Well, you won, brother!" she said, looked at him with a smile of disappointment and tucked her dress back under her legs.

"I thought that was a very good race!" he exclaimed and continued on emphatically. "Our new pony's fast for his size but not fast enough to beat old Buddy, today or any other day of the week," he smirked, in attempt to needle her. Ethan and his sister had always been close; however, a fierce competition exited between them because of their very different personalities and their gender. He was a jokester and a bully and she was serious minded, opinionated and stubborn.

"You're right," she answered, "but if I remember correctly, the race was all about you wanting to ride Rocky. It had nothing to do with how fast he might be," she said and slid off onto the ground so that she could trade horses with her irritating brother.

Ethan gave her a lopsided smile. "Yeah, I guess," he said without fully agreeing and got down off Buddy.

They decided to ride a shorter way home by cutting through the edge of Mossberger's woods where a tree-shrouded farmer's lane would bring them out into a wide swath of recently mowed clover which separated them from their family's farm buildings.

Side by side, Marianne and Ethan rode under a canopy of overhead limbs down the lane. It was a nice relief from the heat. At the end of the green tunnel they could see the clover field. The transition from the shade into the bright sun suddenly made them squint and shade their eyes. Grasshoppers and other bugs swirled up in small clouds as they rode along in the sweet fragrance of the clover for a couple of minutes lost in their individual thoughts.

Marianne peered off in the direction of town where the high school sat on the farm's southern boundary. "Are you looking forward to going into high school this fall?" she asked.

"Yeah, kinda, I guess," Ethan replied.

His sister shook her head in bewilderment. "I know that if I were starting high school, I'd be looking forward to it and really excited... but you don't seem to be!"

"You're right, I suppose," Ethan said without committing himself in any real definitive sense. "School's alright, but...oh, you know," he said and paused a few seconds before he finished his thoughts, "I just don't do very good!"

"If you'd just quit messing around and decide to study, you know you could do much better," she scolded.

"But I just don't like school," he stated flatly. "The only reason I go is because my friends are there and we do things," he explained, speaking as much to himself as to his sister. "Besides, Mom and Dad won't let me drop out and you know that! If I dropped out they'd have a conniption fit. They'd say I'm too young."

"And they're right! You are too young and anyway, how would you support yourself?"

He shrugged his shoulders without answering.

"Why don't you study, try to stay out of trouble and not horse around?"

Her brother chuckled. "I know what this is all about. You're gonna miss me back there in grade school, aren't you?" he joked, trying to laugh off his sister's comments that had hit a sore spot.

Marianne eyed her brother with bewilderment and let the topic drop.

The young riders, using slack reins, allowed the horses to walk and found it became necessary to keep their mounts moving by nudging them with their heels whenever the horses started grazing. It seemed like a losing battle by the time they were halfway home.

Ethan looked across the long length of green towards home and the farm buildings. "Why don't we get off and let the horses nibble the clover," he suggested. "I'll even trade you Rocky for Buddy, if you want," he added.

"Thanks," Marianne agreed happily and reined the nearly stationary Buddy to an easy halt. As he put his muzzle into the lush clover and started munching, she threw her leg over his neck and slid off to the ground.

Her brother sat and watched as she walked over holding Buddy's reins, reached up and offered them with outstretched hands to him. Instead of accepting them, she heard him yell, "The last one back to the barn has to do all the chores tonight!" and whipped Rocky into a frenzy of pounding hooves.

Her brother's surprise move caught Marianne completely off guard and spooked Buddy. He would have bolted away if she hadn't had a firm grip on his reins and the effort to control him almost dragged her off feet and made the leather straps sting her hands. By the time she got him settled down and was back in the saddle, her brother had already crossed the field, circled the barnyard fence and was headed for the barn.

"Damn him," Marianne said under her breath and let Buddy slow trot across the field. When she got back, her brother stood beside Rocky with a fake grin on his face to aggravate her. He didn't succeed. She knew that the only reason he toyed her with mind games was to irritate and get to her emotions. If he ever succeeded, she knew that he would be in control; however, she had become mostly immune to his behavior which gave her some leverage against his antics.

Silently Marianne rode past him and on into the barn. "Don't forget you have to do my chores this evening," he smirked and when she didn't respond, he yelled "I won, didn't I!"

Marianne knew that her brother usually had ulterior motives. Many times his games were attempts to be funny at other peoples' expense, to be ahead of them and be top dog. "Don't hold your breath until you see me do them because if you do, you'll suffocate," she said without looking back.

"Oh, we'll see," Ethan bellowed and his face flushed deep red. He could see that he had been outfoxed when his sister simply ignored his demands. She had just proven to him that he had no way to make her comply to his demands unless he became physical and she knew he would never touch her.

Marianne hitched Buddy to a thick wooden beam inside the barn by his stall. "No! You won't see!" she barked back. There was a long silence until she walked out of the shadows from the interior. "You're not going to bully me!" she sneered.

"You really think so?" he chortled.

"I know so!" she replied calmly.

Powerless, he suddenly became too angry to think. Ethan realized he had made a mistake in his devilishness when he had momentarily forgotten his sister would never do his chores. Seeing that his efforts had backfired, he felt foolish and his shoulders gradually slumped. Quickly he looped Rocky's reins over the top of a fencepost and walked twenty-five feet away before he turned around and said firmly to save a little of his honor, "At least you can unsaddle Buddy and put him in his stall for me!"

Marianne watched her brother walk away without replying.

Standing some distance from the barn, Jonathan and Leon looked at each other. They couldn't hear any of the conversation but they could observe the tension between their older siblings. A few seconds later, their brother walked past them grim faced. The two younger boys pretended not to notice the not-so-unfamiliar angry glare masking Ethan's face.

"We can still ride Rocky?" Jonathan asked.

His sister didn't turn around. "I'll help you two go for a ride once I get Buddy unsaddled and put away," she said, despondently. The confrontations between her and Ethan always left her feeling drained of emotions and the boys could see it. A painting is often better than a thousand words and the picture of her working like an automaton in the dim light wasn't a happy one.

"We'll go wait outside," Jonathan said and turned towards the light. Running after his brother, Leon scattered a small flock of chickens that were in his way.

"I'll hold onto Rocky's reins, Jonathan, until you get up in the saddle and then I'll hand them to you," his sister instructed. Once you're comfortable in the saddle, I'll lift Leon up behind you and you two can ride around while I go up to the house and apologize to Mom for missing dinner." Once her brothers were settled atop Rocky, she took Rocky's bridle, turned him around and led him a few feet away from the watering tank. "Here," she said, "take the reins. I'll come back out in about half-an-hour or so and help you get off," she instructed.

CHAPTER FIVE

July Fourteenth, 1941
Friends and Consequences

After the rain had poured down off and on all night, the morning sky appeared to suggest that it would stay overcast with showers throughout the day. The family sat around the kitchen table having a leisurely breakfast while listening to the local farm report on the old battery operated Emerson radio. The weatherman announced that the heavy rain was over but there was still a chance for scattered light showers during the rest of the morning. The general outlook was for improved weather and clearing skies later in the afternoon.

Working in the fields any time during the rest of the day was out of the question, Milburn realized and contemplated the best course of action to take for the day. The livestock had been fed and he had milked the four dairy cows just after daybreak. Marianne still had her eggs to gather. Ethan and Jonathan needed to do their chores. He also had a few other minor duties to attend to. "Let's go to Decatur today," he proposed to his wife. "The weather's goin' to keep me out of the fields and the other jobs I need to do can wait!" The decision was of no surprise to anyone around the table. The whole family was aware that he was anxious to make inquiries regarding the materials he needed for the large projects he had informed the family about days before. "What do you think, Gloria?" he asked. He knew his wife wanted to shop at Montgomery Wards and Sears Roebucks and also to buy some groceries in one of the big markets in the city. The larger markets like the IGA and Piggly Wiggly in Decatur had more enticing varieties and offered much better prices than the small Atwood market; the trip was a big lure for her. "Give me a little time to get around first," she exclaimed happily.

"I want to stay home!" Ethan stated adamantly.

His mother frowned. "You do?"

"Yeah, I don't want to go to Decatur!" he stated firmly. He knew his parents probably didn't expect him to go along anyway. About a year ago, his attitude and his bellyaching over the infrequent trips to Decatur had finally gotten his parents aggravated and after that they nearly requested him to stay home. Since that episode, he almost always remained home, but he never forgot to speak up and confirm his intentions, just in case.

"Stay home, if you like. In fact, it's probably a good idea!" his father agreed. "And since you're gonna have some time to kill before you go running off, you can go out to the barn and kick five bails of hay down out of the loft, cut the twine and break them apart. I also want you to shell ten gallons of corn and leave the full buckets right there when you're finished."

"If Ethan isn't going, maybe I won't go either," Marianne declared, following her brother's lead. She often liked the occasional trips. Today she wasn't looking forward to spending most of the day in the city and decided to play Ethan's game. She dreamed of having a little free time to enjoy some unstructured activity with her pony. She surprised herself with how easy her intentions flowed out of her mouth.

"You're sure you want to stay home?" her mother asked without demanding that she go along. "I thought you always liked going to Decatur!"

"I do, but Dad's got places to go first which means you probably won't get downtown until later today." Everyone knew that she loved to people watch, look through the stores and admire the window displays.

"If you go gather the eggs and then help me straighten up the house, I'll let you stay."

It was a good bargain. "That's all?" she asked and shrugged her shoulders.

"Yes," she heard her mother reply.

Her mother turned to the younger boys without answering. "You two are gonna go with us, so go change your clothes and put on some shoes."

Standing, looking out of the large living room window, Marianne and Ethan watched their father back the car out of the old garage, pick up their mother at the end of the sidewalk and then pull away down the long driveway.

Excited they had left, Ethan jumped around. "I'm gonna get my chores done before you do," he taunted, and ran out the back door.

He doesn't know it but I couldn't care less, Marianne thought privately, not responding to his challenge. *As soon as I finish with the chores my mom gave me, I'll saddle up Rocky and ride around the section to Stella Mae's house. I haven't seen her since school got out; she hasn't seen Rocky yet and there are some really fun things to do over there. Maybe she'll want to get one of their horses out and we can ride along the river.* "I feel so free, free, freeeee!" she shouted and did a couple of waltz steps.

Marianne was about half finished with her house chores and was just putting the breakfast dishes away when she heard the back screen door slam shut. She anticipated seeing one of her relatives who often stopped by walk in at any second. Some of them came right in without knocking and she hoped that it wasn't someone wanting to visit, because she only had her eggs to gather before she would be on her way.

Instead it was Ethan who walked into the kitchen. It surprised her. "Well, Sis, it looks like I've finished my chores before you once again," he bragged. She couldn't imagine him being finished so soon and felt uneasy. "I'm going over to Donner's house to see Warren. And, oh, by the way, when you go out to gather the eggs, you can finish feeding the chickens for me. I left the buckets of feed just outside the henhouse door."

She slid the last plate into the cabinet and then spun around with fire in her eyes. "I'm not going to finish your stupid chores and you know that!" she spate.

"Well, let me tell you what, little sister," he said smugly. "If you don't agree, your pony won't be around for you to ride him over to your friend's place," he added, chuckling and sat down at the kitchen table. "Oh, by the way, be sure to carry the buckets back to the barn after you've fed the chickens."

"Damn you, Ethan," she said angrily, feeling powerless to his bullying.

To torment her further, he added, "I've got Rocky all saddled up. I'll be sitting on him out in the front yard. If I see that you haven't fed the chickens and carried the buckets back to the barn, I'll ride off over to Warren's and you can walk to Stella Mae's."

Grabbing the egg basket, Marianne headed for the door.

"You better hurry. I want to get going and if you don't hurry up, I might just ride off anyway!" he gloated.

Marianne seethed and hurried to finish Ethan's chores and her own.

"One of these days I'm going to let him have it," she said as she went from nest to nest. "Then on the other hand, I don't want to encourage him with his childish games. The best defense is for me not to get mad. I'll just smile as if this doesn't matter. It'll get his goat.

Some of the nests were occupied with hens and she needed to reach under them to search the warm pockets of straw to find the hidden treasures. Most of the sitting hens ignored her approach but there were always a few of the older hens that would grumble and peck at her hand. The chickens had individual personalities and their varied reactions made her feel as if she was at a social gathering. She believed barnyard animals were more honest than people and would let you know whether they liked or trusted you without any pretense.

Crossing the yard with the heavy basket of eggs swinging on her arm, she noticed that the overcast sky that had brought the rain earlier in the morning was breaking up and she could feel the heat from the sun as it broke in and out of the scudding clouds. "Looks like I won't be riding in the rain over to Stella Mae's," she said aloud, smiled and did a little sideways skip of joy.

She had regained her usual self assured demeanor and felt calm by the time she walked back into the kitchen and put the egg basket down near where Ethan sat eating a slice of toast with jelly and drinking a glass of milk. "That wasn't so hard, now was it?" he puffed. "Wouldn't you enjoy helping me with my chores every day?"

"I hadn't thought about it until just now," she said and smiled, which made her brother's face go blank. "If you ask Dad and he says it is okay for you to give your chores to me and he says yes, then I'll do them. Or maybe I should ask him for you!" she added and watched his face flush.

He shoved the last bite of toast in his mouth and washed it down with big swallow of milk. "Can we leave right away?" he said without commenting.

"Sure, I guess, but first I need to wash my hands and comb my hair. I suppose you still want me to give you a ride over to Warren's house on Rocky's rump?" she said.

"Yeah," he answered, a little off guard that she wasn't trying to retaliate in some way over his threats and added, "I just need to go grab my 22 Remington. Warren and me are plannin' to plink around."

Marianne looked at Rocky, patted his neck and talked quietly to him while she waited on her brother to come out of the house. Every time she looked at her pony's eyes she smiled. It tickled her that they weren't the same color, one being very light blue and the other brown. "You're a good pony," she said, and put her face against his cheek.

"I'm ready," Ethan shouted, ran out of the door and hurried over.

"Why don't I ride behind you?" she suggested, aware her body had taken on a few curves in the last few months and it felt awkward with her brother's arms around her. "It'll be lot easier for me to hang on to you than the other way around."

"Sure. Okay," he said, held the reins tight, steadied the pony and watched his little sister nearly fly up into her position behind the saddle.

Ethan picked up the 22 caliber rifle he had leaned against the tree and handed it up butt first to Marianne. "Can you hang unto that rifle until we get to Warren's?"

They rode down the long driveway to the one-way-slab highway and turned right toward Warrens' house that was located a quarter of a mile closer town. Most of the clouds had blown away and the bright sun made the air hot and humid. The air clung to them like a wet blanket. Ethan guided Rocky along the grassy side of the right shoulder. Marianne held on lightly to her brother's waist with one hand and clutched his rifle in the other. "You said you and Warren are gonna do some plinking with your rifles?"

"Yeah," he answered.

"Anything else?"

"I suppose we'll probably walk into town and mess around some. Maybe we'll go to the Marsh's and see what Dale's up to!"

"If you do, will you say hi to Donna for me?" she asked with a twinkle in her eyes.

"No problem."

"I wouldn't think so...by the way I see the way you eye her!"

"What do you mean by that?"

"Come on now, Ethan; I think everyone I know has seen you nearly trip over your own feet whenever she's around!"

"I don't either!"

Instead of answering his denial, she giggled softly to herself.

Warren's parents' white, clapboarded house with its green shutters stood along the west side of the highway at the very north edge of town. Unlike many farm houses, it didn't face the highway but faced across a small fenced-in pasture towards town. Several apple and cherry fruit trees occupied a small orchard on the south side between the pasture and driveway. A thick stand of oak, hickory and maple trees surrounded and shaded the yard. A long concrete sidewalk, bordered by beds of summer flowers, ran from the driveway up to the front door.

The Donners were good neighbors. The two farm families borrowed equipment from each other for any job, large or small, and reciprocated if help was needed to put up hay or do some other task that required extra hands.

Mr. Donner was ten years older than Milburn, had been gassed somewhere in France during World War I and was in poor health ever since. He struggled with his weak lungs but still managed to work the small farm by himself over the years, only employing a hired hand occasionally to do some of the heavy labor that was beyond his physical capacity. He labored in this way until Warren's body had matured enough at thirteen so that the two of them could do the heavy work entirely by themselves.

Now, nearly two years later, Warren was about five feet seven inches tall, lean, muscular with a medium build, long legged, gray eyed with a head covered in light brown hair. He stood four inches taller than Ethan, who was small for his age.

The two nearly fifteen-year old boys had much in common. They were both independent acting and classmates. Neither was active in sports or in extra-curricular activities. Guns, girls and cars were their favorite things. Each was the oldest child in their families and their shared free spirits and mischievous nature occasionally got them into trouble. Plinking with their 22-caliber rifles was one of the strongest interests and it bonded their friendship.

Ethan looked up and down the highway across from Warren's house to make sure he didn't ride out in front of a car or farm truck. Only the west lane on the side of the road going into town they were riding along was paved with a concrete. The concrete slab was intended to protect the road surface from the heavy loads of grain farmers hauled into town to the elevator. The opposite, east side of the road was oiled because the grain haulers traveling out of town were generally lighter and weren't as likely to tear up the weaker surface; however, many vehicles leaving town drove on the left side of the road, the slab side, unless there was an oncoming vehicle that forced them to move back to the right. He needed to be careful.

Encouraging Rocky into the short driveway of his friend's house, the pony's hooves made a crunching chatter as Ethan reined him to a halt in the gravel. "He's all yours, Sis," her brother said and slid out of the saddle. "Hand me my rifle."

The first street on the north side of town ran east through two unincorporated villages and ended at Tuscola and to the west it passed just north of the village of Pierson Station and Hammond, seven miles away. Marianne turned west on this road, passing the high school and a half-mile later she crossed the high, iron girder-supported Mackville Bridge over the shallow Lake Fork River. Rocky's hooves drummed on the bridge flooring as they rode over the short span. Two bicycles leaned against the guardrail on the right side at the opposite end.

Marianne guided Rocky close to the railing so that she could peer down into the water to see if the recent rain had raised the water level. Other than silt mudding the water the river didn't seem much higher. Two boys not any older than Jonathan, one standing and one sitting on a log, were fishing with cane poles on the bank in the shade of the willows. One was Barb Clark's younger brother Danny. The drumming of Rocky's hooves made them look up. "Hi," Danny said and waved, recognizing her.

"Hi," she said and waved back. "Are you catching anything?" she asked and halted Rocky momentarily.

"Nah!" the other one said. "I think the rain's messed the fishing up bad!"

"I've heard that's possible," she answered, "but the water hasn't risen that much, has it?"

"Nope," the first one responded, "I don't thinks that's the problem today though. It seems like the hard rain last night must've knocked lots of bugs in the water and now the fish ain't interested in our bait!"

She contemplated what he said for a couple of seconds and then answered him. "I guess that makes sense," she said. "Do you know what Barb's doing today?" she asked about her friend.

"I'm not really sure. I left before her and my mom. All I know is they were planning to go berry picking someplace up north of here today along this river. I suppose she went with my mom."

Marianne snapped Rocky's reins lightly. "Good luck!"

"Thanks!" Danny said, waved weakly at her and lifted his line out of the water to check his hook. "Dang it, these stupid fish just ain't hungry," she heard him complain.

Shortly she came to a crossroads where she needed to turn right onto an oiled road towards Stella Mae's house located a half-a-mile to the north. The little, one-story, white, wood-frame farm house sat on a narrow strip of land hidden in a stand of trees between the country road and the river. The front of the house faced the road and was rarely used, while the back of the house with a closed-in porch had been designated the main entrance. A circular drive filled most of the space behind the somewhat plain, single-story house and a medium-sized red barn rose on a low embankment across the driveway by the river. Inside the white picket fenced-in yard, and beside the path to the house, stood a water pump where a well-used, tin, community cup hung from a hooked, rusted wire.

Marianne loved where Stella Mae lived. It was so remote compared to her house which was only across a twenty-acre field, north of the high school. The location was close to town and combined with the friendly nature of her parents there was a constant chain of friends, neighbors and relatives stopping by to share some pertinent news, swap stories or gossip. Relatives, friends and neighbors were never outwardly discouraged to visit. It was different with traveling salesmen: doors didn't usually open very wide for them. Sometimes Marianne found the traffic intrusive. The worst time for visitors was early mornings when she had just gotten up. Sometimes she felt as if she were in a fish bowl; however, out here at Stella Mae's she didn't think life was likely to be as scrutinized.

Well before she got to her friend's house, Marianne heard dogs barking. They were the family's good watch dogs and always seemed conscious of any new sound, smell, or movement within a mile of their domain. In front of the house she reined Rocky off the road and in past the iron, corner posts of the open gate. The farm dogs ran barking beside her. "Hi, Brownie. Hi, Spot," she said. They waged their tails and replied with a few weak woofs. She tied her pony to a hitching post in the shade under a big oak tree by the picked fence, gave him a pat on the neck, patted each dog on the head and went through the white gate of the fence surrounding the yard.

Marianne walked up the narrow gravel walkway to the back door and called out, "Anyone home?" Not getting an answer after waiting a few seconds, she called a little louder through the screen on the door. "Hello! Mrs. Darrian, Stella Mae. Hello! Anybody home?"

About the time she was thinking of giving up, she recognized Stella Mae's mother's voice from the interior of the house with a crisp, "Yes!" Shortly, her friend's mother pushed the screen door open and invited Marianne to step inside.

"I was beginnin' to think there wasn't anyone home," Marianne exclaimed.

"I was off in the back bedroom and didn't hear a car pull up," Mrs. Darrian replied.

"That's because I didn't come over here in a car!"

"You didn't? Surely you didn't walk all that way here in this mucky weather, did you, girl?" Mrs. Darrian asked, continuing to hold the door open.

"Nope! I rode my new pony!" Marianne stated without moving.

Mrs. Darrian looked over the girl's shoulder and saw the small horse tied to the hitching post. "So that's the new pony you told Della Mae that your father might buy?"

Marianne beamed. "Yes it is," she answered, and felt the need to clarify. "He didn't really have one picked out. He made up his mind after he went down to the sale barn a few days ago and saw this one being auctioned off."

The young girl and the older woman studied the pony for a few seconds in silence. "He looks like a nice pony," Mrs. Darrian commented, and scrutinized the pony more closely. "It seems your father made a good choice."

"You know, you're not the first person that's said that," Marianne replied. "My grandmother said almost exactly the same thing the first time she saw him," she said and glanced briefly at Rocky again, proud that she had the pony. "Is Stella Mae around?"

"Stella Mae's out in the barn cleaning out stalls for her dad. I'll go yell for her," Mrs. Darrian offered.

"No, no, that's alright. I'll go out there and find her myself," Marianne insisted and walked away. Thirsty from the long ride in the sun, she stopped at the well, removed the community tin cup off its wire hook and then worked the long cast iron handle of the pump up and down until it was primed. She allowed the cool, clear water to flow freely from the spout until she was almost certain all the insects had been washed out. She rinsed the cup once, filled it again and drank it dry without removing it from her lips.

Stella Mae moved expertly around the back stall of the barn forking the last remnants of manure and bedding into a growing pile outside the door. While mucking out the stall, she had become so lost thinking of her future and fantasizing about boys, not an unusual pastime for a young girl living on a farm away from her friends in town, that she failed to hear Marianne ride up or to pay any attention to the dogs barking. Cooing pigeons on the barn's roof along with the other usual barnyard cacophony of moos, clucks, cackles, oinks were like an ointment to Stella Mae's spirits; the melancholy of the place made her feel as if she were in balance with the world.

Marianne stepped into the deep shadows inside the barn and yelled, "Hey, Stella Mae. Are you in here?"

"Who is it?"

"Marianne!"

"Hey, I'm back here. Back in the last stall," Stella Mae squealed happily. "God, Marianne, what're you doing over here in the middle of the week?" she asked as her friend walked out from behind a stack of baled hay at the far end of the aisle between the stalls. Stella Mae stopped working and leaned nonchalantly on the handle of the pitchfork she was using. "I can't believe you came out here!"

"I decided when my parents made plans to go to Decatur and Ethan and I convinced them to let us stay home," she explained and paused for a couple of seconds for dramatic effect. "And guess whaaat?"

It was obvious that Marianne was titillating her with the prospect of hearing something good.

"What? What?" her intrigued friend asked and came out of the stall.

Marianne grabbed Stella Mae by the shoulders with both hands and looked deep into her blue eyes. Slowly a smile crossed her face. "You're not going to believe this," she said gleefully.

Stella Mae's eyes twinkled with anticipation. "Believe what? What?"

"I got a pony my dad said he was going to buy and that's how I managed to come over here," Marianne exclaimed and shook her friend's shoulders from side-to-side in her excitement.

"You really got a pony?" Stella Mae asked rhetorically, hardly believing Marianne was so lucky. "I don't believe it!"

"It's true; it's really, really true!" Marianne exclaimed. "Come outside and I'll show you. I've got him tied to the hitching post up by your house."

Her friend rested her pitchfork against the front of the manger, closed the stall door and the two young girls quickly fled the strong odors of disturbed manure and stepped out into the fresh air and the glaring brightness of mid-day.

"He's not a very small pony, is he?" Stella Mae observed.

"Just the right size," Marianne stated with pride and walked over to Rocky's left side, patted him on the neck, rubbed his left ear and ran her fingers through his mane.

Stella Mae walked around to the other side and looked across the pony's shoulders at her friend. "What's his name?"

"Rocky," she answered demurely and braced herself for her friend to react.

Almost as if she were on cue and seeming amused, Stella Mae asked, "You mean like a little rocking horse?"

"No, silly girl, of course not!"

"Well, don't you think that's what most people are gonna think," Stella Mae replied. "So why name him Rocky?"

"After Mr. Cartwright delivered him, he asked me what I would call him, and without thinking, I just blurted out that I'd call him Rocky. I don't know why," she explained. "I suppose the name must've been floating around in my subconscious thoughts or something. I don't think Rocky necessarily means he's a rocking horse though. Rocky can mean a lots of things, like unsteady, difficult, shaky or dizzy, but most of all, it means strong as a rock," she explained. "It doesn't really matter to me what others think, anyway," Marianne stated firmly. Deep down in her heart she knew why she had named him Rocky and it was a secret she would keep for a long time, maybe forever. "I need to give him some water," she said, changing the subject.

"You've made me jealous," Stella Mae said, opened the gate and ran to the enclosed back porch and went inside. Before the door had entirely closed behind her, she had bounced back out, swinging a galvanized pail in her right hand. "This is just the right size for a pony," she quipped, stopped at the brick-lined well, hung the pail under the cast spout and vigorously primed the pump until the water gushed and squirted water high into the air.

"Have you had anything to eat?" Stella Mae inquired and placed the pail of water down on the ground in front of Marianne's pony.

Marianne hadn't given much thought when she would show up and now she felt embarrassed. She had been so excited about her freedom that she hadn't thought ahead. Normally, out of simple country courtesy, people tried to avoid dropping in at meal times. It was okay to stop by at breakfast for a cup of coffee, but arriving at dinner or supper should be avoided. "I ate just before I came over," she lied.

Stella Mae knew her friend wasn't being totally honest. "If you're not hungry, then at least you can sit at the table and nibble and talk."

"Are you sure?" Marianne asked humbly.

"Oh, you know my mother. There's no way she's gonna let you run off without passing the breeze for a while. She told me that she'd have lunch ready after I did my chores. They're done; she knows you're here and I know she's gonna insist you stay and eat. Mom's always interested in my friends and for some reason she seems to take a special interest in you," Stella Mae said and rambled on, trying to convince Marianne to stay. "I don't understand why! It's nothing I've encouraged, I can tell you," she said teasingly, placed her feet apart, put her hands on her hips, pushed her chest out playfully and then folded over laughing and giggling.

"No. I," Marianne responded, still resisting.

Stella Mae cut off her friend in mid-sentence. "Don't even say it!" she stated adamantly. "You're not riding off just after you just got here! You're coming in the house to eat and I'm not taking no for an answer!" she continued.

"You're sure your mother's not going to mind?" Marianne said.

"Yeah, I'm sure. I don't have any more chores to do this afternoon and, if you leave now, I'm never going to forgive you," she said and puckered her lips into a fake pout. "If you leave, we won't be able to catch up on things," she said, "and you're not gonna go anywhere until I ride Rocky!"

The two girls went into the house. It was a small but airy, homey house where intricately stenciled, lime and dark green designs decorated the pine floors in the living area. Linoleum floors and wallpaper with a motif of pale, multi-colored parakeets and flowers brightened the kitchen. A bright, blue stove with shiny trim stood among the white, wood cabinets and in the middle of the floor stood a rectangular Formica-topped table surrounded by four chairs framed in shiny tubular steel and seats padded with slick, lemon yellow plastic.

Polly, the big, gregarious and intelligent African parrot eyed them carefully from his perch as they walked into the house. The charming household pet bobbed his head swiftly up and down to show he wanted some attention. "Hello, Polly," Marianne said, coaxing him to talk. "Hello," she repeated several more times.

Instead of responding to her efforts, he picked up a large sunflower seed in his left claw, cracked the shell off nimbly and ate the kernel.

"Bye, Polly," she said and followed her friend towards the kitchen.

"Bye, bye bye," he finally repeated, bobbed his head up and down several times more, stretched his neck out and rang the bell that hung next to his head.

"I just knew that Stella Mae would convince you to stay so I took the liberty to set an extra place at the table for you," Mrs. Darrian said and winked at her daughter. "It's always good to have unexpected company out here once in a while."

"You really shouldn't have bothered," Marianne answered meekly. I only rode over here to show Stella Mae my pony and I failed to pay any attention to what time it was," she replied apologetically.

"Listen here now, child! You're always more than welcome here…any time. Remember that!" Mrs. Darrian replied warmly.

Marianne looked down at the floor, a little embarrassed. She was afraid Mrs. Darrian would notice her reaction to the smell of fresh bread baking and the anticipation of its mouth-watering flavor. Her stomach rumbled. "At least let me help with something," she offered.

Mrs. Darrian noticed their guest felt uncomfortable. "I don't have much more to do, but if you'd like to you can help Stella Mae set the table and fill the water glasses. I've made some iced tea and it's on the counter over there," she said and motioned with a slight tilt of her head.

"Where's Mr. Darrian?" Marianne asked while filling the last glass.

Stella Mae's mother turned around from the old, unique, blue stove where she was checking her unique goulash, a ground beef and elbow macaroni casserole. "He will be right in I'm sure. Lordy, I do swear, you could set your watch by his schedule when it comes a time to eat," she chuckled and opened the oven door to check on her baking bread. "Sometimes I think he can smell my cooking a mile away even if the wind's in the wrong direction!"

The wonderful aroma filling the quaint little kitchen almost overwhelmed Marianne and it didn't make her doubt what she had just heard.

"Oh…Stella Mae, we almost forgot the butter. Can you get it out of the ice box?" her mother asked and tilted her head slightly. "I think I just heard the gate squeak and I suspect it's your father."

CHAPTER SIX

Skinny Dipping

After they finished eating, Mr. Darrian excused himself to go rest. "I'm going to take a nap and rest my weary bones," he said and they weren't surprised how easily the words tumbled from his mouth; it was his favorite trademark expression after lunch.

The three females stayed at the table and chatted. Half-an-hour later they were still engrossed in small talk, ignoring the clutter on the table, when a car pulled slowly up in front of the house and parked. The big barnyard dogs, familiar with the car and its occupants, woofed softly a couple of times and went back to rest in the shade. The women heard the motor stop, a door slam shut and a brief time later, a familiar voice yelled in from outside the screened porch, "Hello, Wilma. Anybody home?" a clear female voice inquired and was followed by a firm knock on the loose frame of the door.

"Isn't that's Mary Clark's voice," Stella Mae whispered and peered quizzically at her mother. Mary Clark and Mrs. Darrian were two old friends and Barb, her daughter, would more than likely be with her.

"I believe it is," her mother answered.

"Hello," Mrs. Darrian replied loud enough to be heard. "Just a minute and I'll be right out," Mrs. Darrian said just loud enough for the visitor to hear and yet soft enough not to wake her husband in the back bedroom.

Mrs. Darrian stood up, straightened her dress, brushed the hair back from her forehead and went to the door while the two girls rushed to clear off the table and put the dirty dishes on the counter to be washed later.

"Well hi, Mary," Mrs. Darrian greeted her friend pleasantly.

"Hi, Wilma," Mrs. Clark responded. "I hope we didn't catch you at an awkward time."

"Oh, for heaven's sakes, of course not!"

"You're sure?"

"Of course, I am! I'm so glad you stopped by!" she said emphatically, looked at the car sitting in the bright sun and noticed a figure sitting in the passenger side of the front seat. "Is that Barb out there in that hot car?" she asked.

"Yes, it is!"

"Barb coming along with you is going to make Stella Mae happy. She's been chomping at the bit for days to see some of her friends and it looks like today she's finally got lucky," she declared and motioned for Barb to come up to the house.

"We can stay only for a few minutes," Mary Clark replied.

Wilma didn't respond. Instead she said, "Well, don't just stand there, come on in!"

"You're sure we're really not intruding on anything?" Mary said apologetically, appearing reluctant to step in and be social.

"Of course you're not!" Wilma answered and noticed that her friend looked a little disheveled. "What've you two been up to this morning?"

Mary apologized for her unkempt appearance. "I'm sorry I look like such a mess," she said and straightened her dress unconsciously. "I would never have stopped by looking like this if we didn't know each other so well!"

"I'm a little jealous because you're one of those people that could wear a gunnysack dress and make it look good," Wilma complimented, attempting to make her friend feel comfortable.

"Don't flatter me…I know I've definitely looked better. I'm sort of a mess because Barb and I were up on the south side of the Crane Bridge picking blackberries most of the morning."

"Out in this heat and humidity?" Wilma asked.

"We had planned to get an early start this morning and hoped to finish before it really got hot and steamy but we didn't get around early enough. You know how that is…the best laid plans often go astray."

"Was it worth your effort?"

"We did real good!" Mary answered. "There were so many berries, we were able to pick three gallons by the time it got so hot we almost fainted from the heat. Not only was it hot but the dang bugs became such terrible pests. We felt we were either going to melt or get eaten alive…but we got more berries than I could've ever dreamed of picking Once we were satisfied with what we got and we went back to the car and started driving home and decided to meander around to this side of the section with the windows rolled down to cool off. Well, let me tell you…the air felt so good, we slowed down to enjoy it, seeing no need to hurry!"

Mary's attractive daughter, Barb, a very feminine, freckle-faced, doe-eyed girl with long black hair framing an acorn-shaped face stood several inches taller and slightly behind her mother, spoke up, "When we came around the little curve up the road I told Mom we had to stop by and visit."

"Well, I'm glad you suggested it to her," Wilma answered, pushed the screen door wide and motioned them to come in. "That sure sounds like a great place to pick berries. The only ones we have are out behind the barn down by the river but they've not produced many berries this year for some reason and I haven't had the gumption to go looking any place else."

"Then it's a good thing we stopped because I'm sure we can spare enough for you to have a nice cobbler or make some jelly."

"No, No! You really don't need to do that!"

"I know I don't, but it's our pleasure. I wouldn't do it for many people, though," she confided and before her friend could protest further, she said, "Barb, run back out to the car and bring in that small bucket of berries from behind the front seat."

Wilma cherished her friend's generosity. "Well then, I guess one good turn deserves another," Wilma said pleasantly. "We were just getting ready to have some iced tea and to sit out here where there's a breeze and you both look like you're due for some cool refreshments too," she added and directed her visitors to sit down on a white wicker settee.

"What a nice porch," Mary observed. "I don't think I've ever been in one that's as cool on a hot day or that's any more comfortable or more pleasant!"

"I believe so too and we're so lucky to have it when the house is broiling on hot summer days like this," Wilma replied. "If you two sit still and relax I'll go hustle the girls along with the iced tea."

Mary undid the top button of her high-necked dress, pulled out a plain handkerchief from her pocket and wiped perspiration from around her collar. "You're sure we're not interrupting," she said.

Wilma paused. "You're not going anywhere until we visit for a spell and have some iced tea!" she answered, and left to prepare a tray with glasses, a pitcher of sweetened iced tea, some slices of warm homemade bread, butter and some fresh rhubarb preserves.

"I want you girls to go out and entertain our company while I get some refreshments ready," Mrs. Darrian explained to them, even though they were still putting things away. "Go on now; we'll finish cleaning up in here later!"

Wilma took two small hand towels, dipped them in water and wrung the excess water out in the sink. These she would offer her guests so that they might wipe some of the berry stains and grime of their hands and fingers.

The girls happily left to greet their friend and mother and found Barb just returning from the car with the pail of blackberries her mother had sent her to fetch. "Hi," they said to each other.

Stella Mae held the screen door open for Barb.

"Golly," Marianne exclaimed, "I get to say hi to almost all the Clarks today."

Mrs. Clark looked puzzled. "Who else did you see?" she asked.

"I saw Danny!" Marianne replied.

"Where in the world did you see him?"

"Over at the Mackville Bridge."

Mrs. Clark arched her eyebrows. "So that's where that boy ran off to instead of going berry pickin' with us like I asked him to. I swear he can slink away faster than a sly fox being chased away from a chicken yard. He knew I was going to make him come along with us and skedaddled before I insisted," she stated, sounding perturbed. "Did he say if he was catching anything?" she asked as if she might forgive him if he were to bring home a nice stringer of pan fish.

"He didn't say!" Marianne answered.

Stella Mae, Marianne and Barb sat together around a small green wicker table talking in whispers and occasionally laughing loudly or giggling about their summer adventures or lack of. Mrs. Darrian and Mary sat on the wicker chairs catching up on local news. After discussing all of the local juicy topics, they arrived at a few others that were as dry as the Mojave Desert. Eventually they switched to world events and the war in Europe. The subject was constantly in the news, making the headlines almost daily and was extremely troubling to most people. Germany's invasion of the countries surrounding its borders worried people. Japan and the Orient were also of grave concern and the United States was an accelerated process of building up its armed forces as insurance in case it might get drawn into either of the conflicts. The effort was making the country take on a much different character.

Stella Mae interrupted the older women. "We're going out to show Marianne's pony to Barb."

"Don't be long," Barb's mother answered. "We need to be getting on the road back to town now!"

"Okay, Mom?" Barb responded excitedly.

"Why don't you stay a while longer?" Wilma asked persuasively, seeing the girls having so much fun together.

"We really should be going home soon," Mrs. Clark said although she really had no intention of leaving until she and Wilma had dredged the barrel dry of every bit of interesting news they could set their minds on.

The mid-day sun glared high in a cloudless sky, baking the rain-soaked earth, raising the humidity higher and creating a moist heat that clung like an extra skin. The wind had completely died and the day had taken on the quality of an open oven.

Rocky stood in the shade where Marianne had hitched him before lunch. As the three chattering girls approached him, he tossed his head and swooshed his tail a little harder.

"From the way he is acting, I believe he must've thought you'd forgotten about him," Stella Mae commented. "It's either that or he's happy to see us coming out to give him some attention...which he seems to like."

"You can say that again," Marianne replied, happy her friends were taking such a keen interest in her pony.

Barb half skipped as they moved closer. "Marianne, you're so lucky to have a pony. I wish I had one, but since I don't, the only thing that'll make me feel better is for you to let me ride him!"

"Be my guest!" Marianne offered.

Stella Mae elbowed her way between her two friends and placed her right hand on Rocky's saddle. Play acting, she said, "No one touches this mighty stead until Stella Mae rides him around the courtyard of this magnificent castle!" For emphasis, she made an exaggerated arc with her arm in a sweeping motion around the dusty area between the barn, house and other outbuildings, pretending that she was in a royal setting. Her pretense made the other two girls snicker.

Marianne untied Rocky from the hitching post, held his bridle and patted him on the neck. "Okay, Princess Stella, just swing your royal butt up into the silver saddle and be careful not to drop your tiara!"

While watching their friend ride around in the rutted, circular turnaround of the driveway between the barn and the house, Barb and Marianne stood in the shade and talked. "Wouldn't it be fun if you could stay out here this afternoon?" Marianne said. "The three of us would have so much fun!"

"Golly, Marianne, I'd love to. I just don't know how I'd get home if Mom lets me stay and I doubt she would, anyway!"

After contemplating for a couple of seconds, Marianne said, "I have a couple of easy suggestions to offer. First, we'll convince your mother that it won't be a problem for you to get home. I'll explain that we can ride Rocky together since I need to go home the same way you need to go. It's only about a mile and a half from here. That's no big deal. We'll also remind her that we haven't seen you for some time."

"But what if..." Barb started to argue another point and Marianne cut her off.

"Please, Barb, you know we'd have so much fun!"

"I'd really like to but I just don't think my mom will let me," she stated reluctantly and looked over at the house with a long face. After thinking for a few seconds, she exclaimed, "You know, maybe because she likes you and Sella Mae so much, she just might consider me staying."

"What are you kids up to?" Barb's mother asked as the screen door creaked open. Barb looked meekly at her mother. "Marianne wanted me to ask if I could stay out here and hang around with her and Stella Mae for a while this afternoon."

"I don't think it's such a good idea, Barb! I'm going to be busy when I get home and I don't believe I'll have time to come back and get you."

Barb whined, "Pleeeassse, Mom!"

Her mother pursed her lips and shook her head slightly from side to side. "Really, Barb, I don't see how it'll be possible."

Marianne cautiously waved her hand from side to side as if she were in a classroom trying to get the teacher's attention.

Mrs. Clark asked, "What do you want to say?"

"She can ride into town with me on my pony when I go home this afternoon,"

"Please, Mom! It'll be so much fun to stay out here. Please! Please!" Barb pleaded and got down on one knee and put her hands together in prayer. "Pleeeease!"

Mrs. Clark looked at Mrs. Darrian. "Would it be a problem for you if she stayed? I don't want her in the way if you people are busy."

"We're not busy and it's your decision whether she should stay or not. I actually think the girls will have fun being together," Mrs. Darrian added in defense of the plan. "If she doesn't want to go back to town with Marianne, I suppose I can give her a lift into town this evening. I've been needing to go to the store all week and this might give me a good excuse," she said and shifted her body slightly on the lumpy, well-worn, cushion under her.

"Okay, you can stay, I suppose, but I want you to behave yourself and if you decide to come to town with Marianne, make sure you come in well before dark! It's awfully dangerous walking or riding a horse along the edge of a road in the twilight and after dark!" her mother stated firmly. "Make sure you come back to town before sunset, you hear me?" she repeated admittedly.

"Yes, Mom, I promise!" Barb answered cheerfully, jumped up, spun around and hopped out through the open screen door that Marianne was holding open. "Thanks, Mom," she called back.

"It's my turn to ride Rocky," Barb reminded Marianne as they ran out through the gate and let it swing shut with such loud bang it woke the dogs.

Stella Mae rode into the shade under the tall tree, slid off the saddle and listened to how her friends had convinced Barb's mother to permit her to stay.

"I was thinking of suggesting the same thing while I was riding around in circles," Stella Mae told them. "Why don't we go swimming over behind the old scout cabin; the banks aren't muddy and there's some short grass to sit and stretch out in," she said enthusiastically. "Marianne knows the place I'm talking about, don't you?"

"It's a really great swimming hole," Marianne happily confirmed.

The girls heard the old gate rattle. "Shhh," Stella Mae whispered.

Mr. Darrian, appeared to be half-asleep as he slowly made his way out to the twenty-acre field across the road where he was cleaning out some light brush along its edge. "What are you kids up to?" he asked.

"We're just chatting and messing around, Dad," Stella Mae answered. "Nothing very special!"

"Hi, Mr. Darrian," the other two girls said in unison.

"Hi, girls," he said somewhat distractedly, concentrating on adjusting the straps on his bib-overalls. The girls silently watched, waiting for him to move on. Instead, he stood and fiddled around with the straps for some time. Finally satisfied that he had arrived at the correct comfort zone for length, he yawned and started to walk away. "Nice pony you've got there!"

"Thanks, Mr. Darrian!" Marianne answered.

"It sure is danged hot," he observed, raised the back of his clenched hand to his mouth, yawned again, and placed the farmer's straw hat on his head.

"Dad, please careful you don't work too hard over there in this heat," Stella Mae reminded.

"I promise to be careful," he replied and slowly walked away.

Stella Mae waited a few seconds for her father to get some distance away. "Are you mermaids ready to go get wet?" she chided.

Barb studied her friends' faces, puckered her mouth sideways and pinched up her face. "You're kidding me, aren't you?"

"No, we're not!" Stella Mae answered.

"But I don't have a swimming suit!" Barb sputtered.

Stella Mae gave Marianne a devilish smile and replied, "Does it look to you like either of us has one?

Barb swallowed hard. "You're, you're joking!" she gasped.

"Nope. I'm not!" Stella Mae answered.

"You, you mean, you, you go n, nu, nude?"

"Nude? No silly girl! Of course we don't! We wear our panties!" she giggled.

Barb's eyes grew bigger. "But aren't you afraid of being seen?"

"NO! Why would I!" Stella Mae said emphatically. "Where we swim is a very secluded swimming hole way back off the road, hidden in a thick stand of trees where we can't be seen!"

Marianne saw that she needed to add some encouragement and play up how much fun it was going to be without being too daring. "Stella Mae is the only one of us that nature has endowed big boobs, so she sometimes wears her bra, but you can swim anyway you like, even go the way nature created you if you want."

"Nude? No waaay! Skinny dipping? No waaay! Nooo way!" Barb fretted, still unconvinced. She was starting to see that she had only two options: either to take the challenge her friends offered or go home with her mother, but if she did that, she would seem very modest and also miss an afternoon chumming around with two of her closest friends.

The other two girls giggled and looked at each other. Barb blushed but managed to force a weak smile. "You're sure no one will see us?" she said.

"I promise!" Stella Mae said and crossed her heart, but she knew there was no guarantee.

"W, well, okay," Barb reluctantly concurred.

Marianne and Stella Mae walked on each side of the pony as Barb rode him on the oiled road towards where the dirt lane went back to the swimming hole.

Mr. Darrian was working a short distance off the road along the edge of his twenty-acre field. "Hi Dad," Stella Mae yelled and he stopped working, waved back and proceeded to wipe his face and neck with a large, red handkerchief.

Puffy, white clouds silhouetted against a clear, pale-blue sky and drifted slowly past overhead. Fields of soy beans and corn grew on each side of the road, forming an avenue of lush green walls. A freshly-cut clover field added a pleasant fragrance to the summer air. Scattered around the perimeters of some adjacent fields were small clumps of tall weeds, brambles and an occasional tree. Meadow larks, dickcissels and tree sparrows found perches on these handy elevations to survey their territories and sing beautiful notes, warning other intruders of their species to stay away. Engrossed in small talk, the girls were oblivious to this peaceful, serene landscape. Most of what they discussed were little tidbits of inconsequential gossip until Barb got caught up in the moment and offered a bigger bit of news.

"You know, I have this really nice, beautiful cousin, Margret… Margret Hannison, that I've only met twice in my life and she's coming down here from Minnesota to spend a few months with us," Barb stated just as they were turning into the dirt lane which was straddled by tall grass. It led back to the river where they planned to swim.

Marianne walked along holding on lightly to a dangling strand of the leather decoration that was part of the saddle. She glanced up, very intrigued with what she had just heard. The small town of Atwood didn't get many interesting outside visitors. The only strangers were mostly the usual passing salesmen or delivery truck drivers. "You're so lucky to have a visitor coming. Why didn't you say something before now?" she asked.

"Mom told me not to tell anyone…so I just couldn't say anything in front of her." She looked at the two girls walking on each side of Rocky. "Promise you'll not tell anyone, please! I, I…p, p, probably shouldn't even have mentioned her," she stuttered nervously, as she contemplated what she was about to say. Now she was caught in a conundrum. If she didn't explain entirely, she realized that they might reveal her secret without knowing the full story. On the other hand, if she explained the full context of the secret, it would explain why they shouldn't say anything to anyone. Tidbits of ripe news had a tendency of spreading quickly along Atwood's small-town grape vine.

"Barb, you know we'll keep your secret," Stella Mae responded; although she wasn't known for keeping many secrets, Marianne trusted her completely. She was known for behaving much as she appeared with her well-developed, curvaceous and feminine body. Her friends knew her to be flirtatious, popular with the boys, extremely social and not the kind of friend anyone with forethought might confide in.

"How long is Margret going to stay?" she asked, prying further.

"For several months, I suppose," she answered.

No one said anything for four or five seconds until Marianne asked, "Several months? Why is she staying so long?"

Barb was caught up in the intrigue she had perpetrated with her announcement and decided to continue telling the story of why her cousin was moving. "My cousin's from Fertile, Minnesota; she's pregnant and she's coming down here until she has her baby."

"Why doesn't Margret just stay up there with her husband and family?" Marianne naively asked.

"That's the problem! She doesn't have a husband," Barb informed them, suddenly speaking so low her two friends had a hard time hearing her.

"What my cousin's going through is really a great tragedy. Mom told me that Margret got pregnant during the last couple of days while she was so emotional during the time that her boyfriend was preparing to leave for boot camp. It wasn't until sometime after he left that she started not feeling well and when her mom took her to the doctor, they discovered she was going to have a baby!"

"Why don't they just get married?" Marianne asked.

"Their romance was filled with a lot of turmoil and bickering from the stress of him leaving. They were talking of getting married sometime in the future, during one of his leaves or whenever. Nothing was for certain!"

"Being from Fertile you would think your cousin would have been more careful," Stella Mae teased and the other two looked at her in disgust.

"That's not funny, Stella Mae! I'm sure that you'd really like her. Mom said she's a very nice girl and I feel deeply sorry for her. Fertile is a very conservative little religious town that's way up near Fargo, North Dakota and many people up that way think getting pregnant without being married is an awfully big sin!"

Marianne added quickly, "Probably a lot like around here!"

"Sometime after I learned Margret was coming here I overheard my parents say they didn't think that her family would be able to stand all of the whispers and stares from the righteous members in the community. That's why her parents are sending her down here to stay with us and made the excuse that Margret's coming down here to go to school."

Marianne angrily kicked a small rock off the lane with the side of her shoe, causing a small cloud of dust to puff into the air. "I don't think it's much different around here," she uttered again. "I get so tired of righteous and holier-than-thou people!"

"What will happen to her baby," Stella Mae asked sympathetically. "Do you think she'll give it up for adoption?"

"Mom told me she'll keep it if her boyfriend marries her but she'd have to give it up if he doesn't. Anyway, my mom doesn't want people around here to know the real reason she's staying with us. It is no one else's business, she says. Mom's going to explain that Margret is looking for a job while she waits for her boyfriend to come back from the service."

Marianne listened to the explanation and looked troubled. "You know, in two or three years we'll be her age. God forbid that something like that would ever happen to one of us."

"God! That's for suuurre!" Stella Mae stressed.

Squirming nervously in the saddle and looking from one of her friends to the other, Barb said, "You're my best friends. I'd just die if my mom found out I told either of you. I don't want to lose her trust," she added.

"And we don't want to lose yours," Marianne answered. "Let's take an oath on our mothers' lives that we'll never tell," she said, to reassure her friend that her secret would always be safe.

By the time they arrived at the grassy area by the secluded swimming hole, they all had sworn an oath to never divulge the secret about the unfortunate pregnancy.

Marianne took Rocky's reins to steady him while Barb swung her right leg over the pummel of the saddle and hopped off to the ground.

"Last one in's a slow poke," Stella Mae shouted, quickly stripped her clothes off down to her panties and dashed off like a deer towards the water. She jumped with her legs tucked up to her chest and made a large splash.

"You're not being fair. I'm still trying to tie Rocky to a sapling," Marianne shrieked and ran for the river. As she ran she unbuttoned her blouse and threw it aside, kicked off her shoes, yanked her skirt up past her knees and at the water's edge pulled it off also.

Her two uninhibited friends demonstrated such an easy abandon that Barb could only watch transfixed with her mouth gaping open.

Stella Mae had swum nearly across the deep quiet pool in the otherwise shallow river before Marianne had so much as rippled the river's surface.

"Wow, the water is really great," Marianne commented as she eased herself into the refreshing clear liquid.

Once Stella Mae reached the opposite side of the pool where the water was shallow over a sand bar and found her footing, she stood up until she was partly out of the water. Her silky hair plastered the side of her face and Marianne noticed that her friend, now glistening wet, had developed the full figure most girls their age often dreamed about. "Come on over," Stella Mae cajoled, very much looking like a water nymph. She scooped water by skimming her cupped hand over the surface of the water and sprayed it high in the air.

Marianne knew she wasn't a strong swimmer like her friend who teased from the other side. In fact, she had only learned to swim overhand the summer before and she still wasn't confident in her ability to go any great distance, although, swimming to the other side of the pool looked like it wouldn't be difficult.

Marianne paused and tried to build her confidence so she could rise to the challenge that Stella Mae continued to present from across the deep pool. She looked back at barb. "Aren't you coming, Barb?" she asked.

"Come on in the water, Barb," Stella Mae repeated, diverting her attention away from Marianne.

"Just as soon as I finish slipping this skirt off," Barb shouted back, standing awkwardly with her back to the other girls.

Last year when Marianne and Stella Mae had gone swimming, only Stella Mae had started developing breasts and now here Marianne was suddenly feeling as if she needed to cover up when she saw her other friend remove her skirt and turn around. It was very obvious that Barb had also developed a few curves. *Why haven't I started filling out?* Marianne thought to herself. *I look like a stick compared to those two!*

"Golly, Marianne, are you going to come over?" Stella Mae asked when Marianne didn't swim across. "Are you coming over, or not?" Stella Mae taunted, giggled and splashed water again. "Are you, or aren't you? Tell me, are you coming over, yes or no?" she pattered.

"Okay, okay I'm coming! Just hold onto your horses," Marianne insisted and pushed off with her feet. She plunged her right arm into the water and made swift strokes towards the far bank. Halfway across she heard a big splash and knew that Barb had plunged off the bank behind her.

Stella Mae still was giggling and splashing water when Marianne finally reached the far side and was happy that Stella Mae had turned her attention back to Barb, tantalizing her by chanting over and over, "The water's nice! Come on over, Barb. You can do it! The water's really nice…sooo come on over!"

The three girls eventually stood together on the long narrow sandbar that had formed over the years in the lee of the current where the water came around a sharp bend, creating a deep pool in the faster current along the west bank and depositing sand in the eddy of the current along the east bank. The deep pool made a safe place to swim and the sandbar made a great place to frolic around in because the water level only came up to their waists there. The girls played tag, swam, teased and laughed until they eventually tired of their playful games.

While her friends sat nearly up to their shoulders in the shallowest water near the bank and talked, Marianne began to swim up and down the length of the sandbar to practice her swimming techniques and the rhythm of her overhand strokes. Eventually fatigue made her struggle to swim smoothly. She felt winded, her muscles ached and she decided to quit and rest.

Stella Mae stood up, and before Marianne had an opportunity to object and explain that she was exhausted, she heard her friend say, "Line up next to me and on three I'll shout go. The last one back across has to kiss the pony!"

Still trying to catch her breath from the strenuous practice laps and before she could say, "wait," she heard Stella Mae command, "One, two, and three, go!" Without thinking, Marianne dove into the deep wide pool and started swimming. A third of the way across a knot formed in the deep muscles in the calf of her right leg. She gritted her teeth and tried to fight off the sharp, hot, stabbing pain of a cramp in her right leg. For some reason she felt too embarrassed to call for help. Two thirds of the way across, her left leg also developed a cramp and she knew instantly that she wasn't going to make it to shore. Panic completely overwhelmed her reasoning. She thrashed briefly at the water before going under. She struggled underwater for what seemed like a lifetime before breaking the surface, but just long enough to gulp a mouth-full of fresh air. Then she sank again. Her lungs were burning and she felt starved for air when she came up the second time. "Help me!" she managed to scream before thrashing and sinking again.

It seemed like a miracle that she made it up the third time and was equally surprised to hear Stella Mae, who had responded to her call for help and had swum back out, demand firmly, "Relax and don't panic!" All Marianne wanted to do was to clutch onto anything that would keep her from sinking, so when she felt an arm reach around her neck from behind, she put her hands up and took a firm grip. "Relax! You're going to be okay," Stella Mae stated authoritatively. "Stay on your back. We're only a few feet from shore."

Marianne felt her head bump against the bank. It did little to settle her fright and she continued to clutch onto her friends arm.

Stella Mae looked at Marianne's contorted face and reassured her. "You're okay now! Relax! Put your feet down," she soothed and felt her friend shiver. "You're okay! You can touch bottom here!"

Whimpering in pain and grimacing, Marianne pleaded, "Please hold on to me. I've got cramps in my legs and I don't think I can stand up!"

Stella Mae kept a firm grip on Marianne and helped her slither more than crawl out of the water. Barb rushed over to help and grabbed Marianne's left arm. Both girls pulled their exhausted friend up onto the bank where she flopped down side by side with Stella Mae on the warm grass, their arms stretched straight out from their shoulders. Their bosoms heaved up and down, enjoying the freedom of being able to get all the wonderful air they could hold while their hearts thumped in their chests. "Oh, my God," Marianne whispered between short gasping breaths. "I thought I was really going to drown!"

Stella Mae stared up at the blue sky and clouds thinking how close she had come to losing a good friend. "Why didn't you cry for help earlier?" she asked.

All three girls were silent for a considerable length of time and waited for Marianne to give an answer. Presently she shook her head vigorously from side to side in disbelief of what had transpired a few minutes before. Tears welled up in her eyes and ran off her flushed cheeks. "I don't know. I really don't know!" she answered with a quivering voice.

Barb stood over her friends. "Gees, Marianne, you scared us half to death!"

"Please don't tell anyone about this!" Marianne said. "I don't know what my mom might do!"

Looking at the smooth glassy surface of the river, Barb picked up a small stone, tossed it high in the air into the middle of the pool, where it made an audible splash and created circular ripples that seemed to define how their lives were changing. "I guess we're now bound to keep not only one secret but two from this afternoon."

Raising up onto her elbows, Marianne sat forward and reached for her blouse. "Friends forever!" she said as if she were making an oath.

"Friends forever!" the other two sincerely mimicked and placed their hands over Marianne's.

CHAPTER SEVEN

Late Again

The afternoon had flitted away until the low sun and the lengthening shadows cooled the air and dimmed their surroundings while the girls sprawled in the deep grass while their underwear dried, unaware of the passing of time and distracted by their varied and animated conversations.

The first to notice the late hour was Barb. "It's getting pretty late," she observed. "Maybe we ought'a be going?"

Marianne looked around and saw the long deepening shadows. "Oh God, you're right, it must be really late," she agreed, and jumped up. "I've really, really gotta be getting home!"

Mostly unaffected with the time, Stella Mae calmly said, "And I've got chores to do."

Barb watched Marianne jump up and rush around looking for the rest of her clothes. "My parents are probably worried and mad too," Barb said and casually got to her knees, "but they'll have to get over it!"

"I can't believe you can stay so calm!" Marianne replied, frantically flitting around like a small bird picking up her clothes. "My parents have no idea where I am unless Ethan told them."

The three girls led Rocky back up the lane to the road and prepared to part ways. Stella Mae watched Marianne slide up into the saddle and then she helped Barb climb up behind her. She gave her pony a little nudge to get him moving. "Bye," the two riders said almost in unison.

Stella Mae stood in the middle of the road. "Bye," she responded and watched her friends ride off into the deepening twilight. "Be careful out on the main road," she shouted. "It may be hard for people to see you!"

"We'll ride on the shoulder wherever we can," Marianne yelled back and gave her pony another nudge to speed him along.

"See you later," Barb yelled.

The familiar smell of dust and road oil heated from the sun seemed to challenge the sweet lush odors wafting off the adjacent fields of green corn, soybeans and clover in that moisture-laden atmosphere. Stella Mae stood in the middle of the oiled road and watched her friends ride away until they turned off onto the highway. "Bye!" she yelled at the top of her lungs.

A faint, "Bye," drifted back out of the darkening twilight.

"I haven't had this much fun since school let out," Barb said softly in Marianne's ear.

Marianne still felt the effects of her near drowning and answered, "It was an experience!"

"I hope no one ever finds out we went skinny dipping. It would be so, so embarrassing!"

"You know what would have really been embarrassing?" Marianne asked and waited for Barb to guess.

"What?"

"If we'd been discovered by a troop of boy scouts!"

"Oh God! That would've really been aaawful!"

"If they saw us in all of nature's raw splendor do you think it would've helped them earn their merit badges for anatomy?" Barb asked and they cackled.

"I don't think I would've been of any help to them," Marianne replied, "but if they were to see Stella Mae, I'm sure it would've!"

The rest of the ride into town was quiet and uneventful. Marianne encouraged her pony into a slow trot and very shortly they were in front of the high school. A few seconds later, she pulled back on the reins and commanded Rocky to stop, ready to turn onto the one-way slab towards home. "Barb, I need to drop you off here because it's not safe to ride Rocky into town after dark."

"I understand, Marianne. And anyway, I'll be home almost as soon as you are," Barb stated and added, "Take hold of my arm and help me slide off this animal."

Before Marianne rode off, she stopped, leaned back in the saddle and said reassuringly, "Don't worry, Barb, the secret about your cousin will always be safe with us!"

"Thanks," her friend responded for the reassurance and touched Marianne's leg as if she were sealing a pact between them. "That was such a great afternoon and thanks for helping me talk my mom into letting me stay out there."

"See you later," Marianne said.

"Bye," Barb responded and walked off towards the small business area six blocks away.

"Sis," a soft voice called out from the dark shadows in the Donner's driveway. "Sis, Sis, wait up!" the voice repeated again, slightly louder.

"God, Ethan, what're you still doing over here? I thought you'd be home by now already," Marianne said and reined Rocky to a halt.

"You're wondering about me and you're ridin' home after dark!"

"Yeah, I made a stupid mistake by talking and not watching the time!"

"And that'll be your excuse to Mom and Dad?"

"Well, it's the truth and I'm not going to lie. Are you?" his sister asked.

"Yeah, I probably will…if I can't think of something between here and home that'll keep me out of trouble! Maybe I can say that Mr. Donner needed my help to do something."

"I just can't believe you can lie so easily!"

"Telling the truth sometimes is like fueling a fire, so why do it?" he answered. "A little lie sometimes can be like throwin' a bucket of water on a raging blaze in a futile attempt to calm it down. It doesn't put it out. It only gets rid of some of the heat long enough so you might luckily manage to control it until you find a way to put it out," her brother philosophized. "It seldom works though!"

"Unbelievable!" she replied.

"Slide your butt back over the back of the saddle and give me a ride," he said.

The steady clomp of Rocky's hooves on the gravel driveway was like a dull bell marking their doom. Off in the short distance up to the house the soft glow of lit kerosene lamps defined the kitchen windows where they witnessed their mother passing back and forth preparing the evening meal. "Thank God we're not late for supper," Marianne said, "that'd really be hell, and can you believe our dad's still out in the barn doing his chores."

"It looks like they must've been late coming back from Decatur," Ethan stated. "I'm gonna go on out to the barn and do my chores before Dad ends up doing them…if he hasn't already. If he has, he'll really be upset!"

"Let me off," Marianne said. "Take Rocky and put him in his stall for me?" she said. "Tell Dad that I'll go out and take care of him after I help Mom with supper."

Although both had been concerned about getting home late, their parents said very little to either of them about it. Ethan's father didn't look up from his milking when he walked past. His younger brothers hardly noticed him. Leon, his youngest brother sat on a bale of hay petting a calico kitten while Jonathan fed ears of corn through the small hand-cranked corn sheller. Ethan could see that Jonathan had nearly finished the chore of shelling enough ears to fill up the two five-gallon metal buckets that would be his duty to carry out to the chicken house after Jonathan finished, but he had other chores to do first. The air seemed heavy with tension. Although Leon had been the first to notice Ethan walk into the dim glow provided by the two old kerosene lanterns, he hardly looked up. It was then that Ethan suspected his parents probably had had a heated discussion concerning his and Marianne's tardiness in front of his younger brothers.

Marianne walked into the kitchen to find her mother standing in front of the hot stove working at frying a meal of home-cured ham and potatoes in two separate big iron skillets. A sauce pan of green beans simmered on a back grate. An uncut loaf of bread sat in the middle of the otherwise bare table. "I'm really sorry I'm late, Mom," she said apologetically and waited for her mother to reprimand her. "I rode Rocky over to Stella's. Mrs. Clark and Barb were there and I just forgot to watch the time!" she said, attempting to explain her actions without going into details.

When her mother didn't respond, Marianne's shoulders slumped and she stood awkwardly not knowing what to say or do. Her mother's silence was painful. A reprimand would have been a relief. At least it would have come and gone; furthermore, silence wouldn't help resolve the distance that seemed to be growing between the two of them. She wished for an opportunity to have their differences aired instead of letting them simmer like the beans slow cooking on the hot stove. "I'll set the table and cut the bread," she finally mustered to say and went to the cabinet.

Their father and the three boys came in, washed up at the sink with hot water from the stove and took their places at the table. Like automatons, Marianne and her mother served the meat, potatoes and the fresh, snap beans flavored with onions, salt and pepper. The kitchen smelled of rich mouth watering food, but the usual conversations and joy were absent. Only three-year-old Leon seemed immune to the atmosphere and pointed at the tray of thick-cut fried ham. "I want that slice," he said and pointed with his fork. "The one that's brown on the edges with crunchies," he said, requesting his favorite kind, and waited for someone to help him. "And will someone give me a big slice of bread," he asked and waited anxiously.

After supper Marianne cleared the table while her parents enjoyed their usual cup of coffee and her three brothers drank cold milk and finished off the last of the left-over blackberry cobbler from their Sunday dinner. Between bites, Jonathan sympathetically watched his sister working across the kitchen. "If you want to go out and take care of Rocky, I'll do the dishes!" he offered.

Marianne gave him a smile and mouthed, "Thanks."

Leon took a bite of his cobbler and washed it down with a big swig of milk. "I'm gonna go out to the barn with you!"

Marianne scraped the last plate clean, staked it on the counter next to the sink, looked at Leon and motioned towards the door. "Come on Leon, if you're still going out to the barn with me you'll need to hurry up," she said to her little brother. "Thanks, Jonathan," she said and gave him a simple smile. Inside the back door of the house she picked up one of the kerosene lanterns hanging from a row of wooden pegs, opened its bail and lit it with a big wooden farmer's match she extracted off the shelf above. They walked along surrounded by the night, enveloped in a cone of light from the lantern swinging at the end of her arm, making their surroundings sway and dance around them in rhythm to their steps.

Leon reached over and took his sister's empty hand in his. "Mom and Dad were really worried about you!"

"I know."

"They were so upset it really scared me a lot!"

Marianne looked at him and smiled. "I know they were but I learned a lesson from a friend today. They'll get over it, and I will too!"

"But aren't you afraid?"

"Afraid of what? I'm only troubled about things you're too young to understand. Everything's gonna be alright...don't worry!"

Her pony was in his stall where Ethan had left him. The familiar smells and peaceful sounds of resting animals in the barn at night and her pony eyeing her over the top of his stall had an immediate calming effect on her and she felt some of the tension across her shoulders leave. "Good pony," she said and hung the lantern on a metal hook that protruded out from a beam.

Leon followed her into the stall. "Do you want to help me, Leon?" she asked. He peered around at the dark shadows, fighting his fear of being in the barn at night. Unforeseen things might be lurking around. "Go around to the other side of the manger and you'll see a big bucket with feed in it. There's a tin hand scoop stuck into the feed. Pull out the scoop and use it to put five full scoops into Rocky's feeding trough."

He looked into the darkness and swallowed hard. "H, how m,many?" he asked.

"Five," she repeated. "You tell me every time you put a full scoop in the trough and I'll count it. Okay?"

"Okay!" he said without moving.

Watching her youngest bother hesitate, Marianne understood his reluctance to leave the stall. "There's nothing in here that's gonna get you, and anyway I'm right here for your protection!"

Everything seemed to have gone back to normal by the next morning. The mood at the table gave little indication of the tension that had permeated the kitchen the evening before.

"Since we're at a standstill with the crops right now, I think today's as good a time as any to start tearin' down them old outbuildin's over at the other place," Milburn said and looked across at Ethan working on his pancakes and bacon. "We got a couple of weeks here during the growin' season where we can get some of our other work caught up," he explained.

Curious to see what else he might have to say, everyone sat quietly and waited for him to continue. "We're gonna need as much of the lumber we can save from those buildin's. Until we get enough lumber we won't be able to build the forms to pour concrete for the foundation. The old sheds we don't get to now, we'll tear down later this fall or during the winter. After we finish eatin', we might as well get the truck, grab some tools and go over to the old horse barn and get started!"

Sometime a little later, Marianne went to gather the eggs. As she crossed the side yard she heard her father back the big truck out of the garage, shift gears and drive off down the lane with her two bigger brothers; it was then that she finally realized their lives were never going to be the same.

"When you were at Stella Mae's yesterday, Mrs. Darrian didn't happen to say anything about Mary Clark's niece coming down here from Minnesota, did she?" her mother asked as Marianne carried her basket of eggs into the kitchen.

Marianne almost stumbled. "No," she answered. "Why do you ask?" she said, caught off guard. Luckily, she thought fast enough to use the tactic of turning a question back into a question without spilling any details, but her mother's inquiry threw her mind into a tangle of knots.

"Well, only because I know Mary and Wilma are good friends and I thought maybe she might've said something or maybe Barb might've said something to Stella Mae recently. I'm curious because I heard someone say, just yesterday in town on our way to Decatur, that Mary has a niece that might be coming down from Minnesota to go to school here this fall," she explained. Marianne felt relieved that her mother was only pulling short straws out of a hat and actually knew nothing about anything that had transpired yesterday.

"No one told me anything," Marianne lied and put the basket down on the table. "Can I go take care of Rocky before I help you in here?" Marianne asked.

Her mother turned away and went back to doing the dishes. "If you want to, but don't be too long...we've got lots to get done."

Pondering her mother's question about Margret, Marianne slowly ran the currycomb over Rocky's neck and shoulders before doing his mane and tail. "You know I've always wanted a horse like you of my very own that I can tell all my secrets to," she whispered in his ear, led him out through the stall door into the barnyard and turned him loose. He walked off a few feet, shook his head up and down, whinnied and looked back at her as if he understood everything she had said.

A wide smile crossed Marianne's face. She didn't just see the changes that were taking place around her; she felt them deep down in her soul, but what she didn't comprehend was how twisted the road to the future might be.

CHAPTER EIGHT

August Twenty, 1941
A Neighbor's Sorrow

Lightning flashed, sending a rumble of thunder through the house that made the corner bedroom shake where Jonathan and Leon were asleep under a thin sheet on a double bed. The older of the two, snapped awake and sat up just as the first gusts of wind whipped in through the window, making the curtains flap and flutter. Jonathan looked over at his brother, curled up with his head buried deep into his feather pillow. "Wake up!" he said and punched Leon lightly in the ribs. "I smell bacon cooking and I hear Mom and Dad talking in the kitchen."

Several simultaneous lightning flashes followed almost instantaneously by large claps of thunder, shook the entire house, making the boys' dresser mirror rattle. Jonathan smacked his brother hard on the arm. "Wake up!" he cajoled, jumped out of bed and rushed over to close the window just as the first rain drummed across the roof, blew in across the window sill, pelted the floor and dampened his feet.

"I'm still sleepy," his little brother responded groggily, rubbed his eyes with the back of his clenched hands and slowly sat up.

"How can you sleep in all this noise," Jonathan asked, pulled his pants three-quarters of the way up and sat down on the edge of the bed with them unbuttoned while he put his socks and shoes on. "I've got to run to the outhouse!" he said and stood up to button his pants and buckle his belt. "Leon, if you get up now you can go with me," he exclaimed and pulled the pillow out from under Leon's head to further encourage his brother to get out of bed.

"It's raining and we're gonna get all wet," he protested as if his brother didn't already know the ramifications of going outside in a downpour.

"Well, wouldn't you rather get a little wet or pee in bed?"

Somewhat like a defensive snake, Leon slithered out from under the tangled sheet and started to get leisurely dressed.

Impatiently, Jonathan stood by the door. "Won't you hurry up? I've really got to go!" he said.

The boys hustled towards the back door across the corner of the kitchen. "I'll have your eggs ready when you two get back up here to the house," their mother promised. "Before you two go out you need to throw one of those rain slickers on."

They each took one, but only held them over their heads in a meager attempt to stay dry. The gusty wind instantly whipped the loosely draped coats around. They found it fun, laughing, running and getting drenched through the warm downpour. Minutes later they came back into the kitchen, dripping wet and giggling.

Their father, mother, older brother and sister studied them. "You two look like a couple of drenched chickens," Marianne noted, emphasizing drenched chickens.

"Don't get water all over the floor," their mother ordered and shook her head in mock disbelief. "Now," she said, "go change those wet shirts before you catch a death of pneumonia and make sure you wash up."

"They're already clean!" Marianne teased further.

The boys were still giggling when they sat down at the table while rain continued lashing at the windows. The kitchen was cozy and dry. It smelled wonderful from the hearty breakfast that everyone but the two late boys were indulging in. On the table sat a pitcher of cold milk, a stack of toast, a big, shallow bowl partially filled with fried potatoes and a platter, thinly covered with bacon. Ethan nonchalantly dipped the corner of his toast into the yolk of his sunny-side-up eggs and used the tired family cliché occasionally given to anyone coming to the table late, "We waited on you like one hog waits on another!"

Leon looked at his brother and curled up his nose. "Oink, oink," he said and turned around to address his mother at the stove. "I want two hard eggs, some bacon, a slice of toast and lots of fried potatoes."

"I want a soft egg and one piece of toast, and a bowl of cereal," Jonathan said. His mother wasn't surprised with his last request because after most meals, he had cereal with creamy, whole milk ladled over it.

"You can get up and get your cereal while I'm frying your egg," his mother said to him.

Marianne and her mother worked quietly clearing off the table after the breakfast was finished. Her father, somewhat engrossed in deep thought, sat pensively enjoying his last cup of coffee while the boys chatted. Everyone but Jonathan was having fresh strawberry jam on homemade bread and was washing it down, depending on one's age, with either hot coffee or cold milk. "I think I hear someone knocking at the door?" Marianne said, stopped drying the cup in her hand and tilted her head.

"Is it Saturday?" Jonathan asked automatically.

His father looked at him. "Yeah, it's Saturday. Now go see who's out there and tell them to come in...unless it's a salesman, and if it is, then you can tell'em I'm out at the barn cleanin' out cattle stalls and that I don't want to be disturbed."

Everyone listened in anticipation as Jonathan went to the door. "Hi," they heard him say.

"Hi Jonathan," came a muffled response they all recognized as their mother's brother, Edward. "Are your parents home?"

"Sure. Come on in," he said and stepped out of the way. "Is there anyone with you?"

"No. Not this time," his uncle said.

Edward was a thin, thirty-year-old, lanky, chisel-faced man with a head of thick, dark, wavy hair. He was the youngest of Gloria's siblings and had lived with her and Milburn for six months during the second year they were married, just after their parents had died. He took off his raincoat and tossed it over the back of an empty chair. "Hi," he said to no one in particular and they each answered back casually in one way or the other. "Wow...that rain is comin' down in sheets out there and I don't think I've ever seen so much water standin' around all over the place like it is now!"

"Yep, and it don't look like anybody's gonna get much done outside today," Milburn commented.

"That's for sure and I have a house I need to finish painting," Edward replied, wiping some rain off his face.

Milburn sat up straight. "If it's raining as hard as you say, this rain's changed my plans for the day too!"

"The slab between here and town is nearly under water," Edward exclaimed, explaining the conditions of the countryside he had observed coming from town. "In fact, I almost turned around when I looked up your flooded lane and couldn't hardly see the house, but then I figured a cup of coffee and a good visit was more important."

"This storm's gonna cause all kinds of problems, I suppose," Milburn agreed and gestured towards the chair next to him. "Move down and let your uncle sit there, Leon," his father said, "and Marianne, pour your uncle a cup of coffee."

"You can wait until you're finished there," her uncle told her. "I'm really in no hurry."

"No, that's okay. I'll get you one."

"How's Helen?" Gloria inquired about her sister-in-law.

"She's fine."

"And how about the kids?"

"Oh, they're fine too. Restless from the heat we've had all week and now they'll be bored and fussy because they'll need to stay in all day!"

Milburn leaned forward, tapped his spoon on the table lightly. "At least this rain'll bring some relief from all the heat!"

"Maybe it will, or just make it hotter, humid and uncomfortable," Edward replied.

Marianne put a brimming cup of strong percolated coffee and a spoon down on the table in front of her uncle. "You want some sugar or cream for that, Uncle?"

"No. I usually don't use the stuff," he said and it seemed that for no apparent reason he acquired a pained expression on his face and looked up at his sister busily cleaning the stove. "Maybe I could use some cream I suppose, if it's handy," he added. He stared down at the cup sitting in front of him for several long seconds and said, "I guess I should get to the bad news that I came to give you because it's something you'd want to know!" he said. His sister instantly turned to face him. Their eyes met. "Morris's baby girl died last night!" he announced.

"No! Oh no," she gasped, twined her hands in her apron, sucked in a deep breath, swallowed hard and said, "The poor little thing was only six months old. They've been worried about her ever since she turned ill two weeks ago," she reflected sadly. "You know, from birth she was never very healthy. The doctor's had been giving them very little hope. I know they've been going out of their wits with worry...and now this!" she said and started to cry, knowing the pain that Victoria, her neighbor and friend was surely going through. Her open hands went to her mouth to cover up a sob that seemed to erupt from deep within her chest.

Edward slowly stirred cream into his coffee and looked down at the table. "I wasn't meanin' to come out this morning, but when I found out about the baby at the drug store, I knew you'd want to know, the Morris's being such good friends of yours and all!"

Gloria looked at her brother through tear-filled eyes.

"What a tragedy it has to be for them," Edward stated.

"They're such nice folks," his sister whimpered. "They don't deserve all the heartaches they've had!"

Edward placed his spoon slowly on the table. "Someone said in town this morning that she'd always wanted a girl. They finally got one and now look what's happened," he said, shaking his head in disbelief. "Nearly everybody in town was talking about nothing else, even though, the newspapers on the news stand blazed in large type that the Russian's were strugglin' to hold back the German invasion. That's really awful news and nobody hardly even mentioned it!"

"That war's a bad thing, but this thing with the Morris's baby is a tragedy that's a lot closer to home," Milburn stated frankly.

"It is, and I think most people in the United States believe, like I do, that we have no reason to get any more involved in the war than we are now!" Edward replied.

Everyone had an opinion. Even so, a large number of people believed that there was at least a fifty-fifty chance that the United States would be drawn into the flaming conflicts raging in Europe and in Asia. The majority of Americans developed a positive outlook for the future as the national economy expanded. Over the last couple of years the country's industrial output was growing to satisfy its need for war materials as insurance for its defense just in case the country was forced to go to war. Although the preparations had been controversial from the start, and still were, the government had created jobs, bought about a sense of security and partially lifted the population out of the Great Depression. Yet, despite all this, no one suspected at the time that in less than six months from that day, Japan would bomb Pearl Harbor, Germany would declare war against the United States, and aggression would stretch around the world.

Gloria leaned against the edge of the counter and looked off into space through the kitchen window. "I bet she's really in bad shape. Victoria told me last year that she couldn't get pregnant again after the hard time she had delivering her youngest son, Lonny Junior, five years ago!" she whimpered, tears running down her cheeks. "Then getting pregnant again was like a miracle, especially after her oldest son, Jake, died in that motorcycle accident a year ago last May. She told me she was totally overjoyed after she gave birth to that little girl," she said, continuing to look outside, "and then that beautiful little thing became sick. Now this!"

Gloria turned away from the window. "We need to prepare some food for them and go give our condolences," she added in a hushed voice, more to herself than anyone else. Dormant emotions were surfacing and she wasn't sure she could hold herself together if she didn't get her mind occupied with some physical activity. The news that her brother gave had also brought back some lingering and unhappy memories of her first pregnancy which ended in a miscarriage of a baby girl. "I think I'll make a potato casserole and devil some eggs," she said and went to work in an attempt to pull her emotions together.

The Morris's farm was just half a mile away across the section west of their farm. Milburn had been friends with Lonny Morris since early childhood and, although he was also visibly shaken by the child's death, the discussion between the two men drifted to other topics while Gloria worked around the stove. The two younger boys, initially very interested in the adult talk, grew weary. "Let's go play," Leon said to his brother and punched him lightly on the shoulder.

Ethan watched his two brothers get up from the table. He couldn't make up his mind to stay or leave. The adults' conversation would take many interesting twists and turns before it ended, but he finally decided to get up and leave anyway. From experience, he figured that if he hurried out to get his work done, he might be lucky enough to go to town later in the morning and run around with his friends, since the rain would probably change his father's work plans for the day. "See you later, Uncle," he said and proceeded to remove himself from their presence and their interesting discussion about America's neutrality. "I'm going to go and get my chores done," he announced, although he didn't think anyone was listening.

Milburn noticed Ethan moving towards the door. "While you're out in the barn doin' your other chores, you can kick four bales of alfalfa down outa the hayloft. Break them up and feed the cows," his father instructed, not looking up, "and don't forget to feed the horses."

Standing at the sink wiping the last plate of the breakfast dishes dry, Marianne listened to the depressing topics that her father and uncle were discussing. What she heard made her feel as if she were being suffocated. "Wait up, Ethan," she yelled, and started to walk across the kitchen towards the door.

"Marianne, you need to finish the work in here first!" her mother reminded her. "We've got to make up the beds and I need you to help me cook a couple of things to take over to the Morris's." While it appeared that Gloria's emotional state over the death of the baby had settled down somewhat, she still looked distressed and frustrated. "No one gives me much help around here!" she complained softly to herself.

In case she was tempted to say something she might regret later, Marianne decided to find look for some fresh air in the out-of-doors. "Please, Mom, I wanna go help Ethan and gather the eggs and I need to feed Rocky too…that's all!" she said and bit her bottom lip after mentioning the pony. She knew that today, under the circumstances, it would take no more than a small slip of the tongue to have a confrontation with her mother and she realized that she had just opened the door to an uncomfortable topic.

"Rocky seems to be the only thing you're interested in around here! Your father should never have brought that animal onto this farm!" her mother stated emphatically.

Marianne felt her blood rise and knew she needed to control herself but could not. "You never want me to do anything other than work around the house! All my friends get to do things that I don't get to!"

"You seem to think all this work can get done by itself!" her mother retorted.

"No I don't. I just think I should get to have a little more freedom than I do!"

"This world wasn't made just so you could run around and have fun. You should realize you're a very lucky girl. You're a lot luckier than I was at your age!"

Marianne had heard her mother dwell on her hard life many times.

Ethan watched his mother remind Marianne how she, at a young age, always had to put her family first with little time to devote to her own interests. She felt no one seemed to fully appreciate her work ethic nor sympathized when she complained about her rough childhood.

Ignoring his mother's comments, Ethan yelled from just inside the back door, "Come on, Marianne. I'll think I'm gonna need your help," he said. "That's okay, isn't it, Mom?" he asked, and snapped the last clasp closed on his raincoat.

"Just make sure you get right back in here when you're done, Marianne," her mother said. "I can't get all of this work done by myself," she stated, getting in the last word.

The tension in the room was beginning to feel uncomfortable for Edward. "Maybe I should run along. I've takin' up too much of your time already!" he remarked.

Milburn decided to overlook his wife's emotional state. He and Edward had seen her get tied up in tangents before. "Finish your coffee first," he said to his bother-in-law. "I'd really like to hear what else has been going on in town!"

Ethan and Marianne skirted around the many puddles of water. "I don't know why she's always throwing up to me about how I have things so much better that she did when she was my age," Marianne said once they were a distance from the house. "It's not my fault she had it so bad!"

"I can see why she feels cheated and sorry for herself!" Ethan said, offering his judgment.

"Her parents were sick with little money and it made her very insecure. It's hard to imagine the responsibilities she must've had with sick parents and for them to try living on her family's meager income. I do feel really sorry for her," Marianne said and walked around a deep puddle. "I can see how she could be jealous of the things we have. "We're living in a way that reminds her constantly of her deprived childhood!"

CHAPTER NINE

Later on August Twenty, 1941

Brother and sister walked through a water soaked world. Rain ran off the driveway in rivulets. Puddles dappled the yard and small lakes stretched across large portions of the barnyard's flat surface. The closer Marianne and Ethan approached the barn, the stronger were the odors permeating the world around them. The fragrant smell of wet grass, the damp aroma of barn wood and the harsh smell of manure and wet livestock mingled and hung in the air. A few very wet cows stood next to the barn, their heads lowered, chewing their cuds.

Stepping in through the barn door was like crossing into an entirely new world. The smell of dry hay, the sound of a stray chicken clucking and scratching around with her clutch of little ones, pigeons cooing in the rafters and the soft moo of young steers sheltered in a stall made the rain outside feel distant. Only the murmuring patter of the rain falling on the steel roof, running off in torrents and falling from the eaves in sheets to the ground gave them a sense of security.

Ethan hurried to do his chores, anticipating he'd have more time to run around afterwards. "I'm going up into the loft to kick down some bales of hay before I do anything else," he said. "You need to shoo those chickens out of the away and watch out below!"

Marianne took off her raincoat and used it to scare the chickens a safe distance away. Once they were out of the way, she hung the coat on a wooden peg by a grain bin. "Okay, they're shooed away," she yelled. "You can kick the bales down anytime you want!"

"Look out below!" she heard Ethan shout and barely had stepped back out of the way before the first bale shot out of the hayloft, landed with a thud on end, bounced and cartwheeled across the floor in a shower of loose straw and dust. By the time the second one came sailing out into the center aisle of the barn, Marianne had escaped back by the horse stalls where she felt safe and completely happy. She loved everything about horses, even the sharp musky smell of their stalls. The atmosphere started soothing the anger and tension she had carried out from the house. Anticipating being fed, her four legged friends tossed their heads and lined up in their places at their feeding trough. Rocky stood against the outside wall, having been relegated to that position by his two larger stall mates. He eyed her with his miss-matched eyes as she approached.

Beginning with Maude, the largest, Marianne rubbed each of them on their velvety noses with her finger tips. "How are you guys doing this morning?" she asked and started rambling aloud about her complaints. "You wouldn't happen to know why my mother treats me like a servant, would you?" she said and pulled a section of loose hay from a bale. "She makes me get so frustrated that I could scream, you know. Why can't she understand that I shouldn't have a deprived childhood like hers? Why take it out on me!" Marianne said dejectedly and tossed some sweet smelling hay into the manger. Verbalizing to the horses made her feel better.

"Who are you talking to back there?" Ethan yelled, carrying two five-gallon buckets of feed for the cows.

Marianne filled a bucket with sweet smelling oats from the grain bin by the horse stalls. "It's just the five of us!"

"The five of you?"

"Yeah," she yelled back, "me, myself and the three horses!"

"Well, if you can spare some time after you finish, I could use a little help moving some bales around up in the loft."

"You know I don't have much time! I've still got to go gather eggs before I go back to the house to help Mom. If I'm gone too long, she'll have a conniption fit," she yelled.

"You've got time, Sis. It won't take very long!" he responded.

"Hope to see you guys later today," she said, briefly touched and patted each horse on the side of his head and walked away from them.

Ethan was up in the hayloft again already. "Are you going to help me or not?" Ethan hollered.

"I told you I don't have much time. Mom's waiting!" she reminded him again. "Why do we need to be moving bales of hay around up there anyway?" she asked, hesitating at the bottom of the ladder, one hand resting on a rung and debating whether to leave or climb up.

"Because, if we drag several from the back and stack them over here above the driveway, I won't have to be doing it every time I'm up here," he explained. "And, anyway, Marianne, I wanted to talk to you about Mom always climbing all over your back about everything."

Marianne yielded and shrugged her shoulders. "Fine, but I don't want to talk about Mom anymore." She climbed the perpendicular ladder into the hayloft and picked up a hay hook. It was easier to complain to the horses than discuss with Ethan the ongoing cycle of conflict between her and her mother. "I don't want to talk about it!" she stated firmly again and slid a bale of hay across the floor for Ethan to stack. After she moved several more, she became aware that the rain pattering on the tin roof was letting up. "Listen, I think the rain's stopping!"

"Well, if it does, I hope Dad doesn't still want to start tearing down that old cob shed next to our back door today," Ethan moaned and looked up at the roof high overhead.

His sister slid another bale about as big as she was across the floor. "I know Dad said he'd start working on those old buildings today but maybe the rain has made him change his mind."

"God, I sure hope so! We've torn down all those old outbuildings over at Grandma's place and now he wants to get started on the ones over here. Not only that, he keeps saying that he wants to tear the summer kitchen off the west side of our house," Ethan stated disgustedly and kicked the side of a bale.

"He says it has to be done before he can raise the house," Marianne reminded him. "Everything depends on it!"

"We been working so hard I haven't had time to do anything with my friends," he complained.

"At least you're not in my shoes," Marianne said sarcastically and hung up her hay hook. "I really gotta go," she stated flatly.

"Wait up and I'll go with you," he replied.

"Why do you want to do that? I'm just going to the chicken house to gather the eggs," she said.

"Well, I might as well carry a couple buckets of feed over to the chicken house so I don't have to do it later and also help you gather the eggs!"

Marianne was very much aware that Ethan was often unpredictable but she was taken aback with his rare nice gesture.

Marianne walked across the loft to the ladder and started to climb down. "What do you think Mom and Dad'll decide to do about today?" she inquired.

"I wish I knew," Ethan answered. "I just hope whatever it is doesn't include me!"

On their way across the soggy yard to the house after gathering the eggs, they noticed their uncle's car still parked out in front. A few drops of water continued to run off the edges of the roofs around them and plinked in the puddles underneath. In her head, Marianne toyed with plans for the day. "Do you think we could be lucky enough that Mom and Dad might decide to go shopping again and let us stay home?"

"If they do, I wouldn't have to help tear down that crappy old shed over there!" Ethan said, as he hopefully dreamed, his eyes fixed on the drab, unpainted old building standing by the sidewalk next to the back door of the house.

"Well, let's pray things work in our favor!" she answered.

In the kitchen they found that their uncle was about to leave. "I really need to be getting along," he said and stood up. "Helen's probably worried not knowing where I've been," he fidgeted. "She's probably got her dandruff up by now because I told her I wouldn't be gone long." Most people thought Edward's wife had delicate senses and was easily upset, which put her in a mood to have a migraine or throw a tantrum.

"Thanks for letting us know about Morris's baby," Gloria said sadly.

"You don't need to thank me; I felt it was very important to let you know," her brother said and put his hand on the back of his chair, ready to push it under the table. "I'm sorry I couldn't have brought you better news," he added. "It's a terrible shame about the bad luck they've had," he added and paused before he continued, "It's really a bad thing!"

"The worst is that children shouldn't die before their parents and they've lost two!" Milburn stated.

"That's very true, and just think about all of the young men that'll be lost if we don't stay out of the war!" Edward exclaimed and picked up his raincoat. "I guess I don't need to put this on right now...the rain seems to have stopped," he stated and hung it over his arm.

There was temporary emptiness in the atmosphere after he left. No one spoke. They listened to the outside door close, his car door slam shut and his car's motor kicked over and start before anyone spoke. A roll of thunder rippled in the distance. "It looks like the rain isn't finished yet," Milburn said as if he alone had heard it. "Maybe this'll be a good day to take care of some of the things I've been needin' to take care if I'm gonna get started on the basement before winter sets in," he stated.

"Remember, we've got to go to the Morris's this morning before we do anything else!" his wife reiterated, worried that he might put his projects ahead of his social responsibility to go with her and offer their sympathy for their neighbor's misfortune.

Puzzled that his wife would consider him so thoughtless, he declared sharply, "I meant later! I can't believe you would think that I wasn't goin' over there!" He gruffly pushed back from the table.

"Let's get around and go over there and be back here by nine-thirty, ten or so!"

"Your father and I are going over to give our condolences to the Morris's as soon as we get cleaned up," their mother reaffirmed. "Marianne, there are some boiled eggs sitting in cold water over on the counter. I'd like you to peel and devil them while I'm getting dressed. The scalloped potatoes should be ready for me to take out of the oven by then also. You'll need to clean up the kitchen and straighten up the house while we're gone so we can leave for Decatur just as soon as we get back from the Morris's.

These were jobs she could quickly finish. "Okay," Marianne chirped, anticipating the freedom she was going to have later.

Ethan stood beside his sister at the end of the table ready to ask his father a question. He shoveled his feet nervously, suspecting he was going to get an answer he didn't want to hear. "Dad, can we stay home today?" he asked.

His mother spoke up instead. "Not today." she answered emphatically. "We need to do some necessary shoppin' after your father's done with his business. You boys need new school shoes and clothes."

"Can I get a new outfit too?" Marianne pleaded, more than asked, hearing her mother indicate that the boys would get new clothes and not mentioning her.

"There's no need to spend extra money when the clothes we bought you last year still fit you fine, but we can look to get you a new pair of shoes," her mother said, calculating the value of a new dress only in dollars. "I've been thinking of sewing you up a nice blouse, a skirt and a pretty dress from the fabrics I already have!"

Being practical minded, her mother hadn't planned to buy her daughter any ready-made clothes; instead, she planned on using the cotton, floral-printed fabrics that she had acquired from the chicken feed sacks Milburn bought from a company which used it as an incentive to purchase their feed. It fit her tight fisted nature and reasoning, clouding her sensibilities. Somehow over the years she had either forgotten or chose to dismiss how a new garment from a store mattered to a young girl's pride and self-esteem.

"Please, just one new thing from the store. All the girls will be wearing something store-bought when school starts.

"Ethan, you'll need to go milk the cows right away," his father said and took one last sip from the cold dregs in the bottom of his coffee cup. "And, Ethan, be sure to wipe their udders with a clean towel before you start."

"When I'm finished milking, which one of those cans in the cooling shed should I pour the fresh milk into?"

"The large one on the far right. And while you're at it, you can empty the vat and refill it with cool, fresh water."

"Okay," Ethan answered.

"We're not going to be gone very long," their father instructed. "You kids will need to get them extra chores done before we get back, cause your mother and me will want to get goin' as soon as possible," he told them. "There's several people I need to see today and a couple of other places where I need to go!"

Shortly after their parents left, Marianne sat down at the table, put her head in her hands and contemplated the consequences of the discussion she had with her mother. She looked depressed. Ethan came out of the boy's bedroom and took a chair across the table from her. The two sat quietly waiting for the other one to say something. Ethan watched as a tear rolled down his sister's cheek and dropped off her chin.

"Maybe she'll change her mind and get you a dress after she thinks about it," he said softly.

"Oh sure! Like she always does!" Marianne whispered sharply, sighed, looked her brother sternly in the face and wiped her cheek. "It's not my fault our grandparents didn't have much and died young!"

"I'll tell you what. When she buys us things, I'm gonna tell her I don't think it's right if you don't get something too," Ethan promised. "Maybe she'll see how unfair she's being!"

"You think doing that will make me feel better? And you really, really think I want her to buy me something only because you might shame her into it? If she bought me one for that reason I'd wear rags first…so don't do me any favors," Marianne snapped, red faced and irritated. Her spirits were really being pulled down very low.

With nothing more to offer, Ethan screwed up the corner of his mouth, bit his bottom lip and shrugged his shoulders. "I gotta go get my work done before they get back or I'll be in real trouble!" he answered meekly.

Marianne stood up. "Thanks for the thought anyway," she said as an apology and went to do the dishes. She worked nimbly, brooded over the unfairness she felt and tried to understand equality. By the time she put the last dish away, she concluded that her mother's decision to not get her a dress was because she favored the boys.

CHAPTER TEN

Decatur Shopping Trip

The family's black, four-door sedan, splashed water out of the pot holes as it lurched from side to side carrying the family slowly down the long gravel driveway toward the highway. In the back seat Ethan and Jonathan sat on either side of Marianne. Leon sat up front between his parents and watched the wipers flicking the rain away. Everyone sat silently, lost in thought. It wasn't until they had driven across the B&O Railroad tracks bisecting the small town, east to west that anyone said anything. "First, I need to stop past the saw mill and order up six large, long beams I'll be needin' for raisin' the house. After that, I have a couple of other things I need to do before we do any shoppin'," Milburn said.

There was a long list of stops imbedded in his head. They stopped at the saw mill. After that, he went by to see Mike Jones, a carpenter and an all-around handy man who several years ago had moved up from Kentucky in the early thirties during the first stages of the depression. Mike now lived in a small, tired, old four-room house with gray clapboard siding across the railroad tracks on the south edge of town. He had often worked on Milburn's farm doing odd handyman jobs and also occasionally helping in the fields. A week earlier Milburn had approached him about removing the summer room off the west end of the house and

Mike had responded that he would need a couple of days' notice before starting.

The two men stood talking on the small, plain porch of Mick's house. "I jest need to finish installin' a window in the back of the barber shop," Mike stated, "and if y'all ain't thinkin' of startin' until the first of next week, I can take on some small job until you all is ready for me," he said.

"Monday'd be fine," Milburn replied, confirming their agreement made earlier. "And you'll help do the basement later this fall after the room's torn off?" he asked, testing Mike to make sure that no holes lurked in his plans that might need to be plugged somehow.

"Sure nough!" Mike answered. He had promised to help raise the house after the beams were delivered and be responsible to get the basement dug, construct the forms for the concrete walls, pour the concrete, build the upper level of the foundation out of cement blocks, and settle the house back down on the blocks before pouring the basements floor. It was a big job and Milburn wanted to make sure Mike would see it through to the end. "That's what I was planning on doin'," Mike said. He was enthused about the work and the interesting nature of the project plus it was a steady job that he had been praying for. "If you all could afford takin' on my son to help with the project, I think we could finish the whole thing, includin' the basement, around Thanksgivin', I s'pose!" he said.

Milburn considered what he had heard for several seconds. "I don't know if I can afford another hired hand," he confided, caught off guard by Mike's suggestions, but he seemed warm to the idea. "You do need to understand, Mike, that doin' this thing is goin' to be a big expense for me right now!" he said, being honest.

"I see's how you can be worried bout the added expenses an' all, but I don't see's how it'd really cost that much more by usin' the both of us. With two of us wokin', we'd finish the work more than twice as fast, don't you see? It's gonna save y'all money in the long run. More efficient this way to, you know, and keep in mind that once we get started workin' on somethin' like this, it's easier and cheaper if you do it all at one time. This fall we should even have the stairwell to the landing roughed in and weather tight.

"I don't know!" Milburn answered.

Mike frowned. "Don't trust my judgment?" he questioned.

"No! No! It's not that!" Milburn answered.

"You knows I'm right!" Mike argued.

"You may be right!" Milburn said, "but I just need time to think on it some," he added and looked away into the distance for a long awkward minute. Mike was about ready to interrupt when Milburn responded, "I think I might be able to put my hands on enough money to do it but only if you really think it'll get finished this fall. The bank hinted that maybe they'd give me a ten-year note for any extra funds I might need, if I can keep the costs within reason."

Needing work and trying to offer the best solution for his friend, Mike suggested, "If, after we get goin' and y'all happen to see along the ways you can't afford doin' all of it this fall, we'll cork it like a bottle and come back in the spring or next summer!"

"You'd agree to that?" Milburn asked, his tight expression softening on seeing the plans working out better than what he had foreseen.

"Sure 'nough," Mike answered. He felt good that they had arrived at a workable solution which would benefit the both of them: Mike for the job and Milburn for the faster and more affordable construction.

"You know," Milburn replied, considering the extra benefits in Mike's proposal, "if you could get all that work done as you say, then maybe we'd be able to get a furnace installed and have central heat in the house before this Christmas time."

"It's a fair assumption, but only if y'all gets right on it," Mike responded.

"This is workin' out much better than I ever expected!" Milburn said happily.

"Then you agree?" Mike asked.

"Yep, I do!" Milburn answered amiably and shook Mike's hand to seal the deal.

The last stop Milburn made was on the edge of Decatur at a large construction company where he needed to reserve twelve large railroad type screw jacks to lift the house on the oak beams that he was having cut. After talking to Mike, he decided to stop and check on the price of a furnace.

"Are we there yet?" Leon asked each time his father stopped. His mother would tell him they would be there in a little while, and his three siblings in the back seat would roll their eyes. Finally, his father said, "Guess what?"

Leon slumped low in the seat and answered, "We're gonna be there after we stop ten more times!"

"No," his father answered, "I'm done with my errands and we'll be downtown in just a few minutes."

"Goody," Leon answered and sat up straight.

"I'll park in the lot across from Sears, if that's okay with you," Milburn stated and looked across the seat at his wife. "If you don't find the stuff you want in Sears, you'll be close enough to shop at any of the other stores."

Just the mention of shopping left Marianne feeling humiliated. She knew that she was going to feel even worse just tailing along to watch her brothers get new school clothes while she stood by and observed. Not even slightly being considered for getting a new blouse, skirt or dress to wear to school on the first day left a hollow pit of resentment in her stomach. All of the other girls in her class, except two of the poorest, would show up flaunting something new from their wardrobes and she knew that she would wilt with envy. She felt that the shoes her mother mentioned getting were only a token to pacify her.

Once more, Leon asked, "Are we there yet?" Marianne looked over the seat at the back of his head and it dawned on her that he wouldn't be getting anything new either; his wardrobe totally consisted of hand-me-downs. He was only three and he didn't seem to mind wearing worn-and-ill-fitting clothes. He hardly ever complained and seemed happy in his own small world, either that, or he realized that he didn't have any other choice and had accepted his fate.

"I've got things I need to buy at Blacks' Hardware," Milburn said.

"Help me pick out the kids' shoes first," Gloria remarked and looked at the big Sears department store across the street. "Sears has the better prices. Afterwards, you can go over to Black's while I check around to see what they have in boys clothing. If I can't find any to my satisfaction, we'll walk around to Montgomery Wards."

Marianne slid lower in her seat.

Leon liked shopping. He was entering the stage of his young life where all things in the world fascinated him; he couldn't seem to get his fill of the city's smells, noises, shapes and sizes of people, pigeons flying around or the whoosh and thump of the vacuum tubes at Montgomery Wards that sent bills and receipts back and forth. Buses, neon lights that looked bright even in the daytime and all the other things that made up the tapestry of the big city awed him.

While they waited for the crosswalk light to change, their mother informed her family, "When we're done shopping for clothes, I'd like to go to Kreske's Five and Ten for some needles and things and we can also grab some hot dogs at the stand-up counter at the front of the store. We'll be hungry by then and your dad can meet us there at twelve."

Two hours later Marianne had a new pair of practical shoes, her two oldest brothers had new shoes, two pairs of pants, two shirts each and some new underwear. Jonathan also had a new belt. The family stood around inside Kreske's eating their hot dogs and drinking their Dad's Root Beers. Marianne was so moody that the joy of eating was lost; taking a bite, she felt it might catch in her throat.

Milburn noticed her long emotionless face and it got to him. He watched her struggle with her food and suspected what was going on in her mind. "You know somethin'? After gettin' everything I needed I still have some money left in my wallet. I wouldn't want to carry all those bills back home with me, would I?" he said with a wily smile and winked at her. "I'm thinkin' that when we go back over to Sears, we should take a look at the clothes in the young girls department...maybe we can find a couple of things affordable enough to buy. What do you think Gloria?"

His wife was caught in an awkward position and was forced to agree. "I suppose," she answered.

Suddenly the food tasted so much better; a twinkle replaced the dull dispirited look in her eyes. Discovering a ray of hope, Marianne chirped, "Can we reeeeally?"

"I'm sure we can," he replied and took a big bite out of his hot dog. "Would anyone like another one?" he asked, buoyed up with a euphoric feeling that life was working out in his favor.

"Could I have one of those doughnuts instead?" Leon asked. He had been watching the automatic doughnut machine add a circle of dough into a tray at one end of a hot oil bath, allow it to cook on one side and then like magic, flip it over and let it cook on the opposite side before a mechanical arm lifted out the cooked delicacy. A young attendant would then dip one side of each with chocolate, vanilla or strawberry glaze and place it on a tray where its visual allure and wafting aroma tempted customers.

Leon pointed to a new chocolate one. "That's the one I want!" he exclaimed to his father.

His father stuffed the last big bite of his hot dog into his mouth. "We'll get a dozen," he replied and ruffled up Leon's hair with a calloused hand.

The ride home in the car saw a much happier group of kids than when they had started out on the trip. Everyone occupied the same seats as before. Marianne sat in the back between her two brothers enjoying the warm evening air blowing in through the open windows and was holding a bag containing two dresses that she peeked in from time to time. "I don't see why we spent money buying them dresses when I could've made them at home," she heard her mother rebuke her father.

As a man, maybe her father didn't understand all the things Marianne felt, but at least, he understood her girlish pride and it had encouraged him to purchase the dresses even though he anticipated it would upset his wife.

"It's like Barb said," she thought, remembering the comment her friend had made about her mother being worried and upset, *"She'll get over it!"* Her father must have used the same logic, she reasoned. Rocky's big ears were going to be available to her during evening chores and she decided that she was going to fill them with her day's experiences and give him a very detailed description of her new dresses.

CHAPTER ELEVEN

September Second
First Day of School, 1941

Rocky tossed his head and pranced sideways under Marianne and she suspected his behavior indicated that he felt the changes that were about to take place with school ready to start the next day.

Earlier, she had given him a couple of extra cubes of sugar and a carrot as a special treat, saddled him up and made over him even more than was her usual attentive nature. While getting him ready for their last long summer ride, she explained that she was beginning her last year in grade school. "I'll miss your company," she said and reminded him how she eagerly sought him out all summer whenever she had time. "Thanks for letting me share my thoughts and secrets with you," she said and felt a knot develop in her throat.

Two hours later, she rode up to the watering tank, swung out of the saddle and slid down to the ground. While Rocky drank and flicked his ears, she undid his cinch strap, pulled the saddle off and tossed it on the ground. She stepped into the barn, brought out a rag, a stiff brush and a currycomb which she used to groom her pony's coat. When she finished, she led him out through the gate and took off his bridle. "I'll see you in the morning before I leave," she said, slapped him gently on the rump and watched him trot away.

As the sun came up early the next morning, banging and ripping noise's intermingled with loud voices roused Marianne out of her deep sleep. She lay awake and listened for two or three minutes until she realized that she had forgotten about the construction that was to take place starting today. Mike Jones and his son had arrived and were continuing with the preliminary work they had started two weeks earlier which they needed to complete before they could tackle the renovations on the house. The cob shed next to the sidewalk had been dismantled, the boards saved and its rubble carried away. It had taken another four long days the week before just to remove and drag the summer kitchen from the yard and out into the front pasture.

She visualized her world coming apart like the house and doubted whether the work and mess were worth the misery it might bring. All of the improvements her father planned were good things but she worried that her mother would feel more than a little stressed until everything was completed. There would be repercussions for her during the next few months and Marianne steeled herself to endure her fate and the consequences.

Their father pulled up in front of the grade school to drop Marianne and Jonathan off. Loaded with the books and other necessities which she needed for the eighth grade, she stepped anxiously out of the car and looked at the front of the familiar red-brick, two-story, rectangular school that sat imposingly in the middle of the wide, deep block surrounded by small, mostly white, wooden-framed houses. The long front half of the schoolyard was tree shrouded. Several areas were occupied with slides, teeter-totters, swing sets and other schoolyard paraphernalia. Out in the open space behind the school were playing fields. Clustered in small clutches along the wide sidewalk leading up to the front entrance were all ages of school children. Only a couple of students were unrecognizable; they were probably new students who had moved there over the summer.

The transition of returning from summer vacation to the classroom made her feel as if she had her two feet in two worlds at the same time. Marianne took a couple of hesitant steps away from the car, stopped, paused and turned around to look at her father; motioned goodbye and strode off towards the old building and a new year.

Jonathan and his sister walked elbow to elbow towards the school and past the American flag limply hanging from the top of its pole in the hot, early-September-morning air. She glanced at it briefly and decided it looked the way she felt: cool, bright, pretty, but somber. Maybe the excitement of the first day of school would finally perk her up the way a fresh breeze could liven up the flag.

Marianne scanned the clusters of students for her close friends. She said hi to a couple of seventh graders standing among the first group of girls she walked by and paused for a couple of seconds to make sure they noticed her new outfit.

Once she saw the subtle cues that they noticed her new clothes, she smiled to herself and walked on. She was already being drawn out of her doldrums. Jonathan touched her on the arm. "I'll see you later, Sis," he said and headed off toward a group of his third-grade classmates standing over by the north front corner of the building. Just as she started to walk up the steps into the building to get rid of her heavy load of books, she heard Stella Mae's familiar voice screech in the distance behind her, "Marianne, over here, over here!" It took a moment for her to locate her friend standing behind some shrubbery.

More interested in visiting with her friends than getting rid of her books, she lugged them over and found that none of the other girls who Stella Mae was standing among had bothered to take their books inside either; instead, they had placed them in stacks on the ground by their feet. The excited girls chattered away sharing their expectations of the new school year and of their summer experiences.

"I must be the last one to make it here," Marianne observed, looking around the circle of girls.

"Almost," Stella Mae corrected, "because Barb's the only one not here yet!"

"You mean I'm really here before Barb? She's always the first to show up for things and she loves school!"

Donna Marsh, the most loquacious of her friends, interjected, "I saw her yesterday afternoon and she told me she'd probably be a little late," and then nearly out of thin air Donna, unaware that the other girls knew she had a crush on Marianne's older brother, asked, "Was Ethan looking forward to going to high school today?"

Marianne looked directly at her friend. "I'll ask him when I get home and I'll also be sure to tell him you were very curious to know!"

Several of the girls tittered and smiled. Since fifth grade, Donna, a flirty girl with an athletic figure, brown hair and dark eyes had been making eyes at Ethan. Although a lot of boys vied for her attention, she seemed to only melt around Marianne's brother. There weren't many secrets or tidbits of gossip that stayed private very long around the small eight-room school and the attraction between the two of them was very old news. She glanced around the circle of friends and her face turned a deep crimson.

"What's so funny, anyway?" she asked, trying to reclaim a cat that had long ago already gotten out of the bag. "He's just a friend of my brother's, that's all!"

Marianne looked around in an attempt to find Barb. "It's almost time for the bell to ring," she said, looking concerned. "I wonder why Barb hasn't shown up yet. It's not like her!"

Evelyn, a shy, dishwater blond with pale blue eyes spoke up first. "Since her pregnant cousin showed up from Northern Minnesota six weeks ago, none of us have seen her very often. It's like she's been avoiding us on purpose. And..."

One of the girls who lived in the same end of town as Barb interrupted. "I thought Barb was trying to avoid me last week when I walked past her house. I saw her standing by the car in their driveway and before I got close, she hurried to go inside and glanced back. Although I waved and yelled at her, she seemed reluctant to come back down the driveway at first. We chatted for a few minutes and when I brought up her cousin, she told me that Margret feels like everybody in town is whispering behind her back about her condition and she refuses to leave the house."

"What a pickle of a situation her cousin has gotten herself into," Stella Mae observed with little forethought, and giggled at her own inappropriate comment and then became embarrassed when no one else found her slip of the tongue funny. "I didn't mean to make an awful joke," she said apologetically. "I'm really very sympathetic about her cousin's condition!"

"I saw both of them at the drug store last Friday and I couldn't tell her cousin was carrying a baby!" stated another classmate. "She's not showing at all!"

"Maybe she isn't showing, but that doesn't keep people from talking," Evelyn interjected. "It only makes people curious and to look or stare even more. People love gossip and they can be really cruel. Barb told me the first week her cousin got here her family went to church and the preacher made a point of talking about the sin of having a child out of wedlock," she exclaimed. "I'm sure the gossip had already gotten around town and he knew about her!" she emphasized. "Barb's mom and dad haven't been back to church since, and I haven't seen Barb or Margret around town either."

"What a nasty thing for him to do!" Marianne replied. "I can't understand why people gossip so much or why they're so interested in condemning someone who made a mistake when they may have something to hide themselves. Wouldn't you think a preacher would be more understanding and willing to forgive? I thought that was what preachers and good Christians were supposed to do...especially about the forgiving part!"

Alice, a snide, platinum-blond girl who had moved into town from Kansas City in the middle of the previous year, and who considered herself much more popular and influential in the group than she really was, rolled her eyes slowly and commented, as if she hadn't heard a word the other girls had said, "Her cousin has sure stirred things up by coming here. Barb acts like her cousin is a princess, but everyone knows her cousin was the one that got herself in that condition. She has nobody to blame but herself! Maybe Barb's a little embarrassed about the whole thing. It wouldn't surprise me if she might think that by coming late she can avoid us asking her questions," Alice added.

A loud agitated voice commented behind Alice, "I don't suppose anything would really surprise you!" Everyone froze. "I'm not embarrassed about anything, but maybe you should be!" Barb replied sharply.

It was a very awkward moment. Several girls shoveled their feet and lowered their heads. Marianne, on the other hand, glared at Alice and remarked, "We're glad you're here Barb and no matter what you might've heard, most of us are concerned about your cousin."

"Alice didn't sound very concerned," Barb said angrily. Her statement was followed by a long uncomfortable silence, leaving only the broken conversations and bits of laughter coming from other small clusters of students some distance away

In an attempt to break the tension, Marianne said in defense of the group, "You only heard what Alice said and not how the rest of us feel. I'm not going to apologize for Alice. She needs do it herself, if she wants. The rest of us were actually discussing about how concerned we've been for you and how we thought you've been avoiding us for some reason, and then today, when you were so late, we got worried...that's not like you!"

After hearing the explanation, the tension eased somewhat. One of the girls turned to pick up her books, but before she could do so, Barb sniffled and held her hands up to her face which made the entire group of girls feel uncomfortable. They stood around hunching their shoulders as if the sky was about to fall.

Stella Mae, clearly becoming emotional also, spoke up, "We thought you were angry with us after the gossip got spread around and we figured you might've thought that me or Marianne had spread the news!"

"We didn't!" Marianne quickly interjected.

"It's true that I've been confused and upset as I contemplated about who might've started the rumor, but that's not the reason why I was late getting to school this morning," she said and then continued. "It's because...well it's...be...be...because," Barb stuttered, "Margret went away this morning and isn't coming back for a long time...if ever! She couldn't stand it here any longer with people t...talking b...behind h...her back and looking at her the way they do," she added and shook with emotion as she tried to explain fully. "She was very nice and so much fun to be with. Why couldn't people just have left her alone?" she added more to herself than to those standing around watching. "Now she's moved to Decatur to stay with our Aunt Minnie and help her keep house. I'm going to really, really miss her!"

Evelyn handed Barb a white hanky embroidered with pale yellow flowers along the edges. "Thanks," Barb said softly and dabbled at the small pools of water gathered in the corners of her eyes. Before anyone had time to say anything more, the first soft ding of the school bell echoed off the surrounding houses. Instantly, it was followed with deeper clangs as the rope in the school janitor's hands brought the arc of the bell up to its full momentum. The ringing created a river of students anxiously flowing up the steps and in through the wide front doors. Barb stayed behind holding her books and dabbled at her eyes while all the other girls but Stella Mae and Marianne picked up their books and scampered inside.

"You can give me my hanky back later," Evelyn said, and hurried off after the others.

The three close friends stood behind the screening shrubs until they were alone outside. The only sounds that could be heard were those coming from inside the school and out through the tall, open classroom windows above them. The room just above them was the first-grade classroom and it was subdued, considering those students were nervous in their new strange environment. The upper grades on the second floor were much louder, a natural phenomenon caused by their self-assurance after surviving the first four grades on the first floor.

The next person to pick up her books was Stella Mae. "I want you to know that I never let our secret out," she reiterated. "I never would've done that. I've really kept the promise I made to you this summer!"

"I hope you believe me when I say I didn't say anything to my mom or anybody else either," Marianne interjected and picked up her books. "The only one I told it to was Rocky," she said, "and he doesn't gossip!" she added.

Barb looked at her two friends and gave them a weak smile. "It doesn't really matter anymore, I guess. The fact of her pregnancy was bound to be discovered sometime anyway. Now she's gone to live in Decatur. The only time I'll get to see her is when we go over there and that's not very often," Barb said dejectedly. "Maybe we should go inside," she softly added, crushed the hanky into her palm and awkwardly used the knuckle of an index finger to rub at the corners of her eyes one last time. "Thanks for being my good friends and standing up for me."

Stella Mae jokingly said, "You're going to tell that pony about today too, aren't you?" and it lifted their spirits somewhat.

Marianne brought her right index finger up to her lips. "Shhh. Don't tell anyone, but I go home and tell him all of my secrets," she said, acting sheepishly.

Barb's face brightened and she sniffled one last time. "I sure wish I had a pony to share my secrets with!" she candidly remarked.

"You're free to come out anytime you'd like and share any and all of your secrets with him that you want to," Marianne stated in all seriousness. "And as I've just said, he never tells a soul about anything you say to him."

Barb managed a weak smile. "I might take you up on that!"

"Does that go for me too?" Stella Mae asked.

"Sure," Marianne answered. "He's got big ears," she added and the three friends laughed hysterically for several seconds before they calmed down.

Anyone watching these three teenage girls walking proudly up the steps might have imagined them as crusaders going up through the portals of Jerusalem to reclaim the city and all of the Holy Land for Christianity.

Marianne grabbed the brass handle on one of the big white ornate doors, swung it open for her friends and they were greeted with the familiar odor of freshly waxed floors, the cacophony of teachers giving out instructions and desk tops banging down. Suddenly all thoughts of summer and the outside world were erased just as clean from their minds as the slate on the unused chalked boards in the classrooms. The interior of the building was like a cocoon shrouding them from any outside influences. Each of them contemplated the new school year as they wordlessly climbed up the terrazzo covered steps to the wide-wood landing between the four-corner classrooms on the second floor. Distinct teachers' voices were giving instructions in each room as students noisily sought to get their desks organized. "I love your dress, Marianne," Stella Mae whispered at the last second before they entered the eighth grade classroom.

"Thanks," she mouthed and surmised that eighth-grade year was going to be the best one ever.

CHAPTER TWELVE

End of the First Day of School, 1941

In the warm classroom, Marianne daydreamed under heavy eyelids, hardly hearing what Mrs. Holtsman had been saying for the last five minutes, was startled when the sharp clang of the hall bell ended the first day of classes.

"You're excused," her teacher said and suddenly the room became alive with a mad fury of activity. Desk tops were thrown open and the students' books and papers were either carefully laid, randomly shoved or tossed into the small storage spaces. A few impatient people hurried for the door.

Marianne watched the commotion for a few seconds before gathering up her homework. She watched the activity without much thought, selected what to take home, slowly lowered the top of her desk and waved bye to Stella Mae and a couple of other classmates who were standing in the front of the classroom talking to Mrs. Holtsman.

The simple gesture of closing her desk somehow caught her teacher's attention. "See you tomorrow," she said directly to Marianne, making her feel special. Mrs. Holtsman was well liked and respected because she was always fair to her students and they knew she tried to treat them all equally.

"Bye," Marianne mouthed back.

She hadn't seen Jonathan since they had walked up the sidewalk in the morning and she had no idea where he was now but suspected he might have walked home alone. *Maybe Ethan's still hanging around outside the high school and he'll walk home with me*, she thought, but when she arrived there five minutes later, she discovered that most of the high school students had already left. A couple stragglers she knew waved out of car windows as they drove by on the street in front. The driver of one car loaded with students, beeped his horn and someone she couldn't see from inside shouted, "Hi, Marianne," and then they were gone before she could wave back.

Marianne didn't see her older brother anywhere. *Oh well,* she thought, *it would've been nice walking home with one of them but it's also nice having time to be alone to think. It sure seemed like a long day...I'm tired. I guess the hardest part of the day was just being around lots of people again. And sitting in the classroom all day really took some adjusting, but I have to admit, it was exciting getting back together with my friends and listening to what they did all summer.*

This fall, the walk home was somewhat shorter for Marianne; after her father had harvested the oats in the twenty-acre field between the high school and their house, it eliminated the need to walk around the field and along the highway.

Halfway across the stubble field, Marianne paused and gazed at her family's farmstead. Everything looked perfectly normal. Puffy clouds dotted the blue sky, a meadow lark sang somewhere off in the middle distance and a car sped down the highway off to her right, going north and fast. She looked up at the blue sky and then back at the house and suddenly became aware of the changes that had taken place since she left for school that morning.

She recalled seeing only the long wooden beams and large jacks in the yard for the work that was to be done. Now the summer kitchen sat in the pasture between the house and the highway, leaning at an odd angle, open on one side. It was like an apparition, like the partial hulk of a small shipwreck sticking up out of a sand dune. The beams and jacks were gone from the yard and the house sat much higher in the air and she could see underneath it even from where she stood.

She had a hard time grasping the many changes that had been happening over the last couple of weeks. Standing in the stubble of the oat field and seeing the house higher, the summer room removed, the cob shed gone and most of the other outbuildings torn down the view gave her an eerie feeling. A shudder ran up her spine. She visualized all the buildings flying around like leaves in an autumn wind, swirling and rustling in a blue sky and then gently settling back to earth in odd places. But unlike leaves, she knew that the wood from them would be reconstructed into different shapes and forms to be put to better uses.

That seems strangely like me, she thought. *I feel like I'm being blown around in the wind, flipped end over end and round and round. Maybe in time I'll land somewhere else and be transformed into a different self. I wonder what I'll become!"* Several images fluttered through her thoughts. A couple of the images made her smile and reflexively she looked around to see if anyone was watching.

The smell of the disturbed brittle oat stubble underfoot and the sensation of the straw brushing against her legs distracted her for a second or two and before she could resume her train of thought, a meadow lark, probably the mate of the one she had heard moments earlier, flew up out of a dense patch of short, matted grass a few feet away, startling her and making her heart thump. she shaded her eyes with her hand and followed the bird's flight towards the pasture in front of the house. She saw its mate fly up off a fence post and join the other one in mid-air; her eyes remained focused on them until they landed on top of the hulk of the discarded summer room.

I know those old buildings Dad tore down were past their usefulness and weren't needed any longer, she surmised, *but I miss them anyway. A part of one building just became a bird roost,* she supposed and smiled because she was keenly aware and delighted to be going through some kind of a metamorphosis herself. Finally, her body was acquiring some lumps and curves. Sometimes she blushed around boys and although she didn't fully comprehend the emotions she often felt, she didn't resent feeling them either. *Sometimes I can hardly keep my emotions under control,* she thought.

"I think later this evening I'll just go confide these new thoughts to Rocky," Marianne said aloud and sprinted the last few yards across the field to the pasture toward the wooden gate separating the field of yellow stubble from her house. In spite of the fact that she was wearing her pretty new dress, she put her left foot up on the gate like a ladder and used the top board for a hand hold. Gaining the top, she swung her right leg over and hopped down to the ground, making the hem of her dress fly up around her waist like a parachute. Several chickens ran, cackling this way and that. She ran across the pasture to the second gate and propelled herself over it much the same way she had the first one.

Standing just across the wide driveway studying the house, she was better able to observe the major transformations that had taken place during the day. The long beams had been placed under the house and the large railroad jacks had been used to lift it several feet higher. Where the summer porch had been, rough ends of wood marred its edges. Stained, old wallpaper stood open to the elements and defined the shape of the room. One large and two smaller, lighter, off-color, rectangular shapes dotted its surface where framed pictures had hung years before. The flowered print inside the rectangles contrasted sharply against the gray and faded print over the rest of the wall. The original, inside door between the kitchen and the summer room now acted like an outside door. Underneath it some very rough steps had been hacked together.

She studied her father and his two hired hands as they were going through the last stages of raising the house. The three of them were going from jack to jack, turning the screw mechanisms only a quarter turn on each while constantly checking to keep the house level.

Mike, the older of her father's two hired hands held a long bubble level against the bottom beam of the house. "How's it look?" she heard her father ask Bill while his father, Mike, braced himself and slowly turned one of the long, steel, rod handles on a jack another quarter turn. Marianne was mesmerized.

Smiling because of their excellent progress, Mike said, "I'd say we've jest about finished a real good day's work! Real good! That old house is still jest as level as a ship in dry dock!"

"We still need to check the jacks on the other side" her father responded. "We should be done here in a couple of hours, and then if we get our stuff put away and get the mess cleaned up, and you two will be ready to get start excavatin' the space under the house early tomorrow mornin'," he added.

Marianne watched the two hired men work while her father stood back and admired their handy work. She discerned that they were doing a big job that needed to be carried out carefully. After a few moments of watching, she said, "Hi."

Bill looked around, touched the bill of his cap and said, "Miss Marianne!" he said to acknowledge her and to show respect in the manner he had learned while being raised in the Deep South.

Busily concentrating on the work he was doing, Mike raised his gloved hand in a cursory wave. "Home from school already?" he asked while he double checked his level.

"Yeah," she answered.

Her father kidded, "Well, your timin's sure good…just when all the hard work's finished, you show up!"

"I tried to come home in the middle of the afternoon to help but recess wasn't long enough," she joked, making the three men chuckle.

Playing along good naturedly, her father lifted his hat in an exaggerated motion, scratched his head in mock seriousness and replied, "I guess tomorrow we'll have to go to that school of yours and see if we can do somethin' about it!"

Holding her homework in her crossed arms, Marianne smiled and rocked on the balls of her feet. "I've gotta go. Mom's probably got some things for me to do inside."

As she walked away, out of the corner of her eye she noticed Mike pull a metal half-pint flask out of his bibs, unscrew the cap and hold it up like a toast to the house and exclaimed, "Here's to a job well done," and took a long swig.

"Let's pray the rest of our work goes as smoothly as it has done today," she heard her father reply.

Bill yelled after her, "Be careful you don't fall on them temporary steps we constructed back there! We didn't get much of a chance to finish them jest right," he apologized.

Walking towards the door, Marianne saw scraps of lumber, old tin cans, bent nails and shards of glass littering the barren ground where the summer room had once been. A musky odor wafted up out of the dirt that had been covered for so many years under the summer kitchen addition, moldering, hidden from the sun and closed off to the wind.

Mike was right in telling her to be careful on the steps leading into the house. She could see how they had been cobbled hastily together with various lengths and thicknesses of scrap lumber. They seemed solid enough when she stepped up on them, but to her eye, they only replicated the destruction around her. She opened the squeaky door, stepped inside and noticed that a large rug had been placed on the pine floor just inside the threshold.

Gloria sat at the kitchen table breaking the last of the season's green beans. "Make sure you wipe your feet," she commanded in a tight voice.

Marianne wiped her feet again and said, "Hi Mom."

"I just don't know what I'm gonna do with that father of yours!" her mother carped without looking up or returning Marianne's greeting. "He's made a big mess out of this place today!"

Marianne had no desire to get caught up in a whirlwind of her mother's emotions from anticipating the turmoil of the construction. It had already created stressful fractures in her parent's relationship and had made it necessary to appease her mother whenever she deemed it essential not to get into a conflict with her. *I guess now would be very good time to start,* she thought. "You're right, Mom, it's really a mess around here!" Marianne said consolingly and prided herself with her answer. "I only think

Dad's just trying to make life a little better for all of us and for you especially!" she added.

Before her mother could reply, the door banged open. Ethan and Jonathan nearly fell over each other trying to be the first one inside. Their mother, although nearing her limit of self-control, ignored them.

"Why don't you two knock it off and grow up!" she exclaimed loudly, but neither of them paid any attention.

"I would've been first if you hadn't grabbed my belt and shoved me off the steps," Jonathan flared, and punched his brother hard on the shoulder.

Ethan gave his brother a big shove that sent him flying into the wall so hard the dishes in the cabinet rattled. "The next time you hit me, you'll get more of the same!" he snapped.

Standing his ground and glaring, Jonathan retorted, "I think you'd better get some help first!"

Previously Jonathan had almost always backed down and his unusual stance this time took his brother by surprise. The unexpected change caused a big boost of adrenalin to pump through Ethan's veins and it made the whites of his eyes flash with red hues; instantly he took an aggressive stance and stepped closer to Jonathan.

Many times Marianne had seen her two brothers at odds with each other and more often than not it was due to Ethan's compulsion to irritate. The behavior he was demonstrating was a classic example of his normal behavior and she stepped between them. "I don't think either of you has a brain!" she stated firmly. Her assertion caught Ethan off guard which gave Jonathan a second or two to contemplate the outcome of the ongoing conflict, and he backed away.

Leon walked into the kitchen as nonchalant as if he were walking into a peaceful park. "I'm sure glad you're all home cause Mom made me stay in the house all day with nothin' to do," he complained. His presence and attitude, only seconds before the confrontation reached the flash point of a physical fight, helped to deflate the anger welling up inside his older brother.

Although their mother didn't reprimand either of the boys, Marianne noticed she had stopped snapping beans and noticed her hands were shaking and she was biting her lower lip nervously.

A small, warm hand slipped into Marianne's when Leon's little fingers took a firm grip on hers. "What's the matter?" he asked.

"Nothing much, just some of the same old stuff," his sister answered and squeezed his hand lightly to give him reassurance that everything was going to be fine.

"One of these days I'm going to take care of you for good!" Ethan vented, hissing his words out between clenched teeth. Jonathan just ignored him, walked over and sat down at the far end of the kitchen table.

"I can't take this anymore!" their mother said, and started to whimper.

Leon leaned protectively against his sister and tugged at her hand. "Everything's going to be okay," she whispered and ran the fingers of her free hand through his thick hair. "Would you like to go outside with me for a while and I'll show you what our dad did today," she said, finding a reason to extract both of them from the uncomfortable situation.

Twenty minutes later they returned to a kitchen that had taken on a much calmer atmosphere. Marianne's mother had regained her composure and her brothers sat at opposite ends of the table drinking glasses of cold milk and eating graham crackers.

"Your dad needs your boys' help. After you two finish your snacks, you'll need to go back there and see what he wants," their mother stated, her voice still quivering slightly. "He has some jobs for you two to do," she added. "And, Marianne, I want you to carry in some water from the well and help me get dinner started."

Marianne looked at Leon. "Since you've been so bored, how'd you like to help your big sis get some water?" she asked. "I'll even let you pump the handle," she added teasingly, trying to be as cheerful as possible under the difficult circumstances.

Leon grabbed one of the two tin water pails. "I'll carry this one," he stated happily and swung it back and forth in a big ark, banging his knee. "Oowee! That hurt!" he yelped and set it down to rub his leg.

Once the pails were full, Marianne lifted one in each hand for balance. Leon ran and held the door open with his shoulder, but even with his help, she came close to losing her footing on the temporary steps. Water sloshed out of the pails, getting her legs wet and Leon's overalls spotted. "Soorryyyy," she said apologetically, steadied herself and stepped inside. One pail she placed on the floor by the stove and the other up on the counter next to the sink. Their weight had numbed her fingers. "There's going to be a lot of extra work to do until Dad can get the basement built," she said casually to her mother.

"I reckon we'll just have to learn to get used to it until he's finished," her mother replied in a steady, firm voice and Marianne could see that her mother was slowly accepting the fact that she had no control over the consequences created by the construction. "They promised me they'd have most of the work done by Thanksgiving. That's only about three months off from now, but if it takes longer than that, I'll be ringing some men's necks!" her mother chuckled.

"Can I go back outside?" Leon asked. "I wanna watch what they're doin'!"

"No!" his mother said.

"Why not?" he pestered.

"It's too dangerous for you to be out there by yourself. The men are too busy to be watching after you! Maybe later! We'll just need to wait and see."

Anxious to see her pony, Marianne baited her mother by suggesting to her brother, "I'll tell you what, when I go out to do my chores, you can go with me, if you wanna...but I gotta help Mom get supper first." Her mother didn't respond. Seeing that her ploy didn't work and not wanting to waste time by being idle, she asked, "What do you want me to do?"

"You can fetch me the enameled roasting pan from the cabinet and go get twelve large potatoes and peel them."

Her mother placed a small cast iron skillet on the stove and started frying four thick-sliced strips of home-cured bacon in it which she planned to break up and add with a little grease into the green beans that were already boiling. For supper she wanted to have two other side dishes along with the large roast beef, a hardy meal that would please her husband. Gloria wasn't a fancy cook but everyone who had eaten at her table could agree that she was a great regional cook. "Your father wants to have a late supper tonight. He said they probably wouldn't finish their work until about dark. I know he's going to be starving because he hasn't eaten nothing since the light lunch he gobbled down at noon."

"It's amazing how much they've done today," Marianne stated.

"They've been working hard because they needed to finish everything they've started today before they can begin excavatin' under the house tomorrow morning. I decided that we might as well get used to Mike and Bill being here early every day for a while," she sighed.

Getting up at daybreak was the usual routine for their farm family and even though that routine was normal, the two extra men working on the basement in close proximity around them would change their living pattern. It would continue that way until the basement and the other work on the house was completed.

"I suppose," Marianne said. Since her mother hadn't asked about her first day in school, she decided to bring the subject up. My new teacher, Mrs. Holtsman is really nice," she said in an attempt to entice her mother into showing some interest in her day and life. "You know her, don't you?"

Her mother didn't comment. Instead she said, "Your father went to town this morning for something he needed for work and when he came home, he brought back a big roast beef from our locker. I've got it thawed out and I plan to get it in the oven in a few minutes," her mother added, and Marianne gave up any hope of enticing her mother to ask about her school day.

"Yumm," Leon said, sitting at the table drawing doodles on a scrap of paper with a pencil stub. "Could I have a big end piece for supper?" he asked, always reminding his mother, just in case she might forget.

"Of course," his mother replied and turned to her daughter. "You need to peel me four big potatoes and quarter them so I can put them in with the roast later. The other eight you can peel for mash. After nearly completing the simple, time-consuming task, Marianne asked, "What's next?" she asked.

"Put all of the potatoes in pot of cold water when you're done," her mother answered.

"Is there anything else you to do after that?" Marianne asked, and shifted her body nervously. "I'm gonna be stuck in the kitchen for all eternity or at least until the world's made several more revolutions on its axis," she mumbled softly under her breath. She was anxious to see her pony and to share with him the events of the first day of school.

"Yes." Her mother answered and placed the several-pound chunk of meat into the large, speckled, blue-enameled roasting pan.

Marianne waited patiently for several seconds without an answer. "You said there was something else you wanted me to do?" she asked once more.

"Oh, I almost forgot; you can get the carrots out of the ice box and clean them too," her mother instructed. "Also, you need to get eight or ten medium-sized onions, peel them and cut them into quarters for the roast."

Presently Marianne finished and held the pan with onions away from her watering eyes. "You want these now?" she asked.

"Just put them in the roasting pan," her mother instructed. "Like I said," she continued, "we're not gonna have supper 'til after dark when your dad quits for the day, so why don't you go do your chores?"

Marianne's eyes brightened. "Okay," she said, and turned to leave.

"But don't forget," her mother added with emphasis, "I need you back here in good time to help with the table!"

Marianne was surprised that her mother gave her this break and to affirm what she had just heard, she replied, "So I guess I'll have about two hours before you'll need me again?"

"That's right, but don't be gone any longer than that," her mother answered and pointed to the peelings and scraps stacked in a small heap on the counter. "On the way out to the barn can you throw them scraps over the fence to the chickens?"

CHAPTER THIRTEEN

Freedom

Marianne couldn't believe her good fortune. September days were still long and she knew if she hurried to get her chores done, she would still have ample time to saddle up her pony and go for a short ride. "Aren't you coming along with me, Leon?" she inquired, knowing he was looking forward to getting out of the house.

Without answering or drawing more lines on his paper, he sat thinking. At the very last second before she left, he yelled, "Wait up!" and bounced down off his chair.

To be alone with her pony would have been her first preference; however, she cherished her younger brother, enjoyed his company and his lackadaisical attitude and, anyway, he liked little adventures as much as she did. He would be a good companion and more fun than trouble.

Ethan and Jonathan were working in the bare spot of soil where the old room had been, picking up nails and other small pieces of debris and throwing them at a metal bucket to see who could make the most successful shots. Engrossed in their game, neither of them acknowledged Marianne or their little brother as they walked past.

"My turn," Ethan said and tossed nail at the bucket. It clanked on the rim and fell off on the ground.

"I'm ten ahead," Jonathan bragged.

Standing in front of the house beside the gravel sidewalk, their father and Mike Jones were conferring over their plans. Mike, a short distance away, moved the level slowly along the bottom sill of the house, double checking to make sure they had accomplished their mission of raising the house perfectly level.

"She's high and jest as straight and ready as she'll ever be," Marianne heard Mike say to her father. "Don't need no more adjustments today, but we'll be needin' to be checkin' her ever so often jest in case one of them jacks happens to settle some. We don't want no trouble, do we?"

Overhearing Mike's comment, Leon's eyes got big. "The house is gonna fall?" he asked his father.

Engrossed in their deliberations, his father didn't acknowledge Leon's question. "Well, Milburn, we're ready to start excavatin' the basement in the mornin' like we planned," Mike assured him.

"Dad," Leon asked. "Dad!" he exclaimed louder, trying to get his father to respond. "Dad!" he repeated. Finally becoming frustrated, he stepped between the two adults. His father put his hand lightly on his son's head, signaling him not to interrupt.

"You've been right so far. Let's hope you're right about the rest of this project."

"I'm thinkin' ever thing is gonna go fine. Unless some act of God or nature, like an earthquake or tornado comes along, then we shouldn't have no problems!"

"While you two finish this work here, I'm gonna get Maude and drag the slip scrapper up here to the house," Milburn mentioned. "I don't want to have to worry about doin' it in the mornin'."

"Now, Leon, what'd you ask me?" his father inquired.

"Is the house gonna fall down?"

"No. It's not gonna fall down. The fact is...it looks like it could fly away, it's so high in the air."

A distraught look came across his small son's face. "It could...It could really fly away?"

"Come on, Leon, let's go," his sister pleaded, and nudged him on the back with the flat of her hand. "Dad's only kiddin' you," she soothed in a soft voice. "The house can't fly away!"

Neither of them spoke for several seconds until Leon stopped and looked somberly up at his sister. "You sure the house won't fly away?" he asked, wide eyed.

She wanted to explain to him about how some things could fly away: things not seen, such as dreams and his youthful innocence, but she didn't want to confuse his young mind. "No! Believe me! The house is not gonna fall down or fly away!"

"Goody, goody, I'm really glad it isn't, 'cause I was scared!"

The big barn doors yawned open and seemed to beckon them to step into the deep shadows within. Marianne had gone there thousands of times and she had never gotten tired of the smells, sounds and atmosphere. She always felt peaceful watching barn the swallows fly in and out, the cattle drinking at the trough, the chickens talking to each other and pigeons cooing in their special language. If someone were to ask, she could probably give a thousand other reasons way the atmosphere in and around the barn pleased her.

They went straight to the horse stall and found that the horses were outside. "Let's put their feed in their trough first and then go do the other chores. When we come back, they'll be inside eating."

"We're not going to ride Rocky?" Leon asked.

"Only after I get my other chores done," she answered and added, "and then we'll go riding, and if you help me, we can go for that ride even sooner."

Marianne gave Leon some simple duties to perform to keep him busy while she did the heavier things. She felt good that her mother gave her this token of freedom. For reasons she couldn't decipher, her mother was devoid of having much interest in her life outside of the immediate family circle and it was disappointing and confusing to her.

"Because you've helped so much, we're almost done with these chores!" Marianne said and thought about her other two brothers working outside the house. It made her feel guilty. "Before we leave the barn, I think it'd be a good idea for me to do some of my brothers' chores," she said knowing that they would be a little upset if she rode off on Rocky while they still worked; a good deed might appease them. Fifteen minutes later she had finished enough of their chores to give herself a clear conscience.

Marianne opened the door to the henhouse.

"Please don't let those big roosters get me!" Leon pleaded.

She was very sympathetic to his plight. "I'll keep them shooed away if you stay close to me," Marianne promised and became happy when she found the henhouse void of them. The roosters had become extremely mean after being tormented by Ethan and his friends, and in defense of themselves. Using their bodies, beating wings and long sharp spurs, they would fly up and flog any person they saw as a threat. To be attacked by even one of them was a very traumatic, painful and frightening experience that no one wanted to experience, especially a small boy.

"Did we get all the eggs?" Marianne inquired.

"I think so," Leon answered and automatically stuck his hand into an empty nesting box to double check.

Eventually, they walked across the yard with the wicker egg basket swinging from Marianne's arm. "We sure got lots of eggs today," Leon observed.

"We sure did and you were a great big help!"

"And it was fun too...but I don't like bein' around them mean old roosters!"

"I don't like the mean ones either!" Marianne answered, although the roosters almost never were interested in her. They seemed to seek revenge on the youngest male gender of the human race, even more than their true tormentors.

"I'd like to ring their necks," he declared, grimaced and made a motion with his hands as if he were actually achieving the feat.

"I'd like to wring a neck too!" she said, referring to Ethan who was responsible for having started the problem.

They walked on a few steps in silence until Leon stopped and looked back at the chicken house. "Why are they so mean?"

Without using too much detail, his sister explained, "The first reason is that they're old roosters whose jobs are to protect the flock and the second one is because Ethan teases them all the time."

"I know he does," Leon agreed. "Ethan catches them, puts their heads under their wings and spins'em round, round and around until they get dizzy," he related. "Then he puts them on the ground, they fall over and their heads weave around. After they get up, they run in circles and fall over sometimes. He thinks it's really funny!"

"And that's why they flog you," his sister explained. "They're just trying to defend themselves and the flock. What if someone spun you around and tormented you like that, wouldn't you want to fight?"

"Yeah. It'd make me real mad too!" he answered.

Marianne looked at the basket. "I don't believe I've ever gotten this many eggs in a long time," she said, changing the subject. "The chickens must be happy for some reason and that's why they're laying so well. It's gonna make Mom happy!"

"Why happy?" he asked.

"Well," his sister said, "when the chickens are happy and contented they seem to lay more eggs! The more eggs they lay, the more money Mom makes. She looks forward to the extra money to buy things she needs."

Leon smiled. "Happy chickens, happy Mom!"

"Well, most of the time!" she answered.

Their brothers, Jonathan and Ethan, were still busily picking up scraps and raking debris into small piles when Marianne and her little brother got to the back door. They had quit playing their tossing game, wasting time and had become serious in an attempt to get their job finished. The fun had gone out of it.

"Where've you been?" Ethan asked and stopped racking.

"Mom told me I could go out early and do my chores because we're not going to eat until after dark," she explained. "I just finished them and she said she won't need me until later."

"If you're finished with your chores, why don't you help us finish so we can go do ours?" Jonathan inquired.

"No, thanks," she answered. "But I already did some of yours to help you out. Now, Leon and I have other plans," she added and opened the door to the house.

"What chores did you do of mine?" Ethan asked, surprised she would do any of his after the devilish tricks he played on her.

"Oh, I really didn't do any," she smirked. "Actually I hid your big buckets in a place where you'll never find them and I left you two little ones so you'll need to make twice as many trips between the barn and the chicken house. I decided today'd be a good time to return the favor you did for me the day I went to Stella Mae's!"

Looking suddenly agitated, Ethan barked gruffly, "That's not fair. I helped you gather the eggs the other day, didn't I, and that should've made up for it!"

"Yeah, yeah, yeah, I know!" Marianne said and set the eggs down inside the door. "Come on, Leon, let's go!" she said and walked off without looking back.

The two walked quietly along halfway to the barn quietly before either said anything. Leon looked questioningly up at his sister and asked, "Why'd you tell Ethan you hid the big buckets when you really didn't?"

"O, that was just for the fun of it," she told him, but the main reason was to remind Ethan that he didn't have the control that he thought he had over her. She hoped that by turning his trick back around on him would send him a strong message demonstrating her attitude and resolve.

Leon picked up a small rock off the driveway, hauled his arm back and gave it a hard toss at the big, wooden, corner post of the pasture fence. Clunk, it went on contact. Marianne walked off toward the barn. "Can I stay out here while you go get Rocky?" he yelled after her, bent over and picked up another rock.

"Sure," she answered, "but, you're still going riding with me, aren't you?"

"Uh huh, why?" he asked, threw the stone and missed the target.

She was grateful her brother stayed outside while she saddled up Rocky; his absence, she thought, would give her a chance to tell Rocky about her day and rid her of some of the new emotions weighing down on her. She planned to explain them to Rocky, even though she wasn't sure she could describe them very well even to herself. However, be as it may, his big receptive ears would soon give her some comfort.

Marianne guided Rocky slowly around the clover field where she and Ethan had raced across earlier in the summer. Only recently her father had cut and baled the clover for the second time and it still retained the wonderful aroma and filled the air with its natural sweet fragrance. Leon sat behind the saddle with his feet hanging off each side. Neither of them spoke. The sun, still intense in the evening's September sky, made their faces warm while a steady light breeze made their ride very pleasant.

Leaning forward and reaching down, Marianne patted the pony on the side of his neck. "Thanks for listening," she whispered in his ear, sat up straight, leaned slowly back and tilted her head back for her brother to hear her. "You okay back there?" she asked.

Leon was too sleepy to reply. He put his arms around her waist and leaned his head into the middle of her back. "Don't you fall asleep because you might fall off," she said and nudged Rocky to trot a few steps to jolt her brother out of his stupor. As the rhythm changed, she felt his arms release from around her waist and then grip the back of the saddle for support.

Later, when the two of them returned to the house, they found that Ethan and Jonathan had finished picking up nails, splinters, and other debris and were now involved in helping their father lay out the long chains to the slip scraper and were generally getting things ready for the next morning.

"Can I stay outside and watch?" Leon asked, pausing at the door.

"I don't know," Marianne answered, "but yeah, I guess so, if you go ask Dad and he says that it's okay. I'll wait here until you go find out," she said.

"He'll be fine!" their father yelled and waved. "We're almost done. Tell your mother I'll be comin' in for supper in less than an hour.

"Sure thing," she yelled back and said softly to herself, "and I'm happy I wasn't late!

CHAPTER FOURTEEN

The Next Morning

The next morning, Marianne heard the horses before she perceived the softer sounds of muffled male voices. She lifted her head off her pillow, peeked out from beneath the light blanket covering her and witnessed the very beginning of early dawn through her east window. "Oh God, what's happening," she whispered to herself and pulled the blanket up over her head protectively. "Yeah, I remember," she whispered into the air and kicked at the blanket. "Dad told us last night at the supper table that Mike and Bill would be here very early this morning to get started on the excavation. I guess he meant what he said!" she groused. It had never entered her mind that they would be there at the very crack of dawn. She grabbed her pillow in both hands, wrapped it around her head and held it tightly over her ears to block the sounds. After a few minutes of trying to hold the feather pillow against her head, her arms got tired and the effort made her so awake she knew that she would never be able to go back to sleep.

"Auugh," she gasped in frustration, punched her pillow twice, threw the blanket off to the side and bounced out of bed. *Dads gotta be outside. Mom's probably in the kitchen and my three brothers are still asleep, I hope, because if they are, I'll have a chance to go out to the outhouse without needing to wait in line or have one of them knock on the door while*

I'm it. "Maybe I'll have some privacy this morning," she mumbled under her breath, brushed a curl back off her forehead and looked with trepidation into the mirror of her small dressing table. "Oh no," she said and stuck her tongue out at her reflected image.

A few minutes earlier, Marianne was experiencing reservations about waking up so early, but now that she was up, she threw her clothes on and headed for the outhouse. The sun peeked over the eastern horizon, its rays struck little spheres of dew clinging to the stems of grass and made them sparkle. She was enthralled with the glistening shine and fantasized that she was a princess strolling to her *toilette* across a green carpet littered with diamonds.

A short time later, a perky Marianne bounced into the kitchen. "There's some hot water on the stove for you to wash up with," her mother said cheerfully.

Marianne placed the enameled washbasin in the sink, poured hot water out of the kettle from the stove and mixed it with cold. She tested it several times with her fingers until she got the temperature just right and only then did she wash the night's sleep from her face.

"When you're done, I'd like you to set the table," her mother said. "Mike and Bill surely must've eaten before they came out, so don't set a place for them. If they happen to come in, it'll only be for coffee," she stated, reassuring herself that she was making the right decision under the circumstances. She reasoned that the two semi-professional men working on a long-term project wouldn't require meals; however, she believed that coffee, iced tea or some other beverage might be a hospitable offering at appropriate times.

Just about the time that the family finished eating, they heard a sharp rap on the door and a squeak as it slowly opened. "Okay, Milburn," Mike yelled, projecting his voice enough for his employer to hear, "I think we're jest about ready to get started out here. That's if y'all are," he said, correcting himself.

"I'm just about done," Milburn shouted back. Before doing his chores he had brought the two workhorses up from the barn so that Mike and Bill could prepare to excavate under the house.

"Milburn," Gloria whispered low enough for Mike not to hear, "it isn't polite not to at least ask them in for coffee."

Her husband nodded in agreement. "Why don't you and Bill take a minute or two off and come in here for a cuppa coffee," he said loud enough for Mike to hear. Within seconds, Milburn got his answer. "Hey, Bill," they heard Mike yell.

"What?" a distant voice replied.

"Come aroun' here. Milburn jest asked us to go in fer a cuppa hot Joe."

His father instructed Ethan to make room for two chairs at the far end of the table. "No. That's okay," Bill replied. "If we sit down now, we'd get spoiled and we sure don't want sittin' to get to be a habit! If we did we'd never get nothin' finished, isn't that right, Dad!"

"Yup," Mike agreed.

"Habits do die hard," Gloria agreed. "That's for sure!"

"And that's why I don't need any more'n the twenty or so habits I've already got," Bill added, making everyone smile.

"You're soundin' like y'all has the habit of pickin' up habits," Mike said to his son.

"They sure do come easy, I reckon. Maybe I should try gettin' rid of more of my bad ones so I have some room for good ones!"

"An, how many bad ones do you suppose you have left?" his father asked.

"Maybe ten or twelve!"

"You must be doin' some serious subtractin'," Mike jested and everyone had a good laugh

"It looks like we've managed to pick a good day to get started on the basement," Milburn abruptly switched topics. "You two didn't happen to stop past the drug store on the way out here this morning, did you?" he asked.

The drugstore in town served many purposes. They offered some over the counter drugs, as well as shampoos and simple cosmetics, a pinball machine and a jukebox, plus a news stand, a counter and five booths that were a big part of the business. Usually, at meal times, all the stools were occupied with customers sharing gossip, news and having a simple meal. During breakfast the usual customers were merchants and farmers. Later in the day a much more varied clientele came and went. Because he did not subscribe to the Atwood Daily Herald, Milburn had raised his question to probe for the latest news about the war in Europe. At the drugstore on Sundays, he picked his subscribed copy of the Decatur Herald and Review which he read from end to end.

"Why?" Mike asked.

"I was wondering what people might be saying about the war!"

"I heard a few things," he answered.

"What'd you hear?" Milburn asked and leaned forward. "Shuu," he said to his restless youngest sons. "If you don't wanna listen, then go into the other room!"

"I heard them sayin' somethin' about Malta...wherever that might be. They was discussin' how important it was and wonderin' if it could hold out against the Nazi's bombin'."

"Where's Malta?" Milburn questioned softly to himself.

"I think I know," Marianne replied. "We studied the Mediterranean in geography class and I remember that it's an island somewhere between France and Italy."

"Well anyways, they was talkin' about how the Germans have been blockadin' the place and bombin' it cause it's been hurtin' their efforts in North Africa," Mike said. "Oh, and another thing I heard was that the city of Len, Leni, Len," he said, prying his brain, trying to remember the place. "Leningrad. That's it," he finally reasoned. "The Germans've been blastin' it with artilliry, bombs and everythin' else."

They all looked over at Marianne, wondering if she was knowledgeable about that place also.

"Where's Leningrad located?" her father asked, seeing that she hadn't taken the cue.

"All I remember is that it's someplace deep in Russia up north of Moscow."

"I can sure feel sorry for all the people suffering in those countries. They deserve our prayers!" Gloria interjected. Her comment struck them all as an ominous omen and the kitchen grew deathly silent for several seconds.

"I hate to think about what might be in store for us in the future. I just don't see how we can stay out of this dang darn war forever," Milburn added without reservation, "but at least it's helpin' our economy a lot!"

Mike set his cup down on the counter. "You're right about things gettin' better aroun here, but I'm hopin' you is wrong about us goin' off and fightin'. I remember the last big one. Anyhow, I needs to get back to work," he said, ending his vague briefing. "Anyone's interested in watchin' the first trip we'll be takin' under the house should come outside! We've got the slip scraper ready."

The slip scraper he mentioned was like a big two-handled scoop. The one they were using was about forty eight inches wide with two handles, one along each side facing backwards. A vee-shaped, hinged steel bar with a loop in the middle ran across the front and protruded forward about four feet. A long chain was hooked onto the loop. The other end of the chain ran under the house and out of the opposite side to Milburn's team of horses. Once everything was in position, one of the men would walk the horses slowly forward and drag the scraper under the house. The handles would be lifted by its operator, causing the scoop to dig into the soil and fill with dirt. Once the bucket was full, the man under the house would push down on the handles and guide the bucket up out of the soil. On reaching the other side, they would slide the scraper out some distance, then by lifting the handles again, the front edge of the scoop would catch in the soil and flip forward, emptying it. The process was very labor intensive and time consuming but it was much more effective and faster than digging with spades and shovels in the low overhead space under the building.

Eager to see the men get started, the farm family stood in a group close to Bill, who was ready to follow the scoop under the house. The technology was old, practical and simple, but fascinating. Mike and Bill already had the aligned their equipment and positioned the horses before they had been invited in for coffee.

"Okay, Mike. We're ready on this side," Bill shouted, gripped the handles and prepared to be pulled under the house. Being the younger and more agile of the two, it would be his job to guide the slip scrapper through the endless passes underneath the old farm house.

"Start walkin' the horses real slow," Milburn shouted.

"Get up," Mike commanded the team and gently slapped the horses' reins. Slack gradually came out of the chain and the scoop was slowly pulled into the dark cavity. Bill lifted the handles. The scoop dug gently into the dank soil and filled up.

Everyone walked hurriedly to the opposite end of the house and waited for the first load of dirt to emerge. The long, taut chain, gradually, link by link came out of the darkness, until a heaping scoop of soil emerged with Bill scrunched over, clinging to the handles. The two workers walked the horses thirty feet out from the house and dumped it by briskly lifting the handles on the slip scraper.

"Okay," Bill said, "that's one!"

"And many to go!" Milburn exclaimed. He knew the job was going to be a long nearly endless and arduous task. Each time the scrapper brought out a load it had to be manhandled back under the house.

The plan was to get enough dirt removed so that eventually they could stand up underneath the house and shovel the rest out by hand.

Gloria smiled for one of the few times since her husband had first mentioned his intentions weeks earlier. She had never fully revealed that she was anxiously looking forward to having a warmer house and a deep basement where she could do her laundry, store her canned goods, and have a place to perform messy jobs. "You kids need to get your chores done or you're going to be late for school."

"Come on, let's go," Ethan said. Marianne left to get the egg basket. Ethan walked off briskly towards the barn and left Jonathan standing, transfixed with the excavating. Leon stood beside his mother and watched the men prepare to make another pass under the house.

"Don't forget you've got chores to do, Jonathan!" his mother reminded.

"Huh?' he answered absentmindedly.

"Your chores…You've got to get them done!" she repeated.

"Oh, yeah," he said and ran off towards the barn.

Marianne checked the last nesting box. "I'm done!" she said to herself, picked up her egg basket, stepped outside and noticed her pony standing forlornly beside the barn. "Hi, Rocky," she shouted. He raised his head, looked her way and switched his tail, causing her to smile.

Their normal route across the stubble field was so moist from dew that the three siblings were forced to walk around on the highway to school. "I hope they finish the basement before it gets really cold in the fall," she said. "I'd love to have a warmer bedroom this winter!"

"So would I," Jonathan remarked.

"You two are just softies," Ethan joked and flashed a teasing smile. "I've gotten used to seeing my breath in the mornings when I wake up!" he added and blew his breath into the air.

Jonathan laughed. "Sometimes I get so cold my dreams freeze and I see the same picture all night long!"

"What Dad's doing will make it so much better for us and I hope it makes Mom's life a lot easier!" Marianne added.

They walked along quietly for a few seconds, each seemingly lost in their own thoughts. "Oh, Ethan, I forgot, Donna was asking about you yesterday," Marianne announced to bait her brother into reacting.

She waited for his response as they walked on several more steps. "What'd she say?" he asked.

"She asked me if you liked high school," she answered. "What do you think I told her?"

"I guess you told her I think it's okay!" he answered and walked on nonchalantly for several steps. "She didn't happen to say anything else, did she?" he suddenly asked, unable to constrain himself.

"Uh huh; she did," Marianne answered and walked along quietly.

After a long pause, he asked, "Well, what'd you tell her?"

"I don't think you really wanna know," she answered, toying with him.

"Come on, Sis! What was it?" he pried apprehensively.

"She said you are the cutest thing!" she lied and watched him turn slightly red from embarrassment, an unusual emotion for her brother and a reaction she would enjoy thinking about all day.

CHAPTER FIFTEEN

Early October

Marianne lay awake, unable to go to sleep. She had been lying in bed for three hours staring at the ceiling and contemplating her day in school and what had taken place. She thought about herself and six other girls, including Stella Mae and Barb sitting on the back steps in the warm autumn sun chatting about nothing in particular, making jokes and whispering about who they thought were the cutest boys in class and other bits of small talk until the happy picture fell apart.

What stayed clear in her mind was that Evelyn, one of her closest friends had seen a group of kids running to look at something up in a tree. She concentrated very hard to recreate the episode in her mind as clearly as she could recall and she tried to visualize the entire episode clearly.

"Look over there," Evelyn said and pointed. "I wonder what they're all looking at," she exclaimed, stood up to get a better look and brushed some dust off the back of her skirt.

"What's going on?" Donna asked.

"I can' tell," Evelyn answered, rolled up on her toes and shaded her eyes with her right hand so she could see better what was going on. "I think someone climbed a tree and can't get back down or something."

"It's probably that dumb kid in the sixth grade that nobody likes," Alice responded.

"What do you mean?" Barb snapped back and caught Alice off guard.

"You're not stupid, Barb, and you know what I mean!" Alice responded.

"He's not too bright and he can't help the way he is, but he's okay," Barb shot back.

"Yah, suuurre he is!" Alice said smugly and made a face as if she had a bad taste in her mouth.

"You seem to find something negative about lots of people, do you know that?" Barb reminded her. "People like you are always looking for flaws or open wounds in people...and they're easy to find if you put your mind to it!" she added, becoming angrier with each breath. "Just like you did with me and my cousin," she added, showing she had not forgotten the episode that took place on the morning of the first day of school.

"Your cousin got herself a bun in the oven up in Minnesota and then she comes down here thinking no one would notice!" Alice flared in defense.

"Like I said, you're always looking," Barb spat, red faced and took a couple of steps towards Alice. "You have a total lack of feelings for other people, don't you?"

I believed they were headed for a fight of scratching and hair pulling, Marianne thought, as she continued reconstructing the scene.

I remember now, *Alice shifted her eyes away from Barb's penetrating stare, raised her arms and put the flat of her hands forward to show she yielded. "I'm, I'm," she said and backed away.*

Evelyn suggested, "Let's run over and see what's going on," and she and the two other girls walked off towards cluster of students gathered around the base of the tree. I believe her action helped break the tension somewhat.

"I don't think you're sorry!" Barb stated.

Marianne lost her concentration momentarily but continued to stare at the ceiling, thought hard and the images started flashing across her mind again.

"Oh, I remember now!" *I remember that Donna nervously stood up. "I'm going over there too," she said and pointed towards students milling around under the tree.*

Alice lowered her arms. "Wait up and I'll go with you," she said, and stepped away from the tense situation she had created.

Stella Mae, Barb and I remained on the small concrete landing by the back door of the school. "I thought you had gotten over Alice's comments she made about Margret on the first day of school," I told her.

"I thought I had too until I heard her being so cold about that poor kid up in the tree and also acting snotty and aloof again," Barb confided.

"But she says things like that all the time, doesn't she?" Stella Mae pointed out.

"She doesn't say things like that because she's stupid. She knows what she's saying…and she means to be hurtful." Barb looked sad and she bit her lower lip. Instead of giving Stella Mae an answer, she tried to avoid looking at either of us, shifted her eyes down at the ground and started to sob.

Confused, Stella Mae and I looked at each other. Something new seemed to be distressing our friend. Neither one of us moved or said anything. We watched her for several very long seconds. "Are you alright?" I finally asked and put my hand on her shoulder.

Barb slowly nodded and said, "I guess."

"You're sure?" I asked.

"No I'm not, and no one can do much to make me feel better," Barb whispered so low I barely heard her

"Why not?" Stella Mae asked her.

Frustrated and angry, Barb replied between sobs, "Because! Because, because!"

Marianne fought deeply in her mind to recall. *In an attempt to comfort her I slid my arm across her shoulders. "Maybe if you tell us, you'll feel better," I said to her.*

Barb just shook her head back and forth several times.

"You know we're friends you can trust forever," I reminded her. "We all feel awkward about sharing…even…!"

"I don't mean that I've got another secret. I'm upset about my cousin Margret and her crappy situation."

"Her situation? I thought everything was working out for her," Stella Mae remarked, "especially now that she is living with her aunt in Decatur.

I thought she was going to get married when her boyfriend comes home on his furlough."

"They were, but it isn't true any more!"

I remember I had a difficult time believing what I was hearing.

"They broke up?" Stella Mae asked.

"I wish it was that," Barb replied and wiped her cheeks. "Yesterday Margret got a phone call with some terrible news!" she sniffled.

"And?" just slipped off the tip my tongue.

"My aunt told Margret that her boyfriend got killed in a training accident while learning to throw hand grenades. She said one of the enlistees must've panicked, and when he threw his arm back to toss the grenade, the thing somehow slipped out of his hand and flew backwards."

"Killed?" I asked.

Barb started sobbing again. "Yeah...killed!"

"Oh, noooo!" Stella Mae whispered.

"It was a rare accident. Margret's boyfriend was standing to the rear behind some sandbags where he should've been safe, but when the grenade exploded, he had his helmet off to wipe the sweat from his brow and because he was tall, his head protruded slightly above the top of the sandbags and a small piece of metal hit him in the temple, killing him instantly!"

Stella Mae and I were momentarily lost for words. "How terrible! What an awful tragedy!" I stated.

"A real tragedy," Barb said.

"How is Margret handling it?" Stella Mae asked.

"My Aunt Minnie said Margret was depressed and her aunt couldn't get her out of her misery."

"What do you think will happen now?" Stella Mae asked.

"My aunt said that Margret's not going to go back to Fertile, not even for his funeral. She said she plans to stay in Decatur until after the baby is born and hopes to finish high school or she gets a job in some factory."

"Work in a factory?" Stella Mae asked. "She's a girl!"

"Yeah, but there's such a shortage of men because they're going into the service so factories have started giving women jobs," Barb replied.

"I really feel sorry for her," I told her and wondered what I'd do under the same circumstances.

The school bell clanged above our heads, signaling the end of recess and drowned out any further discussion between us. Everyone out in the playgrounds walked, ran, or skipped towards the front or back entrance.

"So do I!" Stella Mae shouted over the noise and rushed through the door a few feet away.

Marianne looked into the darkness above her head. She tried to understand her feelings. *I see how awfully unfair life can be, and yet, I complain about my mother just because she just doesn't understand me. I should look at it as no big deal. I guess I have it good compared to some girls my age,* she concluded and fell into a restful sleep.

CHAPTER SIXTEEN

November Fifteenth, 1941

Thanksgiving vacation was a week away and the weather turned unusually cold, more like January. The rock-hard, frozen ground under the stubble in the field was covered with a light dusting of powdery snow. A few lingering snowflakes continued falling from the clouds after the heavier snow moved eastward during the middle of the day. A flake occasionally blew against Marianne's face as she walked towards the house with a purposeful stride while holding her head down against the wind's unrelenting fury. She kept a soft mitten tightly pressed against the left side of her face to keep it warm, but even so, her small nose was bright red and her eyes were watering. Strong gusts of icy air ripped across the vast space of the open field and took her breath away. Although she had only been walking home for eight minutes, her feet were numb inside the light saddle shoes she wore. Her ears stung so much that tomorrow she decided to definitely take her thick wool scarf and colorful knit hat with earflaps to school with her.

Nearly across the field and shivering, she chose to stop and look at the progress made on the house. She could no longer see any space underneath it. "They must've lowered the house down onto the cement-block foundation," she whispered between shivers. Mike and Bill kept their promises so far. *I pray they keep the others. It'd be so nice to have a furnace in the house by Christmas. That'd be enough of a gift for me. Forget all the others. There would be no more below freezing temperatures in my bedroom at night and no more shaking, teeth clattering mornings. I wouldn't need to get partly dressed and run into the warm kitchen to finish putting on my clothes.*

Two minutes later Marianne stiffly climbed over the two gates of the pasture in front of the house, ran across the driveway and hurried up the sidewalk towards the door. She glanced at the back fence and noticed Rocky standing in the pasture, hunched and facing away from the wind. With the bare trees of the woods behind him and wearing his shaggy coat of winter hair he looked forlorn. She agonized that she hadn't found time to ride him much lately, not since the days had grown shorter. Only Saturdays and Sundays was there enough time available in her schedule to do so and the guilt of not riding him pained her, but later, to ease her conscience, she decided to take two carrots plus some sugar cubes out to the barn as a treat.

A rough, temporary wooden floor had been placed over the open area of the foundation where a hole for the new stairwell would lead to the basement. Some unused cement blocks had been placed conveniently on top of the floor as steps to gain access to the door of the house.

Even though the house was being buffeted by a cold swirling wind, a steady staccato of hammering still echoed between the buildings. Mike and Bill were busily driving some of the last nails into their handy work. "Hi, Marianne," Bill said without looking up and hammered another nail into the floor.

"Hi," she replied and added, "Golly! You guys sure made a lot of progress today."

"Well," he said. "Yeah…I reakon so. It kinda does look that'a way don't it. It's 'cause our big jobs are mostly done, so anythin' we do now shows more."

Shivering and numb in the cold, Marianne eyed the door of the house and dreamed of the heat just beyond it. "How long is it gonna take for you to finish the room?" she asked.

"If God and nature don't interfere too much, we think it'll be boxed in and out of the weather in about a week. We expect to finish everythin' up just after Thanksgivin' and have the furnace in 'fore Christmas," he said and took several nails out of his carpenter's apron.

Marianne put her mitten back up to her face. "Aren't you cold?" she asked, her knees knocking together.

Mike drove another nail. "If y'all have noticed, we're dressed a little better for the weather than y'all are," he said, matter-of-factly.

"Yeah, I know," she said and gasped when a sudden gust of icy wind whipped around the corner of the house. "Gotta run!"

"Go get warm," Bill advised, "before y'all freeze to death!"

Marianne bounced more than walked across the exposed subflooring, opened the door and stepped into the warm kitchen. The familiar smell of beef stew steaming in a big cast-iron pot on the stove gave her a feeling of contentment while in the back of her mind she wondered if she could ever get herself warm again. Her bones felt brittle and her face was stinging. She peeled off her mittens and rubbed her hands together over the warm stove before she attempted to take off her coat. Leon was playing with his toys on the living room floor. She didn't see her mother and guessed she was in one of the cold, closed-off back bedrooms.

"Hi," she said to Leon.

"Hi," he answered back.

"Where's Mom," she asked, holding her arms and hands out over the stove.

He pointed to his parents' middle bedroom.

"She been in there long?"

"Noooo," he answered. "Vrrrooomm," he said and pushed a small block of wood across the floor pretending it to be some kind of imaginary vehicle.

Marianne watched him discard the block and become engrossed in stacking his wooden blocks into a fortress.

"Where's Ethan and Jonathan?" he asked and grabbed another block.

"I don't know, but they should be home soon, I suppose," she answered. "I didn't wait for either one of them. It was too cold!"

Marianne stood close to the stove, relishing the heat and watched her brother play until she lost her chill. "I need to go change my clothes and put my coat away," she said and stepped around her little brother.

Her bedroom on the northeast corner of the house had been closed off all day and now seemed noticeably warmer than in the morning. The floors weren't as cold and some of the drafts were gone. She couldn't see her breath. "Thanks for the basement under the house, Dad," she exclaimed, feeling a surge of happiness.

Her mother still wasn't in the kitchen when she returned from her room. "Leon, if Mom comes out before I get back, will you tell her that I went outside and that I'll be back shortly?"

"Sure!"

"Just be sure you do, okay!"

"Okay," he said.

Marianne grabbed two carrot sticks and three sugar cubes on the way to the door.

"Well…the basement's finished," Milburn announced proudly and broke some buttered crackers into his bowl of stew. "They've got the house lowered down unto the foundation, pulled beams out and have temporarily filled the spaces in where the beams were. Tomorrow mornin' I think I'll load the large jacks onto the truck and take them back to Decatur and pick up another tall floor jack for the basement. The two we placed under the joists to keep the house from sagging in the middle aren't enough."

Marianne took a spoonful of steaming stew and blew across it to cool it down while her father explained what still needed to be done. Everything he said held her interest.

"The main thing now is to get the furnace installed. That's what all this work's been about since the beginnin' and I think that with any luck, by the middle of next week Mike and Bill will have the landin' boxed completely in and out of the weather. Once that's done, I'll have them do the inside walls and finish it off. It's been a rough corn harvest this year. If I can get it picked by then, I'll be able to lend them a hand."

"Could I have another glass of milk?" Leon asked, and spooned some stew into his mouth. "Will our bedroom be warmer when we get a furnace?" he asked.

"It might even be a little warmer tonight," his father answered.

"Good, because my nose gets cold and I can see my breath in there!"

"It's not going to be a lot warmer just yet," his father corrected.

"Why not?" Leon asked.

"It's only warmer because the cold air can't get under the floors," his father explained.

Marianne felt warmer all the way down to her toes anyway. The stew in her belly, her father explaining about the furnace, and the warmth of the kitchen was wrapped around her like a blanket. Even though the warmth was having a wonderful effect on her body, and even as comfortable as she found herself, she had other things on her mind. She looked out of the window and saw streaks of red in the clouds to the west. This time of year, once the sun started setting, twilight would be short lived. She hurriedly spooned the last bits of stew in her mouth and swallowed. "Could I go do my chores before I do the dishes?" she asked and looked expectantly across the table at her mother.

"Just don't be gone too long," her mother answered.

Marianne grabbed a heavy Mackinaw coat off one of the temporary hooks her father had placed on the wall by the outside door of the landing. She threw it on. A jumbled pile of gloves, hats and scarves were piled haphazardly underneath the hangers on the floor. She rustled through the pile until she found a suitable stocking cap and some warm work gloves. She buttoned the coat, pulled the cap down over the ears, shoved her hands into the large gloves and grabbed the egg basket. She started to go outside and then remembered that she wanted to give the pony more attention because she was still feeling guilty for not spending more time with him.

"Mom, I'm going to gather the eggs before it gets dark and give Rocky a carrot.

"You're spoilin' that dang pony," she remarked.

Marianne grabbed four carrots and ran outside. The late evening sky was dim which caused the interior of the barn to be subdued. Gone were the sounds of contented chickens, cooing pigeons and the familiar sounds of livestock during warmer weather. Replacing them was a low moaning of the wind blowing through the barn's rough siding and of an occasional coughing cow. Every animal seemed hunkered down, trying to conserve energy. Rocky was in his stall with the other two horses. A few snowflakes blew in through the open, outside-stall door.

Marianne looked at the three horses lined up at their trough. "I have some carrots for you," she announced to them. "I'm going to give Maude and Buddy a whole carrot," she said, "but Rocky, you're going to get two carrots that I'm gonna break into quarters," she said and gave him a piece. You'll get the rest of your carrots, one bite at a time, as you listen to my secrets!"

Rocky shook his head up and down and flicked his ears.

She held a whole carrot in front of the large horse's lips and watched them quickly disappear. "While you guys crunch on those, I'm going to go get the rest of your feed," she said and picked up a bucket to go get the oats.

After she poured the grain into the horses' feeding trough, she broke up a bale of alfalfa, threw several sections into the manger and while all three horses were busy munching, she went into the stall and pushed her way between Maude and Rocky. She patted Rocky on the rump, ran her hand over his thick winter hair and gave him a gentle pat on the side of his neck. "You really like those oats, don't you," she said. "You never ever seem to get enough of them, do you? In a couple of days I'm gonna have some free time and then we'll go for a couple of long rides. Here's another thing I want to tell you," she said and leaned close to his ear and started whispering. "Those feelings that I was having early this fall are getting stronger and some days my emotions seem to be really, really, uncontrollable.

"You're the only one I've said this to, even though I think some of my friends are having some of the same problems," she continued nearly breathlessly. "But I just can't talk to my friends about such things," she added and patted his neck again. "Those things are just too private and are going to stay just between the two of us. Another thing I've noticed is that me and my friends are acting more serious. Everyone's favorite subject is boys and who's dating who! Yesterday, I heard that one of the trashy girls in the eighth grade was dating a twenty-year old guy. Everybody in school was talking about her! I don't understand why her mother would let her do such a thing!"

Another piece of carrot disappeared into Rocky's mouth. "Barb's still very defensive about her cousin and she won't share her thoughts with any of her friends other than to me and Stella Mae. She's smart that way! Barb said she saw her pregnant cousin Margret Hannison a week ago and thought she looked good but sounded depressed. She told us that Margret can't get her dead boyfriend out of her mind because she loved him so much and that's all she wants to talk about!" She patted Rocky on the side of his neck one last time, tweaked his ear and gave him the last bit of carrot. "Gotta go," she said. "Gotta go gather the eggs and then I gotta go help my mom."

CHAPTER SEVENTEEN

Thanksgiving Day 1941

The house felt much warmer now that the cold air wasn't seeping in through every crack in the floor and made the beginning of the holiday even more special. By ten o'clock, several sauce pans sat on top of the stove simmering and creating an aroma that was beyond wonderful.

"Marianne, will you go in and set the dining room table?" her mother asked. "And when you're finished in there, I'd like you to peel about ten or twelve large potatoes for me." Marianne had already peeled yams, cut them up and left them sitting on the counter in a flat pan covered with brown sugar and pats of butter, ready for the oven. In a large bowl she had broken up some chunks of semi-hard bread and mixed in heaps of fresh cut up celery, onion, a lot of sage, two eggs and salt and pepper for her mother to use as a base for the special dressing. This year, her mother had fresh oysters that she loved to add to the dressing. After cleaning out the shell bits and strange little sea things from the pint can, Marianne placed them in a small bowl. Those and turkey broth would be added just before the dish went into the oven.

Her mother opened the oven door and peered inside. "I think the turkey'll be done right around twelve.

Marianne looked over her mother's shoulder. "Golly, it's so big and it looks and smells delicious!"

"Doesn't it! You know, I think I'll baste it again if you'll hand me the ladle off the counter," she said. "Your dad says that this is the biggest turkey we've raised in three years," she remarked and ladled the hot juices from the bottom of the roasting pan slowly over the browning bird.

"When do you think Ethan, Jonathan and my dad'll be back from hunting, Mom?" Leon asked, sitting at the kitchen table nibbling on a soda cracker. The wonderful aroma had made his stomach growl and he was impatient to have something more substantial in his mouth. His father and brothers were out across the highway in their eighty acres of corn stubble, trying to bag pheasants and rabbits. Ethan was carrying the single- shot, twelve-gauge and his father was using his Remington pump. Jonathan had gone along to act like a bird dog to retrieve and flush out game.

"I told your dad and the boys to be home no later than one," his mother replied. "I really suspect they would've come be back before now since it's so awfully cold and windy out there!"

"I wish they would," Leon answered, thinking the sooner they came home the faster the meal would be on the table.

Marianne chopped a stalk of celery in half, smeared some thick butter lengthwise on it and handed it to her little brother. "That should hold you for a little while," she said and winked.

"Thanks," he said and sniffed the air in anticipation of better things to come.

Their mother picked up a quart Mason jar of home-canned green beans and poured them into a heavy sauce pan. "Marianne, I need you to help me get more broth for the dressing," she said.

Just before one o'clock, the three hunters returned from the cold and stepped into the stark, unfinished addition which the two workmen had built onto the house. Leon blurted, "They're back," and rushed out to the door, eager to see what they had bagged. "What'd you get?" he asked without any luck of getting a reply from any of the three red-faced, cold hunters; they were too busy putting their guns down, taking off their gloves, heavy mackinaws, and shoes to heed his curiosity.

"What'd you get?" he tried finding out again.

"Dad got three pheasants and Ethan got two rabbits and a pheasant," Jonathan stated and pointed to the game they had dumped in a heap on the floor just inside the door.

Leon's eyes grew big. "Could I have a couple tail feathers?" he asked.

"Sure," his father said, "take all you want. Maybe one of the boys can help you pull some out."

"Milburn, as soon as you and the boys get warm and cleaned up we should be about ready to eat," his wife yelled from the kitchen. Everythin' but the giblet gravy'll be ready by the time you sit down."

All of Gloria's plans, the menu, the preparation of the dishes and the promise her husband had made to be home at the designated time had gone smoothly. "Marianne, could you go get the good China serving dishes out of the buffet cabinet. The bowls and platter are on the right side," her mother asked.

Marianne inspected the table one last time. Everything her mother asked her to do or had suggested, she had done. Her mother's good China sparkled, the silverware glistened and the crystal glasses, filled with water, stood proud in front of each place setting.

A little later, everyone watched open mouthed as Gloria carried the golden, roasted turkey in from the kitchen and placed it at the top of the table near her husband.

"Thankgivin' has been around since Lincoln made it a national holiday, but this is the first time Thanksgivin' will be officially celebrated on the fourth Thursday of November every year!" their father declared. "President Roosevelt's signed a declaration so that it'll always be that way. Him doin' that and us getttin' our basement finished makes this Thanksgivin' more than a little special. Yes sir, he did the right thing and I'm thinkin', so did we! I can't imagine us wanting any more than this, can you?"

"I can," Leon said.

"And what would that be?" his mother asked.

"I think if some Indians had come to our house for Thanksgiving, it could've been better!" Leon answered. "Then we would be just like the Pilgrims!"

"You're silly," Jonathan replied. "There ain't any Indians around here anymore!"

"There is so!" Leon argued. "They can't all be gone!"

Jonathan shook his head in disbelief. "Yes, they are! They're all gone! You haven't seen any, have you?"

Confused, his little brother said, "No I haven't, but you're lyin'!"

"No I'm not!"

"Where'd they all go?" Leon asked, perplexed that there could be no Indians remaining around anywhere.

"Many died from disease, some died fighting to defend their land and the others were put on reservations!" Jonathan commented without showing any emotion.

Leon still couldn't accept what he was hearing. "There really aren't none left at all?"

"Okay, that's enough!" Their father said, not feeling comfortable with the dialog because the history of his Christian faith in dealing with other races pained him; it conflicted with his social ideals and standards, and for that reason it was a topic he avoided.

"Before I give thanks, I want each of you to tell us what you've been thankful for this year," he said and took a few seconds to look at each face around the table. "Well, since I don't hear anyone speaking up, why don't we just start with the youngest and work up," he proposed. "Leon, you can start and I'll go last."

Leon looked at his father and put his hands over his eyes to concentrate. Everyone's eyes focused on the little boy and they waited and waited for him to say something.

"Okay, say what you're thankful for!" his father eventually asked.

About the time Leon's father was giving up and was going to direct Jonathan to recite, Leon received his inspiration. He peeked between his fingers and gradually took them away, looked around at all the faces waiting for him to respond. No words came from his mouth, although his face beamed with a big smile.

"Well," his mother said, "are you trying to keep it a secret or will you tell us what you're thankful for, before the food gets cold?"

"I'm still thinking," he said and stared at the ceiling.

"Come on, Leon," his mother pleaded, "tell us, please!"

"Okay!" he finally said with pride for what he was about to say. "I'm thankful I'm not an Indian and I'm thankful we have a really big turkey to eat," he said, paused for a second before he added, "and for the pheasant feathers."

Jonathan, shadowed by his brother's drama, was unable to find inspiration. "I'm thankful for everything!" he said.

Ethan remarked hastily, "I'm thankful I got a pheasant this morning and also that I don't have school today!" He hadn't been very careful with his selection…his mind had been more focused on responding before his sister did, next in line.

"Sis was supposed to be next," Leon said, correcting his brother. "You didn't wait your turn!"

Ethan glanced sheepishly at his mother and then over at Marianne sitting directly across the table and then smiled like the Cheshire cat from Lewis Carroll's book, "Alice in Wonderland."

"That's okay," their father said. "It don't really matter. Marianne, you can go next."

Her eyes danced over the surface of the table filled with delicious food and every face briefly. "I'm thankful for this day, the food, my warm bed and the pony!" She said, putting an extra emphasis on pony.

Her mother studied her family briefly. "I'm happy to have all my family here and healthy, and I pray the furnace will be in by Christmas!"

"Thank you for those thoughts!" Milburn said. "They were good thoughts," he stated and looked around the table again. He let his eyes stop momentarily to study each of his family's faces. When he was done, he said, "I'm very thankful for my family and in everything God's grace and wisdom has given us. Now I'd like to offer a prayer."

He waited until the table had grown completely silent and all heads were bowed. "Father above, please bless this food that we are about to receive. Thank you for the bounty you have provided to my humble family and our good health. We pray for those less fortunate than we are in the world and for those still strugglin' from the depression. And, dear God, please help them countries fightin' against the Germans, Italians, and Japanese, and may they win!" he added for emphasis. Milburn paused and searched deeper into his thoughts. "Please keep us out of the war!" he prayed and paused again, wondering if he should add more before he closed. "I ask forgiveness for the way we've treated the Indians!" he stated, sat in silence with his head bowed for several additional seconds and then said, "Amen."

"Amen," was repeated around the table. Milburn picked up the large carving knife and fork and started carving the big, roasted golden bird he had raised from a little poult, its wonderful aroma filling the air. "What a great looking bird," he said, cut off a wing, placed it to the side and proceeded to slice off thin slabs of breast.

The children loved turkey and all the traditional dishes that went with it. Their mouths watered as they watched their dad carve and slice the big bird. Marianne's thoughts drifted away momentarily and she wondered what her friends were doing or if any were as contented as she was right now.

"Why're people fighting?" Leon asked, holding a big spoonful of potatoes and gravy in front of his mouth.

His father didn't understand the political motivation of the Nationalists ruling Germany or exactly why Italy and Japan were seeking to expand their territories either. "I don't think some people are ever happy. There's people in this world who always seem to want someone else's things. They're greedy! They're acting like big bullies to get control over others," he simply explained so his son might grasp the answer.

Leon continued to hold the spoon in front of his mouth, mesmerized by what his dad was saying. He waited until his father finished. "I think I understand," he replied and shoveled the potatoes into his mouth.

"You do?" his father asked.

Leon nodded, swallowed and answered, "Yeah, I guess it's kinda like what happened to the Indians!" he answered.

Later after the food had been passed around for the last time, Gloria, sitting close to her husband, said contentedly, "Jonathan, you can help your sister clear the plates and some of these other dishes from the table. Marianne, I'd like you to set the percolator on the stove. It's already got the coffee and water in it. Oh…and Marianne, you can cut the pumpkin pie also."

"How's pumpkin pie sound to you?" Milburn teased his always hungry youngest son.

"Yumm, I like it! Specially when it's got lots and lots of whipped cream on top of it!"

His mother smiled. "Why don't you go into the kitchen and fetch it for us. It's in a metal bowl up on top of the counter."

"Ethan," his mother said, "while they're getting the coffee and the pie ready, I'd like you to run out to the well and get two buckets of water."

Marianne placed the pie in front of her mother and Leon placed the big bowl of whipped cream down next to it.

"Me and your mother are gonna need to drive the truck to Decatur Saturday and pick up the new furnace," their father said, putting his fork aside, choosing the moment as opportune time to make a pleasant announcement. "As you know, Mike and Bill have the landin' all enclosed. They'll be finished sidin' it and have the roof shingled by next weekend. As soon as they're done with that, I'm gonna have them start installin' the furnace."

"Will I have time to do some grocery shopping?" his wife asked.

"I don't think that'll be a problem," he answered.

"Can I go?" Leon asked, afraid he might be left behind with his older siblings. He liked the farm and found lots of adventures on his own, but he also liked a little extra excitement when an opportunity presented itself.

"I'm sure we can fit you in," his father said agreeably.

"Can I go too?" Jonathan asked. He knew in this cold weather he could have a long day just hanging around the house. Ethan would likely go over to Warren's house and his sister would ride

Rocky, go to town or spend most of the day messing around in her room.

"I suppose," his father answered. "It'll be a tight fit with the four of us in the cab but I'm sure we can make room. We'll manage somehow!" he said and took a sip of his coffee.

The pumpkin pie had turned out exactly the way everyone liked, just a little spicy with generous portions of nutmeg and cinnamon and a perfect flaky crust because of all the lard their mother had used.

Hearing the plans her parents were making for the day after tomorrow made the pie taste even better to Marianne. She knew that there would be no obstructions to keeping her from riding Rocky as much as she wanted. Even if it stayed cold and windy, she decided she'd dress for the weather and ride him twice, once in the morning and again in the afternoon.

Marianne carried the remains of the large turkey back to the kitchen. Only about half had been eaten and it made her think about her grandmother and two cousins from down the lane. As far back as Marianne could remember, there had always been hard feelings between her mother and her grandmother. She thought it was a shame that grudges and resentments could fester for so long; this was Thanksgiving, and with such an abundance of food, she felt that her parents should've ignored their feud and invited them over. It would have been a good time to let old wounds heal!

CHAPTER EIGHTEEN

The Saturday Following Thanksgiving

The bright sun shined in through Marianne's east window, making her curtains glow and slowly drawing her out of her slumber. From under heavy eyelids, she peeked at the sunlit room. Sometime during the night she had pushed or kicked the heaviest quilt down and was surprised to have stayed warm, and although it was now time to get up, it felt wonderful just lying there enjoying the comfort, the solitude and letting her mind wonder.

However, in the back of her mind she knew that if she didn't get up soon her mother would come in shortly and say, "We need to get the beds made!" It was an unwavering rule her mother observed: rise early and get your work done unless you happened to be too ill.

Marianne stretched, yawned and kicked the rest of the covers away and found the room was actually surprising cooler than she expected. It wasn't so cold that she had to dash into the kitchen for warmth, though. The pleasant smell of bacon frying beckoned her and the sound of muffled voices made her curious but hesitant. She slipped quickly into her clothes, looked into the mirror and saw a reflection she never appreciated in the mornings. "Thank God no one but my family is going to see me like this," she said to herself, took a Kleenex, dabbed at the sleep in the corner of her eyes, ran a brush several times through her hair and studied her image again.

Somewhat less disappointed with what she saw, she said, "I look okay, I guess," but then decided to run the brush through her hair a few more times. "At least now I won't make anyone puke up their breakfast," she kidded and smiled at her image in the mirror. *The sooner I get moving, the sooner I'll get to be alone and ride my pony,* she envisioned.

Slowly Marianne cracked her door open and listened. She detected that some of the muffled and indistinct voices were visitors. "Well, I can't stay in my bedroom all morning or stand here listening forever!" she whispered and took reluctant steps toward the conversation in the kitchen and found her aunt Emma and Uncle Thomas, still in their coats, chatting and having coffee with her parents. They were two of Marianne's favorite aunts and uncles and she suspected that they only had stopped by on their way into town to say hello.

Marianne cherished living close to town and in a house that had a large kitchen. The combination lured people to drop in for a friendly visit. There were loose rules of etiquette to observe between the people of the small towns and amid the rural farmers. People believed that one should rarely stop to visit at lunch, supper or at Sunday dinner time or during work periods, such as planting or during harvest. Their kitchen was occasionally like a coffee shop. Visitors dropped by to gossip, bring news, share opinions about politics and life in general. These visits had become important threads in the fabric of her family's life. "God, I must still look horrible!" she said under her breath, steeled herself and walked into the kitchen with trepidation. It gave her pause because she needed to wash her face at the kitchen sink. "Hi," she said hurriedly. "Hi," her aunt replied back pleasantly, only glancing her way and Marianne was thankful that no one else acknowledged her. Keeping her back to the room, she quickly snatched warm water off the stove and proceeded to wash her face and hands as unobtrusively as possible.

She picked up a wash rag, applied warm water to her face and listened to the conversation around the table behind her. Her Uncle Thomas slowly stirred his coffee and clanked his spoon in his cup.

"I think Roosevelt wants us to get more involved in this war and it concerns me to no end. The way I see it, he'll have us up to our necks in it before too long," he commented.

"And, you know, it worries me too," Milburn said, "and I agree about Roosevelt's administration. I think they'll do everythin' possible to stay out of it," he added and motioned for his wife to pour more coffee. "I can't say I'm not concerned the Axis powers won't attack more countries. Germany took France and I believe they'd like to take over England too. What's to say that they'll not be wantin' to come after us next? America needs to do more than just lend Britain and Russia war materials with this…oh…you know… ah…you know…the thing being called lend-lease, lend-lease, that's it! From what I've been readin', the English might not be able to hold out much longer on their own without more help from us! We need to be ready and prepared for war in every possible way!" he stated, showing he had given the subject considerable thought. "We sure wouldn't want to get caught with our pants down around our knees," he added, using a common local euphemism.

"You're probably right about us needing to be prepared. But I think we should just stay neutral and not poke our noses into it anymore than we already have," Thomas argued. "Look how well the country is doin' right now. We're doin' okay!"

"We're comin' out of the depression!" Milburn stated. "The only reason we are is because our companies are buildin' factories and producin' so much war material that it's makin' jobs for people. Two or three days ago I saw several flatcars loaded with army tanks bein' shipped through town on the B & O Railroad. Those were the first tanks I've ever seen in my entire life," Milburn replied, "and from what I've read, the military's draftin', recruitin', modernizin' and expandin' at an incredible rate."

"What you say is true," Thomas answered.

"I don't think lending war materials to England and Russia, calling up the draft and manufacturing war materials at the rate we are shows we're still doing enough of the right things. We may need to start doin' even more!" Milburn concluded.

"I still think we need to be very careful!" Thomas remarked.

"Well, think about this! If we're only gonna help our friends with this lend-lease thing and don't prepare ourselves in case the war swings our way, we could even end up havin' to fight them all alone. What chance would we have? The Russians are about ready to lose Moscow to the Germans," he added to bolster his argument as his thinking drifted more towards America taking some direct action.

"Russia's a long way over there. That's all the way across the Atlantic and Europe!" Thomas stated.

"Yeah, but France isn't. That Atlantic Ocean's not as wide as it used to be and the fightin' isn't just over on that side of the world. The Japs have occupied Korea, invaded China and are at work in Manchuria. They been killin' Chinese civilians by the thousands and our president told them they need to withdraw their troops," Milburn stated. "You think they're listening to Roosevelt? Of course they're not! They're not like us! We're a democracy! We stand for things that're good! We can't just sit by and let the Fascists and the Imperialistic Japanese do whatever they want! No sir, sometimes it takes more than just lip service to make people do what's right!" he said, surprising himself with his fervor. It seemed as if in presenting his statements, he had decided to change his rationale somewhat.

Thomas picked up his cup, swirled the coffee around with slow circular motions a few times to stir up the sugar better while he contemplated. "Well, I reckon what you said has some truth to it," he reluctantly agreed.

"Where are you people off to today?" Gloria interrupted in order to get away from a subject that was making her feel distraught. Discussions about the war, the thought of pain and suffering was making her anxious with worry. She had heard enough.

"Mattoon," Emma answered. "We're going to Mattoon. Thomas needs a new set of tires for the car and I want to get fabrics and do some sewing," she stated.

"That sounds nice," Gloria answered.

"Would you like to come along?" her sister asked.

"Thanks for asking me. That'd be nice to do some other time, but not today. I'm riding along with Milburn to Decatur when he goes to check on our new furnace and I plan to do a little shopping."

Emma looked enviously at the door into nearly finished addition. "I'm amazed how much you people have done around here in the last few months. There's so much we need to have done at our ole place. I wouldn't know where to start and even if we did, the money just isn't there right now!"

"It was all Milburn's idea," her sister admitted.

"I think he made the right decision!"

"I hope so!" Gloria answered.

Milburn had been half-listening to the women. "Gloria thinks it's been a mess around here and I have to agree with her, but it'll be well worth it and all the expense when we're finished," Milburn stated. "Gloria can tell you the house is already warmer and she has a lot more space in the house now that we have a basement!"

"I just think we could've waited another year," his wife responded, showing some lingering doubts. "Just look at this place; it still won't be done 'til spring."

"My blessed stars, girl, you're so lucky," her sister stated. "Don't complain! It won't be long before you'll have central heat just like them big houses in town," Emma said, looked at her husband and tapped him on the arm. "Thomas, we should get goin', these people have things to do and I wanna get back home early enough to do a couple of things I've been puttin' off."

Marianne had listened to the conversation behind her. Their exchange of opinions were exciting, although the war, she had to admit, sounded ominous. She dried her face, and once she decided she was as presentable as she could make herself, she fetched a bowl of oatmeal, two slices of bacon and sat down next to her aunt.

"How's my niece?" her aunt asked.

"Fine," Marianne said, and gave a weak smile to indicate that she had no desire to talk. *It's a little too early for a discussion, but I should be polite.* She thought and said, "It's nice seeing you, Auntie."

"And it's nice seein' you too!" her aunt replied pleasantly and took the subtle hint that her niece wasn't in any mood for talking.

Her Aunt stood up and gave her an affectionate squeeze on the shoulder. "Come on, Thomas, we need to go and leave these people be," she repeated. "They've got things to do and I think you and Milburn have talked long enough about the war!"

After their company left, Ethan and Jonathan walked into the kitchen wordlessly and sat down at the table. "Ethan, right after you and Jonathan have some breakfast you two'll need to go get your chores done. And, Ethan, since you're stayin' home today, you can milk the cows this mornin'", his father ordered. "Your mother and me need to get goin' cause I'd like to get back early enough this evenin' to unload the furnace before dark. And Jonathan, you'll hurry with your chores if you're still plannin' on goin' with us."

"Should I go do my chores now, also?" Marianne asked and wasn't too surprised with the answer.

"No, you need to help your mother straighten up the kitchen first so we can get movin'!" her father answered.

Gloria picked up the dirty breakfast dishes from the table and stacked them on the counter.

Marianne finished her oatmeal and handed the bowl to her mother.

"Before you do anything else, you need to put some fresh water on the stove for doin' the dishes," her mother said and added, "and then go wake up Leon."

Two hours later Marianne had finished all her house chores and was on her way out to the barn. She felt a definite chill in the air, but thankfully, only a light breeze stirred and the sky was clearing. Scattered clouds were slowly drifting by overhead but whenever the sun peeked out between them, she could feel the welcome heat on the side of her face. A small flock of pigeons warmed themselves on the sunny side of the red, metal, barn roof. *What a really nice day to go for a long ride,* she thought and figured she would have five hours alone to go wherever she wanted. Ethan had already left for Warren's with his rifle. She figured that he would be gone the entire day and she could picture them target shooting. Later, Marianne suspected, Ethan and Warren would walk the short distance into town and visit with Dale Marsh as an excuse to see Donna, Dale's sister. The thought made her chuckle.

Just before twelve, Marianne led Rocky out of his stall, into the driveway of the barn, saddled him up and gave him a healthy helping of oats before she went back to the house to get warm and fix an early lunch for herself.

Full and warm, on her way back to get Rocky she saw a low bank of dark clouds that stretched low across the horizon in the northwestern sky. "I'm glad that weather front's still far off and won't get here until later today," she remarked to herself and looked up at the warm sun.

Dressed comfortably, wearing a heavy coat, a thick stocking cap and work gloves, Marianne rode along the dredge ditch that ran north and south through the middle of the section of land their farm was on. She followed it north towards Van Fleet's woods which was a thick timber like the many others that dotted the flat endless farmland. These ancient stands of trees were like sentinels of the prairie, filled with giant oaks and hickories that for logical reasons the pioneers had left standing and all of the generations since hadn't bothered to cut down either. She remembered her father saying to her once that the land quality under these dense growths wasn't worth the labor or cost of removing them.

Coming out of her daydream, Marianne encouraged Rocky to trot. She tried to visualize the Indians that might have once camped among these ancient sentinels of the prairie and she could almost smell the smoke from their camp fires. She liked the solitude away from the roads. It gave her time to think, air to breath and a feeling of freedom. *Horses are about my favorite things,* she guessed. *Well, maybe not just horses. My friends are important also but horses don't demand very much: they don't argue or gossip, hold grudges or tell lies.*

Eventually the two of them came to woods and a dirt lane that had been laid out by someone long ago that circled back through the understory of the tall, bare trees in a loose and meandering fashion.

She turned Rocky onto the lane and headed into the woods. The outer edge was thick with brush but once inside among the trees, the ground was more open; although there were briar patches scattered around which could entangle and rip at the flesh of anyone careless enough to step into one of them.

Not being in any hurry, she slackened her grip on Rocky's reins and let him walk at his own pace. It was somewhat warmer among the trees than it was out in the open air. The atmosphere and the slow gentle sway of the saddle relaxed her until an angry flock of crows at the far end of the woods started making a ruckus over the presence of a large red-tailed hawk. The noise and commotion they made was irritating. The hawk didn't seem too affected by them, so why should she be, she thought. She rode on several more minutes until, in the sky, behind this conflict, she noticed that the grey cloud bank had moved much closer and now acted like a darkened scrim one might see behind a stage play. The black crows, some sitting while others flying madly around, seemed symbolic, like an omen of something bad about to happen. The scene playing out in the tops of the trees made her apprehensive about the weather front that was moving much faster than she had calculated.

Marianne scanned the sky. Maybe I should hurry up Rocky's pace, she thought for a brief second or two and then rejected the idea. *This ride is too nice and I may not get a chance like this again until next spring,* she reasoned. Suddenly, a complaining blue jay burst out of the brush a few feet in front of them, startled Rocky and made him skitter sideways. His abrupt movement made her nearly fall off. Luckily she was able to grab the pummel with her left hand as she slid roughly to the right. "Whoa. Whoa. Easy, it's only a bird!" she gasped, seized Rocky's reins and quickly patted him on the neck to settle him down. "It's okay," she soothed. Her left wrist started to throb. She took the glove off that hand, worked her fingers in a gripping motion and winced from the shooting pain. "I bet I've sprained it," she said aloud, and rubbed her wrist very carefully, unbuttoned the two middle buttons of her coat and shoved her left hand and forearm inside through the gap between them, making it work like a sling.

She gingerly wiggled her fingers and decided her wrist should be fine in a day or so.

The young girl commanded the pony to stand perfectly still until she could get herself situated firmly in the saddle. It had gotten surprisingly darker in the short time she had been distracted. She looked up at the sky again and noticed without a doubt that the cold front had arrived. A cold, sharp wind now whispered through the tops of the trees and a few dry leaves swirled around in the air. "I think it'd be a really good idea for us to ride towards home," she remarked to her pony, and coaxed him into a slow trot just as the first big snowflakes skimmed by her nose.

Exiting back out of the east end of the woods from where she had entered, she was sheltered from the blast of the wind from the west. Large snowflakes swirled around where she was in the ebbing air in the lee of the trees. Her house, a mile away, was completely lost from sight and Van Fleet's farm house, only a hundred yards away, was nothing more than a dim shadow buried in the heavy, white swirling snow. She stopped Rocky again and pulled her coat collar up as high as she could, knowing that once away from the protection of the thick trees, they would face the full fury of the storm and be much colder.

"I wish I had worn even more clothes," she screamed with frustration into the wind. "Come on, Rocky, let's get going," she shouted and urged him to head home.

Once they left the sheltered air behind the trees where the snow had already thickly blanketed the ground, they rode out into the full fury of the storm and found it nearly impossible to tell which direction would take them home. The snow swirled, whipped and blasted them. By keeping the wind on her right side Marianne reasoned that they would be riding generally south and by doing so they would eventually end up bisecting the dirt road on the north edge of their farm. From there it would be easy to go home. Seconds later, the impossible seemed to happen. Snow started to come down harder. The wind died somewhat and shifted directions several times. Marianne could only pray they were still going south but obviously she had lost her sense of direction. A few very cold minutes later, she looked down and saw nearly snow covered tracks where another large animal had left a trail in the snow. "Oh no!" she exclaimed when she realized that they had crossed their own path and were going in circles.

A thick layer of snow covered both of them. Marianne was cold, wet and shaking; her teeth chattered uncontrollably. Snow blew against her face, melted and created tiny rivulets of icy water then ran under her upturned collar. A minute or two after that, Rocky started acting strangely. Whenever she tried to make him go one way, he would try to go in another. A little later, when she thought they were making progress, they crossed their own tracks a second time, and then, shortly after that, Rocky balked every time she tried to make him move where she thought they should be going.

He was trying to tell her something, but she didn't know what. Marianne tried to coax him on. He would take two steps and try to turn left or right. *Maybe*, she thought, *just maybe, it might be a good idea to let her horse try to find the way home before she froze to death*. She loosed his reins and gave him his lead. Instantly, she felt as if Rocky had a new purpose in his steps. Thankfully, a few minutes later, she saw the vague contours of the snow-buried lane and knew approximately where they were. "Thank you good ole buddy," she uttered and nearly cracked her frozen face with a wide smile. "Let's go home!"

The sight of her family's barn had never looked better. Marianne pulled her left arm out of her coat, slid off Rocky and opened the barn door. As she led the pony into the center aisle, she found her father milking his cows in the warm, dim glow of two kerosene lanterns. "Your mother has been worried and waiting for you," he said, not turning around. "You need to get right up to the house after you put your pony away," he added, sounding more as if he were giving an order instead of reminding her of her responsibilities, and yet she knew from the tone of his voice that he had been worried about her. She assumed her parents had a confrontation over her whereabouts because she hadn't told anyone where she was going. Although she didn't know what had transpired, she suspected that her father had tried to defend her lack of responsibility, but was disappointed he didn't at least say he was happy to see her safe.

Ethan and Jonathan were in the back of the barn feeding the livestock. "Gees, Sis, you look like a snowman," Ethan commented. "Are you okay?"

"I'm so numb, I can't tell for sure!" she answered without mentioning her sore wrist as she attempted to unsaddle Rocky without putting much strain on it.

"Mom and Dad got real concerned about you being out in this weather. When you didn't show up right after the storm started, they argued and then the more it snowed the more they both hoped you'd ride up soon. They didn't know what to do!"

"Yeah," Jonathan agreed. "And then they seemed to get madder the more they worried," he added.

"Mom said you don't use much common sense when you're with Rocky. Dad didn't think the pony had anything to do with it!" Ethan added as a caution so she could anticipate what to expect later. "Mom also said a couple of other things about Rocky and I could see Dad was upset. He didn't say anything; he just grabbed his work coat and told Mom that he was going out here to do his chores. When we got here he was already milking the cows!" Ethan related.

Marianne wanted to remind Ethan of how many times he had done stupid things and their mother rarely admonished him for his dumb actions. Now, above the fray, he was acting like a good brother, so why make a negative comment at this moment.

Another inch of snow had fallen from the time Marianne walked into the barn and the time she left for the house. The heavy snow blocking the sun made it appear much later in the evening than it was. She was so cold her legs felt like logs, her feet didn't seem to exist and her ears needed to be touched to see if they were still sticking out from the side of her head. She wasn't going to take her stiff, numb fingers out of her glove to check on them. Having a penchant to talk to herself, she said, "I've been cold before but I can't imagine anyone ever being colder than I am right now!" Actually she didn't care whether her mother would show her any sympathy since she was more miserable than she had ever been and imagined that she probably looked like a cartoon of a snow queen she had seen in the comics; the thought made her smile.

"I'm glad you're okay," her mother said glancing around. "Be sure to hang that wet coat up and then go get some clean dry clothes on!" Other than those brief comments, her mother hardly turned away from the stove.

Playing with his toys in a corner of the kitchen, Leon looked at her. "Do you know you have some snow in your hair?" he asked.

"I know," Marianne said and ran into her room to shed her cold, wet garments. "Thank God I made it home. Now I don't care about anything other than getting into something dry and going back into the warm kitchen," she said under her breath. "I'm going to forget about everything else!"

After changing her clothes, she felt only slightly revived and needed to get warm. The kitchen beckoned. "When you're warm, I want you to set the table," her mother instructed. "We're only havin' potato soup tonight, so don't put on any plates. Be sure to get the soda crackers and butter out and there's a large chunk of cheddar cheese I bought in Decatur today. Cut it in thick slices and put it in the middle of the table."

"Okay," Marianne acknowledged. "Potato soup sounds really good to me!"

"I was worried about you," her mother said matter-of-factly and Marianne felt that her mother was trying not to become emotional; she thought that if her mother threw her arms around her it would sooth both their souls. Her consolation was to be safe and warm and have ample portions of her mother's hot, steamy potato soup made with large chunks of potatoes, bits of onion, salt, pepper in a rich creamy milk base. If there was one time she needed hot soup, tonight was it.

Neither parent asked where Marianne had been or why she was out in the snow storm. For the rest of the evening she was generally ignored. She knew that she had made a terrible miscalculation and yet she would have been relieved to have heard an admonishment.

They didn't ask why I hadn't come home earlier. I bet they think I was in town where I could've gotten home sooner! Sometimes I just can't figure them out! They treated me the same way when I came home from Stella Mae's house last summer. If they'd asked, I might've told them I nearly drowned and today they could've asked for an explanation too. Maybe their silence is a sign that they think I can't handle my freedom?

CHAPTER NINETEEN

Sunday, December Seventh, 1941

Just as Milburn was easing the family car up to the sidewalk to park on the street in front of the First Baptist church, the bell in its steeple rang into the cold crisp air, announcing the beginning of Sunday school.

Marianne liked Sunday school, the Bible lessons, and especially the way her Sunday school teacher, Miss Janet Baker, made each lesson interesting and fun. What she didn't like were the long sermons presented by their minister during the church services where he would present an occasional theory that went against her reasoning. One of the biblical stories that troubled her in particular was about the prodigal son who came home and was given everything while his younger brother, who stayed home and worked tirelessly, got nothing. Marianne didn't think parents should have favorites and she deeply resented her parents overlooking Ethan's misbehavior while finding fault so easily with hers.

She was glad her minister had never offered a sermon about pregnant unwed mothers as Barb's pastor had and she suspected hers would've been even more judgmental. When Marianne thought about Margret's misfortune and her ordeal in church, she wondered why tolerance and forgiveness was sometimes so hard to find in a humble Christian mind.

Marianne's mother and father were not zealots about their faith. They were strong, conservative Baptists and went along with most of the church's teachings and insisted that their entire family go to church every Sunday. Ethan was the exception, able to wiggle out somehow by getting lost while the rest of them got cleaned up and dressed. He would just walk out of the house and not return. Their father rarely reprimanded him, Marianne reasoned, because he found the hassle of Gloria's defense of Ethan contentious and aggravating. Today Ethan rode in the car next to her.

A gust of icy wind took everyone's breath away as they stepped out of the car.

Marianne peered at the two-story, faded-white house and the small neighborhood grocery store standing next door to it that belonged to Mrs. Wades, the single mother of her friend Evelyn and of Ethan's close friend, Matt. She knew that there would be just the slimmest possibility for her to run over and visit her friend after church.

Several more cars pulled up and parked along the street before they climbed the church steps. Jonathan reached the door first and held it open for his family and the line of people following behind. The sound of horses' hooves clomping down the street caught Marianne's attention and caused her to pause outside the door briefly and watch as Charley Dorset went past, the last man in Atwood to use a horse and buggy, other than the Amish families south of town. He was a pathetically thin man and was hunched over in an attempt to stay warm in his open buggy. The fact that someone could stay stuck using the old methods of transportation in the rapidly changing world fascinated her. But she also knew the reality; he was a poor, old man who couldn't afford a better means of getting around and was trapped in a lifestyle from which he couldn't escape.

On an extremely cold night four years earlier, her father had caught Charley stealing two chickens. Her father could have had him arrested, but he didn't; instead, he told the grizzled old guy to never step foot on his property again, then gave him two chickens to feed his hungry family. Milburn never told anyone other than his wife about the episode and the only way Marianne had learned about the incident was through overhearing the conversation between her parents later the same night when they thought none of the kids would hear. She felt good for what her father had done and smiled because she was happy that he had such high ideals, didn't hold grudges, was genuinely sincere and stood behind his Christian beliefs instead of being hypocritical.

The six of them passed two boys ringing the bell high in the steeple above the entrance as they filed into the church with its high, arched faux-stained-glass windows gracing the high front wall on the east end of the pews. The altar was located in the middle of the long north side of the rectangular floor plane. It was a unique layout, one that gave the optimum arrangement for the pews, divided into three sections with wide aisles and which allowed the back rows to be closer to the pulpit than if the pulpit had been at the end.

Milburn led his family towards the center section of pews and stopped at the fifth row. He stepped aside and let his wife go in first. He followed her into the pew and their four kids trailed along after him.

The minister offered a prayer, gave a brief welcoming statement and then excused the congregation's sixty to seventy people to go to their Sunday school classes.

The adults remained in the main auditorium. The unmarried and school-age members of the congregation who had been divided into groups by age went to separate basement rooms. The youngest, like Leon, were taught in a small room beside the pulpit by one of the church's most cherished teachers, Miss Dianna Baker.

Marianne liked the bible lessons of John the Baptist who wore a camel hair robe with a leather belt and who went out into the wilderness to live on locusts and honey. He preached to his followers that baptism, in the name of the Lord, offered the possibility for redemption by having one's sins washed away. People far and wide heard about his wondrous message for the forgiveness of sins and flocked to him to be baptized in the Jordan River.

After Sunday school, their minister, Alan Presley, walked up to the lectern. "What a glorious morning this is," he said and paused for emphasis, "because we learn from the letters of John the Baptist that our worldly sins can be forgiven by our Lord in Heaven…and our Lord knows we all carry a load of sins around with us!"

"Let's do the biblical readings together," he said and opened up his Bible to the correct passages. He waited momentarily while the congregation took the books of readings distributed along the backs of the pews. "You'll also find the readings for today on page one hundred and twelve," their minister instructed and waited a few more seconds for everyone to get settled before he started.

After the Bible readings were finished, a collection plate was passed before the minister gave his sermon on baptism and how the path to salvation began with immersion in water. He stated that baptism washed one's sins away and lifted a large weight from one's soul after achieving redemption. The congregation sang the most moving hymns and Preacher Presley, towards the end of his sermon, held up his hand to stop the singing mid-verse while the pianist continued to play the hymn softly. He would pause dramatically for several seconds and then invite those not baptized to step forward and accept the Lord as their true Savior.

She had refused to take the step many times for various reasons. Her major excuse was that by even thinking about something immoral made one a sinner and reasoned that if it were true, then how could the lifting of one's sins last for more than a few minutes. She felt caught in a conundrum, unless she could change her reasoning somehow. It was as if she were standing on a slippery slope that was slanted towards hell. The way she always avoided stepping forward was to either think of green Jell-O as a distraction or determine to ask for forgiveness every fifteen minutes in case a meteoroid might hit her while going happily about her day. Baptism didn't seem like an easy fix.

Marianne's mind became so actively contemplating right and wrong that she hardly heard the fleeting parts of the first half of the sermon and nearly forgot where she was. Gradually, her attention returned to her immediate surroundings and she became keenly aware that she was standing up with the congregation singing,

"Tenderly He is Calling" as the reverend motioned for them to repeat the words over and over softly while he raised his voice in increments. "The lord is your Savior. Come forward. He's calling you!" he said, repeating this invitation several times, each time a little louder. It was a dramatic effect and it worked sometimes. "He's offering you a chance to be born again!" he said very forcefully, trying to pull any sinners into the fold, as Jesus did with fish in his seine.

His words pulled at her like a magnet, but gravity held her feet in place. This moving enticement, even more so than many others and combined with the emotional hymns, was designed to work on one's guilt and stir up emotions. Each member of the congregation was supposed to feel as if the church held its arms open to them. All you had to do was to step out and walk forward. It took only one step to find salvation. *Should I?* Marianne contemplated and felt a rush of anxiety. Her entire body grew warm for a moment and then she thought, *No I think I'll wait until sometime later when I don't feel as if I'm being manipulated through my emotions. I already have rules that give me restrictions, which I sometimes break, so why would I want to make promises to God that I know I couldn't keep and I'd end up carrying more guilt around.*

After the final collection was taken, Reverend Presley offered a simple prayer. "Heavenly Father, we humbly thank you for looking after us in this world of turmoil and strife and for everything good that you have given us. We pray that you will look after those in need and give comfort to those stricken with ill health. And Lord, we pray that you will help the many people fighting against the oppression of the Axis Powers and with your heavenly help we also pray, with your guidance, that America can avoid the wars raging over across the oceans and around the world. Please guide us in the ways of righteousness and help us keep our faith...Amen."

With his final act, the congregation exited the pews and slowly filed out through the wide front doors. The minister stood just inside the vestibule, shaking hands, praising children, complimenting the people for attending and making a dozen or so other practiced remarks. Rarely did he deviate from his pattern, but sometimes he did. "I thought you might step forward today," he said to Marianne who was trying unobtrusively to slip by him. "I think the Lord's calling your name!" he said. She gave him a weak smile, reached out and gave him a limp handshake as a clue that it would be her decision to be saved and not his. She wasn't one to be pressured, manipulated or cajoled into things. She jostled her way between two slow people and walked out through the door into the cold air. She instantly felt free and took a deep breath.

Marianne sat in the back of the car with her two older brothers and shivered for several long minutes before the heater warmed up enough to throw a little warmth into the rear and take some of the chill out. The back seat was never warm or comfortable on really cold days and it wasn't until they'd driven over to Main Street and stopped at the drug store for him to pick up his Sunday subscription to the Decatur Herald that everyone's breathe stopped hanging like miniature clouds in the air each time they exhaled, causing the windows to frost over. Bundles of papers were stacked in the drugstore waiting to be picked up by individual subscribers.

Milburn bought the local paper once or twice a week, but the Decatur paper with its supplements, editorials, color comics and other odds and ends offered him a couple hours of reading. Left alone in his easy chair, first he would spend a couple of relaxed hours reading through the large in-depth news section and a then read the lighter sections.

For Milburn, Sundays were a time set aside for worship, as a day of rest and free from work. He followed the tenet of resting on the Sabbath as closely he could but the reality of running a farm and having animals to tend conflicted with the work rule. Not doing any work on Sundays was an impossible task that God asked of him and he surmised that a farmer's role exempted him from guilt. He didn't work his land on the Sabbath but he could not ignore his livestock and poultry. He had no recourse.

This Sunday was a typical December day with cold morning temperatures, only warming slowly into the low twenties by mid-day with snow on the ground and a sky filled with broken clouds. The wind had become stronger since they left for church and it now whipped between the farm buildings, making the cold seem much worse. Jonathan and Leon jumped out of the car and raced ahead for the house.

Gloria looked towards the house and pulled her coat tighter. "I can't wait until spring comes," she said.

At first her husband thought she was talking about the weather and replied, "So you can work in your flower beds?" he replied.

"No, Milburn, so you can get them two porches finished," she answered.

"I supose, but we got started too late in the season to finish everythin'. We were lucky to get the basement finished and the furnace installed," he answered and looked proudly at the house perched nicely on its foundation. "I reckon everythin' should be done by June, including the porches," he added.

Coming home to a warm house was a wonderful new experience, Marianne believed. In the past, the rooms were never warm because of the inadequate stoves and a poor foundation under the house which allowed cold air to seep in under the floors. Cold air also came in through, over, under and around every conceivable crack or opening from the outside. The coldest rooms had been the unheated bedrooms. Since the furnace was installed, she could go into her room and casually change clothes without rushing. Now, whenever she had enough time, she could even sit at her vanity and primp in the warmth for as long as she liked.

"Marianne, would you give me some help gettin' our Sunday dinner finished," her mother said while taking off her coat.

"Sure," she answered happily and hurried off to her room. She and her mother hadn't been at odds with each other lately and besides, she enjoyed the kitchen's extra warmth where the family gathered. Jonathan and Leon often chose to sit at the kitchen table drawing or playing games while their father sat reading and sharing with his family bits of information he found newsworthy.

Marianne took her time getting undressed and hanging up her Sunday clothes in her wardrobe. She slipped into a more casual dress, sat down at her vanity, brushed her hair, primped and proceeded to forget to keep track of the time. A princess couldn't have appeared happier than she was at that moment. She primped until Leon knocked on her door and stuck his head inside. "Mom said for me to tell you she needs your help."

A few minutes later Marianne found her father in the living room reading an article from the front page of the Sunday paper and commenting to her mother about it. "The front of the paper today is just full of war news," he was saying. "Most of it is about how bad things are going for the English, although it goes on to say the Russians are having some successes against the Germans. Things are a mess in this old world!" he stated.

"Let's hope and pray the best for England," his wife replied. "What was it you were saying about the Russians?"

Her husband adjusted the pages of his paper. "It says here," he said, and pointed at a large column with his index finger, "the Russians launched a big counter-offensive yesterday against the Germans just outside Moscow and they're drivin' the German army back. It says the Germans are in a massive retreat while tryin' to hold off the Russians. The fightin' is takin' place in terrible winter conditions, some of the worst ever. It was something the Germans weren't very well prepared for. There seems to be some doubt whether the Russians can stay on the offensive," he explained

"What do you think?" she asked.

"I think it's a situation that could turn around at any time," he quipped, contemplated for a moment, and then he let his pessimism show a little more, remembering what the German Army had accomplished with historic swiftness over the last couple of years. Maybe they're drawing the Russians into some kind of a trap or somethin'!"

"But isn't it good what the Russians are doing now?" Gloria asked nervously and sprinkled some pepper on the big ham she was preparing that her husband had brought home from their rented locker at the Atwood Meat Market & Slaughter House the day before.

"Uh huh! Of course it is," he replied somewhat reluctantly. "The paper's reportin' it like it's favorable news," he answered a little more positively. "I agree I suppose. If they can keep the German's retreatin', it'll be the best news anyone's heard since this war started!"

Marianne walked into the snug kitchen with its windows steamed over from the condensation of cooking her mother was doing. The wonderful aromas wafting off the stove were so seductive they made everyone's stomachs yearn to be indulged. "Sorry, Mom...I just lost track of time!" she said apologetically. "What do you want me to do first?" she asked.

The week before, Milburn had requested that his family treat today's meal special with all the usual trappings of a holiday since he knew the church service today was to be about John the Baptist who had preached that total immersion in water was necessary to wash one's original sin away which Adam and Eve had committed in the Garden of Eden and left mankind stigmatized.

Jonathan and Leon were given the task of setting up the dining room table with the family's formal china and the good silver flatware. At two o'clock Gloria announced, "Milburn, will you and the boys stop whatever you're doing and go to the table?"

The table was covered in an appetizing assortment mid-west farm foods. At the head end of the tale, in a big platter, sliced ham was heaped up next to a metal tray of baked Jonathan apples. Broiled potatoes, creamed corn and a bowl of seasoned beets were scattered around in separate dishes. A large porcelain bowl of green beans with bacon was positioned near the middle of the of all those dishes. There was also a slab of churned butter, a pitcher of cold milk, thick with cream and a big loaf of home-baked bread cut into thick slices. On the counter top in the kitchen, just out of eyesight but on everyone's mind, a chocolate sheet cake sat cooling.

Once everyone was seated Milburn indicated he was ready to say grace. First, he offered special thanks for the Lord's help in making it possible for them to have their house finished and for the furnace to be functional to warm the house on the first Sunday since its installation. "Please help the Russians in their struggle against the Germans," he prayed, "and also we thank you for our health and the bounty of food before us," he added with a strong, "Amen!"

Milburn forked a thick slice of ham unto his plate. "Since this platters too big and heavy to pass, you can hand your plates down so I can give you a helpin'," he said.

"That was a great service today," he remarked as he took a plate. "I think our new ministers doin' a good job and I expect he'll be around for a while," speculating the man possessed a good mind and humble traits.

"Can someone read me the comics after I finish eating?" Leon asked, waiting for his plate to return. He loved the big pages of colored comics that included *The Phantom, Li'l Abner, Terry and the Pirates,* and others. It was a treat he got every Sunday and would pester until someone agreed to read them.

"Of course I will, after I help Mom," his sister replied.

The atmosphere in the dining room became a scene of contented people chitchatting and enjoying the abundant food. "It might be a good idea to turn on the radio and catch up on the news or listen to some music while we're eating," Milburn suggested. Their old radio was a battery-powered model that was used mostly in the mornings to get farm reports and the weather. Sometimes, on rare occasions like this special Sunday, the vacuum tubes would be warmed up.

"We don't need the radio on right now," Gloria commented. "You know them batteries are expensive!" What she said was true, but sometimes in the evenings, especially on Saturday nights, she would encourage Milburn to turn the radio on and tune in one of the mystery broadcasts like *Inner Sanctum, The Shadow* or a comedy program like *Amos and Andy* or *Fibber McGee and Molly* as they sat around with large bowls of popcorn in the soft light of the kerosene lamps while listening spellbound to every word. It was great family fun and a good distraction from a week's hard work. "Please, Dad! Please turn it on!" Jonathan pleaded.

"Please, Mom!" Leon, puppy eyed, begged. "Pleeease!"

She looked around and saw only long faces. "Okay," she reluctantly acquiesced.

"So now, everyone's in agreement," their father said and turned on the switch. The vacuum tubes slowly warmed up. The radio crackled with static. Milburn slowly turned the tuning dial, passed a music station and caught a fraction of "Begin the Beguine" being played by Artie Shaw.

"That was really nice! Go back!" Marianne stated enthusiastically.

"Let me look around a little more," her father replied, and turned the dial in search of something he really wanted to hear.

"... planes have swept in over the mountains from somewhere offshore and they seem to have caught the naval base completely off guard. Only sporadic fire is being returned as I watch," the broadcaster was saying and Milburn instantly stopped twisting the knob. "What I see happening has to be a great catastrophe for our Navy. Not only can the explosions be heard from where I'm standing quite a long distance away, but I can also feel the concussions from them even here. The whole area around the naval base is blanketed in a layer of dense, thick smoke," he said and the station faded out.

Milburn fumbled hurriedly with the dial and picked up the broadcast again. "...veral ships seem to be on fire but I can't tell if any have been sunk. A heavy plume of smoke is rising thousands of feet into the air as Japanese planes continue to roar overhead, diving in and out, strafing and dropping bombs!" the broadcaster said in a staccato voice, never wavering but filled with deep emotion.

Distracted from eating and concentrating on the words that flowed from the small speaker, Ethan leaned forward on his elbows. "What's he talking about?"

"Shhhh," his father shushed, struggling to keep the station tuned in.

Ethan and Jonathan disrupted by talking between them.

"Please!" Their father implored and kept turning the dial and got even more static. He became visibly frustrated as each station faded in and out. Gradually, and ever so carefully, by slowly moving the dial back and forth, he finally managed to get a station to come in clearly.

"Just after seven-o'clock Hawaiian time this morning and only a little while ago, the Japanese attacked Pearl Harbor with what must have been from a carrier-based aircraft. I can see the base several miles away and there are still a few enemy planes strafing and dropping bombs. The entire island was just put on alert in case the Japanese are planning to come ashore in an invasion. Honolulu is panic stricken..."

Although the family wanted to hear more details, the civilian newscaster was limited to report only what he could see and hear from a distance of several miles. No other details were yet coming from the military for him to relay because of the confusion of the action taking place at the base as well as the issue of national security. It would be days before the public would be more informed of the devastating damage to the Pacific fleet and many years before the whole story of why the military had not taken better precautions against an attack.

In time it would be reported that the older battleship West Virginia was one of the ships sent to the bottom of the bay. About two years later, on May 17th 1943 it would be refloated. Seventy bodies would be located. In one compartment, a calendar was found that had been marked with each passing day from the 8th of December to the 23rd. The ship was eventually repaired and put back into service to see heavy action. Donald, the children's first cousin would be assigned to her crew. After the war, he came home with his nerves shot from the naval battles he had witnessed in the Pacific from West Virginia's deck as a member of a gun crew. During heavy fighting he later related to them how he wished he could have dug a foxhole in the steel deck. He recounted how he had been with his crew when they fired at a Kamikaze plane flying directly towards their position. "It seemed to fly straight down our gun barrel," he stated with great emotion. "It was my duty to fire when the order was given but I fired in a panic, without waiting for the order...I blew it out of the sky. It was only because there was a direct hit and the plane blew apart in mid-air that I was never reprimanded or court marshaled for that serious offence," he admitted.

News gradually filtered out of the War Department over the next few days of the terrible losses suffered at Pearl Harbor and that the great battleship Arizona sat in the bottom mud beyond any hope of being salvaged. The grand ship had taken most of her crew into Davy's Locker with her and the ship would forever sit as grave to those entombed and as a memorial to all those who lost their lives that day. "A Day of Infamy" President Roosevelt would tag it.

The bad news tainted the excellent meal they just started to consume with gusto and what had started off as a festive Sunday for the family, a soothing religious service and coming home to a warm house had suddenly put them into dismal moods. For the next few minutes not much was said. The silence was so profound that little creaks could be heard in the house's framing as it adjusted to the recent construction.

While they strained to hear every word being said on the radio by the commentator speaking in short precise phrases, their tension was further heightened by the sound of the wind whispering around the outside corners of the house, further adding to their feeling of doom.

"Who are the Japanese and where's Hawaii?" Leon asked, looking from one face to the other around the table.

His sister held an index finger up to her mouth. "Shhh," she whispered and shook her head. "Listen and I'll tell you later," she added.

CHAPTER TWENTY

Monday, December Eighth

The next morning the breakfast table looked normal, but the atmosphere felt different. Their conversations had changed and the eggs, bacon and toast didn't taste as appetizing. Milburn had the radio tuned to a news station he had chosen after listening briefly to several others. Every station he passed was reporting on the attack of Pearl Harbor. On this station the commentator was questioning what would be the American government's immediate response to Japan's aggressive move. Ever since Germany had invaded France, the American public had been debating whether the United States should intervene in the war by joining its European Allies. The general consciences had been for United States to stay neutral and non-involved in any way; Japan's attack more or less ended that belief. Just one day later most Americans were calling out for retribution and Germany would declare war against the United States on December eleventh. Suddenly, war would loom on both coasts.

"I was afraid somethin' like this was gonna happen," Milburn stated, and bit into his buttered toast. "I never really thought there was any way we could've stayed out of the war even if the Japs hadn't bombed Pearl Harbor. It's been obvious to me that Roosevelt's been leanin' that way ever since he started buildin' up the military."

Their father would listen to a broadcaster for awhile, switch the station to other broadcasts and then make offhand statements of his personal views. Everyone else ate and watched him struggle with his notions about America's role in world events. "I thought he was right for buildin' up the military but I have to admit I always thought he was goin' a little too far and spendin' too much money. It was a good thing he did, though," he admitted, "or we would have been caught out in an open field with a tornado approaching!"

"I'm going out to gather the eggs and feed the horses," Marianne announced and looked up at the clock. "I don't want to be late for school," she stated needlessly because no one was listening and she had more than enough time to go do her chores. The news of her country going to war had really unnerved her, so to escape from more tragic news reports, she put on her coat and gloves, picked up the egg basket and headed for the door. "I need to go see Rocky!" she said softly to herself.

"Later today President Roosevelt is going before congress to make an announcement," was the last thing she heard of the broadcast before she stepped outside.

Marianne knew that Ethan and Jonathan would be along shortly, so she walked hurriedly to the barn. Time was a precious commodity she couldn't spare if she were to have some moments alone with Rocky. She knew if her oldest brother ever caught her talking seriously to him, she would be teased relentlessly. Once or twice in the past Ethan had quietly come around unseen and asked whether she was talking to herself. Surprised at the time, she had gotten red faced from embarrassment but had managed to play coy. "I didn't realize that I must've been talking to myself again," she told him with a smile and then bolstered her claim by purposely talking from time to time to herself around the house. She continued to remain very guarded about being surprised again as it would surely lead to silly and tiresome teasing. She could just hear Ethan telling his friends, "Do you know my sister talks to her pony and asks him questions and blah, blah, blah?"

"So, what if she does?" they might ask, she theorized. She could picture the whole thing clearly in her mind.

Ethan would laugh at their reaction and say, "Well here's the problem…I believe she even thinks he understands what she's say telling him and even expects him to give her an answer!"

Only to her trusted friends had Marianne admitted sharing her secrets and thoughts with Rocky. If the special relationship she had with her pony became general public knowledge, she was afraid that people might interpret her as being afflicted with some kind of a mental condition. If Ethan knew, with his devious nature, he might encourage the idea without worrying about the consequences it would have for her.

Once she was sure that she was ensconced securely in solitude, she said, "Hi Rocky," and poured a measured amount of oats into the horses' eating trough. "Boy, do I have a lot to tell you today!" she added quickly. "I'm scared," she whispered and then rambled nervously on about Japan bombing Pearl Harbor, how she worried that her older male friends might be called to serve in the military and how she was afraid the war might even come to the United States. She explained about her anxiety of going to school that day; everyone, she was sure, would be talking about nothing else but the war. Her rambling occupied several minutes and just as she was finishing, she heard the barn door slowly creak open.

"Hey, Sis, are you still out here?" Ethan called out at the other end of the barn's driveway.

"Yeah, Ethan…I'm still here and I'm just about done," she shouted back.

"Dad told me to tell you he'd drive us to school if we hurry," he yelled, rushing to do his chores. "He seemed impatient and explained he wants to leave real soon!"

Most mornings they had to walk to school unless it was raining, snowing heavily or extremely cold. "Why and where is he going?" she asked.

"He told me that he wants to go to town, get the Decatur paper and have coffee at the drug store."

"He never goes to town to have coffee!"

"I know, but I think he wants to hear what other people are saying about the Japs!"

Suddenly Marianne was in a rush. "I'll see you up at the house," she said, threw another small scoop of oats into Rocky's side of the trough, picked up her egg basket and ran off towards the hen house.

Marianne was surprised to find Donald, her seventeen-year-old cousin, standing at the end of the table in the kitchen across from her father. She could tell from the way he postured himself that he had something serious on his mind because, instead of sitting down, he had both hands on the back of a chair and was leaning forward. "What do you think, Uncle?" she heard him ask and then he added emphatically, "There's not much for me to do around here!"

She watched as her father contemplated for a moment or two before answering. "No, Don, I don't suppose there is, but you must know that joinin' up for the service will be a life changin' decision and it's one you need to make by yourself. Your grandmother and Anna Lee don't depend on you much for their financial support, so that isn't a problem."

Marianne put her egg basket down and pulled out a side chair. "Hi, Don," she said softly, trying not to disrupt as he mulled over what he should do.

Instead of replying, he paused only long enough to dart his head partially around and nod slightly toward her in acknowledgement.

"I know Grandma doesn't depend much on my income," he said. "I give her money for room and board and take her places in my car!" he defensively added.

"If you join the Navy, it's gonna be a big step you'll be takin', you know," his uncle stated. "I sure do hope you give it a lot of serious thought first!"

"I have already! I've been thinking about joinin' the Navy for some time now and I've decided that there ain't nothin' I need to be hanging around here for. I'm working, but it's not a good job and I don't have a wife and family to hold me back and besides, I could get drafted pretty soon, anyway."

In a contemplative mood, Milburn thought for a second or two and then confirmed Donald's logic. "You're probably right about being drafted. You're the right age, healthy, and you don't have a job that'd qualify you for a deferment. The draft'd put you into the army and you'd probably end up in the infantry."

"That's what I've been thinkin'. It seems to me like the Navy beats the Army hands down in lots of ways and besides, I don't like the idea of sleeping in no cold, miserable tent or muddy foxhole and being dirty all the time."

Marianne was having a hard time believing what she was hearing and then it dawned on her again of how much the bombing of Pearl Harbor was going to create untold consequences. Coming in and hearing this conversation caught her off guard, even though Donald often sought her father's advice. *Where would all the turmoil, mayhem and violence swirling around in the world end?* she wondered, as she watched Donald, with all his misfortunes, make the final decision to go off to war.

Donald and his sister, Anna Lee, had become wards of their grandmother after their parents had died of typhoid fever about eleven years earlier. Marianne often thought about how unfortunate they were to have lost their parents at such a young age and Donald had, as far as she could tell, always been deeply affected by their untimely deaths. He carried a lot of anger and resentment around with him and she was sure it and his impetuous nature had brought him here today. She could understand how he might equate the unjust act by the Japanese to the unfair loss of his parents and maybe he was seeking to vent his anger and get revenge as a sailor.

"Have you talked to a recruiter yet?" his uncle asked.

"No! But I did run into Johnny Jones who just got back from the Great Lakes."

"You mean Willard's son?"

"Uh huh, and he encouraged me to join up in the Navy," Donald replied. "He thinks joining up was one of the smartest things he's ever done. Says he gets three good meals a day…a warm place to sleep and lots of other benefits. He told me that after his leave is over, he'd be going to San Francisco and wait for further orders."

"Then I guess from what I'm hearin' you telling me is that you've pretty much got your mind made up?"

"Yeah, pretty much, I suppose! Johnny even said he'd be willing to go over there with me to the recruiting station in Decatur sometime this week."

"I think you've made the right decision," Milburn told him.

"Thanks for listenin' and the advice," Donald replied, excused himself and left only minutes before Ethan came back to the house.

"I'll take you kids to school as soon as you can get around," Milburn replied. "I have a couple of things I need to get."

As promised, Milburn dropped Ethan off at the street corner in front of the high school before driving Marianne and Jonathan another block and a half away to the grade school. During the short ride into town Ethan was curious about Donald's visit and his father only told him, "Don has pretty much made up his mind to enlist into the Navy," and let the subject drop. Their father seemed to have a lot on his mind and the kids took his short answer as a clue that he wasn't in any mood for long discussions.

Marianne walked into a school charged with an electric-like atmosphere. Where she normally saw students scurrying around here and there purposely, she now witnessed them looking somewhat confused. The four upper-grade teachers were in a huddle talking in the middle of the wide, wooden floored area between the adjoining classrooms. They appeared so engrossed in their animated conversation that even after the last bell rang, they continued to talk without moving.

As Marianne entered her classroom, she briefly acknowledged a couple of her classmates, waved at Stella Mae, raised her desktop and put her homework and her sack lunch inside. By the time Mrs. Holtsman walked in and closed the door behind her, the students wondered what she had been talking about for so long. She strolled along the outside aisle between the desks and the blackboards towards the front of the room. "Good Morning!" she said when she reached her desk. "Good Morning, Mrs. Holtsman," the class answered in unison.

She smiled, moved around to the front of her desk to be in closer proximity to her class and said, "I know you've all heard what happened yesterday and I think you should all realize the Japanese attack is going to bring about many, many changes in this country. It's going to affect each and every one of our lives in some way. Today we'll be following our normal procedures, but at the same time I think it is imperative that we keep abreast of the new events swirling in the bigger world around us. We're witnessing history in a very profound way. Many of you probably know that President Roosevelt is going to make a speech today about how the United States is going to respond to the awful attack the Japanese made yesterday. For that reason, I've gone to considerable trouble to bring a radio in here. That's it, sitting over on the table in the far corner," she said and nodded in that direction. "You might've noticed it," she said and a few students turned and looked. "And as you know, we're living in troubled times and they've been made worse because of Japan's actions," she pointed out and continued. "I think it's vital that you hear the voice of our president as he explains, live and in his own words about how he thinks America should react to this terrible crisis. I'm planning on turning the radio on low, and when we hear something that relates to world events or hear the president, we'll stop whatever we're doing, turn the volume up and listen," she added and walked back to the radio. "Now," she said, "take out your math homework and pass it forward. Barb, you can collect it and put it on my desk," she instructed and dialed the radio for a clear station. Once she found a good one, she set the volume low and walked back up to her desk.

The students worked quietly. The mood in the classroom stayed fairly somber for most of the morning until one of the boys near the radio suddenly announced, "Mrs. Holtsman, I think the president's getting ready to speak."

Their teacher stopped what she was doing and walked swiftly to the back of the room and turned up the volume of the radio so that everyone could hear. First, they listened to a few brief comments from the news commentator before the president was introduced. Shortly thereafter President Roosevelt gave his famous "A Day of Infamy" speech.

Yesterday, December 7th, 1941--a date which will live in infamy--the United States of America was suddenly and deliberately attacked by naval and air forces of the Empire of Japan. The facts of yesterday speak for themselves. No matter how long it may take us to overcome this premeditated invasion, the American people in their righteous might will win through to absolute victory.

I ask that the Congress declare that since the unprovoked and dastardly attack by Japan on Sunday, December 7th, 1941, a state of war has existed between the United States and the Japanese Empire.

A few brief statements followed Roosevelt's address and once their teacher felt her class had heard all the key components of the news, she turned the volume down and walked back to the front of the room. The room buzzed. Everyone wanted to make a comment or ask a question.

Mrs. Holtsman, the good teacher that she was, responded to her students' enthusiasm. "Put all of your work away," she stated and waited a good minute until the room had grown quiet. "And now," she said, "since you've heard that we're obviously at war, I believe there is no better time than now for us to discuss America's role in world events!"

Over the next hour hands constantly shot into the air to be recognized, illustrating the keen interest their teacher had created by bringing her radio to school so that her students could witness the once in a lifetime event. Many beliefs, ideas, and concerns were respectfully debated openly until it became necessary for them to stop for lunch.

CHAPTER TWENTY ONE

June Sixteenth, 1942

The United States was rapidly becoming a nation tuned to the war. In May, gas rationing had been imposed on all citizens. Businesses and factories were critically short of help and jobs that recently had been hard to find were now available just for the asking. Women were taking positions that traditionally hadn't been open to them because the draft was sweeping so many young men up into the armed services.

The farmhouse, sheltered among tall trees, looked reborn like the spring flowers blooming along the back fence of the yard. At the end of March, with the improving weather, Milburn's two workers had returned and completed their interior projects and then moved outside to finish the porches in early June. A faint hint of new grass sprouted in the excavated soil around the foundation, turning it a soft velvety green. Two weeks earlier the schools had recessed and the summer of nineteen-forty-one was stating off like many other past ones. If anyone were to stand in the house and look out through one of its windows, the world would look deceivingly unchanged and tranquil.

Across forty miles of farmland to the west of Atwood, in Sangamon County, between Decatur and Springfield, was the little town of Illiopolis where a large industrial war plant was under construction. Several local men had jobs at the site and carpooled there every day. Any hint of the recent great depression was quickly fading. Cousin Donald, looking very trim and fit in his new blue uniform came home a week earlier on a furlough from boot camp at The Great Lakes Naval Training Center north of Chicago.

Nevertheless, in all outward appearances the farm was mostly unchanged. Ethan worked with his father doing the mundane jobs around the farm, while Marianne felt trapped in the house working with her mother. She hadn't seen any of her girl friends since school had let out nearly two weeks earlier because she and her mother were putting the house back in order with spring cleaning.

Jonathan and Leon also assisted with the house cleaning, always an important event for their mother. Rugs had to be taken out, hung over the clothes line and beaten with a wire paddle, aired and then brought back inside. Cabinets needed to be emptied and scrubbed and windows washed. Those normal chores got followed by countless other tasks, nearly all of them distasteful to the boys and Marianne, now a fourteen year old and more restless. Thankfully, today their mother had promised them that all the work would be finished.

Her pony was the one thing that kept Marianne happy. After supper, most evenings she would saddle him up and go riding, feeling unbound for a brief time. While riding, she often dreamed of endless things she would like to do when she got old enough. At the present, she was mostly contented with her life and looking forward to going to town on Saturday night.

The surrounding farming community used Saturday nights as a time to go into town to shop and visit. Their mother, Gloria, also seemed cheerier at the end of the week when she started to anticipate another Saturday night where she would find the social atmosphere pleasant, purchase her groceries and exchange some humorous stories with her friends and neighbors.

These nights were like mini celebrations with an occasional band concert performed by local musicians. Often, roving entrepreneurs put movie screens up in the middle of a side street, vacant lot or church yard. The movies were free and the profits they acquired came from the selling of candy, popcorn or snow cones at the portable concession stand.

"We should be finished with this mess today," Gloria told her daughter. "Next week we won't have extra work to do!" she added and turned to Jonathan. "You need to go out to that field across the road and tell your dad to get in here for lunch," she instructed.

Jonathan and his little brother walked down the lane towards the eighty-acre field across the road. Halfway there, they heard the roar of planes overhead and stopped and looked up. They became utterly fascinated as they watched two fighter-trainers from Chanute Army Air Base, north of Champaign, fly in circles, looping, hiding in clouds, diving and doing other maneuvers. The two brothers stood for a long time, totally mesmerized, until the planes leveled off and flew, side by side, back north from where they had come. "Wasn't that something?" Jonathan said. "I wonder how they keep score."

Confused, Leon looked at his brother with a curious expression on his face. "Score?" he asked.

"Yeah! I think they were practicing dog-fighting and were trying to get into positions where they could shoot the other one down…that's if they had real ammunition and were enemies; so they must keep score, don't you think?"

Leon shrugged his shoulders as if he should know the answer but couldn't come up with it at the moment. "I dunno," he said seriously, "but wouldn't it be fun to fly like that! I want to shoot down some Germans and some Japs!" he stated very seriously.

"The war's gonna be over a long time before you're old enough to fly. The Nazis and Japs will be defeated long before then," Jonathan remarked.

Leon pondered. "Yeah, I guess you're right!"

Jonathan realized that his mother would probably have lunch on the table by now, but he didn't say anything to Leon. Instead of performing their duty, they dillydallied, transfixed, watching the planes fly wing tip to wing tip north until they lost sight of them behind the trees in the woods. He didn't know how much time they had wasted by watching them and he contemplated concocting an excuse, even if it meant telling a lie his mother might accept. He figured that he could get by with a well-rehearsed fib, although, his younger brother had not learned the finer nuances of deception yet and might trip him up. Lies were like a sieve, and especially when their mother might decide to pump them with questions. Gradually the truth would dribble out and they would be in trouble. They had wasted enough time. "Let's go." Jonathan barked and ran towards the eighty to fetch his father.

The two young boys walked into the kitchen with their father and luckily found only cold foods arranged on the table and saw that their mother had no need to ask where they had been.

"I'll try and have all my work done early today so we can leave for town by seven," Milburn announced and put together a spiced ham sandwich with his favorite condiments. "If any of you kids are gonna' be riding into town with your mother and me this evening, you'll need to get your chores done early."

That evening, after the early supper was over, the table cleared of dishes, washed and put away, Marianne took a sponge bath and went to her room. She dug through her meager wardrobe and picked out her favorite dress, a soft pink one with Peter Pan collar and short puffed sleeves. She sat down at her vanity, combed her hair, pulled the right side back and clipped it with a small red bow to hold her hair in place. She looked at herself closely in the mirror, studied her reflection as someone might study a painting for faults, and grimaced. An added little touch of rouge gave her cheeks a slight blush of needed color. She studied her image again and gave a sign of approval Still feeling somewhat plain, she chose three large Bakelite colored bracelets, one red, one yellow and one blue, slid them on her left wrist, stretched her arm out and shook them, making them clank against each other. She loved the way they looked and sounded. *I think I'm ready to go,* she thought and smiled happily.

Milburn needed to work later than he intended and doing so delayed the family's departure until dusk which meant that he had to park on a side street because all the spaces along the small, two block business strip of Main Street were filled with earlier arrivals. Luckily, he found a vacant space just around the corner next to the International Harvester dealership. "I want all you kids back here by ten-thirty," he said as he pulled in. "Gloria, I need to go in here and check on a part for my tractor. I'll catch up with you later," he said and opened his door.

Leon started to follow his father and then hesitated when he eyed his mother crossing the street to the Atwood Grocery Store. He was conflicted about what to do. He took three steps towards his father, stopped again and then ran after his mother, hoping he would be able to talk her into buying him some candy.

Ethan and Jonathan jumped out and split up. Jonathan planned to hang out with his friends on the sidewalk. Ethan headed for the smoke-filled pool hall, a popular male hangout in the small town. Two pool tables and a lone billiards table overhung by green shaded lights occupied most of the dim space of his destination. In a small alcove set into the back wall of the pool hall a group of old men sat playing dominos and talking in hushed tones. Several spittoons were spaced around the floor for tobacco chewing patrons and ashtrays were spaced handily along the walls next to the racks of cue sticks. Smoke hung in thick undulating layers across the large space of stale air. Ethan stepped into this nearly toxic atmosphere and managed to locate Warren Donner at the last pool table.

Marianne opened the car door, stepped out, and headed for the soda fountain in the drug store a block away where she planned to find Barb, maybe Stella Mae, and some other friends she hoped were keeping the seats warm in one of the booths. If they were there, she knew they would be sipping Cherry Cokes, Green Rivers or having an ice cream soda. The image of them made her smile. She pictured Barb with a bottle of Coke she preferred instead of one from the soda fountain because, before she drank any, she'd tear open a small bag of Tom's Peanuts and pour them down the neck of the bottle. *It must be a city girl thing,* Marianne thought, laughed aloud and then nervously looked around to see if she had called attention to herself. Two old ladies coming out of the Atwood Herald's newspaper office gave her a strange look, whispered to each other and hurried away,

Marianne noticed the headlines, pictures and some war memorabilia arranged in an interesting display in the large window. The war intrigued her deeply and she wanted to know more about what was going on and stopped out of curiosity. It had been several months since Pearl Harbor was bombed and the editor wisely had chosen to display some large photographs recently released to the press by the government. A picture of the Arizona engulfed in smoke brought a lump in her throat. On a second bulletin board were clipped-out headlines of related articles that described recent battles in various places around the world. She stood in front of the lighted window and read the details, not compelled to move even though she yearned to see her friends.

The big banner across the top of the display stated, **WAR NEWS** in big, black, bold letters. Directly underneath the large banner was a smaller one that read, **Keeping You Informed.** Tacked underneath those two banners and covering the boards were clippings from some of the paper's most recent articles.

The first newspaper headline stated, *B-25s Raid Tokyo on April 18th*. The article described Lt. Colonel James H. Doolittle's flight of B-25 bombers that raided Japan, hitting Tokyo and other targets. It was dated April 21, 1942.

In chronological order was the second heading, *Corregidor Falls* and was dated May 7th, 1942. She knew about the surrender of the Americans on the little island of Corregidor in the Philippines a short time after the troops on the Bataan Peninsula had surrendered. When the news broke of the surrender, America's morale tumbled to a new low level. In the classroom the day after Corregidor fell, Mrs. Holtsman found it pertinent to spend part of the morning discussing America's failure in the Philippines. Marianne briefly scanned the text and went on to the next headline.

The third headline stated, *Gas Rationing Imposed on 17 Eastern States.* Marianne didn't look at any of the adjoining text and moved on to the next article.

American Victory at Midway read the fourth headline. It was dated June 7th, 1942. The article stated how the United States Navy had won a decisive engagement against the Japanese at Midway Island. Four Japanese aircraft carriers had been confirmed sunk by the Navy, plus several other Japanese ships had been reported either sunk or damaged. The United States hadn't gone by without its own losses either: the great aircraft carrier, the wounded *Yorktown,* was sunk the next day by a torpedo from a Japanese submarine.

Marianne walked into the drugstore and saw little indication of the war. Only if she had taken the time to study the place she might have noticed a sales poster that stated in bold letters **Lucky Strikes Green has Gone to War** and she would have noticed a uniformed man in the third booth. A steady patter of talk and laughter rose and fell in volume as if the world were a contented place. The soda counter stools were filled as were the booths across the aisle. The two noisy pinball machines by the door were being played by amateur experts nimbly flipping the steel balls, causing the lights of the machines to flash, make tingling sounds and occasionally orchestrating a deep thump that indicated a bonus game had been won. Several other young boys stood around watching, gesturing and making comments.

Pinball experts and the maze of people were standing around just inside the door. In the last booth she saw Stella Mae's blond hair which she could recognize anywhere because it was combed into such a unique style. As she drew closer she saw that Stella Mae, Barb and Alice, a classmate she wasn't necessarily happy to see, occupied one side of the booth on the far side facing her. Two boys sat with their backs to her, across from the girls and she didn't believe that there would be any space left for her to sit down.

After turning fourteen in April, Marianne started feeling awkward around some guys after their attitudes had changed and sought her company, showing interest in what she had to say.

Before she had the opportunity to acknowledge her friends, Stella Mae looked up, squealed loudly, "Marianne's here!" and made her feel self-conscious, and although usually not shy, she blushed and forced a big smile. "Hi, everyone," she answered.

"We've been saving a place just for you and were getting worried you weren't gonna show up," Stella Mae breezed and motioned for her to sit down next to Bobby Roberts, one of the cutest boys in Ethan's class.

Feeling self-conscious when everyone's attention stayed focused on her, she said, "I wish I could have been here sooner." The unexpected attention rattled her to the point that she almost sat on Bobby's leg before he jerked it out of the way. Her face flushed again and she prayed no one noticed. "I wouldn't have missed tonight for nothin' or nobody!" she said lightheartedly, trying to regain her composure.

Bobby threw his arm lackadaisically over her shoulder, gave her a gentle squeeze and said, "So you're going to be in high school next year!"

Marianne felt her face start to warm up again. "Yeah, I guess so," she said. *"God, I hope the whole evening isn't going to go on like this,* flashed through her mind and noticed Bobby's friend, Richard Shaw from Tuscola was the other boy in the booth.

"Look at her," Alice commented. "I don't think I've ever seen Marianne blush so much!"

Bobby yanked his arm away. "Sorry," he apologized meekly. "Does anyone else want something from the soda fountain?" he asked and nudged Marianne lightly with his elbow to let him out.

"Yeah, I do!" Marianne said, opened up her small red wallet and handed him a nickel. "You can get me a small Cherry coke with only a little ice!"

"Keep your nickel…it's on me," he said and grinned.

"Why haven't you come into town once this summer until tonight, Marianne?" Stella Mae asked.

"I haven't been able to get away because we've been…" she said and started to explain why but Barb cut her off in mid-sentence and said, "We've missed you!"

"We've had this big mess to clean up at home and I haven't had much time..," Marianne related, trying to continue her explanation and got interrupted by Bobby when he overheard the conversation as he was putting her Coke down in front of her. "What kind of mess are you talking about?" he asked.

"Well," she said, "my dad has had a lot of construction done over the last few months and now that it's finished, we've had to clean up the aftermath and I haven't had the time to run around because of it!" Being made to stay at home made her angry, but tonight she was determined she wouldn't complain about her personal life. "And what've you guys been doin'?" she asked cheerfully.

Stella Mae was the first to answer. "Somewhat the same as you, I suppose. I've been helping my mom around the house and my dad do some of his work. I guess I'm just the lucky farm girl that gets to go to town once every three or four days, either with my mom or my dad."

Barb giggled. "There's no way anyone can keep Stella Mae down on the farm. I think she'd crawl into town if she had to!"

"Hush," Stella Mae retorted good-naturedly and kicked Barb under the table. "And I don't suppose you considered staying home tonight either, did you?"

Barb giggled and her face flushed a deep crimson. Marianne didn't comprehend what the issue was about. Alice thought that Marianne understood what was taking place and rolled her eyes in a knowing fashion. Less than an hour would pass before Marianne would discover, on her own, that Barb had a crush on Richard, which explained all the giggling in the booth.

Barb blushed lightly and then she glared at Stella Mae. "I went to Decatur this week and saw my cousin's new baby," she said, effectively stopping the innuendos.

"She's had her baby already?" Marianne asked, surprised the birth was possible so soon, until it dawned on her that it had been over nine months since Margret moved down from Minnesota.

"It has actually been about eight weeks ago already. You should see him! He's such a cute little guy, with big blue eyes and a full head of silky blond hair."

"Why didn't you say anything before now?" Marianne asked and calculated the months. "That would've been at the end of April when she had him, wouldn't it have?"

"Actually it was the first week in May. I never wanted to say anything because Margret had been given such a hard time while she lived here in Atwood. I've avoided saying anything about her to anyone. But now, after the baby arrived, she's a lot happier, probably feeling the best she's felt in a long time and I'm so happy for her too. She said the baby looks just like his dad and that seems to really make her the most happy!"

"I'm afraid there's going to be a lot more very tragic stories before this war's over with," Bobby opinioned and quickly changed the subject. "You know, I think Richard and me are going out to walk around a bit and see what's going on," he added and proceeded to stand up. "It's getting a little too stuffy and noisy in here," he stated, "and the smoke's really getting to me...I've gotta get some fresh air," he added. "Would anyone else like to tag along?" he asked and looked from face to face around the booth.

Alice and Stella Mae replied that they were happy just sitting and talking. "Why don't you and Marianne go along," Stella Mae suggested and nudged Barb to slide out of the booth. "Alice and I have some juicy and private things we want to share with each other, don't we?'

Alice became tongue tied for a split second before she finally answered. "Yeah, yeah, that's right! I guess so!" she answered.

"I want to go," Barb said, brightening up. "How about you, Marianne?" she asked, reached across the booth, took Marianne's hand and pulled, encouraging her to get up and go along. "Come on!" she pleaded. "Come along with us!"

"Okay. Sure!" Marianne responded without a clue yet that her friend was interested in Richard or that she was intentionally being teamed up with Bobby by her friends. "The smoke's getting to be a little too much in here like Bobby said," she answered naively, totally unaware of being manipulated.

Stella Mae looked at Alice and arched one eyebrow as a silent gesture that everything was working out as they planned. Barb and

Marianne walked toward the door, followed by Richard and Bobby. They squeezed through the crowd standing in the aisle, walked past the pinball players and went outside. On the sidewalk, they had to walk between several small groups of people. Laughter erupted from one of the groups and a heated debate was taking place in another. Bobby took a few steps toward the street corner. "Why don't we walk down to the high school and back and get away from all this commotion for a while?"

"I don't think I have time to go that far," Marianne commented. "My dad said he wants me back at the car by ten-thirty!"

"I could give you a ride home if we're late," Bobby offered offhandedly.

Marianne considered his offer for a moment and weighed the option against how upset her parents would be if she wasn't back to the car at the designated time. She was afraid that they might sit and wait for her before they would finally decide to go home. "Not tonight," she answered, but really yearned to say yes to this tall, nice-looking boy.

They walked on in silence for half a block. "So, how's life on the farm?" Bobby asked, breaking the awkward silence in an attempt to start a conversation. "Isn't it kinda boring out in the country where there's so few people around?"

"No. No, I think it's great! Actually, I live on a farm that's almost in town and I also have lots to do and a pony to ride," she answered. "And how's life in town?" she joked. They both laughed. *That literally slipped out between my lips,* she thought and was happy that it hadn't sounded sarcastic.

"It's great," he answered with a sheepish grin. "I'll bet your house is the one right behind the high school! It is, isn't it?" he asked.

"Uh huh," she answered unenthusiastically.

"Do you ride much?" Bobby asked.

She brightened and smiled. "About every time I get a chance to!"

A few minutes later they were walking down the sidewalk of the dimly lit street on the back side of Main Street. Low watt bulbs glowed under the shaded street lights hung on wires stretched across the middle of each intersection. Barb, talking in whispers, sauntered along next to Richard several feet in front of Bobby and Marianne. It was a tranquil setting. In the soft light Marianne watched Richard's right hand reach out and take Barb's left in his. A few steps later, Barb nestled up close to him.

Bobby took Richard's move as an opportunity to step closer to Marianne and put an arm over her shoulders. He quickly removed it after he felt her body stiffen. They walked on in silence for another half block without either one of them making an attempt to converse.

So Barb must really have a thing for Richard, raced through her mind and she felt Bobby's fingers groping for hers. She pulled her hand away, even though a rush of blood made her body feel warm. "I should get back," Marianne replied in a near whisper, breaking the awkward situation. "I don't want to be late."

Main Street was noticeably less crowded when they returned. "It must be after ten already don't you think. Maybe I should be getting to the car!"

Bobby tried one last time. "You're sure you can't stay longer? That ride I offered is still good," he said.

"No, no, I don't think I should," she answered. "I can't, really. At least I better not," she said, fumbling for the right answer, correcting herself and started walking away.

"See you," Barb called out, so engrossed in her conversation with Richard that she had hardly noticed Marianne leaving.

Bobby followed along for a few steps. "Maybe I could stop out sometime and you can show me that pony of yours."

"Anytime!" Marianne answered and walked on for some distance alone before she turned around. "Bye! I had a really good time," she said so softly that Bobby almost needed to read her lips to tell what she had said. He stood unmoving and admired her cute figure until it became just a distant silhouette after she passed a group of young boys in front of the pool hall.

CHAPTER TWENTY TWO

Friday, June Twenty Second

After several warm sunny days interspersed with puffy cloudy skies, a thunderstorm rumbled in during the night. Heavy rain sat in, leaving ponds in the front pasture and drenching the fields, bringing fieldwork to a halt again. By breakfast time the downpour turned to scattered showers. Marianne was happy to see the heavy rain and when she walked into the kitchen, she found disappointment. Her mother informed her that she still had one or two projects to finish in the house and until they were done, she wouldn't be able to do anything else. Sitting at the table listening, Ethan thought he might be luckier, but there were no guarantees; there was always a barn stall or a chicken house to clean and if those didn't require attention, there were other tasks that might require his time, such as, helping to repair equipment or one of the other odd jobs that were set aside for days like this.

The family ate quietly and listened to the radio and were halfway through their breakfast, they heard Donald drive up in his shiny black car, one of his few possessions. He had only a few days left of his leave after finishing his naval training. Once his leave was over, his orders were to take the Illinois Central Railroad to Effingham where he would catch another passenger train on Nickel Plate Railroad to St Louis. A troop train using the Union Pacific's tracks out of St. Louis would transport him to San Francisco where he would receive his orders of deployment. After parking his car as close to the sidewalk as possible, Donald swung the car door open and made a mad dash for the house, just as the rain started pouring down again.

He knocked on the door briefly, out of courtesy, and let himself in. "Anybody home," he yelled up into the house from the doorway to make sure his uncle's family knew who was out there.

"Yeah, Don," his uncle responded loudly in acknowledgement.

"Wow. What a rain!" his nephew commented, wiped some water off his rain-streaked face and shook his arms like a wet chicken. "A person could drown out there!"

Since he had been home, his uncle and aunt had seen him only briefly in passing, just long enough to say hello and to congratulate him on finishing boot camp. Ever since he returned, Milburn had been curious and anxious to hear about his training. "It's a gully washer, that's for sure," his uncle said and motioned for Donald to take a seat. "Glad you decided to stop by before you left," he said. "We were afraid you'd leave and not say bye!"

"There's no way I would've left without seeing you and you know that!" he answered.

"Well, we've been thinkin' a lot about you lately and wonderin' about how everythin' went up at the Great Lakes."

Donald shrugged his shoulders as if it weren't a big deal. "Everything went okay, I guess," he said.

"You're really lookin' good and healthy," his aunt complimented, seeing how trim and muscular he looked. "Would you like a cup of coffee?" she asked and picked up an empty cup.

"Sure, sure…fine!" he answered and pulled out a chair from under the table. "I've had lots of coffee lately but I haven't had a really good cup in weeks."

It took a few minutes, but gradually the conversation drifted around to Donald's experiences. He related how excited he had been traveling to Chicago for the first time and seeing the sights of the big city. Everyone listened intently as he described what his life was like during basic training and the effort it took of him to take orders without thinking. "The food was really good and you had to eat everything they put on your tray," he stated, and went on to explain some of the drills and how hard it was to learn the United States Navy's ways. "There was always another drill to do or something else going on…always something," he complained. "Those were the bad parts. I became good friends with some of the other enlisted guys and I hope I get assigned to serve with a couple of them. Anyway, that's about it, I guess," he said, finishing about forty-five minutes after he started. "Now…I'm looking forward to seeing the world!" he stated enthusiastically.

"It sounds like you worked hard," his uncle commented, although he knew it couldn't be any other way with his determined nephew.

"I didn't work any harder than most of the guys," Donald replied. "There weren't many slackers!"

"Anyway…I'm thankful you're satisfied with the Navy," Milburn stated. "It puts me at ease because I feel somewhat responsible for you joinin' up."

"You don't need to fret about that any, Uncle. I came askin' you only because I needed someone I respected to confirm what I had already planned to do. I had my mind was made up for some time before that and I was committed to signing my papers when I came to see you. I have to admit you made me feel good when you agreed with my decision. But like I said, I would've signed up anyway; it just might've taken me a day or two longer," he admitted and turned to his aunt. "You wouldn't happen to have another cup of coffee, would you, Auntie?" he asked.

Ethan, wide eyed, sat on the edge of his chair listening to every word Donald said. No one else at the table realized that during the last hour he had decided that the United States Navy was the branch of service he was going into as soon as he got old enough. "What're you doing today?" Ethan asked, enthralled with his cousin's stories and hoped to hang out with him.

Donald answered, "I was thinking about going into town, hangout and kill time until tonight when I have a date."

"You're still dating that girl from Arthur?" his aunt asked; she had been listening but hadn't said much since he came in.

"Uh-huh... she's the same one."

"She sure seems like a nice girl to me," his aunt noted, believing she had met the girl twice. "Her name's Delores, if I recall rightly, Delores Kenny it is, isn't it and I'm pretty sure I've met her parents before."

Donald concurred. "Her last name is Kenny, and you've probably met her parents! They live just north of Arthur."

"She has a younger sister named Debra, doesn't she?" his aunt said, trying to get all the details right in her mind.

"That's right," Donald confirmed again and for the next five minutes, he shared his plans for the future. "I'm going to ask Delores if she'll marry me before I leave. She's dropped the hint more than once and I think I need to make my move before I ship out to the West Coast; but, I don't want to get married until I'm home from the service permanently."

"You don't have a lot of time left to ask her, Donald," his aunt replied.

"I know I won't be popping the question tonight. I'll have the ring by the first of next week once I find a suitable one," he said, sounding content with his decision. "Other than asking Delores to marry me, I have only a few other things I really need to take care of!"

Contemplating Donald's decisions his uncle stated, "Maybe you have other things to do, but whatever they are, they're not even half as important as askin' a girl to marry you!"

Donald acquired a very serious look on his face. "I know!"

His aunt recalled how impressed she was with the girl's looks, a tall, blue-eyed girl with wavy, blond hair and an unforgettable smile. "She'll make you a pretty bride and a good wife!" Gloria stated.

"I'm sure she will," he answered.

"You surely don't have many other things to take care of!" his uncle stated.

"I've just got to put my car up on blocks in my grandma's garage and remove the battery until I get back home."

"Listen, Donald, I've got work to do and I'd like to talk some more before you leave," his uncle said and stood, walked over, gripped Donald's big right hand, looked him in the eyes and pumped his arm firmly. "God be with you!" he said and walked briskly out of the house in an effort to hide the somber mood he felt about seeing one of his own go off to war.

He had prayed often that his nephew would come home alive and in one piece after encouraging him to join the Navy. If anything were to happen to him, Milburn didn't know how he'd ever console himself. *I'm going to pray often for his safety, because I know that I couldn't carry the guilt around for the rest of my life if something was to happen to him!*

"I should be going into town to see who's around," Donald said.

"Why don't we go riding? It looks like the rain stopped," Ethan observed, hoping to entice his cousin to hang around.

In the past, the two of them often rode their horses together. Sometimes they acted like crazed cowboys and at other times like mounted stern-faced cavalry soldiers. They would ride across bare fields pretending to be looking for enemy troops or bands of renegade Indians. Until Rocky came along, they had ridden the big horses. Dean rode Maude barebacked, and Ethan rode Buddy, the Morgan, with a saddle. If Donald agreed to go riding today, they would both be riding saddled horses, Dean on Buddy and Ethan on Rocky.

Donald tried to decide. "You know, that sounds like a real good idea! I'm sure it's gonna be a long time before I get to ride a horse again and I know I'm gonna miss it," he added and contemplated for a couple of seconds. "But before we go get the horses, I need to change clothes and look like a civilian. I'll take my car home and walk back over here a little later. If Grandma has some things for me to do, I might not be back for at least an hour or so."

True to his word, Donald didn't return until around one o'clock and for them to have the horses saddled. They changed their minds about riding behind the timber and up the dirt lane, after they considered it would be too muddy. Ethan suggested they ride into town instead.

"That's a good idea," Donald replied.

The wind still gusted in uneven spurts. A few very light sprinkles pelted the young riders from time to time as they rode side by side and chatted. Donald rode along the edge of the highway pavement while Ethan kept pace with him on the grassy apron of the narrow shoulder. Being very curious about boot camp, Ethan persisted to have Donald tell him all the details about his training. Donald's mind was more on his future than on the past and would have preferred to share his thoughts about the great adventure he was embarking on and how he looked forward to his deployment after California.

"I'm looking forward to California. Other than Illinois, the only states I've been in are Indiana and Wisconsin. I want to see more of this country and the world and that's one of the reasons I picked the Navy. I know there's a slim possibility that I might get assigned to some mundane land assignment, but I'm betting I'll be living in close quarters aboard a ship and visiting foreign places!" Donald told him.

Enticed by his cousin's hopes, Ethan asked, "What kind of ship are you hoping to serve on?"

"I want to be on a fighting ship!" he answered, "and not some tanker, supply ship or troop carrier!"

"Did you like boot camp?"

"You sure are interested in what boot camp was like, aren't you?"

"Yeah, I guess I am. I've been wondering what it was like ever since you left!"

"Well, I can tell you one thing that's for darn sure. Boot camp's a far different kind of life than the one I'm used to. You're told how to make your bed, fold your clothes, polish your shoes, when and how to salute, when to go to bed and even when to turn the lights out. They get you up before daylight, have inspection and then have you do endless drills. You have to take classes, do calisthenics and follow every order without any hesitation!"

"Wow," Ethan exclaimed, sounding intrigued. "What else happens?"

Donald searched his mind. "And, oh yeah, every morning they give an order for what the dress of the day will be. You have to wear the clothes or uniform they've told you to wear or you'll get into a lot of trouble. I never saw any boot ever not dressed perfectly like all the others!" he said.

"Did you ever have a chance to get off base to see or do something?"

"Twice, about the time my training was finished. Both times a couple of my buddies and me got short passes and we caught the train down to Chicago for a few hours and walked around. That was it!"

A car came out of town towards them, headed north on the other side of the road. Donald reined Buddy off the concrete onto the grassy shoulder just to be safe. Ethan instinctively guided Rocky off the shoulder and down into the bottom of the wide ditch. After the car passed, Donald continued to ride along the narrow shoulder so that any cars coming up from behind would have room to pass without slowing down.

Halfway into town they came to a small, square, concrete culvert that ran under the road. Ethan was forced to ride around its outside end and as he rode past the opening, he looked down into the culvert. "Hold on," he said and reined Rocky to a halt.

Donald watched Ethan lean forward in his saddle and study the grass-shrouded opening of the culvert. "What're you up to, Ethan?" he asked.

A sly grin slowly etched Ethan's face. There was a long pause and then Ethan pointed down at something inside the culvert. "I see a bottle of whiskey or some other kind of liquor in there," he said and swung down out of his saddle while holding onto Rocky's reins firmly with one hand to keep the pony from bolting and running back to the barn.

"You're kidding me, aren't you?" Donald said and shifted his weight around in his saddle to face Ethan.

"Yeah…sure I am!" he stated, got down to his knees and reached inside with his free hand. "It's a bottle of Wild Turkey Whisky and it's almost half full," he chuckled. "Somebody must've hidden it in there for later," he speculated and lifted it into the air like a trophy. "Whoever it was, it's their misfortune and our good luck!" he exclaimed excitedly.

"Why don't we change our plans," Donald suggested. "Now that we've got whisky why don't we go someplace to enjoy some of it!"

"What exactly are you thinking we should do?" Ethan asked.

"Well, instead of following our plan to go into town, why don't we ride out to the Mackville Bridge and find some secluded spot along the river where we can sample the contents in that bottle," he suggested.

"I don't know!" Ethan replied, doubtful of the decision.

"Come on, Ethan, a little alcohol isn't going to hurt you," his cousin chided.

Not quite convinced that straight whisky was something he wanted to try, Ethan unscrewed the top off the whisky bottle out of curiosity and took a sniff of its golden contents.

"It's not going to hurt you to take a sip!" Donald replied.

Slightly intimidated, Ethan took another whiff, raised his eyebrows, licked his lips and said, "I think it's a great idea, Cousin!"

The two adventurers rode across the Mackville Bridge, reined the horses off the road and down the north embankment of the approach on the west side. They rode a short distance along the bank of the river on a well-beaten, tree-shaded path that was walled in on the left side by a tall stand of corn and to the right by old willow trees lining the river's bank.

They examined several open places where fishermen had cleared the weeds between the willows and left a ring of logs to sit on. Most of these trampled, open areas were muddy from the heavy rain. They looked around and eventually managed to find one clearing that was grassy and with enough room to tie their horses. Some individual, probably someone fishing for catfish at night, had built a fire in the middle of the clearing and now all that remained of the fire were charred bits of wood and the smell of wet embers. They were pleased to be out of sight from any vehicles passing on the road above. "I think this'll do," Donald said with a savvy sense of assurance.

"Looks good to me too," Ethan concurred instantly, having convinced himself to go along with Donald's suggestion and somewhat eager to taste the contents sloshing around in the bottle he carried. He tossed his leg over Rocky's neck and slid off to the ground.

Donald sat down on one of the two large logs facing the fisherman's cold fire. Ethan held the bottle up to the light, sloshed it around and admired the golden liquid. He slowly unscrewed the cap and being very apprehensive, he didn't take a drink. "You, first," he said and offered Donald the bottle. Drinking hard liquor was something entirely new to him. He had taken only a couple of sips from a pint bottle of schnapps that several of his friends had shared and vaguely considered the consequences he might face by taking more than a few sips.

"Okay," Donald said without any reservations. Previous experiences with spirits had taught him a valuable lesson: don't drink too much and pace yourself carefully or you'd face nasty results. He took a couple of very small sips, barely parting his lips and let a tiny trickle flow down his throat. Ethan was momentarily distracted while he positioned himself on another log and assumed Donald had taken a healthy swallow.

"Here you go," Donald said and handed Ethan the bottle without warning his younger cousin about imbibing alcohol too quickly or warning him about the effects one might encounter by doing so.

"Thanks," Ethan said, and took a big swallow that sucked the air out of his lungs. His face flushed, coughed several times and arched his eyebrows. "Wow, that's good stuff," he exclaimed before handing the bottle back to his cousin. Before the day was over, Ethan would learn a hard lesson about the effects of alcohol from the cruel teacher of stupidity as his cousin had a few years earlier.

Why Donald didn't caution Ethan from the very beginning was never known! "Take it easy!" he finally instructed his younger cousin after they had passed the bottle back and forth a few times and noticed how fast the liquid in the bottle was disappearing. "You're drinking too much and too fast!" he cautioned.

"I don't really think so!" Ethan grinned, thinking his cousin was only jesting. "Where do you think you'll be stationed?" he asked, took a much smaller sip, coughed a few more times, pounded his chest with his closed fist and repeated again, "Wow, that's good stuff!"

"Like I said, I hope I get assigned to sea duty on a big fighting ship and not some scowl like a tanker or troop carrier. I also don't want to get trapped being a clerk in some damned shore office in some backwater installation either, or to be shuttling around in the middle of the ocean on some barge. I don't want to miss the action!" he said. "I didn't join the Navy for that," he added, nearly repeating himself. "I'm encouraged because they didn't train me to do anything ashore, so I'm hoping for the best, but I won't really know where I'm going until I get to San Francisco. I've been informed that's where my final orders will be drawn up and I hope I get to go see the world!"

"I wish I was old enough to join," Ethan said.

"You'll be old enough before this war's over the way things are going!" his cousin replied.

Donald tossed a stick into the water and watched its circular pattern grow several feet wide before he spoke again. "Our grandmother told me this morning that she's thinking about moving into town about six months from now," he said, changing the subject. "I think part of the reason she decided to do so is because I'm going into the service and they'll have no way of getting around. My sis doesn't drive, as you well know, because of the damage polio did to her legs and Grandma never learned to drive and never will. She says she would like to buy a place close to Main Street where she and my sis can walk to the stores without depending on other people. I know she and Aunt Gloria have had hard feelings towards each other, but her decision has nothing to do with that, although she told me Aunt Gloria will probably think it does."

"You're probably right about what my mom will think," Ethan said, took another sip and added, "I think it all goes back to when my parents bought the farm and that fall, Grandma and Uncle Joe sued my dad. They lost, but there's been hard feelings between them ever since. I believe what bothered him the most is they saw him as a cheat; otherwise, why would they even think of suing him?"

After taking another short sip, Donald handed the bottle back to Ethan, who attempted to put the bottle to his lips, but before he finished the motion, he screwed up his face, leaned forward, dropped the bottle and vomited three times with only a very brief pause between each upchuck. When he was done heaving, he said, "I don't feel too good!"

"You don't look so good either," his cousin stated emphatically. "Green's a strange color for your face!"

Ethan vomited again and gagged two or three times in quick succession. When he finished, he wobbled over to the water's edge and splashed some water on his face several times until his shirt was soaked in front. "That helped a little," he said, although Donald could tell that Ethan wasn't really sure. "Maybe we oughta get going," Ethan said and tried to walk. He wobbled around and fell on his knees. Donald helped him stand, supported him while they walked over to the horses and he helped Ethan up into his saddle. "Do you think you'll be able to stay on the pony without falling off?" Donald asked.

"Yaaah. Okaaay. I…I…belieeeveee sooo…oo," Ethan answered and vomited again, barely missing his cousin.

Donald shook his head in disbelief. "I think it'd be a good idea if we go home the back way down the old dirt lane even though it's probably still full of mud," he said without asking Ethan what he thought. Donald didn't want to ride back along the main roads where Ethan would be in danger of riding out in front of some vehicle or falling off unto the pavement.

"F…f…fine," was all Ethan could utter as he held Rocky's reins in his right hand and the saddle horn in a death's grip with the other.

The two young men rode the path back to the bridge and up the embankment without any incident. Once they were back upon the road, they crossed over the Mackville Bridge again. In a very short time, they turned north at the tee junction onto the side road and walked their horses down the middle of it for a half mile until they came to the dirt lane that ran behind the two big wooded timbers. Just as Donald had contemplated earlier, he found the grass-bordered dirt lane a slimy ribbon of mud with endless puddles dotting the ruts and short tufts of grass attempting to grow in the raised ridge between them.

Donald brought Buddy to a halt and looked down the lane. He studied it for several seconds before he decided to continue riding instead of dismounting, walking and leading Buddy. "I think if we ride along the side on the grass, we should be okay," he advised. "Don't ride in the mud, Ethan, especially in your condition. If your pony starts slipping, you'd have a real good chance of falling off!"

The sprinkles had stopped two hours earlier, but now, as they rode toward home, the sky grew dark again, almost black and it became ominous looking. Stiff gusts of wind whipped across the tops of the early crops in the wide fields, causing them to undulate in an uneven series of waves like a stormy sea. The dirt lane went straight east for a quarter of a mile, did a slight dogleg to the left for a hundred yards, turned east again and crossed a small wood-planked bridge that spanned the dredge ditch. "We're more than halfway home," Donald said, feeling more confident, "so hang on tight to that pommel."

The words had no sooner left his mouth than the rain came again, quickly becoming a deluge, drenching them both to the bone. Once they gained Mossberger's very thick and overgrown woods, it gave them some protection from the storm, but not much; the wind whipped around with such force it made little difference. Tall trees swayed, limbs whipped in the wind while sheets of rain created transparent curtains across the landscape. Somewhere back inside the woods lightning struck with a loud clap. A limb crashed to the ground amid the fury and the intensity of the storm made their horses nervous and hard to control.

Even on normal days Rocky had a mind of his own. Anyone riding him had to be firm and in command to make him mind. In the rain, with the whining noise of the wind and the clapping thunder, Ethan, in his condition, was far beyond being able to make the agitated pony behave. Donald could see trouble coming if his cousin didn't pull himself together for just another ten minutes and he prayed for good luck.

Two minutes later they passed the clover field and were behind their own timber and within a short distance of the concrete slab highway. Another brilliant bolt of lightning ripped out of the low clouds with a blinding flash and struck very close by turning the world bright white for a split second. Rocky danced around. Ethan tried to control him by pulling back hard on the reins. Rocky sensed Ethan's weak condition and resisted, put his head down and ran a few feet out onto the concrete. Still unable to think clearly, Ethan pulled the reins over to the right side which encouraged Rocky to quickly turn. Thrown off balance and then instead of loosening up on the reins, Ethan pulled them harder, causing the pony to dance around in a tight right circle with his muddy hooves slipping on the slick, rain-soaked, concrete surface.

The world spun around under Ethan. He swayed several times and pulled at the pony's reins haphazardly, sending mixed signals to the crazed animal. Dizzy, weak and sick to his stomach, Ethan wasn't doing well to hang on. Becoming ever more confused, he made one more futile effort to get Rocky under control. When he pulled straight back on the reins, the pony tossed his head and fought Ethan's efforts and suddenly lurched sideways.

The sudden shift in the pony's motion, the slick wet leather of the saddle and Ethan's drunken state of mind all contributed to his falling heavily off and slamming down onto the hard surface of the rain-streaked road. "OOalllllooo," he screamed and started screeching loudly, "OOOhhhh, Ohh Nooo," over and over. Rocky shook his head, trotted off and stood on the shoulder of the road about fifty feet away, pawing and snorting.

"What's wrong?" Donald shouted to Ethan amidst the flashes of lightning and sheets of driving rain. "Ooooh," Ethan moaned. Donald jumped off Buddy, led him hurriedly down into the ditch and tied him securely to the fence while ignoring the smaller agitated horse standing nervously a few yards feet away. He ran back up to the highway and looked down at his cousin. He stood frozen, feeling helpless, having no idea as to what he should or could do.

"I think I broke my right leg way up here," Ethan moaned and gestured. "It reeeeeaaaally huurrrts."

A car approached from the north on their side of the road with its lights only dimly penetrating the downpour, causing Donald to nearly panic. He jumped up and down on the concrete and waved his arms around frantically in hopes the driver would see them and not run over his cousin. Luckily the car wasn't traveling fast and slowed down a safe distance away. It gradually came to a stop a few feet from them, its wipers rhythmically flipping water off the windshield in sheets. The driver rolled his window partway down and yelled, "What's wrong?"

"My cousin fell off his horse! I'm not sure, but I think he's broken his hip or something," Donald yelled over the roar of the rain.

Within minutes, three more cars had stopped and a small crowd had gathered, everyone stood around, huddled against the rain, stymied to decide what would be the best course of action to take.

A fifth car pulled up and sat idling a few seconds before a woman stepped out and covered Ethan with a blanket. "I'm a nurse," she announced, relieving the tension somewhat. "He shouldn't be moved until we get an ambulance, if that's possible, since we're not sure of the extent of his injuries," she said authoritatively.

A voice from among them said, "Charley Bonner uses his hearse for an ambulance. Someone needs to drive into town and tell him he needs to bring it out here so this boy can be moved carefully and taken to a hospital!"

A neighbor from a farm just down the road by the name of Wilson spoke up. "And I think someone should also go immediately and tell this boy's parents what's happening out here! They live right over there," he remarked and pointed between the trees at the nearly invisible house.

"I'll go for the ambulance," someone said that was standing by one of the cars parked closest to town.

"I'll go fetch his parents," a man next to him offered.

Ethan was flooded by light in the glare of the headlight beams from four cars, two on each side of him. His complaining had grown more subdued. Faces in the cars peered out through the windshields. Wipers swished. Rain drummed on car hoods. Time seemed to stand still, until what seemed like ages had passed before the siren of the ambulance could be heard coming through town, its wailing piercing the thick warm evening air like a hawk seeking its prey.

Looking around or Rocky, Donald brushed water out of his eyes and seeing no sign the pony, he assumed Rocky had gone back to the barn.

Without a rider, Marianne, standing inside the open driveway of the barn, watched an agitated Rocky trot in out of the dark. She grabbed his reins and settled him down. Initially she was only upset that her pony had come back without a rider. She stood in the doorway holding Rocky's reins, saw her parents rush frantically out of the house, pile into the car and drive away, and a few seconds later, she heard the shriek of a siren. She had a premonition that something was terribly amiss. A knot formed in the pit of her stomach. "Oh no," she whispered two or three times and hurriedly led the still highly agitated Rocky into his stall. He tossed his head around nervously and pawed. "Shuuu…steady," she said to calm him down. Gradually, coaxing him with soft words, he became less restless. "That's a good boy," she said, loosened his girth and pulled his saddle and his bridle off. She stared at her pony for a few seconds and closed his stall door. "I hope Ethan's okay," she said to herself and grabbed her raincoat hanging on a wooden peg, pulled it up tight under her chin. She ran to the house and found her two younger brothers standing by the back door with worried expressions on their faces. "We're glad you're still here," Jonathan exclaimed.

"Why are you saying that?"

"Because someone came and said something bad has happened to Ethan and then Mom and Dad rushed out!"

"So that's the reason Rocky came running all agitated to the barn. Before Mom and Dad piled into the car and drove off, did you hear what happened to Ethan?" Marianne asked.

"The man said he's hurt and laying in the middle of the road over by Grandma's house!"

"He's hurt and laying in the road?" she repeated to convince herself that what she heard was true.

"Yeah!" Jonathan reaffirmed.

Not knowing the extent of Ethan's injuries, Marianne's mouth felt dry and made it hard for her to talk. "Do you know how bad?"

"All I know is that Jude Mossbarger came to the door and I overheard him tell Dad that something serious happened to Ethan over on the other end of the woods. When Dad asked him how bad he was hurt, Jude said they thought Ethan might've broken his leg or something when he fell off his horse," Jonathan said, relating the little bits of information he had overheard.

"He didn't say anything else, did he?" Marianne prodded.

"I couldn't hear everything Mr. Mossbarger was saying from where I stood. Whatever else he said made Mom so upset she acted like she was going to faint!"

Did she?

"No, she didn't! And I think the only reason she didn't is because Dad told her if she did, he'd need to leave her behind," Jonathan explained. "Mom managed not to...but she looked awful pale. Finally, she grabbed her purse; they put their coats on and told us to stay here and left without saying nothing else!"

The three of them went into Marianne's bedroom, looked out the north window and tried to watch what was happening through the spaces between the trees of the woods. "I can't see nothin'!" Leon complained.

"We can't either," Jonathan replied.

Through the rain-streaked window, Ethan's siblings strained to see what was happening and no matter how hard they tried, they could only make out vague images of people moving around in the cars' headlights and a red light flashing. A few seconds later, the flashing, bright red light slowly started moving slowly back towards town before picking up speed. Shortly, all the cars had driven away and the spaces between the trees were swallowed by the night.

They ran to the front window.

The last set of headlights going towards town drove slower than the others and turned into their driveway. "I wonder who that could be?" Marianne said and ran to the backdoor and waited.

"It doesn't look like our car!" Jonathan said, and looked away from the window. "Wait up, Sis!" he shouted louder and rushed after her.

Before the car made it up the lane to the house, all three of them stood at the bottom of the steps inside the new addition and looked out through the window of the storm door. A light, drizzling rain still fell and glistened the sidewalks.

They watched a man get out of the car. "I think that's Clyde Walker," Jonathan exclaimed, pushed the outside door open and held it there until the manager and telegraph operator at the train depot in town, a lanky, bean pole of a man, came up to the house.

"Hi, kids," he said calmly to relieve their concerns and stepped inside through the open door. "I'm Clyde Walker," he said. "Your parents asked me to come by to tell you that your brother broke his leg and that they're taking him over to Decatur to St. Mary's Hospital."

While Jonathan and Leon huddled up closely behind her, Marianne asked anxiously, "Is he going to be alright?" and studied Mr. Walker's rain-streaked face to decipher whether he was going to answer truthfully.

"I'm not a doctor, so I really can't tell you. All I can say is that he seemed to be in a lot of pain and he was babbling incoherently… kinda like he had hit his head…or like he was drunk. I don't know which it was but something was amiss,' cause I heard him ask if anyone else had been hurt in the accident," Mr. Walker explained. "Your father said, under the circumstances, to tell you that they'd be home as early as it's feasible to do so. That's all the information I have. I'm betting he'll be okay though!" Mr. Walker added when he saw the concern on the children's faces.

"We really appreciate that you came up to the house to tell us," Marianne said to him.

"You kids probably shouldn't wait up for your parents to get back. I know they said they'd be home as soon as they can, but I don't believe anyone can predict when that'll be," he said and to emphasize his concern for their worry he added, "More likely than not, it'll be early morning or thereafter!"

Mr. Walker gave them a smile for assurance. "I'm sure he'll be okay!" he repeated and added, "Wouldn't worry too much!" and stepped out into the misty rain.

"Thanks again!" Marianne yelled after him.

Thirty minutes later, while Marianne was in the process of frying ham slices and scrambling eggs for their supper, they heard several sharp raps on the door. She instantly became concerned because she hadn't seen a car drive up and couldn't believe anyone would walk up the muddy lane on such a miserably, dark, rainy night like this one. "Who is it?" she shouted. No one answered immediately and it raised her apprehension even more. "Who's out there?" she shouted louder.

"Donald," a deep trembling voice answered.

Not able to hear the reply well, Marianne asked, "Who?"

"It's me, Marianne...Donald!" he said more distinctly, opened the door and walked up the stairs into the kitchen.

Marianne and Jonathan quizzed their cousin thoroughly. At first, no matter how hard they tried, Donald only related the same details as Mr. Walker, but the more they pried the more they were able to find out. He finally admitted that he and Ethan had been drinking; however, before he confessed, he had them swear never to tell anyone and especially their parents. "Do you...and I mean... do you swear never to tell anyone if I confess something to you?" he said nervously. His face looked drawn, his hair was matted down and his eyes looked hollow. A puddle of water was at his feet. "It'll have to stay a secret just among us, or I'll never tell you!" he added.

"Yes, we swear to keep your secret," Marianne and Jonathan swore. She turned to her youngest brother and looked directly into his eyes with a cold stare. "Leon, you have to promise me that you'll never tell Mom or Dad what Donald's going to tell us or you'll need to leave," his sister said sharply. "If you ever tell, you'll be in really deep trouble with me and I won't trust you never again!"

He looked at his sister's stern face and gulped. Keeping secrets might put him in a position where he would be forced to lie; it scared him because he wasn't very good at it and harbored doubts that he could keep a secret forever. More than once he had been petrified that he was going to get caught lying to his parents. Leon didn't know what the outcome would be if he didn't keep this secret. He did know that he didn't want to lose his sister's trust.

"Promise me," she said. "You have to promise me, and if not, you'll need to go into the other room where you can't listen!" she repeated.

He took a deep breath. "I promise!" he said, trying to muster all his strength.

"You've got to cross your heart," Jonathan ordered and his little brother made the mark.

There was a long moment of silence. Donald looked weary. "We were drinking and that's the main reason Ethan fell off Rocky. It was because he was drunk!" their cousin stated.

The rest of the evening crept slowly by after Donald went home. The three kids sat around the kitchen table talking, passing the time and waiting impatiently for their parents to come home. Leon drew on some lined writing paper with a pencil to help the time pass. Marianne and Jonathan played rummy and chatted without once bothering to mention Ethan.

Around eleven o'clock Leon yawned several times, rubbed his eyes with his knuckles and said, "I'm really sleepy and I wanna go to bed."

"Give me a few minutes 'till I finish this hand of cards and then I'll pour some warm water, help you wash up and get you dressed for bed," Marianne answered.

At eleven thirty, Jonathan fell asleep on the sofa and slept there for an hour before his sister tapped him on the shoulder and said, "Jonathan, wake up...wake up! Why don't you go to bed? Come on...wake up!" she prodded and added, "I promise that I'll wake you when Mom and Dad get home!"

Marianne extinguished all the kerosene lamps other than the brightest one with a mantle. She placed it in the middle of the small table next to her father's armchair where it would give her the most light so she could sprawl out and read a paperback novel. About one o'clock, she slipped into a deep sleep, her head slumped against the armrest with her legs extended awkwardly out onto the hassock. The book lay on the floor where it fell as she had slumbered off. If someone were to observe her, one wouldn't be aware of how worried she had been, and although exhausted, her dreams must have been peaceful because she barely moved for several hours.

Just as the eastern sky was turning a golden red-orange, the back door opened quietly and the sleeping kids' parents stepped inside. "Careful with the door!" Gloria cautioned her husband. "Don't let it bang shut; we don't want to wake the kids," she added, assuming that all of them were in bed. They tip-toed into the kitchen as quietly as possible and were caught by surprise.

From the next room, Marianne shook the sleep out of her head and yelled, "Mom, Dad is that you?"

"Uh huh," her tired father replied softly.

Marianne jumped out of the chair and rubbed her swollen eyes. "Is Ethan alright," she asked.

"I suppose so if breaking your hip way up here means you're alright, then he is!" her mother said and pointed high up on her thigh.

"He broke it in a bad place," her father stated. "Actually, he's probably lucky he didn't get hurt worse, considerin' he fell off the pony onto the concrete pavement!" he theorized and explained to her that Ethan had broken his leg just a few inches below his hip joint. "The doctor needed to put him in traction so the bone can be aligned and set later."

"How long will that be?" Marianne asked.

"The Doctor explained it could be a couple of days before he'll be able to set the bone. He said it's gonna be necessary to put long pins through the leg and wire them together to hold the bone in place before he can put a cast on it. It'll be a big cast, going from above his hip down to his toes," he explained uneasily.

"The poor boy was in a lot of pain until they gave him something strong to keep it down. Before we left, he seemed to be resting but doing so only fitfully," her mother interjected.

Although what she heard wasn't the best news, it wasn't the worst. "He's going to be okay, isn't he?" she asked again.

"I'm pretty sure he'll be in time," her father answered and walked off toward his bedroom.

Marianne instantly felt her tension waning and yawned.

"Wake us if we don't get up by nine," her mother wearily instructed. "I'd like to get my housework done before we go back to Decatur right after lunch tomorrow. When the boys get up, you'll need to fix them some breakfast," she added.

Her father stopped and leaned against the frame of his bedroom door. Marianne noticed that he appeared really fatigued. "You and Jonathan will need to do Ethan's chores later this mornin' and keep doin' them until he's back up and around, I suppose," he said matter-of-factly.

Late morning found Marianne rushing to help her mother straighten up the house and make the beds. She was just in the process of pulling up the top blanket of her own bed and fluffing the pillows when she heard her mother say, "When you're done in there I'd like you to go shake the kitchen rugs and then get lunch started. Get out the cold-cuts and things for sandwiches and slice some carrot sticks," she said and paused, debating. "Maybe you ought to cut up some celery sticks too and get out the block of Colby Cheese."

"Pass the spiced ham this way, Jonathan," his father said. "And you might as well slide the mustard and the lettuce down this way also to," he added.

Gloria's plan to go back to the hospital right after lunch had been squelched. "Your dad told me he can't spare the time to go back over to Decatur until this evening, so I think I need to go into town and make a telephone call to see how Ethan's doing."

"Can I go?" Leon asked. "I wanna know how he is too!"

"And me?" Jonathan asked.

"Whoever wants to can come!" she replied and looked at her husband.

"I can't go," he answered. "I told you I can't spare the time right now." A troubled expression crossed his face, which showed the weight of the conflict he was under between getting his farming duties done or being at Ethan's bedside. "You know, ain't nothin' I can do for Ethan over the phone and my farm work was already sufferin' before Ethan fell and broke his leg. Them heavy rains we've had has put me behind in the fields and I can use this time for my other chores!" he explained. I'm gonna be workin' out by the barn and when you get back from town, let me know how he's doin'!" he said.

"We will," his wife replied, shook her head very lightly from side to side and stared momentarily at her plate of half-eaten food. "I just can't understand how he could've fallen like that! He's such a good rider!"

"Sometimes things just happen in this old world that we've got no control over and we're not meant to understand!" her husband stated, although he figured his son had been drinking. He had smelled the whisky on Ethan's breath and it was a fact he decided to keep it to himself.

"I still think it was because them three boys went out and shot that black cat that was killing the baby chickens," she suggested dryly, attempting to find some answer for her son's injury other than hold him responsible. Her comment illustrated that she was following a human instinct of being superstitious of things one didn't have answers for.

The two boys smiled at each other. They liked the idea of black cats and evil spirits coming around to punish Ethan, even though they knew that evil spirits had nothing to do with their brother's leg and everything to do with whisky.

Her logical husband didn't put much stock in making wild assumptions unless it dealt with the solid faith of his religious beliefs. Milburn knew that worldly things all happened within the scope of simple reason. He also knew the real cause of his son's accident and wanted to guard his knowledge of Ethan's behavior. Telling his wife would serve no purpose. "Don't be superstitious!" he said. "I don't think that was what caused him to fall off the pony; it wasn't no evil spirit of some black cat!"

"Well, don't you think it's a bit strange that Elvin shot himself, Matt Wades got so sick he had to be hospitalized for four days, and now Ethan broke his hip after one of those three shot the cat?"

Listening intently as their father gave his view, his children were all ears.

"Maybe it does look a bit strange... but just look at the facts! First of all," Milburn said emphatically, "Elvin wasn't thinkin' too clearly when he was out plowin' with that old Massey Ferguson down along the river. He had his twenty-two rifle cocked, with the safety off and had it leanin' over against a fender. I think you can agree, as I believe, that it was an accident ready to happen. So, when it slid sideways towards him, all it had to do was get jarred hard enough to make it go off...and it did, right at him! He's very lucky the bullet missed his heart, all his vital organs and only collapsed his left lung as the bullet passed through him. If there really was an evil spirit involved, he'd be dead, don't you think?" he asked. She didn't answer, as he knew she wouldn't, and stated, "God was looking after him!"

Marianne felt the need to add a detail and interjected, "I heard that Elvin drove the old tractor a quarter mile up to the house, called out to Aunt Emma that he'd been shot and then fainted in front of the door. Aunt Emma said she thought he was going to die for sure!"

"Then explain why Matt got so sick and Ethan broke his leg?" his wife asked, still certain that her thinking was right.

"Them things are just the normal circumstances of life... accidents and diseases!" her husband replied.

"I'll tell you, it was bad luck because they shot that cat!" their mother insisted.

Her husband shook his head in disbelief that he couldn't get her to open up her mind. "Of course those things might have been bad luck, but they weren't caused by some evil spirit. It's only coincidental it happened to all three of them so close together.

That's all it is and nothin' else," he argued. He became so frustrated that he almost told her the truth. "The boys did the right thing by shootin' that feral cat. I wanted them to do it because it was killin' so many of your young chickens," he said, sounding agitated. "Why hasn't somethin' happened to me? You know it was my idea. We're constantly being over-run with unwanted animals that people drop off out here!" He continued to drive his point home. "Look at them two stray dogs that killed your entire flock of seven hundred young pullets last summer. The county paid money for your loss, but they paid you only about half of what you would've gotten if you'd sold them at market price a couple weeks later. Just because the cat was black doesn't make one iota of any difference. It's them people that abandon their pets that become strays who have no respect for the animals…or for us! What kind of a price do they pay for their awful actions? I'd like to put a hex on them!"

"I still don't understand how Ethan could've fallen off that pony and the other boys to have them things happen to them all in one week!" she concluded without seeming to have accepted anything he had explained to her.

Her husband felt the futility of convincing her and ended the conversation. "It was just a coincidence them things happened that way I tell you, and nothin' more!" he stated flatly for no other reason, other than to have the last word. "Sometimes, I just don't understand you," he said under his breath.

Sitting quietly listening to his parents' arguments, a mesmerized Leon suddenly asked, "What's a colancidance?"

"You mean a coincidence," his sister corrected.

"Uh huh, a co…inci..dence?" he asked with trepidation, wanting to get the pronunciation right.

"Let me try to explain it for you," she said. "A coincidence is when two or more things happen that seem to be connected in some way but really aren't. It's like this. If you hit your head on a low limb and then stumbled over something," she stated, "you wouldn't expect to stumble on a twig or rock or something every time you bumped your head, would you??"

"No!" he answered.

"That's why it is only a coincidence even if it happened twice," she said.

"I think so," he answered and took a big bite out of his sandwich. Deep down in his mind he still thought the black cat had caused everything just as his mother said.

"Well, I still think there's something strange about how he fell off the pony like that!" their mother repeated adamantly. "If it wasn't the black cat then it was because that pony was acting up," she added, still trying to avoid blaming Ethan for his misfortune and desiring to pass the blame along to some other cause. The pony had to be guilty if it wasn't the black cat!

"It wasn't Rocky's fault either," Marianne snapped, her face flushing with anger. She resented her mother making the accusation and bit her lip to keep from speaking out further and breaking the promise she had made to her cousin. "Don't you think Ethan might be able to tell you what happened when he feels better?" she argued, knowing that Ethan would never admit getting hurt due to his careless behavior.

Irritated that her arguments hadn't gone the way she thought they should have, Gloria looked Marianne straight in the eyes and said, "I won't need to ask him!"

Milburn shook his head in disgust and pushed his chair away from the table. "I have no more time for this nonsense...I've got to go out and get my work done!"

CHAPTER TWENTY THREE

July Third, Independence Day Observance, 1942

As a patriotic fervor swept across the country in the months following the bombing of Pearl Harbor on December seventh, nineteen-forty-one, most Americans were eager to show their spirit on Friday, the third-of-July, which was an unusual date for the observance of Independence Day. Outrage had worked to pull the various factions of the country together into one cohesive goal: to stand firm against Nazis' oppression and Japan's imperialism. Since December, untold thousands of young men had signed up for military service and there were many others being drafted; however, there were deferments for some individuals with crucial talents, essential skills in manufacturing, or whose labor was crucial to farming.

For this first Independence Day since Pearl Harbor, Milburn and Gloria were carried along on the wave of emotions rippling across the country and decided to have a large country-style, potluck picnic behind the house in their large, grassy pasture that backed up to the edge of the woods. It was a beautiful location and a great place to have a fireworks display. A tall stand of trees stood on the east side and an open swath of grass faced the west. The trees would act as shade and shelter during the day and with any luck there would be clear skies in the evening.

Milburn's mother, Anna Lee, her granddaughter and ward were invited. They had chosen not to attend. Also, his two sisters, Yolanda and Della were invited along with their families, but only Yolanda's family was planning to attend. Two of Gloria's siblings' families were coming, those of Edward's and Emma's. It ended up being a small gathering of family members eager to show the spirit of their patriotism.

With her mother's permission, Marianne invited Barb, Stella Mae and Donna out after she learned that the parents of all three girls hadn't made any plans for the day. She was surprised when her mother actually encouraged her to invite them. "It won't be a problem!" she stated a week earlier. "They're nice girls and since no cousins your age are coming, other than Elvin, it'll be more fun for you and I like them girls!" her mother told her.

Barb and Stella Mae showed up only a few minutes apart. Barb brought news that Donna wouldn't be able to make it out.

"It would've been really nice if she could've come!" Marianne replied, chatted with her friends for a few minutes and then returned to her task of chopping up green onions for potato salad.

"Why don't you give me something to do?" Barb offered.

"I'd like to help too!" Stella Mae added.

"You don't really need to give us any help," Gloria answered.

"Come on, there must be something for us to do. You don' expect us to just sit here and watch while you two do all the work," Barb jested.

Gloria smiled. "Since you insist, there is a couple of little jobs you could help us with, I suppose."

"Name one!" Stella Mae joked.

Gloria pointed to a large bowl. "There's two dozen hard-boiled eggs in cold water in that bowl that need to be peeled for deviled eggs."

Eager to help, Stella Mae answered, "I'll peel them and make them, if you want me to!"

"I'll trust your judgment for the ingredients," Gloria replied.

"What can I do?" Barb asked.

Stella Mae held up the bowl. "Why don't you help me peel these eggs?"

Around three o'clock in the sunny afternoon, the food was laid out over the top of a long table constructed of two saw horses that had long 1x12 pine boards which had been salvaged from the old outbuildings that Milburn had torn down the previous year. Various tablecloths patterned the rough tops. Gloria's and her guest's foods were spread across the surface of the makeshift structure, tantalizing hungry mouths. There were three platters of fried chicken, two kinds of potato salad, macaroni salad, banana salad, a big bowl of green beans with bacon and onions cooked together, canned sweet corn, sliced, marinated cucumbers, creamed peas with small chunks of cheddar cheese, Jell-O with orange slices and several condiments as well as the deviled eggs the girls had prepared. For dessert Gloria had made a large chocolate sheet cake with red, white and blue icing that bristled with forty eight white candles, one for each state. Late in the afternoon, as a special treat, homemade vanilla ice cream would be churned and served with it.

Gloria's brother, Edward, had somehow managed to acquire hard-to-find fireworks which were no longer being manufactured or imported because of the war's constraints. The shortage caused a stiff competition for any that still existed. Edward had been lucky enough to procure his through someone who knew someone…etc., but had managed to get only a dozen small sky rockets, four large ones, ten Roman candles, ten packages of firecrackers and several boxes of sparklers. The numbers didn't really matter because spirits were high and they were all looking forward to a simple display slated to take place once the sky darkened.

By late afternoon the large bonfire, blazing an hour earlier, had burned down and had left only a small fire inside a wide circle of ash. As dusk slowly approached, Marianne and her two girlfriends took a brief break from giving rides and were roasting marshmallows for the younger children.

Barb lifted her long forked stick away from the smoldering fire; a flaming marshmallow was burning and turning black on the far end of it. "Oh no," she giggled, held it in front of her mouth and blew out the flames. She studied it for a few seconds, pinched the crusty skin off and cautiously put the darkened piece into her mouth. "Ummm...good," she said. "I think it's almost as yummy as Richard!"

Wondering what had elicited Barb to say what they just heard, Marianne and Stella Mae looked round eyed at each other and raised their eyebrows. It wasn't a secret that she liked Richard but her comment surprised them because it indicated that she had acquired a serious crush on him. As far as the other two girls had been aware, she had only dated him once or twice; however, evidently, it had been more often than she had led them to believe.

None of their other friends had ever professed of being involved with boys to any extent other than having a coke at the drug store, holding hands or the curiosity of sneaking a kiss. What Barb had just indicated was that she and Richard were becoming emotionally entangled or even intimate.

"Barb! What do you and Richard have going on between you?" Marianne asked without thinking and immediately realized that she had stepped over a social boundary.

"Wha'da you mean by asking me what's going on?" Barb blurted, realizing that she'd revealing something personal with her comment.

Marianne bit her lip. "I'm really sorry I asked," she apologized. "It's really none of my business!"

Stella Mae's eyes brightened, seeing a wedge to get Barb to reveal her secret, if she had one. Being more brazen, she glanced at Marianne and then looked back at Barb and asked, "Why don't you tell us?"

Barb blushed slightly. "Tell you what?"

"About what's going on between you and Richard?" Stella asked bluntly.

"I don't have anything to tell!" Barb demurred, looked away to avoid facing them and held the skinless marshmallow back over the diminishing fire.

Enticed to respond and get back into the conversation which she thought was being dropped, Marianne asked, "So you two aren't serious?"

"No!" Barb stated flatly.

"You don't sound very convincing, and I know you like him!"

"No, I swear!"

"Please, Barb, you know you can tell us because the three of us are such close friends!" Stella Mae said even though she realized that she was stepping beyond the threshold of proper etiquette.

"Well it's the truth," Barb insisted. "Believe me, there is nothing to tell. I've dated him three or four times, that's all!" Barb said, tittered and yanked her flaming marshmallow out of the fire. "When I do have something to tell, you two'll be the first ones to know...I promise!" she said, unruffled by the inquisition and the other girls let the subject drop.

Barb's sweet flaming, marshmallow torches might be an omen of some tragic event that's going to happen to Barb, Marianne suspected, but decided to keep her premonition to herself. She could see in Stella Mae's face that she must have drawn a similar conclusion.

"Is it okay if I ride Rocky again," Barb asked, totally ending the conversation. She pulled another flaming, sugary lump away from the fire and nibbled the tasty morsel.

"Oh sure," Marianne answered, glad that Barb would be riding for a few minutes which would give her time to quiz Stella Mae about her thoughts. "When you go, could you take my little cousin Sarah with you?"

"Of course!" Barb answered cheerfully.

"What do you think is going on with her?" Stella Mae asked after Barb rode off. "You think they're dating seriously or what?"

"I'm not sure...I hope she knows we are concerned about her instead of being noisy. She's only a freshman like us!" Marianne replied, thinking for the first time that one of her best friends was having serious thoughts about a boy.

The day continued to be nearly perfect with moderate humidity and the temperatures in the mid-seventies, making it possible to sit in the sun and just laze around. A few puffy clouds graced the robin-egg blue sky and a light breeze rippled the tops of the young corn in the field across the fence to the west. Near the trees at the top of the slope overlooking the pasture, the adults separated by gender, sat around on old blankets thirty feet away from the fire chatting and drinking iced tea.

A short distance away, Ethan, with his full-leg cast protruding out on the ground in front, sat on a bale of hay which his father had placed there especially for him. Sitting next to him was his cousin Elvin, recuperating from the gunshot wound to his chest which had happened a few days before Ethan broke his hip.

"Did your parents ever find out you were drunk when you fell off your pony?" Elvin inquired.

"Shhhh…not so loud!" Ethan whispered. "If they know, they haven't said anything to me and I'd just as soon keep it that way!"

"They really don't know?"

"I suspect Mom still blames my accident on bad luck she thinks I got from shooting that black cat…anyway, I'm glad that's what she believes!"

"That's what my mom said right after I got shot," Elvin replied and snickered. "But she doesn't think that anymore…I'm pretty sure. She knows it was my fault for having a loaded, cocked rifle with me on the tractor. What I did was careless and stupid. I can't imagine that Aunt Gloria is so superstitious to believe that killing a black cat caused you to fall off your horse."

"Our mothers may be sisters but they sure don't think the same," Ethan observed. "Your mom sees what is going on around her and deals logically with what she's seen. My mom puts blinders on to hide anything that doesn't suit her. What she says about black cats is her way of not blaming me and at the same time she looks at Rocky with suspicion."

"Why would she blame a stupid pony?"

"Haven't you noticed that people many times throw blame around whenever they don't want to believe the obvious?" Ethan reasoned. "Rocky's a good target for her and I think Mom's still mad at my dad for spending money we needed. Dad buying him has been like a thorn in her side that she can't pull out. Now she sometimes confronts Marianne about ridin' Rocky and I believe she'd love to prove Rocky was to blame for my accident, it'd make her happy."

"Holy molly!" Elvin exclaimed. "What about uncle Milburn. Doesn't he know you were drunk?"

"Probably, but Dad doesn't want to tell my mom and have a confrontation and anyway, he probably thinks getting a broken hip, having pins put through my legs and then having them wired together plus a full-leg cast is enough of a punishment. Dad might be fast to judge sometimes, but he also has lots of common sense. I think he overlooks some of my dumb mistakes because I'm sure he made some himself when he was my age."

"My parents never let me get by with much," Elvin said and pointed at Ethan's cast. "How much longer are you going to have to wear that thing?"

"The doctor said it'll be at least until the middle of August."

"That's a long time yet!"

"You're tellin' me! It's driving me nuts. I can't get around and my leg itches like crazy. I can't scratch down inside to make it feel better...and you can't believe how bad the smell is either!"

Riding and no longer roasting marshmallows, Marianne reined her pony up in front of Elvin and Ethan and disrupted their conversation. "Elvin, would you help Sarah off?" she asked.

Wordlessly, because his thoughts were still on the discussion he and Ethan were having, and anxious to get back to it, he quickly stood up and steadied his little cousin, careful not to strain his injury while Marianne held unto her arm as she climbed down.

"Thanks a million," Marianne said and rode over by the flickering fire to pick up another of her young cousins.

"Will you get the cast off before school starts?" Elvin asked and nodded towards Ethan's outstretched leg.

"God, I really hope so!" Ethan replied and slowly pulled a long straw out of the bale and stuck an end in his mouth.

Elvin decided to change the subject. "Have you heard anything from your cousin Donald lately?"

"Yeah! He sends my grandma picture postcards or letters every week or so. I saw a postcard yesterday she got that had a picture of the Golden Gate Bridge on it. He wrote he was being shipped out to Hawaii sometime the next week." Ethan thought about that for a moment and said, "I suppose that means he's about out there by now, since it was postmarked a week ago."

"It'd be real interesting to see what the Japs did at Pearl Harbor, don't you think. I just wouldn't want to join the service to find out, would you?" Elvin asked.

Ethan stared down at his cast and seemed lost in thought. "You want to know something, Elvin," he replied, "I'd join the Navy the first thing tomorrow morning if I could, but with this leg and bein' only fifteen, I just don't think it's possible!" he emphatically stated. "I'll tell you one thing for sure," he added and adjusted himself on the bale. "Just as soon as I get old enough, I'm gonna go into the Navy too!"

"When you turn seventeen?"

"Yep! That's right! In fact, I'd join up sooner if I knew of some way to get by with it!"

In time, only a few embers and small wisps of smoke remained of the large fire. The marshmallows had all been roasted, the sun had gone down and only a gray twilight existed as the sky grew darker by the minute. Milburn threw several large logs on top of the embers to build the fire up for more light and take the chill out of the air. "How soon do you think it'll be before you're goin' to be settin' off them fireworks, Edward?" he yelled to his brother-in-law who was sitting a hundred feet away.

When the younger children heard Milburn's question, they stopped playing tag. The promise of seeing aerial bursts of fireworks in the sky excited them more than their game. "Is he going to do it now," one of them immediately asked.

Milburn didn't hear an answer. "How soon did you say?" he shouted louder.

"If I wait another twenty minutes until it gets really good and dark they'll look better!" he yelled back loud enough for everyone to hear.

Seeing that the fireworks were going to be delayed for awhile, the kids went back to chasing each other in the twilight and lightning bugs began to show themselves, their blinking lights dancing, darting and weaving patterns over the pasture and the adjacent fields.

Edward walked into the circle of light around the fire.

"Your fireworks will be a very special treat to end this Independence Day with!" Milburn praised. "I can't think of anything more appropriate this year than to have some fireworks to honor our country's independence!"

"I agree," his brother-in-law remarked. "There aren't a lot, so you shouldn't expect too much," he stated. "These were the only ones I was able to finagle out of my source...no matter how much I pressed him!" he added apologetically.

"I don't think the number you set off is gonna make much of a difference, because under the circumstances, even settin' off a few will show our spirit and pride. They'll remind us of our freedoms and of our cherished independence, somethin' we're desperately fightin' for right now!" Milburn remarked, summing up feelings that he had been harboring for several weeks and was finally able to release in his humble and straightforward style.

"Amen to that!" he heard Emma's voice clearly ring out from the small semi-circle of women sitting at the edge of the light a few yards away.

Milburn didn't know if everyone had heard what he said, so he added another comment and directed it to everyone around. "Today, more than ever, I think we, as Americans, need to show our support for the United States of America, the war effort and for our president!"

"I'll give an Amen to that!" his wife agreed.

Thomas, Emma's husband, who had always been dubious about the United States getting involved in the war before Pearl Harbor and Germany declared war, said, "I hope we can stop Hitler, Mussolini and Tojo before they manage to put a foot on this land here!"

"People have changed their minds and I never hear anyone mention that we should've stayed neutral. I find it interestin' that some people are even startin' to worry that the Japs are comin' over here; that is they were, until the Navy kicked their butts at Midway last month. Midway was the first defeat the Japanese have had since they started this war and I think we're goin' to make damn sure it isn't their last loss!" Milburn said proudly. A short silence followed among the adults as the kids played loudly around in the light of the fire. "I don't think the Japs ever had any intention of coming here!" Milburn stated as an afterthought.

"Okay! It's time for the fireworks," Edward announced loudly, causing the kids to jump up and down in excitement. He opened a box of sparklers and handed one to each child after he instructed them to have an adult to help with them. "Be careful you don't burn yourselves!" he added. "Don't touch the hot ends and be sure to hold them away from your faces!"

Marianne and her two girlfriends volunteered to assist her young cousins with the sparklers after lighting them off glowing embers at the edge of the fire. Once lit, the children laughed, squealed and ran around in circles waving the sparklers like wands in the air.

Edward fumbled around in one of his big, brown-paper bags. "Where are those Roman candles?" he asked, quizzing his memory and dug deeper. "Oh, here they are," he finally said and handed all of them to Milburn. "Why don't you take these and help anyone who wants to hold one. Just make sure they're held at arm's length away from their faces and are pointed out in the air over the pasture!"

"Who wants to hold a Roman candle?" Milburn asked, picked up one of the slim cardboard tubes and waved it around for effect.

In the process of lighting sparklers for Sarah and Jane, two of her young cousins, Marianne yelled, "I want to do some too."

"And please save some for us!" Barb screamed.

"I think there's plenty for everyone," Milburn replied, offering them in his outstretched hands.

While the Roman candles burped out their multi-colored strings of bright balls into the night sky, Edward walked away a safe distance off to the side into the grassy pasture where he had previously arranged his rockets and mortars. He waited silently until all of the sparklers were burnt out and the last of the Roman candles had thumbed their colored balls into the night sky.

"Okay everybody. It's time for me to light the first mortar! Stand back!" he ordered and looked around to make sure all the kids were a safe distance away. "I'd move back a little more," he commented to those closest to him and made a motion as if he were shooing chickens away. Once he was satisfied that everyone was seated or standing a safe distance away, he struck a match and lit the slow fuse on the first rocket and backed away several feet. A silence fell over the small gathering that was so complete it left only the night songs of the crickets and katydids filling the air.

Everyone waited intensely for something to happen and just when they assumed the fuse had gone out, a bright flash spewed out of the top of the small mortar tube, followed by a soft swish, and the mortar arched high into the black sky on a tail of sparks until it exploded high overhead into brightly multi-colored gems, leaving in its wake a small grayish smudge of smoke where it had burst.

"Oooh, wooow and aaah," his spectators gasped. "More, more, more," the young ones chanted and clapped their hands after each spectacular explosion filled a small space in the sky with pyrotechnic paint.

Edward walked over to the last and largest cardboard mortar tube. "Well, this is my best one and I've kept it for last," he stated and paused, waiting several seconds to be dramatic. "Okay, everybody, get ready?" he said and looked around to make sure that his audience was watching, and lit the fuse. The mortar thumped the shell high into the sky on a string of bright sparkles. Before it exploded, it appeared to mingle with the stars and then burst with a loud bang, creating a wide display of red, white and blue spinning shapes that hung longer than any of the other displays that had been created against the dark backdrop of night sky. Even the adults who had been silent until now, but enthralled, couldn't help themselves from giving out unconstrained, "ooohs and aaahs." The young kids screamed, clapped, ran and jumped up and down.

"That was really, really somethin'!" Milburn exclaimed. "I can't begin to thank you enough, Edward!" he added warmly, acknowledging his brother-in-law's efforts. "We really appreciated that great display and we'll always be grateful for makin' this Independence Day so special!"

"You don't really need to thank me! And, anyhow, I'm not finished yet!"

"You're not?"

"No! I still have several long strings of firecrackers left!"

"Firecrackers? I forgot all about them," Milburn replied.

"I figured we needed to end this great picnic with a bang!" Edward said and lit a string of firecrackers. He threw them up and out into the air several feet away, creating a noisy geyser of flashes that fell to the ground and withered around like a brightly injured snake. The kids went wild with delight. "Stay back!" he ordered and tossed several more, one at a time. Not until he had lit and tossed the last string of firecrackers, and not until the last firecracker on the last string had exploded, did he finally state, "Now we're finished!"

The kids, suspecting there were more, pleaded and screamed until Gloria's brother-in-law, Thomas, gave a loud whistle for attention. "That was a great picnic, a great fireworks display and on everyone's behalf I want to thank Milburn and his family for hosting a picnic and also to Edward for the fantastic fireworks display!"

The women slowly got up, folded the blankets and organized their picnic baskets. Everyone, including the smallest child, carried something back to the house. In a few minutes time, all that was left in the pasture were a few smoldering embers of the fire, three bales of hay, the rough table and some patches of trampled grass.

Marianne led Rocky with one arm and carried one of the folded blankets with her other one. Sitting in the saddle holding a folded tablecloth was her little brother. Her two friends walked along next to them swinging the small, but awkward to carry five-gallon milk can, now empty of iced tea, between them.

"I think my mom'll be here about anytime now," Stella Mae said. "She told me she'd come over to pick Barb and me up between ten and ten-thirty."

"Well, our timing seems to be pretty good because I think that's your mother coming up the driveway right now!" Marianne remarked.

"Yeah, you're right. It's her! She's always on time!"

Marianne tied Rocky to the fence behind the house, lifted Leon off and followed her two friends out of the pasture and into the yard. Della Mae and Barb clanked the milk can down on the sidewalk by the backdoor. "I know Mom won't be getting out, so I think we'd better run," Stella Mae said. "Thanks for the great picnic and we'll see you next Saturday at the drug store, if not sooner, okay?"

"Okay!" Marianne shouted after them.

"Thanks loads!" Barb yelled out of the car window as it pulled away. "I had a great time!" Marianne let her eyes follow the car until it neared the highway.

Everyone except Emma and Thomas hustled off to their cars after pausing only long enough to thank Gloria and Milburn one more time for the picnic. "Let me help you straighten some of these things up before I leave," her sister said and stepped towards the door to go inside.

"You really don't need to!"

"I won't have it any other way!" Emma insisted, held the door open and motioned to Jonathan and Elvin to go inside. "You boys can carry them two picnic baskets inside and then come back out and get this other stuff."

Ethan hobbled through the open door.

"Mom, can I go out and put Rocky away?" Marianne yelled in through the screen door. "Mom," she repeated louder on not getting an answer.

"I heard you, but don't be long," she finally heard her mother answer back. "We could use your help in here."

Marianne untied Rocky from the fence, led him across the barnyard and back to the barn. Two of her right-hand fingers were hooked around a leather strap on his halter and her mouth was close to his big left ear. "When Barb rode you this evening, she told you some secrets, didn't she?" Marianne said.

Rocky shook his head up and down. "How happy I'd be if you could talk!" she whispered and led him into his stall.

CHAPTER TWENTY FOUR

Saturday, July Eleventh, 1942

Was the picnic just last week? Marianne questioned herself. *It seems like so long ago…*

"Are we goin' for a ride now?" Leon asked, interrupting her thoughts for about the twentieth time. "I'mm booorred!" he moaned. Two days earlier, while at the grocery store, Leon had persuaded his mother to buy him a red straw cowboy hat with white stars on each side and he was anxious to act like the cowboy he pictured himself to be. He stood beside her, his red hat firmly planted on his head and with two cap pistols slung in holsters on his hips. "Can't you hurry up?" he pleaded.

"I think it'll be okay if we wait a little longer, don't you? Just as soon as I'm done here we'll go," his sister said, perturbed with his impatience. "Try to wait quietly, okay?" she said sharply. "It won't be much longer, cowboy!"

For what seemed like an eternity, Leon watched his sister curry and groom Rocky. She warned him before they left the house that grooming Rocky was her first priority. It was one of those necessary jobs she needed to do and also doing.

"Go outside and play," she demanded. "Go shoot something or throw rocks," Marianne suggested, trying to use the infliction in her voice for effect. "Don't annoy me, leave me alone and I'll be along shortly," she scolded.

Leon maintained his attitude. "You promise?"

"Yeah, I promise! We'll go riding just like I said we would, but I won't until I'm done grooming Rocky," she answered firmly. "It'll be a long ride, if you don't bother me anymore and it'll be a lot shorter, if you do!"

"Why do you need to do that?" Leon asked, watching her work. He hoped to discover some way he could pleasantly coax her to hurry. Throwing rocks was fun but not nearly so much as riding behind his sister on Rocky's rump.

"He needs it for the same reason you need a bath and have your hair combed," she explained. "Now run along! I'll be out in a little while."

"Oh…all rriiight!" he muttered and walked out of the cavernous space created by the open barn doors. His shoulders slumped and he kicked at a loose pile of straw scattered on the floor.

She heard a rock ding on the metal horse tank beside the barn and she knew her little brother would be occupied for a while longer before he would come back to pester her. She started thinking again. *That picnic must've been the most fun I've had all this summer, although Saturday night a week ago had several interesting moments. It's a good thing I didn't stay home with Ethan after he nearly begged me to, because I would've missed so much excitement. And why is it that just because he can't get around very well with that big cast on his leg does he think I should be obligated to stay home and keep him company. Really…why should I punish myself?* The thought of his demands made her temporarily angry. *He was the one that was stupid. I actually think he deserves what he got! No, oh no…*she thought, reconsidering the thought and feeling ashamed, *I really don't believe that, but I shouldn't have to give up my fun just because he feels miserable.*

She thought back to the previous Saturday night and the fun she had. *I love getting away from here, going to town, hanging out and being with Donna, Stella Mae, Evelyn and my other friends. How lucky we were to get a booth with so many people around. I think we must've gossiped about everything, including the absence of Barb for the first time all summer. And what about Donna...she asked about Ethan again!*

I still don't understand why all my girl friends looked at me when we walked down Main Street and Bobby drove by in his thirty-four, green, Ford sedan, waved and honked. What do they think is going on? One thing I do know is that they all think he's sooooo cute! "Don't look at me," I told Donna and she rolled her eyes dramatically; Stella Mae giggled and punched Evelyn lightly in the ribs. He's alright, I guess, but I don't know why they make such a fuss about things sometimes!

Of course, Stella Mae was her flirty self again and in her usual good mood. I like the fact that she's pretty predictable about so many things: spontaneous, carefree and doesn't take things too personal. She managed to say hi to almost every boy we saw and then would giggle and say goofy things under her breadth like, "I wonder what he would look like with a wart on his nose!" When just the two of us were off by ourselves, she took the opportunity to ask me to go to the movies in Champaign with her family tomorrow night. I said yes so fast I embarrassed myself but Stella Mae pretended not to notice. She said we're going to go see the popular movie, "The Black Swan," about the Caribbean buccaneers starring Tyrone Power...God, is he good looking!. Who else did she say was in it? Oh yeah, I remember...Anthony Quinn and Maureen O'Hara. I love the main features but sometimes I think I almost enjoy the cartoons and the "Movietone News" as much because it shows clips of what's going on in the war and other world events. I can hardly wait!

Other pleasant thoughts crossed Marianne's mind as she ran her curry comb slowly down Rocky's shoulder. *I'm gonna go riding today, going into town tonight and then tomorrow night I get to go to Champaign to see the movie.* Before any further daydreams entered her mind, a very loud clank against the metal horse tank disrupted her tranquility and a loud voice pleaded, "Sis, can we go for a ride now?"

"Yeah! Okay! Sure! I'm putting Rocky's saddle on right now," she hollered back at him.

Leaving the dark confines of the barn and leading the pony out into the bright sun nearly blinded her. She had to stop and wait momentarily with the palm of her hand shading her eyes until her sight improved. "Leon, can you come over here and help? You'll need to hold unto Rocky's reigns while I make sure his girth strap is cinched tight enough."

Leon held the reins firmly as he watched his sister check the saddle's girth strap. "Can I ride him sometime by myself?" he asked.

"Sure," she answered. "You can today, if you'd like. When we ride into town, I'll let you sit in the saddle and I'll ride up behind you," she answered.

"I don't mean like that! I mean all by myself…alone!"

"I really don't think that's a very good idea!"

"Why not?"

"Because you're still awfully small and Rocky's a little bit headstrong, uncooperative and ornery at times. You could get hurt riding him all by yourself!"

He knew what uncooperative meant because Marianne and Jonathan both said that about his older brother. He wasn't too sure about the headstrong part. "You mean his head is full of muscles?"

"No, you silly boy!" Marianne laughed. "Being headstrong means that Rocky doesn't always do what you want him to and instead does what's in his head. Oh…and he can be very stubborn about it too. Anybody who rides him has to be firm and let him know that they're his boss," she explained. "When he behaves well, I like to encourage him to mind by talking gently to him. Petting his neck also helps," she said and reached up and petted his neck. "You're a good pony!" she said.

Leon hesitated until he formed a good reply. "I can be…firm… and do all that," he said with confidence.

"I'm sure you think you can," she answered. "I just don't think it's a very good idea. Maybe you'll be ready in a couple of years."

"Gosh, darn it, Sis, a couple of years is a really long time!" he said and frowned. "That's almost forever!"

"It's not that long!" she answered with a smile. "Now come around here and let me lift you up behind the saddle so we can get going."

Marianne guided Rocky away from the barn and down the lane towards the highway. They road in silence and listened to the pony's hooves crunch in the gravel. The joy they felt was further enhanced by the sight of a half dozen Holstein milk cows browsing lazily in the small pasture on their right and by the giant old oak and hickory trees that shaded the ground in dappled patterns of sunlight and shadow in the wooded pasture on their left. Maud and Buddy, their other two horses, stood a few feet beyond the fence grazing in the long grass of an open glade among the trees.

"Hi Maude! Hi Buddy," Marianne shouted.

"Hi Maude! Hi Buddy," Leon repeated and watched both horses raise their heads and neigh a greeting.

Rocky whinnied.

"Isn't this fun?" Marianne asked.

"Uh-huh," Leon answered and threw his arms around her ribs and squeezed. "Where're we goin'?" he wanted to know.

"Let's ride into town instead of going around to that old back lane. The deer flies and bugs are awful back there and we'd be swatting at them all the time and we'd still get eaten alive!"

"I don't like deer flies!"

"Maybe that's why we should ride into town. There's no deer flies in there and I'd like to see if any of my friends are hanging around."

Leon liked his sister's friends and he liked going into town. Doing so offered adventures the farm didn't have: a variety of people, a train station, grocery stores, a creamery and two blocks of other merchants. Even though his sister didn't always carry money with her when she went riding there was always the distant possibility of having a treat, such as a candy bar or an ice cream cone.

Instead of going straight down Main Street to the small business district, Marianne guided Rocky west toward the grade school and Illinois Street, a quiet street running in front of the grade school where kids came to have fun on the slides, teeter-totters and other playground equipment during the summer. Behind the school, in afternoons and on weekends, older students gathered to participate in softball or baseball games on the ball diamonds. She dearly hoped to find some of her girlfriends watching a game or just hanging around and Leon hoped they might ride on past and have his sister treat him at the drug store.

Even before they could see the ball diamonds, they heard young people shouting and whooping and making a racket.

"Who's doin' all the yellin'?" Leon asked.

"I can't be sure," his sister answered and listened. "It sounds like some guys playing baseball, but I have no idea who they are," she said.

Riding out from behind the houses that were blocking their view they saw several boys engaged in a game of fly balls and grounders. Each person out on the field was yelling for the batter to hit the ball to them. Along the left side of the ball diamond Marianne observed a handful of girls sitting on one of the simple, long, two-tiered wooden bleachers, uninterested in the game and talking among themselves. Three cars, one a deep green, thirty-four Ford sedan, were parked at odd angles behind the bleacher in the shade of tall, American elm trees.

As they rode closer, she saw that Bobby was at home plate hitting a baseball randomly to the six or seven other guys that were attempting to catch or snag it. One of the catchers caught a ball and lofted it smoothly back to home plate. It bounced twice before Bobby snatched it up and prepared to hit it back into the outfield. Marianne watched. Bobby caught a glimpse of her, stopped in mid-action and jabbed the length of the bat in her direction and waved. His action caused the players in the outfield to look her way also, which in turn, prompted one of the girls sitting on the bench to turn and look her way. Bobby turned away, tossed the ball up in the air, swung the bat and connected the ball with a solid whack.

"Marianne," she heard a voice shout and realized it was Barb, sitting with a group of girls.

Marianne waved. "Hang on tight," she instructed Leon and prodded Rocky into trot which was more in keeping with her persona. She reined Rocky up at the end of the low bleachers. "Hi, everyone!" She said.

"Hi," two or three of the six girls responded casually and the others made small gestures of acknowledgement. "Who's the good looking cowboy with the big red hat you've got up there behind you?" Barb asked, getting up and walking over. A couple other girls followed.

"He calls himself Two Gun Pistol Pete!" Marianne related. "He's a tough western sheriff!"

Leon instantly pulled out one of his cap pistols, waved it in the air and pointed the barrel at the tin badge pinned to the shoulder strap of his bibbed overalls. "I'm lookin' fer cattle rustlers," he said. "Yah haven't seen any, have yah?"

"No, none right now," Barb stated, playing along with his game. The few other times that she had seen Leon, she had enjoyed his friendly personality and the way he liked to pretend. She acquired a serious look on her face, squinted and slowly scanned her eyes around. "But, you know partner, I did hear there's recently been some rustling going around here!" she informed him, getting caught up in the drama of the moment. "They must've left when they saw you coming!" she said, imparting a serious edge to her voice.

His sister smiled. In one easy motion she swung her leg over the pummel, hopped down off Rocky and tied his reigns to a brace at the end of the bleachers.

Barb took Leon's chubby bare foot in her hand. "Could I help the sheriff down off his horse?" she asked.

"No, thanks! I don' wanna get down. I'm gonna sit up here where I can see better just in case any of them rustlers might try to sneak back into town!"

"Okay," she said, tickled his foot lightly and gave him a friendly wink. "Don't go riding off looking for them unless you take some deputies with you!"

"I won't, cause Sis said I can't ride Rocky all by myself!"

"Don't tell your sister this, but I think you and I both know you're big enough to ride him all alone," she said teasingly and, although she didn't know it, she was planting a seed in his mind which would grow and ripen in the days ahead.

"I guess I could get to be a little jealous of you," Alice said to Marianne.

It was an unexpected comment that caused Marianne to be temporarily lost for words, and then, since she couldn't determine if Alice was being sarcastic or not, she asked, "Why?"

"Because I've often heard from several people that yours is a really nice place and it's fun to go out there," she admitted.

"I'm glad you heard that!" Marianne affirmed, seeing that Alice was probably curious to know more and a little envious also.

"I always lived in an apartment in the middle of Kansas City until I moved here," Alice said.

"Maybe you could come out sometime and I'll show you around. It's so close you can walk out there!"

"I don't know, I," Alice stuttered and the bravado of a big city girl was lost for the moment.

"Maybe we could walk out there together some day next week!" Donna offered, trying to be helpful and using the opportunity as an excuse to go out to Marianne's also. "I haven't been out to her house yet this summer and I missed the picnic when my parents forced me to go visit my stupid cousins down in Mattoon."

And you missed seeing my brother, Marianne thought devilishly.

"You're sure you wouldn't mind if I come out sometime?" Alice asked hesitantly, not yet accustomed to the more informal culture than the one she left behind in Kansas City.

Marianne was seeing Alice in a new perspective, a new classmate that was still making lots of adjustments after ending up in a small town after the glamour of her previous home. *She acts snide and pretends to be superior because she's from Kansas City, but I'm starting to think it's all one big act. She must feel defensive because she feels so out of place here...she's like a fish out of water.*

"I like it when people come out to the farm," Marianne encouraged, "and I think you'd like it too!"

"Marianne's farm is not only interesting, it's a place where you can have loads of fun!" Donna exclaimed and giggled. "You should see the haymow!"

Marianne looked at Donna in disbelief for making a reference to the fabled stories about farmer's haymows, and then it suddenly dawned on her that maybe Donna's remark came from a personal experience.

"So, that's your pony!" a husky, male voice exclaimed. The girls stopped talking and turned around to face Bobby walking toward them. "I had to come over and apologize after I told you that I'd come out to see your pony sometime and I never have. Just haven't found the time," he said, giving a feeble excuse. "When I saw you ride up, I knew I had to come over and defend myself!" he added and stepped within inches of Marianne's elbow.

Marianne's face turned a light pink. No one could have determined if she was embarrassed from Bobby's attention or mad at him for offering the excuse. Her reaction would make for a good lively conversation among the girls later.

"Hi, cowboy," Bobby said to Leon.

"I'm not a cowboy!" he snapped. "I'm a sheriff," he corrected sternly and pointed at his tin badge again. Leon's fast response caught Bobby off-guard. Very clearly the girls could see that the simple encounter made Bobby feel awkward and that he had momentarily lost his bravado, self-assurance. His demeanor quickly changed and all he managed to say was, "S, s, sorry."

Leon didn't blink. "Y'all haven't seen no rustlers around here, have yah?" he asked and waved his right arm around in a wide sweeping motion.

"No," Bobby replied. Two of the girls sauntered back to the bleachers; three lingered and discussed other topics before following their friends. Only Bobby was left talking to Marianne. The two of them, out of ear shot of the bleachers, talked for several minutes. Eventually Marianne walked over to the bleachers and sat down on the third, top tier.

"He's really a cute guy," Elizabeth, an eighth grader remarked as her eyes followed Bobby back out to the ball diamond and she didn't shift her vision away until he picked up his baseball glove. "I think he likes you, Marianne!" she added enviously.

Instead of commenting, Marianne changed the subject. "You know, summer's already about half over and school will be starting before you know it!" Of the six girls sitting on the bleachers, four of them were Marianne's close friends, Barb, Evelyn, Donna and Alice. In the fall they were all entering high school and they shared their worries about entering the new school. Barb was the only one that didn't seem nervous about the transition.

Can you believe we'll be freshmen?" Donna said.

"Two things that bother me is how the seniors haze the freshmen and also how I'm going to remember where I need to go," Evelyn, shy and forgetful added.

"Just keep a small notebook with you," Alice told her. "That's what I'm going to do, and besides, I don't think going to high school's such a big deal. What's to worry about? We'll all be there together and after a couple of days or weeks, we'll be adjusted and be wondering why we were ever nervous in the first place," she added. "I'm thankful it won't be anything compared to the adjustments my older brother Bob's gonna be making," she interjected.

"Your older brother?" Barb asked. "I didn't know you even had one!"

"Yeah, well, I do!" she said. "I guess I've never mentioned him to anyone because he stayed back in Kansas City when we moved here."

"Why did he stay behind?"

"He's older and had a good job and didn't want to leave. Yesterday he called and sounded irritated and really upset."

Impulsively Barb asked, "Why, because he lost his job?"

"I wish it was. He told my dad he got his draft notice in the mail and he has to report at the end of August."

None of the girls were very sympathetic because so many young men were being drafted that it was being taken for granted that anybody of draft age, healthy and male, unless he had a deferment, would find his draft number coming up sooner, more than later.

"I can't imagine what it'd be like to get drafted!" Donna replied.

"I can't imagine having to fight or to shoot someone," Evelyn added. "Wouldn't it be just awful?"

Yvonne, one of the younger girls spoke up with some sad news that made being drafted seem like a non-issue. "I have a first cousin who was fighting in the Philippines and was on Corregidor last May when it was overrun by the Japanese."

"You really had a cousin on Corregidor?" Her friend, the other eighth grader asked.

"Uh huh!"

The disastrous loss of the Philippines was still weighing heavily on everyone's minds.

After months of heavy fighting on the Bataan Peninsula of Luzon in the Philippines, the American and Pilipino troops, unable to be resupplied and running short of food, medical supplies and ammunition, surrendered to the Japanese forces on April 9, 1942. Earlier, General MacArthur had moved his headquarters two miles offshore to the Rock, as the fortified island of Corregidor was called. He stayed in command until ordered by President Roosevelt to leave the island on February 20, but he stayed until March 11, when he was finally taken off the island by PT boats and transported to Melbourne, Australia. At the time, he was heavily criticized for abandoning his troops.

General Wainwright assumed MacArthur's command and defended Corregidor. Constant artillery shelling, the conditions in the tunnels, his lack of adequate arms, and contenting with a dwindling number of exhausted soldiers and sailors to defend the island against an overwhelming number, Japanese troops finally forced him to contemplate his options. Without any hope of reinforcements or supplies, he sent out a flag of truce and Wainwright found himself faced by the Japanese General Masaharu Homma's threat of the possible annihilation of all the people on Corregidor, if he didn't surrender all of the Philippines, therefore, on May 9, 1942 he signed the surrender document.

The weary, hungry and thirsty soldiers of Bataan were forced to walk in the stifling heat sixty miles to their internment camp. Any sick or tired laggards were shot, bayoneted or clubbed to death. The forced march into captivity became known as the Bataan Death March.

The prisoners from Corregidor were paraded through Manila and sent to various prison camps. Some became slave labors in Japan. General Wainwright was held captive in Manchuria.

"What happened to your cousin?" Evelyn asked.

"We've never actual been able to find out! The last time my aunt and uncle had any news of him was around the first of March. They managed only to find out when they saw his name listed in the news or somewhere. My uncle is really devastated and holds out hope he was taken prisoner and not killed. There have been some sketchy reports about the lucky survivors but no one knows very much about them yet!" she said, repeating what little she knew in much the same way it had been related to her.

Leon, still sitting on Rocky, waved his toy pistols around and pretended to shoot things while slowly becoing bored. "Can we go?" he groaned. She was so engrossed with her friends that she nearly forgot about him. "Okay, in a couple of minutes," she answered.

Two minutes later he pleaded, "Come on, Marianne, less go!" and slid over the back of the saddle and waited impatiently. A few minutes later she said, "Bye," and walked away from her circle of friends. She took the saddle's pummel in her left hand and prepared to put her foot in the stirrup to mount her pony. Instead, still interested in the chatty conversation going on a few feet away, she paused. It was hard for her to leave and Leon read her body language. "Less go! Pleeeease!" he begged.

Marianne finally put her foot in the stirrup and swung up into the saddle. She adjusted her body on the hard leather. "I guess I gotta go!" she said, took a firm grip on Rocky's reins and coaxed him to turn around.

At the last second, before Marianne rode off, Donna quizzed, "You are coming into town Saturday night, aren't you?"

"I'm planning to," Marianne chirped and pulled Rocky's reigns harder across his neck. "Bye," she yelled and gave Rocky a slight nudge to make him move ahead.

"Maybe I'll see some of them rustlers on the way home," Leon said and held on tight as his sister encouraged the pony to go into an easy trot. Before they turned the corner and rode out of sight, she glanced back over her shoulder one last time. Later she would recall that she saw Bobby standing in the outfield, shielding his eyes against the bright sun, watching her.

CHAPTER TWENTY FIVE

Breakfast the Tenth of August, 1942

Leon sleepily entered the kitchen and to no one's surprise, he announced, "I'm really hungry and I miss Granma too," he mumbled, and plunked his body heavily down on a chair. Over the last weekend, his father, Ethan and Jonathan had helped her move into a comfortable, older, single-story house just a block from Main Street near the business district. "Why'd she have to go move into town anyway!" he moaned.

His father looked at him thoughtfully. "I know your grandmother liked livin' out here. It just it just got to be too inconvenient for her and Anna Lee to stay without Donald around to drive them places," he explained. Donald's enlisting may or may not have been the major reason she moved but he hadn't lied to his youngest son either. What he failed to mention was that there were other reasons for her moving. One of the other reasons was that his wife and his mother had their differences; they rarely spoke to each other. Also there was the lingering rift between himself and his mother over other issues and no matter how hard he had tried to mend the fences, she stayed cool to most of his entreaties to find a middle ground.

"Well, I love Granma and I'm still gonna miss her a lot!" he murmured and looked at his empty plate.

Milburn usually refrained from contaminating his children with his personal prejudices. His father was relieved to see Leon feeling so warmly towards his mother. "We'll miss her too and I promise you'll get to see her often," his father said, and it seemed to satisfy his youngest son's concern.

To avoid any further discussion of the awkward, contentious and painful topic, Milburn quickly changed the subject. "It's a good thing we have two oceans separating us from the wars," Milburn remarked to his wife and kids. "Yesterday's Decatur Herald had lots of bad news and we Americans should be truly thankful that most of the destruction is overseas!"

Horrified with his statement, his wife blurted out, "What do you mean most of the destruction is overseas? There isn't any fighting going on in this country, is there?"

"No, not on land, but there's plenty in the water along the Atlantic coast where German submarines are sinking allied ships, many at night and close to land. Some of the torpedoed ships are close to shore!"

Ethan pictured himself standing on the heaving deck of a ship hunting enemy submarines. "When I turn seventeen, I'm gonna join the Navy!" he announced for about the umpteenth time.

His mother frowned and gave him a troubled look.

Bewildered from Ethan's tiresome insistence, his dad shook his head. "We'll see," he replied, skirting a direct answer and went on with his own dialog instead. "There have been several reports of attempted espionage right here on American soil also and it's become a big worry! One article I read gave details about them Germans who came ashore off a submarine, got caught and were givin' the death sentence!"

"They were given the death sentence?" his wife asked, a little stunned that she hadn't heard anything about the story. She rarely read the front section of the paper and relied on her husband to fill in important news items she missed and it surprised her that he had not said anything about this.

"Uh huh, and they were executed in Washington D. C. last Saturday!"

Jonathan, hardly listening, concentrated more on reading the information printed on the back of the Kix cereal box in front of him and deliberately spooned more into his mouth. "Did any of those Germans kill someone?" he asked.

"No, they didn't! They were caught before they were able to do any other harm," his father answered. "I found it interesting that one of them had even turned himself into the authorities before they found him and yet he was executed along with the others!"

"He was?" he asked, looking stunned.

"Yes, they did and I think he got exactly what he deserved!"

"They hung him even after he turned himself in?" Jonathan asked incredulously. He could see that justice in the eyes of the law might have been met; however, he thought it was a moral injustice to hang a man who hadn't done any harm and who turned himself in. "I don't think that was right at all!"

"We're at war, you know!" his father answered emphatically. "At least we gave them a trial first, didn't we? I'm sure the Germans execute every spy they catch and don't do it until after they've also tortured the person for hours or even days!"

Ethan, always feeling uncomfortable, shifted around on his chair in an attempt to find a decent position for his leg to relieve some of his aches. "I wonder if there's any more spies around!"

"I have no idea, but if there is, I'm sure they'll get caught by the FBI," their father answered, having total faith in the country's security and in Jay Edgar Hoover's FBI. "Yep, I'm sure they will if they're here!" he added, trying to sound reassuring as the thought flashed through his mind of how ill-prepared the country had been prior to Pearl Harbor.

Gloria put her fork down. "What do you think them spies would have done if they hadn't been captured?"

"Well," he said and stopped to contemplate for a few seconds. "For one thing, I think they were probably goin' to blow up some of them large electrical towers that stretch across the country. That would've been the easiest thin' for them to do that would have the biggest and most immediate impact on our industries."

Marianne interrupted, "It wouldn't have affected this place very much, because we don't have any electricity."

"Maybe it wouldn't affect many rural areas, or us directly, but it would've slowed down our industries!" he stated authoritatively. "It'd be really tragic if someone managed to blow up very many of them towers. Nearly everythin' would shut down, factories, entire cities and even some of the country's transportation...it'd be a catastrophe," he concluded. "Almost everythin' we do depends on electricity in one way or the other!"

Jonathan got a twinkle in his eyes. "Even schools would need to be closed, I suppose," he said with a smile, thinking that might not be so devastating to him personally. He put his cereal bowl up to his lips and drank the sugary milk from the bottom. "So electricity's that important?

"Don't joke about such serious things that way!" his mother interjected.

"Yes, it is," his father answered gruffly. "And by the way," he added since he had everyone's attention and decided to use his daughter's observation about not having electricity on the farm to his advantage, "I think it's time we start thinkin' about gettin' electricity ourselves. You might've heard of the REA, the government's program to bring electricity to all of the rural areas in the country. They've been runnin' the main lines in many places. Well, I think it'll shortly be our turn. I've got some solid information about how they're gonna be puttin' feeder lines along our highway sometime soon…maybe within the next month or so. Once they run them out our way, the lines will be standin' there just at the end of the lane, waitin' for us to hook up to them!" he stated enthusiastically. "It's comin' our way at just the right time. Just a year ago I thought we'd never be able to afford doin' such a thing, but thank God, this year the crops are lookin' so good I expect we'll have a bumper one," he said happily. "On top of that, the war's drivin' grain prices up. Things seem to be workin' in our favor and I believe we'll be able to afford to do somethin' like that," he explained and studied his wife's face. "How does that sound to you, Gloria?"

He surmised it might take some coaxing for her to warm up to the idea. When she didn't give him an answer right away, he got up and walked over to the wood-burning cast iron stove for another cup of coffee to give her time to mull over his proposition. The young members of the family anxiously watched to see what her answer would be.

Breaking the heavy silence and not wanting to wait another second for her mother to reply, Marianne asked, "You mean we might really get electricity?"

"Uh huh. I do, everything is gonna be in our favor from the way things seems to be comin' out!" her father answered and queried his wife, "Don't you agree that us workin' towards gettin' electricity in the house is a good idea, Gloria?"

"I'm not sure if just now's a good time for us because of our other expenses!" she answered. "Maybe we should wait a while!"

"I can understand your concern because of the cost," he said, knowing it was usually foremost in her mind. "Would you agree we should at least determine the cost before either of us rejects the idea," he said with trepidation. The previous year he had learned a lesson concerning his wife's fear of spending money and assuming mortgages. He knew now that he had to lead her slowly into accepting any changes that might involve her fear and frustrations.

The eyes of her entire family were transfixed on her. "Let me think," she said and resumed her silence. Obviously, she was caught off guard by her husband's new proposal and needed time to think and hash it out in her thoughts. "Are you sure we can afford it and we won't start until we're sure?" she asked again with little emotion. She showed no indication of the deep turmoil she had shown the year before after learning that her husband planned to put a basement under the house.

Milburn watched his wife and could detect little indication of which way she was leaning. Her face stayed calm. As he watched her contemplate, he figured that she would come around to the obvious conclusion that electricity would have great advantages for her by improving their primitive living conditions and lead to a lot of conveniences.

He decided to add some encouragement. "I've got a pretty good idea we can afford it without bitin' off more than we can chew. Sometime this comin' week I'd like to go over to Tuscola and talk to someone at the power company and get a rough estimate of what it'd cost to have electrical service brought back here from the highway."

"How soon do you think they'll be running them electrical lines down along our highway?" she asked.

"From what I've been hearin', they'll be startin' to run them lines in a month or so."

"And how soon after they do that do you think we'd be able to get electricity into the house?" she asked, sounding nearly impatient.

After hearing her response he surmised that she liked the idea. "I don't know what their schedule is. Let's say, if they do run the lines along the highway in the next few weeks and in the meantime I'm able to get one of their work crews to set the posts and run the electric lines back to the house this fall, we could possibly have electricity and lights by Thanksgiving or Christmas!" he avowed. No one knew that he was playing ignorant. Weeks before, he had made several inquires about this issue and was given an affirmative answer for everything he had questioned the electric company about their plans. They had even agreed to run the electricity back to their farm by mid-October. "If they tell me they can get the lines in this fall, we could go ahead and have the house wired and be ready to hook up. The barn and the other buildings could wait to be wired in the spring," he said.

Having an inclination that her husband had not been totally forthright, Gloria looked at him questioningly and waited several seconds before responding. "And if the house gets wired this fall, do you think we'd be able to afford a wash machine and refrigerator sometime soon after that?" she asked slyly.

He hadn't considered those expenses in the equation. "Those should be two of the first things we buy," he answered, well aware that his wife held a strong bargaining position and those appliances were a big reason to have the house wired.

Another warm humid breeze blew in through the kitchen window, making the curtains flap softly, distracting her for several seconds while nothing was said. "Okay…then I agree," Gloria answered.

Milburn took another sip of his coffee. "Then it's settled and I should check about gettin' electricity."

"I reckon," Gloria said and dropped the subject. "It looks like we're in store for another really hot day!" she added and started clearing off the table.

His wife's easy demeanor lowered his anxiety. "You're right… today's gonna be another broiler," he said, tipped the last few drops of his coffee into his mouth and stretched. "It's already hot out there!" he casually observed and peered at the flapping curtains. "I've gotta go get some work done on my equipment before it gets too dang hot," he said. "Jonathan, Marianne, you two need to go out and get your chores done as soon as you've finished eatin'…and Jonathan, I'm gonna need some help. Right after you finish doin' your chores, I want you to come out to my workshop in the garage."

Thankfully for the family, the daily routine on the farm changed its rhythm somewhat in August, usually one of the hottest months of the year. The grain crops took less effort to tend because they were too tall to be cultivated or walked and it would be couple of months before the corn and soybeans needed to harvested. The clover had been cut, bailed and bucked onto a flat-bed wagon, hauled to the barn and stored in the loft for the winter months. The same had been done with the straw from the wheat and oats. For a short time the crops could be left unattended. There was still the livestock that needed tending to, machinery maintenance to be undertaken and a smattering of other odd jobs to worry about. These slight variances in their workloads during August allowed an interval of time for other endeavors.

"I need to strip the beds and do the wash," his wife stated. Monday was the traditional wash day for many and Gloria was not one to vary from her routines. "I've got to get busy, she said. "If I don't get my wash done early and get the clothes hung out on the line, they'll never get dry in this humidity!"

"That's good, because I'd like go to Tuscola sometime this afternoon," Milburn said in the singular after working alone so much. She knew he intended for her and anyone else to go along if they wanted.

"Why?" she asked.

"Well, I've been needin' to go over there to pick up a part for my truck and with this heat I think it'd be a good time to go get it done!" he answered. "I could pick up the part, and while you do some grocery shoppin', and I'd have a chance to check with the power company to see how soon they could run the lines from the highway back up here to the house...if it's affordable, we could get the house wired and be ready before then."

"That's a good idea," she said agreeably, pursed her lips and stared off into space. "There's some things I could pick up in the big grocery that I can't get in either of the two stores here in Atwood," she added thoughtfully. "And, do you think we'd have enough time for me to run into Ben Franklin's for a few things?"

"If I get movin' and get everythin' done around here, I could be ready to leave around noon time," he commented and got up from the table. "We could leave right after we eat lunch."

Gloria mulled over the changes she needed to make in her days plans. "I think I could be ready by then also," she answered and turned to the kids at the table. "Marianne, when you're done with your chores, you need to come back and help make up the beds and, Jonathan, when you're finished, I want you to take that small basket and go out and pick whatever string beans might be left in the garden."

"I can't!" he said, feeling good to have an excuse. He absolutely hated picking beans or doing any work in the family's garden. Picking beans was almost as bad as walking the endless rows of soy beans or the tall rows of corn to cut weeds out. "Dad told me he needed my help when I'm done doing my chores," he reminded her.

"If you don't pick them now, you'll need to pick them in the heat this afternoon or early tomorrow morning'," she said. "It's your choice!" she added. Finding that he couldn't avoid picking the green beans, he swallowed and slumped in his chair.

Their mother's attention turned to Ethan. He had seemed oblivious to everything going on around him and immune to any work. "Ethan," she said loudly to get his attention.

"Whaaat?" he answered dryly, sounding bored, and yawned.

"I'm gonna get the globes off the lamps, some newspapers and I'll put them here on the table for you to clean."

"What can I do?" Leon asked, the only one of the young members of the family wanting to get involved in some industrious activity.

Marianne nodded towards the door. "Why don't you come along and give me a hand?"

She and her little brother walked out into the warm glow of early morning. The red orb of the rising sun was still low in the eastern sky, trying to get a foothold on the day by penetrating the moisture-laden air. What little breeze existed earlier was calm. Not a leaf on any tree or stalk of corn stirred anywhere. Little spheres of water glistened across the tips of the grass. Clouds of low steamy moisture rose out of the beans in the eighty-acres across the highway. "Whew! And I thought it was hot inside," she commented.

Leon seemed totally uninterested in the weather. "Are you gonna go with Mom and Dad?"

"Probably," she answered. "I'd really like to go into Ben Franklin's and look for some stuff."

"Stuff? What kinda of stuff?" he asked.

"Oh...just some things! Maybe some jewelry, some perfume and other things. Whatever I can afford with the three dollars I've saved up. What about you?"

"Well," he said and hopped happily around. "If I go with Dad, maybe he'll buy me some chocolate milk at the creamery. If I go with Mom, I might get her to buy me a candy bar from the grocery store. That's the stuff I like!"

"You sure have your thinking cap on!" she said.

He looked up at her quizzically. "Are you gonna talk to Rocky when we get out to the barn?"

Marianne almost stumbled when she heard his question. She answered, haltingly, "No, I uh, won't have the time," she said and looked down at him and their eyes met. "Do you think I talk to him?"

"Yeah, sometimes you do?"

"Maybe I do," she admitted. They walked on a few steps. "Can I ask you to do something for me?" she asked.

"What?"

"Don't tell anyone that I talk to him," she said and winked, trying to act unconcerned. "Let's let it be our little secret, just between the two of us, okay!"

"Is it really a secret?" he asked.

"Uh huh," she answered. "It's a secret and secrets are fun to have!"

Leon grabbed his sister's hand and swung her arm in unison with their stride. "I like secrets!" he replied. "Specially fun secrets!"

They walked on a few more steps while Marianne contemplated, searching her mind. "Secrets are very important things and do you know why?"

"Yes, because if somebody doesn't keep a secret his sis won't trust him anymore!" he replied instantly, dropped her hand, picked up a pebble and gave it a toss.

"Not ever!" she added. "Secrets between two people should never be broken and a broken secret between a brother and his sister is maybe the worst!"

"The worst?" he asked.

"Yes!" she answered.

"And you tell Rocky secrets?"

"I tell Rocky secrets, you can too and since he can't talk, you know they'll always be safe," she answered. "People should be more like horses!"

They walked on a little ways before either spoke again. "I wish I could ride him!" Leon said and took her hand again without breaking their rhythm in their stride.

"Maybe tomorrow I'll saddle him up and I'll let you sit on him while I lead him around."

"Ah, shucks. Not that! I mean, ride him all by myself!"

"You're sure persistent," she said. "I've told you before, haven't I, that you're too small to be riding him alone?" She ran her fingers across the top of Leon's head and fluffed up his hair affectionately. "I don't want you to get hurt!"

"How bout around in front of the barn?" he asked.

"Maybe," she answered.

CHAPTER TWENTY SIX

September Seventh, 1942
Labor Day

Milburn and Gloria were in the middle of discussing a wiener roast for Labor Day when Ethan hobbled into the changed kitchen and sat down heavily on a chair next to his sister. A new refrigerator graced the east wall, an electric toaster sat on the counter and a long florescent fixture hung above the table; all were still non-operational without electricity. In about a week, with a little luck, everything would be working. The doctors had taken the cast off Ethan's leg and pulled the pins out of his hip on Saturday. Heavy bandages covered his upper leg, necessitating him to wear extra large pants to fit over them and every two days he needed to have the dressings changed. He walked without crutches now, but needed a cane. His hair was barely combed and he was hollowed eyed from lack of sleep. The over-sized denim bibs, the cane, and his stiff, partially atrophied leg made him look miserable as he tottered around.

"You must be feeling better now that you've got that awful cast off and able to bend your leg some," Marianne observed.

"Yeah. Maybe I am," he grumbled, "but Doc said it'll take a long time for me to get the full use of it again!"

"Did he say how long?" she asked.

Ethan rolled his eyes in misery and replied sarcastically. "Maybe a couple of months or several years!" he said, showing his disgust over a possible long and trying recuperation.

"At least you're not going to have anything permanently wrong," she replied, encouraging him to brighten up.

Angry about his condition and wanting to throw the blame somewhere else instead of taking fault for the accident, he continued to grumble. "If that stupid pony hadn't acted up, I wouldn't be like this now!"

His statement stung because she couldn't throw the blame back in his face. Marianne knew the cause of the accident and it was only because she had promised Donald not to say anything that she held her tongue again; her honor would guarantee her silence. But the worst stab, the one unspoken that went straight to her heart, was for Ethan to use this moment to add weight to her mother's negative opinion of Rocky. She glared at him. He stopped looking morose and smiled at her. "Could I have some pancakes?" he asked.

Marianne ignored his request and decided to play along with his nasty little game. "You're lucky you got to take the cast off just in time for the first day of school tomorrow," she commented. She knew how uncomfortable and self-conscious he felt. "You know it'll still be stiff and you might have a hard time getting up and down the stairs to your classes. I'm sure that you'll enjoy the extra attention!" she said with a casual tone to her voice.

"Don't even bring up school. You know I'm going to hate being there!" he growled.

"Oh, but you shouldn't!" his mother answered frankly. "You haven't seen many of your friends this summer, and now you can even get around pretty good," she said, unaware that Marianne's comment was meant to sting.

Ethan watched his sister's sly smile broaden across her face. "Mom's right, isn't she!" Marianne answered.

"Look at me," he said. "I'm a mess, I look like a cripple and I can't hardly walk," he grumped. "Just pass me a couple of those pancakes," he added gruffly, "and leave me alone!'

Marianne discovered a chink in his armor and she couldn't leave it alone. "You know, Ethan, you really could use this gimpy stuff to your best advantage. Keep in mind that Donna's a freshman this year and I'm sure she'll be more than a little happy to give you lots and lots of attention and loads and loads of sympathy. Maybe, if you ask her, she'll even carry your books around to your classes," she teased and giggled.

Without looking around, Ethan reached out and whacked her on the shoulder with the back of his hand and hard enough to make her wince. "Ooow, Ethan, that hurt!" she complained and rubbed her shoulder.

His father knew the key to Ethan's accident, although he wasn't aware Marianne also knew.

Tired of his son's manipulation, he gave him a hard look and Ethan suddenly understood his being drunk wasn't a secret between just a couple of people.

"Marianne, if you'd leave him alone he wouldn't act like that!" her mother responded sharply.

Ethan gulped, looked at his dad and then at his sister. "Could I have the pancakes?" Ethan asked again, this time more humbly. Jonathan, sharing his sister's pact with Donald and sympathetic to his sister's position, slid the plate of pancakes over to Ethan without looking up. "Don't choke on 'em!" he said grumpily and Ethan slumped his shoulders.

Returning to the earlier subject, Milburn asked, "Gloria, what time was it you told them people to be out here this afternoon for the wiener roast?"

"I told them around six," she answered. "Six should work out just fine because I still have a lot of stuff to get done," she answered and went through the litany of other things she had on her mind. "Don't you go running off someplace this morning, Milburn where I can't find you."

"Why not just tell me what I need to take care of before I go outside?" he answered.

"Okay! We're gonna need a couple blocks of ice from town for the ice cream churn and you need to start chillin' that big watermelon."

"Those things have already been takin' care of," he answered. "Edward's bringin' the ice out when he comes this afternoon and I'm puttin' the watermelon in the water tank of the milk house this mornin'. Yesterday afternoon I drove around to Mossberger's old timber and got up a good load of firewood…so don't worry about them," he assured her. "If I need to do anything else, just let me know!"

Satisfied with what she heard, she looked at the kids. "Marianne, you need to help me around the house and, Jonathan, go grab a small basket, run out to the garden real fast and pick any ripe tomatoes that might be left, pull up a good dozen of the smaller winter onions and make sure you wash the dirt off!"

She wasn't done. "Milburn, do we have sticks for roastin' the hot dogs?" she asked, hurriedly picking up the breakfast plates from the table.

"It's a good thing you asked me, because I've plum forgot about them," he said. "Right after I get my chores out of the way, I'll take the truck over to the river and cut some long willow branches. Jonathan," he said, "you'll need to come along with me and help." He looked over at Ethan. "And you can come along also now that you've got that cast off your leg. Some exercise might do you some good," he pointed out. Ethan shrugged apathetically.

Leon didn't need to be asked or persuaded. "Can I go along?" he chirped excitedly.

"No! Not this time," his father replied, "You're gonna have to stay home!"

"Please, please, please," Leon begged and looked at his father with big pleading eyes.

"Not today!"

"But why?" he asked, crossed his arms and pouted.

"Because there isn't enough room in the truck cab with Ethan's leg like it is!"

"Aw, shucks," he said, copying Jonathan's favorite expression.

Ethan sat up straight. "I'll stay home if he really wants to go that badly!" he remarked, yawned and stretched lackadaisically. "I'm really tired and don't want to go!"

Milburn looked sternly at his oldest son. "I'm not givin' you that option. You've done enough sittin' around…so when I'm done with my chores, you'd better be up and oughta that chair!"

"Why should I go? I can't help!"

"I'll find something you can do!"

"Milburn, do you think them guys are going to show up tomorrow to finish wiring our house?" Gloria interjected to distract him from having another heated confrontation with his oldest son, seeing that her husband wasn't in any mood to have his lethargic son act insolent.

Red faced, and on the verge of losing his temper, Milburn paused briefly and snapped, "Yeah, of course they're goin' to be here! I suppose you think that just because they weren't here Thursday or Friday it would mean they'd forgotten!" he added sharply. "They'll be here, don't worry! Don't you remember me tellin' you what Fred, the boss, told me as they were packin' up Wednesday to leave. He said they had an emergency and as soon as they're finished takin' care of it, they'd be back!"

She could see he was calming down somewhat. "I remember!"

"Fred said they probably wouldn't be back until tomorrow, and he also told me that, more than likely, they'd finish wirin' our house in a week. Anyways, it don't make much difference when it's finished, if the power company doesn't get the wire strung along those poles they placed down our lane last week. Till they do that, we won't have any electricity."

"I'd like to see this mess straightened up and be able to turn a light on!" she said.

"It's possible the linemen could be here early tomorrow also. If they do, we'll probably have lights before this week's over and you can plug in all them new appliances of yours." The stress was gone from his voice and his face looked calmer. "By the way, about what time are you plannin' to have lunch ready?"

"How does twelve thirty sound?" she answered.

Preoccupied with other matters, Millburn didn't answer until he got halfway to the door. "Yeah, yeah...That'll be fine!"

Marianne and her mother had just finished their housework when Jonathan rushed in from the garden. Ethan and Leon sat at the kitchen table drawing with stubby pencils on lined theme paper. "Ethan," Jonathan said, "Dad's done with his chores and he told me to tell you he'll be ready to leave in a few minutes. He's gone to get the big truck and said you'd better get right out there!"

"Okay..." Ethan moaned.

Leon wadded up his carefully executed drawing and threw it on the floor in disgust. "I wish I could go!"

"Maybe the next time!" his older brother said and slowly hoisted himself off his chair. "Draw me something nice before I get back."

"I don't wanna draw nothin'! I'm gonna go outside and play," he announced and picked up his bright red, straw cowboy hat that he had been wearing daily for the last two weeks and followed his slow-moving brother outside and down to the end of the sidewalk. Jonathan and their father were already waiting in the idling truck. The passenger door hung open for Ethan to step up on the running board and slide into the cab.

Leon watched his brother hobble around the front of the truck to the other side and waited motionless until he heard the truck door slam and when the truck started moving forward he waved tepidly at his father and brothers. His eyes followed the truck down the lane until it turned off onto the highway. Not moving and thinking for nearly a minute, he suddenly became very animated and ran across the yard towards the back fence where he had seen Rocky standing.

"Hi Rocky" he said. The pony appeared to ignore him. Leon watched the pony for several seconds. "You hungry?" he asked and pulled some long tufts of grass from along the untended border of the fence and offered it through one of the square holes in the woven wire. "Come on, come over here and take it!" he coaxed and wiggled it around to make it appear more appetizing. "It's good!" he said. "Come on, Rocky, take it!" he repeated several times. Rocky still didn't respond. Leon located some longer stems of green grass which he thought might be more appetizing to the pony and pulled a big fist full and waved the long tufts around vigorously.

Rocky stepped closer, snorted softly, curled his lips, and tugged the grass from Leon's hand, making the young boy smile broadly. The fun lasted only a minute or so until the pony seemed to tire of the game and stepped away. Once that happened, no matter how hard Leon tried to coax Rocky to come back, he wouldn't and each time he tried, Rocky would toss his head, stare at Leon for a few seconds with his mismatched eyes and take another step.

"Where you goin'?" Leon asked and began to scheme. An idea formed in his young mind. A sense of overwhelming guilt made him pause, fearing that someone might be watching. He looked slowly around, even though he knew his mother and sister were in the house working and his father and brothers were over at the river by now. Eventually, he started climbing the fence. He put his hand as high as he could on the wire, his right foot in one of the low holes of the woven wire and began climbing. His heart raced. "Don't go away!" he begged the pony. Leon felt exhilarated from the adventure he anticipated. The guilt of doing something wrong and the fear of getting caught made him hurry. His belief that he and Rocky had just acquired a unique bond drew him over the fence. *I know I can ride him. He wants me to,* he thought without logic. Once on the other side, he walked calmly over and petted the pony on his shoulder, not as high up, or exactly the same way he had seen his sister do so many times in the past. "Nice boy," Leon said soothingly, mimicking his sister's actions and tone of voice. Rocky acknowledged Leon by slanting his head around and tossing it slightly.

A few feet away sat an old orange crate his mother had discarded after using it to carry scraps of vegetables out to the chickens. Hoping to use it to climb up and take a ride, Leon carried it over and placed it next to Rocky and got on top of it. Rocky turned his head around and nipped at Leon's arm. Leon scrunched up his face and reprimanded the ornery animal. "Don't do that," he ordered. "Be a nice pony," he added and patted Rocky's neck again the way his sister had instructed. He recalled his sister saying that Rocky was headstrong and needed kindness and a firm hand from anyone attempting to ride him. Leon put his arms over the pony's back and began to pull himself up; the pony stepped sideways and left him standing three feet away from his four legged objective.

Undeterred, Leon got down, moved the crate again and wasn't any more successful than he was each time before and decided to keep trying. A very determined Leon would move the crate over, start to climb up onto Rocky's back and the pony would sidestep away from the young cowboy.

They each schemed to win and after several long persistent minutes, Leon seemed close to triumphing. The pony gave up the game first. "Please, Rocky...Please don' move," Leon pleaded for the umpteenth time, patted his neck and the pony finally stood still. Leon threw his arms across his back and with great difficulty managed to climb up and straddle the pony's spine. The ornery animal turned his head around, tossed his head and nipped at Leon's bare toes that were extended forward on his short legs. Quickly Leon bent his knees and pulled his feet back. "Stop it!" he commanded in a firm little voice which he deepened to sound more authoritative; he leaned forward and patted the pony's neck again to encourage him to behave.

Leon firmly thought, *I'm a big cowboy and I know how to ride horses.* He straightened up his red cowboy hat as Rocky started walking unguided through the tall grass and weeds that carpeted the ground underneath the big trees. Leon relished his success, looked back at the house and felt totally secure that no one had seen him accomplish his dream. Several thoughts crossed his mind! *I did it. No one yelled at me,* he thought and then a bit of panic sat in. *How am I gonna make Rocky go where I want him to. What if I want to get off?* He contemplated and since he couldn't think of an answer to make himself feel better, he rationalized; *I'll just wait and think about how to do those things later!*

An hour later the men came back from the river carrying a few bug bites and enough long sticks for a small army to roast hotdogs on. "You boys can take them sticks and put them out by the back fence, across from where we're havin' that wiener roast and then go in and tell your mother I'll be in for lunch shortly!"

Jonathan primed the water pump and pumped until Ethan had washed most of the sweat and grime off his face and hands. "Okay, it's your turn," Ethan said and took his turn working the long handle while Jonathan washed. "I guess I'm next," their father said, walking up just as his sons were finishing. "I'm not gonna miss these primitive conditions," he added derisively, took the old towel from Jonathan and dried off. "Electricity is gonna stop this nonsense and change the farm for the better. Give me another two months and we'll have runnin' water in the house from a well I'm plannin' to have drilled," he said proudly. "By this fall your mom will have an inside toilet, water in the kitchen and a shower in the basement." Milburn wasn't a selfish man and the improvements meant a better life for his family; it gave him pride to be able to afford comforts for them.

When they walked in the table was already set with an abundance of thick, sliced slabs of roast beef, soft white Butternut Bread, sliced home-grown tomatoes, American cheese, mustard, wilted lettuce, some condiments and a pitcher of iced tea.

"Boy, am I hungry," Milburn declared and sat down heavily in his chair at the head of the table and waited for everyone else to take a seat. Leon's chair unexpectedly sat empty.

Concerned about the unlikely occurrence, Gloria furrowed her eyebrows and craned her neck around. "Has anyone seen Leon?" she asked.

"I thought he was here in the house," Milburn replied.

"I haven't seen him since he followed you outside when you left for the river," Marianne said.

Jonathan replied, "He's probably just outside playin',"

"He's never late for meals," Gloria remarked and looked at her husband quizzically. "I thought he went with you," she stated apprehensively. "I thought maybe you'd found room in the truck and changed your mind because he was being so persistent!"

"He was standing at the end of the sidewalk when we left, and, don't you remember me telling him, right here at the table that he couldn't go with us?"

"I know that's what you said! I just thought you might've changed your mind when you saw how disappointed he was!"

Milburn looked across the table at his middle son. "Jonathan, run out and yell for him to get in here or his goin' to miss his lunch!"

"Oh, gosh, darn it!" he growled.

"Go on! We'll wait 'til you get back before we start eatin'. Go on out and hurry! He's probably just out there playin' and lost in a world of his own."

A couple of minutes ticked slowly by. They could hear Jonathan outside repeatedly calling, "Leon, Leon!" The first calls were close to the house and gradually they moved farther away. The people sitting at the table looked at each other apprehensively after perceiving that Jonathan wasn't having any luck locating his younger brother.

After another long minute of waiting, Milburn declared, "Marianne, why don't you go see what's goin' on out there!"

Another minute or so ticked slowly by and when neither Jonathan nor Marianne came back inside, Milburn exclaimed, "Somethin' got to be wrong!" His frank statement broke the uneasy silence.

Deep concern etched Gloria's face. She looked at her husband. "Maybe we should all go out and see if we can find him!"

"Maybe we..." he started to agree, but stopped mid-sentence as the back door opened and closed. "I guess they've found him," he said and was surprised to see only Marianne step into the kitchen and shake her head, indicating that she and Jonathan hadn't had any luck locating their young brother.

Marianne shrugged. "He's not anywhere," she said. "We've turned this place upside down!"

"Well, he has to be somewhere, doesn't he?" her exasperated father pointed out.

"Yeah, of course he has to be, but we couldn't find him!" she answered.

Worried, more than perturbed over his son's absence, Milburn asked, "Did you try the barn?"

"Yes!" she replied.

"The hayloft?"

"Yeah, of course!"

"And the garage?"

Frustrated, Marianne snapped irritably at her inquisitor, "Yeah! It was one of the first places we looked. I said we've looked everywhere!"

Unconcerned about his brother's whereabouts, Ethan suggested, "He probably just went over to Grandma's barn to play with those baby goats." Milburn had paid his mother a few dollars for a pair of goats when she moved into town and had been tending to them ever since. The female had given birth to two pure white offspring the week before and Leon, especially mesmerized with playful baby animals, went to play with them often.

"I'll run over there," Marianne offered.

"I think we all had better go outside and look for him," Gloria said nervously.

Marianne eventually came back. "He's not over there," she announced.

While everyone stood in the yard, worried, full of anxiety and wandering what had happened to him, Leon and Rocky were at the other end of the woods where they were partially hidden from view by the tall grass and thick trees. The four-year-old was pretending to be a cowboy, surveying his surroundings for bandits and cattle rustlers while Rocky slowly grazed along.

Once or twice Leon had become concerned when he thought he heard someone call his name but hadn't given it much thought because he was too busy concentrating on his adventure. Bugs swirled around his head, distracting him as he watched a snake slither away through the grass. A few minutes earlier, an angry red-wing blackbird dove at his head, nearly knocking his hat off. Anyway, he had no way to answer whoever was calling and he couldn't get off the pony or make Rocky turn and go home without having a bridle. Each time he nudged the pony to go in some direction with one of his feet, the pony would try to bite it, which left Leon going wherever Rocky desired. Although tired, he was still trying to convince himself that he was having fun and then swatted at a deer fly.

The family stood between the house and chicken coup discussing what other options they had. Marianne, only halfway paying attention to their theories, constantly craned her neck around and wondered what they might have overlooked. As she was doing so, she noticed something red moving along just above the grass and weeds in the back of the woods between the trees. She squinted and shaded her eyes against the sun. "Wait," she said. "Look," she giggled happily. "I think that's him back there by the back fence. I'm sure that's him. He's over there…in the woods, by the back lane and he's on Rocky!" she squealed

Everyone stopped talking and looked where she was pointing and, one by one, they recognized the Leon's bright red hat as it moved just above the weeds. His mother gasped, "I can't believe that boy could manage to get on that darn pony!"

Marianne absolutely never thought of her brother as that boy or Rocky as that darn pony. *Even when I'm mad at Mom I don't think of her as that woman,* she deliberated, *but maybe I'm over reacting!* "I'll go get him!" she said and ran across the lawn and out the gate.

Leon was so busy swatting at the pesky deer flies buzzing around his head that he didn't notice his sister until she was only a few feet away. "Hi," he said and swatted at one of the flies that had landed on the top of his bare foot.

Immediately, Marianne noticed how miserable he looked. "Are you ready to go back to the house, cowboy?" she asked.

Pitiful looking, "Uh-huh, and I'm hungry and really thirsty and I hate them bugs!" he answered and swatted at two more deer flies, nearly knocking his red cowboy hat off in the process.

"Let me help you down," she said.

Rocky swished his tail and with his mismatched eyes he watched her walk away. Shortly he followed along several yards behind.

"Are you okay," his sister prodded.

"Yeah, and I had fun, and I rode him all by myself!" he answered. She didn't reprimand him.

The persistent deer flies had left welts on Leon's face and neck. "We'll need to put some medicine on those bites when we get back to the house," she said and took his hand. "Lunch is waiting and there's a big pitcher of iced tea on the table that'll help quench that big thirst of yours...so we'd better hurry!"

The two walked into the kitchen and found the rest of the family nearly done with the meal. Marianne, perturbed that they hadn't waited, grumbled, "I suppose you people started eating without us because you thought Rocky was responsible for the whole thing!"

Her mother looked straight at her. "Don't be silly. Ponies don't plan things!" she retorted, "We knew it would be sometime before you would be back and we don't have any more time to spare because we've got to get ready for the wiener roast this evening."

Without answering, Marianne plopped down heavily in her chair and poured Leon and herself a tall glass of iced tea.

"Marianne, after you finish eating, I'll still need your help to get everything done for the wiener roast."

The young girl and her mother worked wordlessly around the kitchen for the next hour. Eventually, after the tension faded, her mother asked, "Do you think Stella Mae is still going to make it over here this evening?"

"I believe so. She always does what she says she's going to do and last Saturday night she told me she's really looking forward to it!"

"I really like that girl," her mother commented and started arranging a tray of condiments for the hot dogs. "And you think Barb's comin' out too?" she asked.

"You can never tell about her anymore, not since she started dating Richard."

Many local girls of Gloria's generation had married young. "Are they serious?"

Marianne nodded. "Yeah, I guess so!" she said and hoped the subject would be dropped, although the door had already creaked open. She did everything to avoid gossiping or making negative insinuations about her friends to anyone and especially to her mother.

"I just hope she doesn't make the same mistake her cousin made!" her mother stated.

"That was a natural mistake Margret made and it's a shame it turned into a tragedy. They were in love and he got drafted," Marianne remarked, searching for words to excuse Margret's sad predicament. "Everything would've turned out a lot differently if he hadn't been killed with that grenade," Marianne explained. "They were really in love!"

"Well, like they say and as far as Barb and her cousin is concerned, apples don't fall very far from the tree," her mother theorized, ignoring her daughter's opinions.

"You're not making a fair comparison!" Marianne replied adamantly.

"Well, I think I am!" her mother replied.

"No you aren't! You know it's not right to compare apples with people! Barb's a good girl and so is her cousin and it's not right for anybody to say they're not!"

"I say that many traits run in families!" her mother insisted, not considering how the same analysis would apply to her family. It was a deep belief she carried even though one of her own siblings and two of her first cousins had gotten pregnant before they were married. Now, how was it still possible for her to think this way when none of her nieces or nephews in the younger generation needed to have shotgun weddings?

Marianne felt she was being baited, so she bit her lip to keep from debating the issue any further. It was an unwinnable topic anyway. Her mother often expressed several strange beliefs about sex and reproduction. She thought freaks could be caused by pregnant women being startled by snakes, sharks, wolves or any number of wild beasts, so it wasn't a great leap in her reasoning to believe that the pregnancies of the young unmarried girls ran in some families because of their genes.

To change the subject, Marianne asked, "Who's coming out here today?"

"Your Uncle Edward and his family, the Baker's, your Aunt Melina and Uncle Chuck and their kids," she answered, "and Ethan told me he asked Warren to come out. I don't think there will be any others."

Although leaves wouldn't be turning for another month, Labor Day always reminded the people in central Illinois that fall was slowly creeping south. September was a month during which many changes took place around their farm: crops were left to mature in the fields; schools resumed, days grew shorter, the landscape faded from the green of summer to the reds, yellows and browns of fall and the nights grew cooler. It was under these mild conditions, between summer and fall, that Gloria and Milburn deemed as a natural time for a wiener roast.

The family's plans turned out much as planned. Everyone they were expecting managed to show up. The weather was nearly perfect and the women had prepared a great variety and abundance of food, with everything from baked beans, American potato salad, deviled eggs, sliced tomatoes, creamed peas and lots of condiments for the hot dogs. Several people took joy in roasting the groups' wieners before filling their plates with the nice selection of foods.

Slowly, the brilliant red-orange sky along the western horizon obscured the turquoise sky overhead and ever so slowly darkness encircled the people around the bonfire. After eating and running around playing tag, the younger children mingled with the adults and were entertained by singing campfire songs. "Can we sing *Dum Dum Diddy* again," Sarah, asked her mother Helen.

"I don't think so," she answered. "We've already sung enough campfire songs and it's getting late. Time to go home!" she replied, and her statement acted like a catalyst for all the other adults to start gathering up their dishes, blankets and the rest of their belongings. Individuals slowly got up, said their goodbyes, and made their way back to either the house or to their cars.

As the fire winked out, night steadily closed in over the wiener roast site. Crickets chirped, katydids sang; occasionally a small flame flickered out of the red hot ashes until the only thing left was a steady curl of smoke twisting into the night sky.

CHAPTER TWENTY SEVEN

Saturday, October Tenth, 1942

The chilly October afternoon found Marianne outside the back door of the house watching her mother pluck a big, roasting chicken that Jonathan had killed minutes earlier by ringing its neck and she was happy she hadn't had to perform the distasteful duty.

Her mother dipped the lifeless carcass into scalding hot water for several seconds, lifted it out which created a great smelly cloud of steam that rose into the cool, pleasant fall air.

"Jonathan, can you set that empty, five-gallon bucket over this way so I can throw these chicken feathers in it?" his mother asked and looked admiringly at the lifeless steaming carcass in her hands. "This old hen's gonna taste real good for dinner tomorrow," she contentedly, grabbed a fist full of feathers and gave them a hard yank. "I think I'll make some egg noodles to go with it," she added. Old non-laying roasting hens like the one that she was stripping the feathers from were a cherished source of protein on the family menu, especially when served with handmade noodles, string beans and accompanied with mashed potatoes and gravy.

"It doesn't look very appetizing right now," Jonathan commented, wrinkled his nose and watched as his mother tossed another handful of wet, stinking feathers into the bucket. In a very short time she had stripped the bird down to its pen feathers and then worked carefully to remove those with the tips of her fingers.

Marianne was so intent on watching her mother expertly processing the chicken that she wasn't aware of the thirty-four Ford that slowly pulled up and came to a rest at the end of the sidewalk. Jonathan and Leon, however, standing a few feet away, quietly watched Bobby open the driver's side door and step out.

"Someone just pulled up," Jonathan said impassively and motioned nonchalantly towards the car. Marianne and her mother barely acknowledged him.

"Someone's coming up to the house," Jonathan warned and seeing that his warning didn't register he stated sharply in a low voice, "There' someone here!"

"Whaaat?" Marianne asked, focusing intently on the precision and skill her mother demonstrated from years of cleaning chickens, pheasants, rabbits, fish, and squirrels that were brought to her doorstep. She wanted to learn, even though she thought the job was distasteful. Someday, if she ever assumed the role of a housewife, the knowledge would be useful.

"Some guy just pulled up...and he's walking up here!" Jonathan repeated.

"What," she asked the second time and her brother nodded towards the figure stepping towards and Marianne who was completely caught off-guard by Bobby looking at her. Her face started to grow warm. Oh, no, she thought. *How could I get caught like this? I know he told me several times he might stop out, and now here he is at one of the worst times...right when I'm in the middle of helping my mom pluck a stupid chicken.*

"Hi," he said and flashed an awkward smile.

Marianne glanced awkwardly over her shoulder and wished she could turn invisible. "Hi," she managed to reply.

Totally oblivious to the subtle drama taking place, her mother said, "Marianne, can you roll up some of those newspapers and light them so I can singe the fuzz off this thing!"

The only option Marianne had was to act unperturbed and make the most out of her awkward situation by seeming to be unfazed. "Okay," she answered, picked several sheets and rolled them into a rather tight tube to use as a torch.

"Why don't you let me do that?" Bobby asked. "I help my mom do this all the time," he said and stuck out his hand.

"I'll light it," Jonathan said and grabbed the big box of farmer's matches his mother had left resting up against the foundation of the house.

Once the end of paper was in flames, Bobby held the torch steady while Gloria passed the fowl's carcass back and forth through them.

Jonathan puckered up his face and held his nose. "Yuck! I don't like to smell burning feathers!"

Gloria singed the last of the fuzz off and in almost no time she had the chicken gutted and washed with fresh water. "Jonathan, take these entrails out to the barnyard and throw them over the fence for the pigs," his mother instructed and pointed to the old, blue-enameled, circular basin where the offal rested. "I won't need your help any more, Marianne," her mother said, easily determining the boy was there to see her daughter.

Bobby looked uncomfortable. "I'm sorry I came at such a bad time. I can leave and come back later or some other day," he apologized.

Being unkempt, Marianne felt uncomfortable. Distraught, she stared at him for two or three seconds without answering. *He's here and I'm a mess,* she thought. *Maybe his suggestion to leave isn't such a bad idea, but he has already seen me this way...so what's the difference now?* "No, no, that's okay," she answered smoothly, recovering from her initial reaction. "Why don't you sit down on one of those lawn chairs over there while I wash my hands...and I'll be right back out?"

"You know, I'm not out here by myself," he confessed.

"You're not?"

"No! I ran into Alice at the drug store and she decided to come out with me; she's sitting in my car."

Marianne looked and saw Alice's face staring back from the passenger window. After having been somewhat enlightened of Alice's background, Marianne had come to view her more sympathetically. She smiled, waved and motioned for Alice to get out and come up to the house. Alice was slow to respond. "Get out of the car and come over here," she shouted and motioned again. "I'll be right back," she replied to Bobby and ran into the house without waiting on Alice.

Feeling fresher after washing up, Marianne put her hands under her nose and sniffed. Satisfied that she couldn't detect any lingering smells from the wet chicken, she gave herself a weak smile, changed her blouse, ran a brush through her hair, and applied a light application of perfume and a small amount of lipstick to her lips before she determined that she had done enough to make herself presentable.

Alice and Bobby sat chatting next to each other on the metal lawn recliner and only glanced up briefly when the heavy, wooden, screen door banged shut as Marianne came back outside.

"Hi," Marianne said pleasantly. "I'm glad you both came out," she said and took a seat on one of the two matching lawn chairs.

"Me too," Bobby answered.

"I'd like to apologize for intruding!" Alice replied.

"You really aren't!" Marianne answered.

The early evening air was turning slightly cooler. Alice pulled her light jacket up closer and snuggled her chin into its collar. "I've looked over here at your house many times out of the study hall windows and each time I have, I've always wondered what it'd be like to live on a farm so close to town. This summer, when you asked me to stop out, I just knew I had to sometime and today when I ran into Bobby and he mentioned coming out, I volunteered to ride along with him."

Marianne decided to tell a little fib. "You know, it's odd, but a couple of years ago, although I never told anybody, I would've given about anything to live in town!"

"Why'd you change your mind?" Bobby asked.

"That's easy to answer!" she said happily. "Things have improved a lot after we got a new basement, a furnace, running water and electricity." She didn't mention the toilet or Rocky.

"I think you're lucky," Alice stated without being shown around first.

Marianne felt Alice was only being polite and replied, "I like it!" without clarifying.

Alice was inquisitive. "Do you mind if I browse around?" she hesitantly suggested.

"Why don't I show you around instead of sitting here?" Marianne proposed, sensing Alice's curiosity. "Maybe we should go out to the barn where we'll find lots of interesting stuff on the farm," she stated.

Alice stood up. "I'd like that!"

Bobby didn't appear to have any intention of getting off the recliner. "Aren't you coming along too?" Alice asked him.

"Oh yeah! Sure I am; wait up!" he said and tagged along wordlessly.

Just inside the door, Alice saw several friendly, red hens scratching around in the loose straw looking for tidbits of grain.

A barn cat ran over and rubbed against her leg and she patted it on the head.

The quiet atmosphere was suddenly disturbed by the rapid beating of several startled pigeons that flew out through the open door of a stall.

"That's a beautiful little calf over there!" Alice commented. "Could I pet him?"

"Yeah," Marianne answered.

After spending several minutes petting the calf, they climbed into the hayloft. It still had the strong and pleasant odor of new-mown hay. In a wide gap between two bales, they discovered a mother cat and her young kittens whose eyes were barely open. Marianne picked up a yellow one and Alice picked up a gray one to hold.

Bobby started getting antsy. Although impatient, he sat on a bale of hay and politely listened to the girls chatter away while pigeons cooed in the rafters and down in the barnyard cows mooed. Finally he asked, "Where's your pony?"

"I'd say that he's probably back in the woods with the other horses," Marianne answered.

Alice ignored Bobby's inquiry. "I really like this barn because it's like a peaceful world in here and it's so full of life!"

Alice's unexpected comments finally convinced Marianne that Alice was a more sincere person than she had given her credit for. "Yeah, isn't it?" Marianne agreed. "I just love farms and barns and especially this one!"

"I can see why!" Alice said.

Bobby stood off to the side listening. "I'm sorry to interrupt, but I've got to be going!" he said and unwittingly ruined the unique circumstances that were allowing the girls to become closer friends.

Surprised at his sudden announcement, Marianne asked, "You're sure you can't stay longer?"

"I really can't. My dad's going to be waiting on me now by the time I get home. Maybe I could come back and see your pony and go horseback riding with you some other time, that is, if you don't mind!" he added.

"I'm looking forward to it. Just let me know beforehand!" she replied.

CHAPTER TWENTY EIGHT

Wednesday, November Twenty Fifth, 1942

Every student in the large room where the study hall and library were located adjacent to each other was familiar with the strictly enforced rules governing behavior to maintain peace and quiet. Any disturbance, such as talking or the passing of notes usually brought a swift reprimand. It was understood that the sound of even a pin being dropped on the floor would draw the attention of whichever teacher was the monitor. Several students cautiously tested the rules. Surprisingly, the strictest and most predicable rule enforcer of all, Mrs. White, didn't seem very interested in keeping the students absolutely quiet during last period of this school day and now several students were whispering or passing notes.

Positioned on a high platform behind them at the rear of the hall, Mrs. White occasionally used her wooden ruler to tap the top of her large desk to warn students about the consequences of breaching the rules. The restless students eventually came to realize that she was only allowing minor acts of freedom during the final few minutes of the last period of the day before Thanksgiving vacation was scheduled to start.

Marianne took advantage of the situation and hurriedly scribbled the last line in the note she was penning in response to the one Stella

Mae had slipped across several rows of seats to her a minute or two earlier.

Stella Mae,

Not sure I have answers for everything you asked! Yes - I'd like to go to the Christmas dance - even if I don't get asked, but I really don't want to go without a date. Would you? I'm hoping some brave guy will find it in his heart to save me from such an awful disgrace. Heard you were asked! Yes, I'm <u>sure</u> I'll be able to come into town this Sat. in the afternoon. Try to meet me in the drug store around 2 o'clock. We can talk more then!

Marianne

Marianne read it over once, twice and then folded it several times until it became a little two inch square bundle. She glanced anxiously over her shoulder at Mrs. White and handed it discreetly to the boy in the seat across from her. He gave her a questioning look. Marianne nodded very slightly and pointed her finger unobtrusively at Stella Mae, three rows away and closer to the tall windows. Making sure it reached its rightful destination, she watched the note pass slowly from hand to hand and row to row. How awfully embarrassing it would be for her if it fell into the wrong hands. Not until she finally witnessed Stella Mae getting it from a boy across the aisle from her did Marianne give a sigh of relief, pick up her book and start reading again. Two minutes before the bell rang for dismissal, the boy across from her made a "Pssst" sound to get her attention. "What?" she whispered and seconds later, after glancing back at Mrs. White, he handed her a new note folded in a similar fashion as the one she had handed off to him less than ten minutes before.

Marianne was written on top. She unfolded it and read...

> There's a rumor that two or three boys have been overheard planning to ask you to the dance. I know Bobby doesn't have a date yet. I suspect he'll ask you! Don't worry!
>
> Stella Mae
>
> P.S. Just in case I miss you after the bell rings I'll see you Saturday between 2 and 3 at the drug store.

Marianne looked across the study hall at Stella Mae and saw her friend waiting apprehensively for a signal that she had safely gotten the note. Passing notes was like playing cat and mouse, the students were the mice and the teacher the cat. If a note was discovered being passed, the study hall teacher would most often confiscate it, rip it into pieces and throw it into the wastepaper basket. Occasionally, a teacher would unfold a note and read the contents, which was an embarrassing situation. Although it was hard to read Mrs. White's mind, they knew her motivations and respected her lack of favoritism. At times she was misleading and had a tendency to play students like a cat's play toy: predictable when she had her prey in sight and stalk the offender without making a sound and then pouncing suddenly. The boy who had just handed Marianne the note rolled his eyes, held his fist up by his chest and pointed with a wiggling index finger towards the back of the room.

The metal wheels of Mrs. White's chair rattled on the uneven floor under her desk. Marianne nodded that she understood and tucked the note in between the buttons of her blouse where it would be safe.

Mrs. White stood, stretched and stepped silently down off the raised dais. Her action changed the atmosphere in the study hall instantly. Feet shuffled, sleepy heads rose off desks and strict decorum resumed. She walked down the long, wide aisle dividing the fifteen long rows of student desks in the study hall from that of the library's book cases and tables. Eyes watched her sort of drift along, seeming to be stalking some unwitting prey. There was no disappointment shown when Mrs. White calmly sat down on the leading edge of the small, low stage in front of the room and waited for the bell to ring.

Marianne looked at the library that was on the other side of the large room. A long bulletin board above the bookcases covered about a third of the walls length. On the bulletin board, the history teacher, Mr. Todd and his World-History students were keeping a running news update on the war. Small news releases, the names of enlistments and draftees, the bigger battles and a myriad of other timely war topics littered the board in a rough semblance of organization. At the top center of the board was a white banner that read **GUADALCANAL**. Underneath the banner, on a six-inch strip of red construction paper, someone had printed neatly in smaller block letters America Strikes Back. The display made her curious and unable to read any of the details, she decided to get up to take closer look just as the bell rang.

CHAPTER TWENTY NINE

November Twenty Eight, the Saturday after Thanksgiving, 1942

Brown leaves swirled around in the bitterly cold early afternoon air as Gloria parked the car in the ally behind the Atwood Grocery store. In her purse she carried a shopping list for a few necessities and in the trunk were two crates of eggs she planned to sell. Jonathan, Leon and Marianne had ridden into town with her; the two boys sat on the wide front seat close to the heater and their sister, a little cooler, but comfortable, was in back. The chilly, back-seat ride was far better than the cold walk she had anticipated before her mother had made the decision to come into town.

"Jonathan, before you go running off someplace and get lost, you need to get the eggs out of the trunk and carry them inside for me," his mother instructed. Instead of answering, he shrugged and pushed the door open.

"And be careful not to break any," his mother added.

Wearing clothes more suitable for appearances than for warmth on a cold day, a shivering Marianne asked, "Do you know about what time you're planning on going back home?"

"I'm not sure. I've got to get my groceries and then go down to the locker on the corner and pick up a pork roast from that pig your dad had butchered. After that, I think I'll look for a few other things I need," her mother answered.

Marianne reached for the door handle. "Then in about an hour or so?" she asked, trying to confirm an approximate time.

Her mother studied her wrist watch. "Let me think," she said. "I have other things to take care of besides buying my groceries and picking up the meat at the locker, but I also need to get home and finish making my beef stew. Your dad's picking corn," she continued. "He'll be tired and hungry and wanting some warm food on the table when he quits this evening, so we can't be in town too long," she explained, paused and thought for several seconds before giving Marianne an answer. "Since you're goin' to be over at the drug store, why don't I just meet you there around three?"

"Okay, Mom!" Marianne answered and hopped out into the cold, late autumn air and discovered the first snowflakes of the season drifting down out of the gray sky. *I hope Stella Mae's over there like she promised she'd be,* she thought and stepped into the rear entrance of the grocery store, walked down a short, narrow aisle of tinned goods and out the front door unto Main Street.

The busy summer crowds had long departed and Marianne found Main Street unusually deserted for a Saturday afternoon in late fall. She could see that most people's ability to get around was visibly being affected by gas rationing. The farmers, on the other hand, instead of coming into town were out in the fields trying to get their crops out of the fields after dealing with an extended wet spell.

As Marianne made her way down the street, she saw only two people walking along the store fronts and just a smattering of cars parked along the curbs in broken intervals; the town appeared forlorn.

As Marianne walked into the drugstore she heard, "He Wears a Pair of Silver Wings" by Kay Kyser being played on the jukebox and discovered more people than she expected. She noticed three men sitting at the counter loudly discussing the war, smoking and drinking coffee out of heavy, white porcelain cups. Two other highly animated men farther down the counter were engrossed in some other conversation she couldn't make out. Just inside the door a seventh grader was playing on one of the pinball machines as a couple of his buddies watched and gave encouragement.

Marianne's eyes automatically searched across the top of the high dividers separating the five booths. All she was able to see was a tall boy's head protruding above the last one and some female voices which she wasn't able to determine whose they were.

She and her girlfriends always tried to acquire the first booth and she expected Stella Mae to be sitting in it, but as she stepped around into the aisle dividing the booths and the counter, she saw her friend sitting in the third one and was facing the front of the store. Donna sat next to her and Evelyn sat across from them facing away. They were so engrossed in a giggling conversation that they didn't see her until she got close enough to speak. "Hi," she said, "I told you I'd make it!"

"Golly gee, Marianne, we were beginning to think you might've changed your mind," Stella Mae said.

"Well, I almost did because I didn't want to walk into town. Luckily my mom decided to come in to do some shopping," she said and slid in next to Evelyn. She noticed immediately that they were all smiling strangely at her. She studied their faces for a couple of seconds. "What're you guys talking about anyway?" she asked.

"Nothing really!" Evelyn said, obviously trying to keep a straight face.

"Come on, what is it?" she asked, thinking they had a bit of juicy gossip to offer.

"Oh, we were discussing several things, including you," Donna admitted.

"Me! Why me?"

"Well, because that cute guy, Bobby was in here no more than fifteen minutes ago and he was asking us about you!"

It didn't totally surprise her. "Why was he asking about me?" she asked self-consciously.

The other three girls glanced at each other devilishly.

"Guess!" Stella Mae teased.

For some reason Marianne suddenly felt defenseless and open. "I don't have any idea!" she answered and wished she could hide.

"Come on, Stella Mae, stop the suspense and tell her," Evelyn said.

"Bobby told us he wanted to ask you to the Christmas dance. He confided in us that he was afraid to ask you because he thought you might've gotten a date already or you'd turn him down!" Stella Mae stated. "He wanted our opinion!"

"He's sooo cute when he acts shy!" Evelyn stated as if she wanted him for herself.

Marianne was miffed that he would ask others and felt annoyed. "And, what'd you tell him?" she asked sharply.

Stella Mae shook her head in disbelief at her friend for acting so upset. "Nothing! Nothing! What could we say? We didn't want to say something that might keep him from asking you and we weren't sure how you felt."

"Thanks for that at least!" Marianne answered.

Donna looked as if she were going to explode. Her eyes sparkled with anticipation and she leaned forward. "Marianne, do you know that Ethan asked me to the dance?" she blurted.

"He didn't say anything to me!" she answered

"Well, anyway, if you go with Bobby, maybe we could double," she proposed and giggled.

Caught off guard by Donna's suggestion, Marianne was left speechless over the premature plans.

A new record dropped onto the turntable. "Be Careful It's My Heart" by Bing Crosby filled the air.

"Please say yes if he gets up the nerve to ask you!" Donna begged.

Stella Mae listening to the music and caught up in the budding adventures of every girl's idea of a romance replied, "How appropriate is that song?"

"Very!" Evelyn agreed. "Wouldn't it be wonderful if we each had a guy to ask us to the dance and we could all go together?"

Marianne liked the idea of going to the dance with Bobby; she just didn't like the plotting.

CHAPTER THIRTY

Friday, December Fourth, 1942

Marianne walked in from school and hung her coat in the new closet just inside the back door of the house. She was ecstatic when Bobby asked her to the Christmas dance and now she had a cloud of doom hanging over her head as she anticipated what her mother's answer would be if she asked for a new dress for the occasion. There was only a very slim possibility that her mother would agree to the purchase and Marianne was still searching her mind for a way to ease into the subject without having a confrontation. She found her mother working at the sink.

"Hi," Marianne said. Instead of responding, her mother dried her hands on her apron, pulled the curtains back and looked outside. "I see you got a ride home," she said casually.

"Uh huh," Marianne answered, and found herself lucky that the opportunity to request a new dress was already presenting itself. "Bobby was nice enough to give me a ride home so I wouldn't have to walk in this cold, miserable weather."

"Isn't he that boy who helped me singe the pen feathers off that roasting chicken?"

"Yes, that's him," Marianne replied; he would be her first date to a formal occasion and she was anxious to see how her mother would respond to the announcement. "A couple of days ago he asked me to the Christmas dance. I think it'll be so much fun because we're planning to double date with Ethan," she explained.

"He seems like a nice boy," her mother stated. "Who's Ethan taking?" her mother asked without inquiring further about Bobby. It was a surprise that her mother would show so little interest in her going to the Christmas dance and Marianne rationalized that asking for a new dress might be even more difficult than she had anticipated.

"Donna!" Marianne answered.

Her mother turned around and faced her. "Donna? You mean he asked Donna Marsh?"

"Yeah!"

"That's very nice!" Her mother answered, turned back to the sink and let the subject of the dance drop. "After you change your clothes, I'll need your help."

Faced with making her request, Marianne felt weak in the knees and warm around the neck. "There's something I need to ask about first," Marianne announced reluctantly.

Several slow seconds ticked by. "What's that?" her mother asked.

Deciding to attack the problem head on, Marianne replied, "Mom, you know this is going to be my first really big date…and it's the Annual Community Christmas Dance, so I was hopefully thinking that maybe I could get a new dress!"

Marianne ran her hand along her pony's rough coat of winter hair. "You know…I'm angry, happy, excited and confused," she stated into his big ear. "I'm sure I've told you before how I thought Bobby was going to ask me to the winter dance, didn't I? Maybe I forgot to tell you…well, anyway, you know what? He asked me today! This is my first date where a boy actually asked me to go somewhere really nice." Rocky twitched his ear. "Well, maybe I didn't mention it, but I meant to!" she said softly. "And then tonight, after school, I got up enough courage to ask Mom for a new dress. I was praying she'd agree but just as I suspected, she said no. Her refusal was like a stab in the heart and I found myself lost for words and I stared sniffling," she informed him. "I tried begging. Please,

please, Mom, I asked, but she just shook her head. And then, you know what? I was so mad I put on my coat, grabbed the egg basket and ran out of the house to give myself time to calm down and think clearly."

Marianne went to the grain bin and scooped up a bucket of oats for the horses. *I'll be so happy when I can do things without always asking my parents first; independence would sure be great! If I wanted a new dress and I could afford it, I'd just go buy it,* she thought. She poured some grain into the feeding trough and noticed Rocky was watching her with his mismatched eyes.

"I didn't tell you everything," she said. "As I was gathering eggs, I dropped four of them because I was furious and my fingers were so cold. Then for some reason, I started thinking positively. The profit from the eggs is used by my mother for extras, like Christmas gifts. I had a thought and came up with a neat plan!" Rocky's ears twitched again. "I figured it's so close to Christmas that I might be able to bargain for an early Christmas present and a proposition I could make without a fight. She and Dad wouldn't need to get me anything else, just a dress. Anyway, that's what I did. I went back inside the house...and you know what...my mother said yes! In fact, she wanted to know if I needed some new shoes too!"

Later, while Marianne was helping her mother prepare dinner, she considered the irony of accidently breaking the eggs which made her think of a solution to her dilemma. If she could have saved those broken eggs somehow and scrambled them for dinner, they would've tasted better than the steaks they were having. "Marianne, can you set the table and make sure to get the milk and butter out of the refrigerator."

Jonathan and Leon were still sprawled on the floor in front of the radio listening to "Captain Midnight" while everyone else sat at the table. "Will you two boys get up and come in here right now?" their mother demanded for the third time.

"Just a minute, Mom! We wanna hear the end of this program!" Jonathan replied, and having no intention of moving, he spread his elbows out, cradled his chin on his hands and got more comfortable

"We're not going to wait on you any longer. Remember, your supper's getting cold!" she said sternly.

Milburn leaned forward, sniffed the aromas wafting up from the table and smiled. The abundance of food, his hard labor and young pretty wife sitting to his left, four kids and a warm, cozy house gave him great satisfaction. It had been a cold day working outside taking care of the cattle and performing a multitude of other odd jobs. While working, he contemplated several future improvements he wanted to make around the farm. He picked up a platter of thick, sliced pork his wife had sliced off the roast and passed it on to Ethan. "You know," he said to no one in particular, "the government just announced that furnaces are gonna be rationed. If we hadn't bought ours when we did, we could've had a cold, old house for several more winters," he speculated and scooped a big T-bone steak onto his plate.

When the platter was passed, Marianne smiled at her good fortune and took a small steak.

CHAPTER THIRTY ONE

December Nineteenth, 1942
Community Christmas Dance

At exactly Six-thirty in the evening Bobby pulled up to the front of the house and flicked his lights off and on twice as a signal to Marianne and Ethan that he had arrived and would wait for them to come out. The three of them planned to drive back into town and pick up Donna at seven o'clock and then go straight to the dance.

The unusually large field house had been carefully decorated by a group of community volunteers during the day. They had created the semblance of a cozy café using several round tables inside a short, white, fence in one corner of the basketball court. Two long tables filled with refreshments partially blocked a gap which served as an entrance to the cafe. In the middle of one of the tables was a punch bowl surrounded by small glasses, paper napkins and several trays of decorated Christmas cookies, a special treat because of the sugar rationing that somehow was solved by a few dedicated women. On the other table was a selection of home-made snacks. Instead of pricing the punch, cookies or food, hand-printed signs requested donations for the servicemen fighting for the country.

In the middle of the south side wall of the field house, the large, raised stage was decorated on each side with colorful lighted

Christmas trees. Red, green and white crepe streamers crisscrossed overhead above the band. The lights in the field house had been adjusted for mood and a mirrored globe hung about fifteen feet off the floor in the middle of the basketball court. Three narrow beamed lights, one green, one red and one white were focused on the globe which caused the reflections to dance and swirl around the large space, making the dance floor and walls come alive with motion.

Dressed in a white sport coat, the high school band director stood mid-stage moving his baton in undulating arcs, directing a band which consisted of local volunteer adults and high-school students. A large, American flag was draped across the back wall.

Two men in military uniforms stood in line ahead of Ethan and Bobby. At the door the boys handed the attendant their tickets and the four teenagers walked into a magical dream world of music, swirling lights and romantic shadows. They discarded their heavy coats on a low bleacher and then looked around, taking in the dreamlike transformation of the large space. A very talented, former female student was up on stage singing a rendition of the band's first selection for the evening, "Don't Sit under the Apple Tree," and two or three couples walked out and danced across the floor.

"Wow," Donna said and hummed along momentarily and tapped her foot to the rhythm. "This is really neat!"

Bobby took Marianne's hand and led her out under the globe and into the swirling cascade of dancing lights. He pulled her close in an embrace, stepped back slightly and the two started doing a slow lindy. Occasionally Marianne glanced around and peeked at her surroundings. The new experience of a formal date, her first Christmas dance and the atmosphere created by the gathering crowd, live music and dancing lights thrilled her. Towards the end of the dance, after dancing so close, she was experiencing those reoccurring awakenings in her body, a not so infrequent sensation any longer which she equated as somehow being more adult. She smiled to herself. They danced twice more, stopping after slow dancing to, "You'll Never Know" and left the floor to sit out the next few tunes, have a glass of punch and visit with Ethan and Donna.

Presently, the four of them stood in line talking, greeting friends and waiting for a table to open up in the faux café. "Where do you find the gas to drive your car?" Ethan asked Bobby. "You don't have gas rationing coupons, do you?" Everyone was aware of the rules for purchasing rationed items and gasoline was the one most discussed, debated and watched in order to identify cheaters.

"I've had my ways until recently," Bobby responded. "I've been getting little dabs here and there from people who've been willing to sell me some out of their stored cars. The rest I've gotten from dealers who've been willing to sell me a little at highly inflated prices. Now, it's all coming to an end for various reasons. My dad says I'm either going to have to sell my car or put it up on blocks until the government gets rid of this gas rationing business! Dads got a gas rationing card for our family Ford and he's made it very clear that he won't give me even a pint. I suspect tonight may be the last time my thirty-four will leave the garage for a long time!"

"Why don't you put it up on blocks and sell the tires?" Ethan inquired. "You know, since they're rationed, I'll bet you could get a lot of money out of them!"

"My dad suggested the same thing and they're actually in pretty good shape," Bobby answered. "I'm just gonna put it in the garage and drive it, if and when I find some more gas.

Donna interrupted. "Look, there's a table open," she said, and pointed eagerly. She grabbed Ethan's hand and pulled him away. "Why don't you guys get us some punch and cookies while Marianne and I grab that table before someone else gets it!"

After refreshments, Marianne danced and chatted so much that later she only recollected the sequence of events in short flashes. She remembered conversing with lots of friends and dancing, mostly with Bobby, to many of her favorite songs. Ten minutes before eleven, the lights flicked on and off to warn everyone that there was only one more dance. After they found their coats and stepped outside into the cold, it was difficult to realize how the Christmas gala had slipped by so quickly.

Shivering from the cold, Donna slid into the back seat and exclaimed, "God, is it cold in here!" and snuggled up close to Ethan, encouraging him to put an arm over her shoulder. "The Christmas dance was really loads of fun, wasn't it?" she chirped happily.

"I thought so!" Marianne answered through her chattering teeth and pulled her coat up tightly around her.

Bobby put the key in the ignition and pressed the starter. On the first try the cold engine sounded as if it had no interest in coming to life. "Oh no," Bobby complained and shook his head in disbelief. To have car troubles at any time was a big pain, but to have car troubles at a fun time like this was a horrible thought. "Maybe I should choke it a little," he commented.

"That'd be a good idea," Ethan agreed and leaned forward and looked over the high back of the front seat. "Just be careful you don't flood it!"

Bobby pressed the starter again. The engine caught, ran for a few seconds, coughed and died. "Maybe you choked it too much. Push the choke in a little and give it another try," Ethan suggested as if Bobby didn't know how to start his own car. "I bet it'll run this time!"

A few minutes later Bobby pulled up in front of Donnas' house, turned off his headlights and left the car idling. Donna giggled from the back seat.

"Once the heater warms this thing up, I'll need to turn the engine off to save enough fuel for me to get home on," Bobby said and looked over at his date. "You're not cold, are you?"

"Just a little, but that's all right," Marianne answered without moving.

Early the next morning, Marianne poured a large helping of grain into Rocky's manger and patted him on the neck. "I've got thing's to tell you this morning," she said and started on a litany of topics. "Last night Bobby kissed me on the lips several times. At first I didn't know what to do and then with a little practice I think I finally got the hang of it," she told him and kept on talking for another ten minutes.

CHAPTER THIRTY TWO

Sunday, February Seventh, 1943

About a month before, the Christmas of 1942 offered few gifts and even fewer surprises. Most of the family's gifts had been practical, such as socks, belts, underwear or other mundane items. Everyone got something, even Marianne after accepting the deal for the dress. Their Christmas gifts had been limited somewhat by the conservative nature of their mother and by government's rationing of essential products that were needed by the military. Although the war seemed far away, its effects imperceptibly crept into their daily lives and on this Sunday it wasn't much different. Milburn, as was his habit, was eager to relate events while they were still fresh in his mind after reading the Sunday paper.

Living on a farm and producing one's own food brought an abundance and variety of things to eat that most urban families could only dream of. It was true that some city dwellers grew victory gardens, had chicken coops or raised rabbits to make up for the restrictions, however, none of these people came close to matching the quality or quantity of food a farm like theirs could produce. Many farms in the mid-west produced their own beef, pork, poultry and eggs which they consumed and sold. Their large gardens supplied most of their vegetables, which they ate fresh in season, canned, or stored in root cellars during the other months.

The only commodities Milburn's family didn't have an abundance of were those rationed items which they didn't produce, such as processed flour, coffee, and sugar; honey from their bee hives was a good substitute sweetener.

Anyone living on meager meat rations would have looked at this dinner table with disbelief, bulging eyes and drooling mouths. On a ceramic platter in the middle of the table a big, pork roast, surrounded by carrots and potatoes, ready to be sliced, sat steaming. Other savory fare filled the rest of the table's surface. Milburn studied the food. "It's time to say grace," he said and lowered his head.

"God …we ask that you look after our service men and women and keep them safe from harm. For any who may fall in combat we ask that you take them into heaven with open arms and give them comfort." Milburn felt almost guilty ensconced in his home while much of the world was in turmoil. He paused to gather this thought before continuing, "And please, God, look after those unfortunate souls who are caught in war zones!" He looked up briefly at his family. "Please bless this food," he added and paused a few seconds before concluding with, "Amen!"

"Does everyone have everything they want?" Milburn asked, anxious to start relating what he had learned without having any distractions. "I think the war's startin' to turn around and go our way," he said, theorizing from all the facts he had recently acquired from reports on his new radio and from this Sunday's paper. "On Tuesday," he said, "The long battle over Stalingrad has finally ended when the entire German Sixth Army surrendered. It's a great victory for the Allies," he added. "I read that it's the first time the German people have ever been informed about any of their army's defeats," he emphasized. "The article's author made a lot out of that point," he added. "It's good that the Nazis are beginning to get what they really, really deserve and this war, unlike the First World War ain't goin' to end until they're completely defeated!" he said emphatically.

Interrupting his father, Jonathan put his hands on top of his head as if he were a Nazi soldier surrendering. "Comrade, comrade," he said while Leon pretended to be shooting a rifle. "Bang, bang,

bang," he repeated several times and his father shook his head and rolled his eyes.

"Another thing," Milburn said, "I read that in North Africa, Rommel is still retreatin' and the Allies have Libya under their control. In the Pacific at Guadalcanal, they're sayin' it seems to nearly be secured," he declared, speaking authoritatively. He was never sure where all the places he mentioned were located. "Although I firmly believe the war is going better for us, I don't understand the announcement that some further rationin's bein' considered!"

An immediate response came from his wife. "What kind of rationing are they talking of having now?" she asked.

Her husband's face reflected a reluctance to say. Milburn was one who thought ahead. He took a long satisfying sip of coffee that he had squirreled away over two years earlier, once a common luxury, before rationing started on some commodities during November of forty-two. Four days before, the government had placed restrictions on additional items.

"What is being rationed this time?" she asked.

"You're not goin' to like what I tell you," he said.

"Why?"

"Because startin' this coming Tuesday, shoes will be added to the list!"

"Nooo! That leaves only Monday before they start rationing them she said in disbelief. "You're joking, aren't you?"

"I wish I was...and you know somethin'; I'm thinkin' that maybe it'd be a good idea to pick up the kids from school tomorrow and go straight to Decatur, and, if possible, buy shoes for everybody...that's if we can still find any. I'll just bet you, a dollar-to-a-doughnut, lots of people are gonna have the same idea who have more time or live closer to the stores than we do. Them people will probably beat us to them," he surmised. "I think we have to try anyhow, don't you?"

Without debating the issue, she said, "I think it'd be a good idea to get each of the kids a pair and you some new work shoes also."

"And maybe a pair for you too," Milburn replied, smiled and took a sip of his precious coffee.

CHAPTER THIRTY THREE

Friday, February Twelfth, 1943

Earlier that morning Marianne was given an assignment by her English teacher to do a three page career paper. It was an assignment she thought that she would enjoy yet wasn't anxious to start. Drowsily she looked over at the study hall's frosted windows, yawned, shook her head to shoo away the cobwebs and reluctantly decided that now, instead of later, would be a good time to begin. She gathered up her things and walked to the back of the room and asked permission to use the library.

After putting her folder and the book down on one of the long tables, she went to the shelves and selected a book on nursing and removed the N volume out of the set of the encyclopedias. Taking no immediate interest in the encyclopedia, she opened the book, stretched, put her hand in front of her mouth and yawned again.

After debating what to report on, Marianne still wasn't sure why she picked nursing. When she was first given the assignment she had considered writing her paper on veterinarians because of her love of animals. She took a stack of 3x5 cards out of her folder for note taking and started reading. When another student approached and dropped a tightly-folded square of lined paper on the table next to her elbow, she was too engrossed in the subject to notice. "Pssst,"

Phyllis sounded between her lips, tapped the table and whispered, "In P.E. last hour Stella Mae told me to give this to you."

Slowly Marianne unfolded the note, flattened out the wrinkles to the best of her ability with the palm of her hand pressed against the table top.

> Hi Marianne,
>
> I can hardly believe what I just overheard because you hadn't mentioned anything about it to me. Bobby was telling Billy, one of his buddies who has a locker next to mine that you won't date him anymore. I heard him say that he feels you think you are too good for him. I'm sure he said it loud enough for me to hear on purpose. I suppose he thought I'd let you know how he feels. I grabbed my books and ran. It can't be true, can it? I don't mean that you think you're too good for him. Why won't you date him anymore? You two have had such a thing going? I know it's not any of my business, but He's such a sweet guy! Meet me by the front door... right after school.
>
> Gotta run,
>
> Stella Mae
>
> P.S. If you want to go to the basketball game tonight let me know!

After reading the note twice slowly, Marianne folded it in half and tore it into tiny slivers. She could not believe that breaking up with Bobby would have any repercussions after explaining very clearly to him why she didn't want to date him any longer. Keeping her independence was foremost in her mind and then, after he had tried making some physical advances toward her, she realized that, as a freshman, a committed relationship was all wrong for her.

Granted, he was good looking, a nice guy and fun, however, Marianne was dead serious about not wanting to lose her free spirited independence. She wanted her freedom to succeed and she knew that she would have to avoid romantic entanglements to have it. *I'd rather just date around and test the waters; it's easier, safer and a lot more fun!*

Marianne thought of Barb as an example of what not to do. Barb was restricted in her choices of things to do because of her relationship with Richard. *That's not for me. I don't need anyone controlling what I do, where I go or what I think. Maybe! Uh huh! Just maybe there'll be some time in my future when I might think differently. Tonight I'm gonna explain to Stella Mae and give her the reasons I stopped going out with Bobby. I know she'll keep it a secret!*

"Tonight's basketball game's going to be loads of fun," Marianne whispered under her breath. She walked over, threw the slivers of paper in a wastebasket, went back to the table, sat down and picked up the book on nursing. She flipped it open and started skimming through it.

Just before the game was to start, Marianne, Stella Mae and three other girls found places to sit together four rows up in the bleachers at the far end of the field house and away from the entrance.

The first game had already concluded between the rival freshmen and sophomore basketball teams when they took their seats; Atwood winning against Arcola. During the thirty minutes between the freshmen and varsity games the girls sat and talked as the scoreboard clock ticked off the minutes between the competitions.

On the bleacher, just above them, Joanne, another classmate huddled amid friends, making the large group of girls appear to be like a clutch of baby chicks. She leaned forward and asked, "Are any of you going to stay for the after game dance tonight?"

Halfway turning around, Marianne answered, "We're all staying except Irene because she needs to ride home with her dad! How about you guys?"

"We're all planning to stay," Joanne said just as the Atwood's cheerleaders bounced out onto the floor, rousing the home fans into wild action. The cheers, whistles and shouts drowned out any attempt to talk for several moments.

Once the din died down, Marianne turned to Stella Mae, "Isn't it neat that we've gotta couple of cheerleaders that are guys,"

"I think it's amazing!" Irene replied.

"It seems a little odd, if you ask me," Joanne remarked.

"You really think so?" Irene asked.

"Yeah! Of course I do!"

Marianne looked around at Joanne and said in defense of Dwayne and Bob, the two male cheerleaders, "Colleges have guys on their cheerleading squads, so what's so wrong with us having some on our high schools?"

Joanne shrugged her shoulders. "Yeah, I guess so," she said and tried to let the topic drop.

"Don't you think he's kinda cute?" Stella Mae asked and looked at Marianne for a response.

Which one?"

"Maybe they both are, but I think Dwayne's the cuter of the two, don't you?"

"I can't make up my mind!" she said and studied the two male cheerleaders for a moment. "Yeah, I guess he is, sort of," she added and looked again. Marianne joked, "I don't think any of the upper class girls are fighting over him and if he's not taken, but why would we want to take any of their leftovers!" They both giggled uncontrollably for several seconds.

"Well, I would guess that also leaves Bobby out," Stella Mae snickered.

Marianne chuckled softly. "Yeah, I suppose so!" she replied and all five girls broke out laughing just as the loud warning horn blew for the varsity game to start.

CHAPTER THIRTY FOUR

Friday, April Ninth, 1943
Marianne's Fifteenth Birthday

Marianne came home from school in one of the best moods she had experienced for some time. Two of her good friends, Stella Mae, Donna and a couple other close classmates had given her a small birthday party during lunch period. It was a small but thoughtful gesture. They sang happy birthday, gave her handmade cards, two Bakelite bracelets and some ribbons.

At home there was the promise her mother had made to her that morning: she was going to bake her a cake, even though sugar rationing was making pastries rare.

Walking home she found the spring weather was cooperating with mild temperatures and a bright sky to keep her spirits up. The sun flashed in and out of the scudding clouds as a light breeze blew across the fields from the west. Dandelions blanketed all the grassy areas around the farm and a few daffodils and narcissus were blooming along the fence bordering the backyard. Thick grass had finally filled the scars around the foundation where the soil had been replaced, graded and seeded the year before. "What a beautiful day to go for a ride," she said to herself and scaled the two gates in the fence of the pasture in front of the house.

Baking aromas greeted her at the door and assured her that her mother had kept her promise.

The fifteen year old walked happily into the kitchen. "I'm home Mom," she announced and saw her mother flash a sly, foxlike smile. "Hi," her mother responded with a broad smile. Marianne's head swiveled around in every direction, curious to see what kind of cake was scenting the air. Before rationing, home-baked cakes were common; now they hardly existed. Chocolate cake smothered in chocolate icing was her favorite, but she held out little hope for a cake like that; it was an impossible dream.

"You baked me a cake?" Marianne asked, with little concern.

Her mother responded stone faced, "What makes you think I went and did that?"

Slightly worried, Marianne looked around the kitchen again for any telltale sign of what was making the sweet odor that was lingering in the air. "Because I even smelled it outside and my nose doesn't lie."

"I thought maybe you'd forgotten about the cake. I wanted it to be a big surprise at supper!"

"You can't hide that smell, and anyway, it's still a really nice surprise because I didn't think you had the ingredients to make me one," she confided.

"I finagled with the grocer to get one ingredient. Everything else I had!" her cake loving mother answered.

"Where is it?"

"Look in the cabinet above the plates."

Marianne peeked. "It looks really yummy. Thanks, Mom!"

"Well, it's not fancy, just a small vanilla sheet cake with chocolate icing, considering...!"

Marianne's mouth watered. "I'm going to go change my clothes and come right back in here and help with dinner!"

"I won't need any help until around seven," she replied. "Your dad's busy in the field over across the road getting it ready for planting and I'm pretty sure he won't be in for dinner until after dark. I'm guessing around eight or so," she advised.

"Then can I go riding for a little while?"

"Be back in here around seven and make sure your chores are done," her mother declared.

CHAPTER THIRTY FIVE

June Seventh, 1943
Marianne's First Job

Marianne's car door swung open. "Thanks, Dad," she mouthed softly and walked over to the train platform and stood, surrounded by several other people in the cool morning air. With a ten-cent ticket in her hand she waited for the train to arrive from the west which she planned to take to Tuscola for her first job which she was eagerly looking forward to begin.

Before school had let out for summer break in late May, Melanie, her first cousin from the small village of Garrett, asked if she would like to work as a waitress in a new little restaurant in Tuscola. Melanie informed her that the job paid thirty-five cents an hour and she could keep all her tips, probably no more than a nickel here or a dime there! At first Marianne was apprehensive because she was only fifteen years old, and then Melanie told her that no one would question her age if she said she was sixteen. She also found out that the restaurant was right across the street from the train depot, making it possible to use the convenience of the B&O railroad and that she wouldn't need to bum a ride in someone's car. "It'll be a lot of fun," Melanie promised, "and you'll be making your own money!"

The young working girl nodded and said, "Hi" to a couple of older people she knew and smiled at some less familiar faces. She listened to Clyde Walker's Morse code key clacking away through the open window of the depot and it made her vividly recall the image of him coming up to the house in the rain to tell her about Ethan's accident.

After a bit, she started thinking, yielding to her private thoughts of this new experience she was pursuing. *The thing I'm going to miss most is not being able to ride Rocky as often. I'll never forget the look on my mom's face when I told her I was thinking of working as a waitress this summer. She was so surprised at my announcement she wrinkled her forehead and gave me a blank stare. I thought she was going to ask why or tell me I couldn't do it, but she didn't; instead, sounding a little peeved, she said that I'd still need to do my work around the place and take care of my chores. Her reaction really caught me off guard. I was prepared to tell her I'd be willing to give up almost anything to work with Melanie and say to her that it won't be much different than when I'm in school. I understood there'd still be chores for me to do and things to do around the house. I still have to gather the eggs in the morning, but Jonathan said he'd gather them in the evening for me if it became necessary.*

A train whistle blew a series of warnings as it approached a crossing a half-mile west and blew again, sounding louder just before it crossed the railroad bridge over the Lake Fork River. The deep throated sound snapped her thoughts back to the present and she noticed that her stomach was suddenly churning from the anticipation of the day ahead. In less than thirty seconds the train would blow its whistle at the street crossings a block west and pull into the station with a rumble, screeching brakes and a big release of steam. The conductor would step out, say, "All aboard," and the new adventure would literally move Marianne a big step towards adulthood.

Feet shuffled around her. A young mother that Marianne had seen before but didn't know, picked up a small shopping bag and took hold of her little girl's hand nervously. Two men stepped out of the depot just as the train screeched to a halt.

Marianne followed the lady with the young child up the steps into a middle car and found an empty window seat. Out of her window she watched the conductor check one last time that all the passengers had boarded before he signaled the engineer and stepped aboard also. The engineer released the brakes and applied a little throttle. The steam engine chugged and she felt a slight lurch when the slack came out of the couplings between the cars. Shortly, the conductor came by and took her ticket. Minutes later, farm fields slid by like patches on a quilt as the steel wheels clacked against the rails and smoke from the engine swirled and rolled past her window and drifted off in a string of gray clouds across the landscape.

Twenty minutes later she walked across the brick-paved street towards the restaurant situated above the street on a raised sidewalk. Two large windows peered back at her, one on each side of the restaurant's green-edged, front door. She straightened her dress, fluffed her hair with her finger tips and stepped into the Track Side Café. "Good Morning," she said cheerfully, using her best charm to create a positive impression.

The smell of new paint and varnish mixed with the aroma of food reminded her that this was the first day the small café was open to customers. A counter along the west wall occupied about three quarters the length of the interior. A single dining table sat in the window the end of the counter. Five other square tables were lined up in a row down the middle of the floor space between the counter and four booths along the east wall. Visible in a pass-through from the kitchen at the far end of the counter was Bud Rayborn, the owner and cook. He looked up and waved with a spatula and said, "Morning, Marianne!"

"Good morning," she replied back cheerfully

Already busy behind the counter, Melanie was serving eggs, toast and coffee to two business men, the first customers. "Hi, Marianne," she said and smiled.

The week before, Marianne had spent two days with Mr. Rayborn and Melanie getting instructions, rehearsing and having her responsibilities clarified. Now that she was trained, she was anxious to try her new skills. "Talk to you later," Marianne replied to her cousin and rushed to grab her apron, pencil, and a note pad to take orders. Two railroad workers came in, sat down at a red-checkered, oilcloth-covered table and waited for service.

Shortly, the counter was lined with customers sitting on the stools. Busy at the counter, Melanie hadn't been able to help Marianne take any orders of the people filling the tables and booths. The two young waitresses struggled through the morning rush until ten o'clock. They each took brief breaks and then got nearly overwhelmed again from eleven until one-thirty in the afternoon. It appeared that they would earn every nickel and dime that came their way.

At five o'clock in the afternoon, shortly before their train was to arrive, both girls were relieved of their jobs by a young married woman. Although Melanie had found a ride to work, she had been unable to find another one home in the afternoon, causing her to take the train to Atwood, the nearest stop to her home.

Sitting together on the train, Melanie commented, "God, I'm glad that day's over," and wiped her forehead pretentiously, then she dramatically sprawled out her arms and legs out in a mock state of exhaustion.

"Oh! Me too," Marianne sighed and massaged the side of her neck. "I still can't believe how busy we were all day!" she said, happy to be leaving after thinking that Bud might ask her to stay for the evening rush.

"We really, really were, weren't we?" Melanie recalled. "A couple of times I was worried we wouldn't be able to keep up...but we did it, didn't we?" she stated proudly.

"We sure did," Marianne answered and peered out of the train window. The only changes she detected from that morning was that the fields were drenched in bright sunlight and sliding past in the opposite direction. Anticipating that she would feel more adult and more independent after a day paid to work, she didn't; however, she felt nicely compensated because she met several new people and earned three dollars and seventy-five cents in tips after they divided their money evenly and each gave a dollar from their extra earnings to Bud's son, working as the busboy and dish washer.

The two girls stood on the train platform in Atwood and talked next to the station's black high-wheeled baggage cart. "How're you getting back to Garrett?" Marianne asked, somewhat concerned that Melanie might be forced to walk two miles home, if she walked back down the tracks or closer to three miles, if she walked around the road.

"I'll walk, if I really have to, but I think I'll be able to scrounge up a ride over at the drug store with someone going east, or I'll go out to the filling station on the highway," she said, referring to Route 36 that ran between Kansas City and Indianapolis.

"Are you going to be riding the train in the morning?" Marianne asked.

"I don't think so," Melanie answered. "I can hitch a ride to Tuscola with my neighbor every morning. Maybe I'll to need ride the train home every afternoon...and you know that's a bummer for me. Maybe I'll get lucky and find a ride in the afternoons!"

They walked across the street. "I gotta go," Marianne said.

Melanie took several steps toward the drug store. "And I've gotta go find a ride home!" her cousin replied.

"I'll see you tomorrow at work," Marianne said.

"Okay," Melanie answered. Marianne turned away. On the short walk home, she contemplated how well her day had gone and of the money she had earned. One worry she had and couldn't get out of her mind was what the consequences would be for being gone all day; she was anxious to find out. *I know I reminded my mom this morning that my waitressing wasn't much different than being in school and I think that it might've made her feel better. I'll definitely have to change my clothes in a hurry and help her with anything she asks me to do, just to prove to her that I was right. After supper, when I get all my chores done, maybe I'll still have time to ride Rocky.* She stopped at the end of the lane, looked up at the house, kicked a small rock and ran without stopping until she reached the back door.

CHAPTER THIRTY SIX

Detasseling Corn, Mid-summer, 1943

Marianne paced back and forth across the kitchen, very apprehensive about detasseling corn for the first time and was utterly dismayed at her brother's lackadaisical behavior. She peered at the wall clock for about the umpteenth time. "The truck from DeKalb's is supposed to pick us up at the grain elevator in about twenty minutes," she growled at Ethan. "Why aren't you ready yet?"

"Because," he snapped back while trying to get his stuff together after oversleeping.

"We're going to be late and if we are, we'll probably get fired before we even get started," his irritated sister exclaimed, trying her hardest to prod him to hurry along.

"You should know, since you got fired from your last job," he said sarcastically.

Even angrier now, Marianne's face turned deep red. "It wasn't for me being late; it was over breaking one stupid plate! And I didn't get fired...I quit!" she shot back and returned to jabbing at him with little dart-like comments which she felt justified in doing because she had organized her things the night before and he hadn't. "If you hadn't been so stubborn about not getting your stuff together last night because you stayed out so late with Donna, you wouldn't be in such a rush now!"

"I was too tired when I came home!" he moaned.

"Like lazy, you mean!"

"Could you fix me a baloney sandwich?" he pleaded, still trying to get socks on his feet.

Marianne stared at him in disbelief.

"Come on and do it, please!"

"Okay, but I'll tell you one thing. This'll be the last time, so don't ask me again tomorrow because if you do, you'll go hungry!" she snapped back.

To avoid getting entangled in their squabble, their mother stood silently by watching and listening. Finally unable to stay calm, she said, "Finish your toast, Ethan!"

Ethan forced his foot into his shoe, grabbed the toast, shoved a corner of it into his mouth and held it there while he finished lacing up his shoes.

Playing in the background of their noisy dispute was a new radio tuned to an agricultural station. "Shhh," their father hushed and waved his hand for them to stop fighting so that he could hear the weather forecast. *Expect temperatures in the low nineties today with high humility across the region. Scattered Rain and thunderstorms are expected this afternoon over a wide area of the state with most of it likely accruing across the center section of the Illinois in a line generally running between Kansas City, Missouri to Indianapolis, Indiana. And now for the futures market report we turn*...and before the announcer finished, Milburn turned it off. "Well, it looks like it's goin' to be another hot one today," he stated. "You kids'll need to hurry if you're goin' to make it. I'll be out in the car," he announced and got up from the table.

At two minutes before seven they approached a large, red truck with high sideboards parked along Main Street in front of the elevator office, waiting to transport young crew members out to the corn fields. **DeKalb Seed Corn Co.** was printed on the door in large letters with Tuscola, Illinois printed in smaller letters underneath. Separating the two lines of large type was the logo of an ear of corn with wings and with the company's name printed on the ear.

Looking impatient, the driver sat with his door slightly open, smoking a cigarette. He flipped an ash off the end, took another deep drag, blew a stream of smoke out from between his lips and flipped the butt down on the pavement. It appeared that they were the last ones to arrive. Several teenagers he had picked up along the way from Tuscola were huddled in the bed of the truck while four wide-awake boys horsed around out on the ground.

Milburn slowed, swung in a wide u-turn and parked next to the Dekalb Seed Corn truck. Marianne and Ethan grabbed their lunch boxes and jumped out before their father turned the car around, parked, got out and headed for the drug store. In the calm, warm air a quarter mile away, a deep-throated train whistle blew long and steady. The sound reverberated between the buildings and in a few seconds, a large, steam engine clattered, clacked and rumbled through the crossing behind them, heading east, only slightly disturbing the quite morning of the small, mid-American farm town. At the very end of the long line of box cars were several flat cars loaded with heavy, military trucks and a few Sherman tanks.

Everyone, including Ethan, Marianne and their father turned and watched as the train cars flashed through the crossing and not until the caboose cleared it, did anyone move. Three young military guards with rifles stood out on the rear platform of the caboose and for the few brief seconds they were in view, they smiled and waved. Some of the kids waved happily back and the scene Milburn just witnessed struck him with the fact that the three guards weren't much older than the kids waving and waiting to detassel corn; it was an image he couldn't get out of his mind for a long time.

Six days later, Saturday evening found the fair-skinned, lightly-tanned Marianne with a sunburned nose walking with her date up to the Lamar Movie Theater in Arthur to purchase tickets for the seven o'clock showing. The last six days had been long, hot ones for her. She had gritted her teeth and toughed it out, and was proud she survived. After the first day in the fields, which was the most exhausting one, she had seriously considered quitting. Pride didn't allow her to quit after quitting her waitressing job where she had been making better money, and even though her muscles ached, she cherished her meager pay that made her feel somewhat independent.

Tonight, Marianne was looking forward to tomorrow, her day off, a Sunday and The Fourth of July, yet she was miffed to be working on Monday, the fifth when the country would actually be celebrating Independence Day. This was the second year in a row that Independence Day would be officially designated to be celebrated on odd dates. Instead of a big family picnic and celebrations, she would be back walking the rows of tall corn, her arms over her head, pulling tassels off the tops of seed corn stalks.

Marianne had met Janet, a tall dark-haired girl with pale, creamy skin and hazel eyes from Arthur only minutes earlier. The two stood off to the side getting acquainted while their dates waited in the slowly-moving ticket line to purchase tickets for "Five Graves to Cairo," one of the better war pictures of the year and only now getting around to the smaller theaters like The Lamar. "This is supposed to be a really good war flick with several big stars, like Ann Baxter, who I really just adore!" Janet related. "The movie I just can't wait to go see is the one that's coming out sometime later this month with Gary Cooper and Ingrid Bergman," she added, making small talk.

"Which one is that?" Marianne asked, wondering why she was unaware of the movie she was describing.

"For Whom the Bell Tolls," Janet answered knowingly and carried on enthusiastically with several other details until Marianne had a full review. "Earnest Hemingway wrote the story the movie's based on. The critics are saying it'll be one of the best movies of the year and it's over one hundred and seventy minutes long!"

Quickly calculating, Marianne exclaimed, "That's almost three hours!"

"Yeah, I know!" Janet answered. "They say it's so long that there'll be an intermission in the middle of it."

"Really?"

"Uh huh, and they're also saying it could even win an Oscar for the best movie of forty three!"

"Come on, you two," Roger, Marianne's date said and guided the two girls into the lobby where the smell of fresh popcorn filled the air and several people waited in line to be served. "I'll come back out and get us some popcorn after we find seats," Roger commented and motioned the other three to go ahead of him into the long narrow auditorium.

Although they had been toward the rear end of the line to see the popular movie, they were lucky enough to find four adjacent seats close to the middle of the theater before the lights dimmed.

Marianne liked movies; they lifted her mind out of the sheltered life of her small community and tweaked her desire for independence and adventure and kindled her spirit for new discoveries. After the lights lowered and" Future Features" ended, "Movie Tone News" came on the screen and presented world events using brief film clips and short descriptions. The first news featured American troops in the Southwestern Pacific using the strategy of "Island Hopping" to defeat the Japanese. The second offering of "Movie tone" showed brief shots of Kiska Island in the Aleutians off Alaska, which the Japanese had abandoned as their last foothold in the western hemisphere.

A comedy, "Der Fuehrer's Face," a Donald Duck cartoon was the next feature. It had been released in January and some people in the audience had obviously seen it previously, but the audience reacted with laughter as Donald Duck skewered the despicable Fascist killer. The sharp contrast between the "Movie Tone" newsreels and the cartoon made the audience feel that the protection and freedom of a democracy made them safe and able to laugh at one of the biggest despots of all time.

Later, over Cokes, the four of them sat in the restaurant next to the theater and reminisced about their summer's activities. Joe said he worked at a filling station and related an interesting observation. "You can't believe how people try to cheat on their ration cards," he informed them. "Last week a lady stopped by and asked my boss if she could get a couple extra gallons of gasoline. I'm not going to mention her name, but Gary, my boss, shook his head and pointed at the sign in the window forbidding him to do so. She acted like she was gonna cry and started pleading.

"'Please?' she asked and tried to look as pitiful as she could. She searched my boss's face for some sign that he'd relent and added, 'My husband broke his leg yesterday and now he's at Saint Mary's Hospital in Decatur and I don't have enough gas to get over there and back. Can't you help me...Please!'

"My boss lifted his cap, scratched his head and said to her, 'That's odd,' and looked at her real funny."

"'What's odd?" Joe said she asked.

"My boss answered, 'You mean he's out and about already and didn't let you know?'

"'What...wha...what do you mean?' she stammered," Joe said and gave a thin smile.

"'Well,' my boss said, 'it must be a miracle that his leg has healed so fast because I saw him about an hour ago going into the barber shop without a cast on his leg!'" Joe said, still relating what his boss told her and laughed along with the other three. "Anyway, we don't pump as much gas like we did last year but we're sure busy fixing lots of old worn-out tires like you can't imagine."

"Fixing tires and seeing people come and go all day is better than what I do!" Janet said and explained to them that her summer consisted mostly of hanging around the house, reading, being bored and helping her mother. "What about you, Marianne?" she asked.

Marianne was happy she wasn't hanging around the house and doing chores. Making some money and fluttering her wings at independence suited her just fine. She didn't want to divulge much about herself to Joe or Janet who she had just met or to Roger either, a junior with piercing blue eyes and blond hair parted down the middle who she had accepted a casual date without any romantic undertones. She simply said, "I'm having fun this summer, I guess. Up until a week ago, I was doing all the usual things and now I'm on a detasseling crew in Tuscola."

"That's hard and tedious work," Roger commented.

"Tell me about it," she answered. "It's hot but really lots of fun too!" she said. "We joke, laugh and sing songs to pass the time."

"And what about you, Roger?" Joe asked. "I know you help around your dad's grocery."

"Well," he said and swirled a straw around in his Coke, making the ice cubes clank, "that's true and I get to see people come and go all day just like you do around the filling station. I sometimes get bored stacking shelves and arranging produce. Most people who I see are shopping and don't want to spend much time chit chatting. I finally decided I wanted a little excitement instead of looking at the shelves lined with cans, apples in baskets and cuts of meat on display in a glass case. I weighed my options one afternoon as I was sweeping the floor and came to the conclusion that my dad didn't really need my help because of my two younger brothers...so last week I signed up for the Marines."

The other three stared open mouthed.

"You didn't really, did you?" Joe asked.

"Yeah, I really did!"

"How soon are you gonna need to report?" Marianne asked.

"They promised me I could finish my fall semester of high school first and that I won't have to report until the first of February when I turn seventeen!" he answered.

"Then you won't be in school in the spring, will you?"

"Nope!" he replied.

Even though Roger was only a casual date, his announcement caused tightness in her stomach and she immediately saw him in a different perspective, even though she didn't comprehend all the changes military service would cause him. One thing she knew for sure was that movies, sodas and chumming around with friends would soon be a thing in his past.

CHAPTER THIRTY SEVEN

Saturday, September Twenty-Fifth, 1943

Seeking time to think and wanting an opportunity to share some secrets with her pony, Marianne rode in a slow meandering fashion through the woods behind the house. She was relaxed on Rocky's bare back. Instead of using his reins, she used the pressure of her knees to indicate where she wanted him to go. If anyone were watching them, it might have appeared that Rocky was reacting to Marianne's wishes by reading her mind. To those who knew the two of them, there was little doubt that they understood each other like best of friends.

A half-hour crept by while she was lost in her thoughts. Eventually she patted her pony on the side of his neck. "You're a good boy," she said and ran her fingers through his thick mane. He tossed his head, reacting to her abrupt attention. "We both know you can be a little ornery sometimes, don't we?" she said and Rocky tossed his head again. Marianne patted him once more. "I love you, anyway!" she whispered and coaxed him to turn left by using a little pressure with her right knee.

Another fifteen minutes or so elapsed in silence again before she spoke. They were now away from the main woods and in a narrow three-acre finger of scattered trees that doglegged west and abutted Mossberger's thick, overgrown timber. The sky was clear with a touch of autumn scenting the air. The soft breeze wafting across the soybean fields to the south carried silken threads of spider webs along with it. During the middle of the week a light frost had finally eliminated the deer flies and other biting bugs, making this sojourn even more pleasant than most. She felt free. Varied species of disturbed grasshoppers flew up out of the grass around Rocky's legs. On the ground, the nuts from the hickory and oak trees crunched under his hooves. Eventually they came to the end of the fence and couldn't go any farther. "Whoa," she said and patted him on the neck again.

Marianne stretched out on her stomach along the ridge of Rocky's back, her feet atop his rump and her face resting on the back of her left hand that she had cupped over the top of his mane.

"Guess what? I was elected to the Homecoming Queen's Court," she said and patted his neck with her free right hand. "Everyone says it's such an honor, you know," she added and patted him lightly again and contemplated for a few seconds. "Being elected to the court over several other girls caught me totally off guard. What a surprise it was!" she admitted and grew silent again for a long time. "Let me tell you...I was really, really shocked! I still am, I guess, because the other two names on the sophomore ballot were girls more popular than me," she stated, nearly repeating herself. "I can't imagine winning. I don't know how many votes I got...it might've been by only one vote more than any of the others. I'll never know because a couple of teachers count them and they don't divulge the tally. But guess what? I won!" she said, carrying on with her dialog, a little dazed over the outcome and still working to get the fact to sink in. "That crazy friend of mine, Stella Mae, was the one who put my name in as a candidate. At first I was embarrassed and angry at her for doing it. Now I'm glad and I need to tell her so!"

Marianne carefully slid her feet off Rocky's rump, rolled her legs around and slid off onto the ground. As she did so, she picked up the pony's reins which she had left draped loosely over his neck and hadn't needed to use. Leading Rocky over to a stump of a tree which had been sawed down two years before, she sat down and looked out across the bean field at the family farmstead.

"You know, I'm happy I got elected to the school's homecoming court," she said with pride in her voice. It was unusual for her to feel like a princess but that is how she felt at that moment. "I suspect at least one of my friends might be jealous and a couple of Joanne's friends snubbed me. Mom didn't say much about me winning either and didn't compliment me. At first I didn't feel like I'd won anything. I thought people only voted for me because the other two candidates acted so aloof and sure of themselves! But I won, anyway!" she added.

"Let's go back," she said, got up off the stump and started walking. She held Rocky's reins lightly in her left hand to make him walk close behind where he could nuzzle her shoulder.

"Homecoming's next Friday and I've just got to go find a new dress," she whispered in his ear. "It's hard for me to believe that I can afford to buy my own with the money I made this summer and I won't need to ask Mom again," she said happily. Rocky nudged his muzzle against her shoulder as if he praised her accomplishment. "But, you know," she continued, "Mom will probably complain that I'm being irresponsible with my money." Marianne walked along for several more steps before she hopped up on Rocky's back again. "I'd better be getting back to the house to help with any chores Mom might have for me," she added and encouraged her pony into a trot.

The kitchen was filled with the wonderful odors of pies being baked. Her mother always made the most wonderfully delicious fruit pies with the flakiest crusts using lard rendered from their own pigs. Apple was Marianne's favorite and two tantalizing ones sat cooling in the middle of the table. She could almost taste and feel the wonderful texture in her mouth. Tonight at dinner she'd insist on having a really big slice.

"I'm glad you're back, Marianne, because as soon as dinner's over, your father and me decided to go visit your Uncle Fred's family," she stated. "It's been some time since we've seen them," she said in reference to one of her younger brothers.

"Maybe you might think about coming along too. I'm sure they'd like to see you," her mother remarked.

"They're nice, but not tonight!" Marianne replied, easing away politely from the subject. There was no way that she was going to sit and listen to her parents, her mother's brother and his wife talk about things that were mostly uninteresting to her. Jonathan and Leon would be expected to go along and only Leon would be happy because Ben, his cousin, and Fred's only child was Leon's age. Jonathan, five years older, would be bored. "I'd like to go, Mom, but I've got a date."

"I'm sure they'd like to see you," her mother cajoled again, twisting the guilt screws a little deeper into her daughter's conscience. Marianne easily ignored the comment. Forced occasionally over the years to go with her parents to visit a childless relative, she had more than paid her dues. On those visits she considered herself lucky whenever she had the opportunity to go outside and use a porch swing or some other distraction to avoid the adult conversations that seemed to have no end.

Being older now does have its benefits, she thought. "Please tell them hi for me!" she repeated.

Without urging her any further, her mother said, "Move those pies over to the counter, set the table and then come over here and give me a helping hand."

Marianne was maturing; her attitude was changing and she was learning to get along better with her mother. There still were times when she had to bite her lip and ignore her mother's comments, but all in all, the relationship between them was improving. Nevertheless, there were new disturbing emotions stirring in her which were still beyond her comprehension.

Several days earlier, she found reasons to question her feelings when she had become fascinated watching a mother robin feed its young in a nest in the tall shrub just outside her bedroom window. The mother fed her babies habitually and yet they always seemed hungry. Over time they feathered out and she wondered when they would finally leave their comfortable nest. After several days, she was sure they would be gone the next morning; instead, she found the mother still bringing food to them every few minutes. One morning the brood of baby robins seemed ready to fly away, and one more than any of the others showed more reluctance. Marianne decided that the anxiety of leaving a safe nest and flying out into a world of unknown consequences was holding them back.

That very night a storm with heavy rain and strong winds swept across the farm. The next morning the nest had only three birds remaining. Two of them huddled together, but the third, a more courageous one, stood on the rim of the nest flapping its wings as if it couldn't be held back much longer by the safety of their shelter.

The following morning only two were left and by noon when she checked the nest, it was empty. She peered out of the window into the yard and noticed the mother robin hurriedly flying from place to place feeding each of the three. Later that day, Marianne heard a robin making a loud ruckus in a back corner of the yard and hurried to see what the complaining was about, thinking she might be able to help. One of the farm cats ran past her with one of the babies in its mouth. Her last recollection of any of the four baby robins was two days later when she saw a speckled young robin land in the yard looking for a meal. It hunted stealthily for a worm and after she watched it for a few minutes, she came to the conclusion that leaving the nest early or staying had various consequences. The incident caused her to pose a question to herself. *I wonder if it is the one that was in a hurry to leave the nest, or one of the two that seemed reluctant to fly.*

CHAPTER THIRTY EIGHT

Friday Night, October First, 1943
Homecoming Dance

The light dimmed just as the band played the first notes of the Grand March making a hush fall over the murmuring audience that waited expectantly in the bleachers for the coronation ceremony to begin. Several more seconds passed. Up by the stage a spotlight was turned on and its bright beam slowly swept around the field house, eventually stopping at the entrance to the passageway at the end of the bleachers where the homecoming court was expected to emerge.

Nothing happened for several seconds, making anticipation grow. From the odd angle of the bleachers people struggled to see the king and queen's court enter the field house before filing across the gym floor to the stage.

Marianne waited toward the back of the short line suspecting that she was the most nervous of all because she was experiencing more than a minor tinge of stage fright, and it was messing up her stomach. Of the four girls on the Homecoming Court, only Mary Wilson, a senior, who was slated to be crowned Queen, seemed cool and relaxed? *Maybe she's like that because she was already on the court last year as a junior*, flashed through Marianne's mind and studied Mary's demeanor. If *she can be cool and collected, then so can I,* she reasoned and straightened her shoulders.

"Doesn't she look good?" Stella Mae commented, watching her friend walk out into the bright light and then follow Marianne's every step. "I'm so happy for her!" Stella Mae said.

"So am I," Donna admitted happily. "And me too," Barb added. "I should admit that I'm just a little jealous!"

"You're jealous and I'm a little envious," Stella Mae said, "but I'm still so really happy for her!"

Stella Mae's date grinned, looked at her and teased, "The same goes for me...now will you three hush so I can hear what's going on up there!"

The long rows of eyes watched the court participants file along in pairs, like a procession of royalty winding its way across the basketball court, up the temporary steps and onto the stage where the participants took their proper positions for the ceremony that was about to unfold. Marianne's and her football-player escort's position was just to the right of Mary Wilson.

The student-council president walked upfront to the microphone located mid-stage, paused and waited until the music stopped playing before he proceeded to introduce each individual on the court by name, starting with the freshman representative and ending with the king, John Edwards, and Mary, the yet to be crowned queen.

Marianne's eyes peered across the floor of the field house and scanned the rows of seated people in the bleachers. Never had she sought attention and now that she was getting some, she felt somewhat conspicuous. She started feeling warm and realized her face must be turning pink. *I hope no one notices*, she thought, felt panicky and worked to control her fear. She turned her head slightly sideways and studied one of the other girls on the court to see how she looked while she contemplated her own appearance: her new dress, the touch of makeup she'd applied and her hair style. *I know I look better than she does*, she thought, consoling herself and smiled.

The discomfort of being in front of a large body of people wasn't something Marianne had considered when she left her name on the ballot. She contemplated, *maybe I made a mistake,* and then instead of paying attention to what was happening on the stage around her, she let her mind turn inwards in an attempt to mentally escape her uneasiness and let her eyes scan the faces in the bleachers. *There's Stella Mae, Donna and Barb with their dates.* She looked up and down, back and forth at the two hundred or so people sitting across the floor from her. *I wonder where Roger's sitting. I know he's there somewhere because I've got a date with him.*

Somehow, and against her own judgment, she had accepted another date with him; however, she had held out until the last minute to accept because there were a couple of other boys she was more attracted to and she thought one of them might ask her. He never did. Time had been running out and she didn't want to get stuck without a date...how embarrassing that would have been. Later, through the grapevine, she discovered that both had intended to ask her but didn't because they thought she would have refused. "Why didn't someone tell me," she mouthed silently and then thought, *but, I can't really complain, can I? Roger's a nice guy and I think he respects me and besides, he's lots of fun.* Her eyes continued to search for some sign of him.

A small boy walked out of the wings carrying a purple velvet pillow with a tiara centered on it and his physical intrusion distracted her from searching any longer. Every eye followed his steps, and after a few theatrics, the tiara sparkled on top of the head of the beaming new homecoming queen. Last of all, and in a display of cuteness that nearly overshadowed everything that had happened before, a little tow-haired flower girl dressed like a fairy princess in a pale, blue chiffon dress with a giant, pink bow in the back walked up the steps, approached the newly crowned queen and handed her a large bouquet of deep red roses.

Donna eyed her friend on stage. "She's prettier than the queen," she stated proudly and loud enough for several people around her to hear, eliciting more than one or two smiles.

Later that night Marianne took her diary and sat down at her dressing table. She began to brush her hair, eyed her reflection in the mirror and searched for something deeper than just the image reflected back. Thirty brush strokes later, she put the brush down, emptied the center of the dressing table of her cosmetics, trinkets and other what-knots and started to write.

Entry: Oct. I, 1943
Dear Diary,

I had a really fun time tonight at the homecoming dance. Something I learned about myself is that I don't want to have the limelight...I don't care about being on stage or anything like that!

P.S. Roger is lots of fun but I don't want to get into a close relationship with him or any other guy...goodbye Roger. I hope we can still be friends though.

What Marianne didn't fully understand when inserting the P.S. was how girls her age could easily get tangled up in their emotions that often seemed beyond their control! One comforting option she had, which her girlfriends didn't have, was her four-legged friend. He never asked for anything and was always there to listen. When she shared her thoughts with Rocky, it gave her a release, comfort and the strength she would need to stay true to herself.

Fall came and went. The first snow fell between Thanksgiving and Christmas. Roger reported for boot camp which literally made her pledge valid to never date him again.

CHAPTER THIRTY NINE

Saturday, January Fifteenth, 1944

Life on the farm appeared safely incased in a cocoon of security even as the planet was in the middle of a colossal conflict. The house was warm, the electric lights glowed and there was always a variety of food on the table unlike most urban Americans who still felt the pinch of food rationing. Constant reminders of the war and the families' concern for Donald, the only person from either side of the family wearing a military uniform, seeped into their lives. It was like a gray film of sadness that took the brightness away from their lives and the short cold days of January reflected their mood.

The sun came up in a clear, cold sky and a weak attempt to raise the air temperature above the mid-thirties without any success. Most of their livestock sheltered up against the barn in the sun's weak rays. Across the wheat stubble to the west, a Northern Harrier hawk hovered, looking for small prey.

Around the breakfast table the family was eating oatmeal, toast and bacon and silently listening to the morning news on the radio. A commentator was giving a summation of military actions that had taken place over the last few days. He reported that in Burma the British forces had taken Maungdaw on the ninth of January. Next he stated that American forces were driven back from their attack on

Monte Cassino in Italy. The names of these places would be fixed in many Americans' minds for the rest of their lives.

"We've got a lot of work to do today," Milburn told his family without commenting on the battles, places, losses, gains, costs and endless other bits and pieces of information about the war as was his habit. It had became overwhelming. "Just as soon as you and Jonathan finish breakfast," he said, looking across the table at Ethan, "since we've got this break in the weather, I want both of you to go out and start cleaning the cattle stalls this morning."

Being in no mood to leave the warm kitchen, Ethan resisted. "But I thought we were going to help with the paper and metal drive today!"

"Yeah, we are," he answered coldly. "I was told we wouldn't be needed until around one o'clock in the afternoon because they want to give everyone time to get their stuff out to the street."

Ethan moaned, "Can't cleaning out those stalls wait until next week?"

"No, and if you two lollygag around in here and don't go out and get on it right away, you might not be going with me!"

"Which stalls?" Ethan asked disgustedly, although, he knew which ones his father was referring to, having experienced mucking them out many times before.

"Just the cattle stalls on the north side today. Next week we'll do the others."

The extent of his father's order meant less work and it made him feel better. Seeing no need to hurry, Ethan leaned back in his chair to make himself more comfortable.

Milburn gave his older son a stern look. "Like I said, the sooner you get started, the sooner you'll get finished. If you're not done when I'm ready to go to town, I promise that you won't be goin' with me!"

"Come on, Ethan," Jonathan prodded and got up from the table. He was looking forward to the waste-paper-and-metal drive for the war effort and didn't want to miss even one minute of it. "Let's go!"

Ethan wasn't keen on going out into the cold barn to fork and shovel manure all morning, although seeing that he had no other alternative he pushed himself heavily out of his chair.

Showing no sympathy, his father said, "You'll find the tractor and manure spreader out in the lean-to off the south side of the barn. You know where to find the pitch forks and shovels," he added flatly. "Spread the manure along the north edge of the west twenty and when you're done cleaning out the stall, break up a couple of bales of straw and spread a good layer down on the floor for bedding. When you're done, drive the tractor over to the other place and put it in the barn." They always referred to their other farmstead from which Milburn's mother had recently moved from as "the other place" which consisted of a house, barn, and other outbuildings.

Leon barely listened to the conversation going on around the table. Many times he had heard the conversations of what needed to be done, should have been done better or what had been forgotten to get done, and this one wasn't of much interest to him. "Can I go to town too?" he asked, seeking a new adventure.

"Sure! Why not?" his father answered. "You can ride up front with me where it's nice and warm and keep me company," he told his youngest son, knowing the cab of the truck would keep him warm, out of the way and safe.

"Don't forget, I'm going too," Marianne reminded her father, anxious to see Barb, Donna and possibly Stella Mae and several boys her age who would be there to unload the trucks, promising to make the scrape drive exciting.

Her mother started taking the morning dishes off the table. "Only if"...Gloria began, and Marianne finished her mother's sentence agreeably, "If I help you clean up the house first!"

A few seconds later, Milburn told his wife, "I should be comin' in to get cleaned up around eleven," indicating he wanted to have an earlier than normal lunch. "I'm sure the boys'll be done by then too," he added and pulled on his heavy work coat and picked up his hat and gloves.

The boys had a very difficult morning working in the stall where a stiff wind funneled in through the open door and whipped around them. The heavy, wet manure, trampled into the bedding made the work difficult. Their shovels were of no use because the packed manure, mixed with several layers of straw, had to be loosened with pitchforks. Once the stall was clean of the animal waste, Ethan returned the spreader to the open-ended lean-to and took the tractor over to the barn while Jonathan spread new straw down on the stall floor and put the shovels and pitchforks away. Finished with their duties barely in time, they hastily made their way to the shower in the basement of the house, showered, shampooed and got dressed in clean clothes.

A big block of cheddar cheese, soda crackers, butter and a pitcher of milk sat in the middle of the table. Simmering on the stove was a big pot of hearty beef stew, thick with cabbage and potatoes that also included carrots, celery and onions. Their mother ladled it out into white porcelain bowls which Marianne placed on the table, one at a time, in front of her father and her three brothers.

"Make sure you all dress nice and warm, especially you boys." Their mother remarked. "It'll to be freezing riding up in the back of that truck!"

"Yeah, Mom, we know!" Jonathan answered. Ethan looked knowingly across the table at him and rolled his eyes.

Their mother couldn't bring herself to ignore them. "You may know, but you two had better put on some of your warmest clothes," she reiterated. "And be sure to wear your hats with ear flaps," she added for good measure.

Ethan still wasn't able to resolve his irritation for shoveling manure out in a cold cattle stall all morning, "Yeah, yeah, we know, we know!" he smart mouthed.

Millburn thought Ethan's sarcasm reflected on him. "Dress anyway you want. Just don't forget, you're goin' to be ridin' in the back where it'll be a lot colder than workin' out in that barn stall!" he replied sternly.

Marianne, Donna and three other warmly-dressed girls stood talking inside the old building next to the slaughter house on Main Street, trying to stay warm while they waited over an hour for the first truck to show up. The empty building had been used several years for the storage of dilapidated furniture and other useless discards until recently when a junk man hauled it off. A large, double-sided, sliding door opened into the alley, making it a perfect place to collect and store the old newspapers, magazines, castoff metal pots, pans and other odd scrapes of tin, aluminum and copper the community would be donating to the war effort.

"I remember Barb saying that she was going to show up today!" Marianne replied after she and her friends had chatted for some time. "I wonder what happened to her?"

Donna looked around as if she expected to see Barb walk in at that very moment. "That's what she told me too!"

"Don't you suspect that once she got away from her house and her mother that she might've hooked up with Richard," Donna offered. "He's all she ever thinks of anymore, you know!"

Marianne slapped her gloved hands together to keep them warm. "She's really gone crazy over that guy!"

To get their attention and elicit a conversation, an eighth grade boy stepped over and asked, "Aren't you girls cold?"

Marianne didn't break the rhythm of slapping her hands together. "Uh huh," she grunted.

He gave her a broad smile. "I wonder why anyone would've thought it'd be a good idea to collect stuff when it's so cold," he asked rhetorically as he shuffled his feet around, attempting to stay warm. Donna and another girl glanced at him and Donna gave him a quizzical smile, thinking he had made a weak attempt to flirt with them. Seeing that the girls had come to the wrong conclusion, he stated sheepishly, "It's not really that cold," and blew into his cupped gloves. One of his friends snickered and lightly punched him in the ribs over the awkward situation. "Well, it isn't," he stated emphatically to his group of friends.

Vern, the owner of the building, stood nearby listening and felt compelled to answer the boy. "It was a unanimous decision to do it now. Everyone on the committee agreed that since most people around here aren't real busy this time of year, more people would be willing to give and participate. It looks like our predictions were right because we've got more volunteers than we actually need!" he added proudly.

"This is either going to be a long cold day or a lot of fun!" Marianne remarked.

"Or both!" Donna said and blew into her gloved hands.

The first truck arrived, stacked high with paper waste. Someone outside the building slid the door aside so that the driver could back his truck up until its tailgate extended a couple of feet into the empty cavity of the building. Shortly thereafter, everyone became warmer while unloading the loose piles of magazines and bundled stacks of newspapers. They piled up the magazines against the north wall and the newspapers tied together along the west side. Once the first truck was emptied and had pulled away, it allowed a red, International Harvester truck, heaped with old pots, pans and other metal discards to back in. Wanting to watch the unloading, the driver turned off the engine and hopped down out of his cab.

"Hi Vern," he said and the two men began an animated conversation lashed with laughter while the younger people unloaded the metal. The metal discards, worth more than the paper, grew into a jagged pile along the south wall.

"I can't believe people have so many things to get rid of," Donna said over the din caused by the metal being thrown into a heap. She grabbed a large skillet by its handle and gave it a toss. "Some of this stuff must've been stored for fifty years!"

"Maybe the women are giving them up because they're tired of cooking," Marianne said and aimed a metal sauce pan at the middle of the pile.

"Maybe!" Donna answered, they both giggled and threw two more old skillets that clanked loudly unto the pile.

Milburn's truck, brimming with newspapers and magazines, was the third truck to back in. Ethan, Jonathan and two other boys, stiff, shivering and cold with their faces red from the wind, sat on top of the mass smiling over their success as Milburn partially maneuvered the rear of the truck inside the door and stopped. Immediately, the four boys climbed over the sides and hopped down to the ground. Milburn turned his truck off, got out and walked around to its rear to remove the long, metal rods that held the tailgate in place.

Each new load brought three or four boys along with it and it created a small crowd; the extra arms made the paper and metal fly off the trucks faster. Feeling isolated as he sat in the truck's cab peering out through the rear window, Leon was unable to control himself, climbed out.

Jonathan grabbed an armful of old magazines and noticed that some of the issues went back several years. As he carried them over to the far corner to throw them on the growing heap, he read some of the headlines on the front covers. After he threw the ones down in his arms, he searched carefully through the stack and saw old issues of Look, Life, National Geographic and Colliers scattered everywhere. He paused, awestruck by the number of publications which his family didn't subscribe to or even have a copy of any single issue. There were so many interesting headlines and cover pictures glaring at him they seemed innumerable; he wanted to read as many as he could, especially the issues of Life magazine having pictures and captions of the war printed on the covers.

He grabbed the September 20th, 1943 issue of Life and quickly thumbed through it. What he saw on page thirty-four surprised him as it had many of its readers when it was first published. "Three Dead Americans Lie on the beach at Buna," was the caption under the photograph taken by Geroge Strock in New Guinea. He remembered hearing that it was the first photo of American casualties that was allowed to be printed and that it had upset many people.

Bob, a classmate, asked, "what're you reading?" Instead of answering the question, Jonathan said, "Look at this," and held up the 1943, May 10th issue of Life. "PT SKIPPERS" ran along the bottom of the page under the photograph of three naval officers. He sat down on the pile of magazines and became lost in concentration and forgot about unloading trucks. Shortly, he was surrounded by three other boys who started digging into the pile like gold miners.

Jonathan scavenged until he found twenty copies of Life he couldn't resist, carried them to his father's truck and placed them on the wide seat to guarantee good, future reading.

"It doesn't look like we're needed here any longer, so why don't we go over to the drug store, have a hot chocolate and warm up?" Donna suggested. "Maybe Barb will be over there!"

"Marianne, her fingers and toes numb from the cold answered, "I don't think we'll be missed much, do you?"

"I'm too cold to care anyway!" Donna replied.

"First, let me tell my dad where I'm going so he won't be looking all over the place for me."

The two girls dashed across the street, ran into the drug store and found the place unusually subdued. The pin ball machine next to the door stood silent and only three men sat at the counter having coffee. In one booth two boys and two girls of grade-school age sat chitchatting and eating ice cream out of tall, fluted, stemmed glasses and in another booth they found Alice and two more girls talking softly among themselves.

Marianne and Donna walked over. "Hi," they said.

Whatever their three friends were discussing, they hurriedly finished in whispers before they acknowledged the new arrivals.

"You two look like you've been helping with the scrap drive." Alice remarked.

"I'm sure we do…and we're really cold!" Donna replied and peeled off her gloves.

"One of the girls observed, "Your noses and cheeks are all red!"

Marianne studied her image in the large mirror behind the soda fountain. "I guess you're right about that!" she answered and ordered two mugs of hot chocolate, one for herself and one for Donna before they crowded into the booth. "Did any of you happen to see Barb today?" Marianne asked.

"She was having a Coke with us about a half-an-hour ago before Richard came in. He stayed a few minutes, didn't say much and got up to leave and Barb went with him," Alice answered.

"Did she say anything about working on the scrap drive?"

"No, and she wasn't dressed like she might've been thinking about it either!" Alice answered. "Why do you ask?"

"Oh, for no reason at all, really! I just thought she was going to help, that's all!" Marianne replied. "And you haven't seen Stella Mae either?"

"Nope! The only other people that have been in here since we came in were Barb, Richard and some older guy that came in briefly and left," one of the girls stated.

CHAPTER FORTY

April Ninth, 1944

"Rocky, tomorrow I'm going to be sixteen years old," Marianne announced. "Since it'll be Saturday, you and I'll go for a long ride to celebrate it. Okay? She recently had been ecstatic about reaching sixteen, believing it to be a big pinnacle and a major milestone in her life. In her mind she pictured the sixteen as the time at which a girl becomes an adult; at least she had convinced herself years before that it was true and besides, she wasn't going to bring it up to anyone for a debate.

The previous year her mother had made a special effort to bake a nice cake for her, and now this year, even though this birthday felt more important to her, hardly anyone in her family had even mentioned it. The biggest and best gift she had ever gotten was Rocky, although he hadn't been a true birthday present because her dad bought him two months after her birthday and he wasn't meant just for her enjoyment. It didn't matter any longer because no one else other than Leon took interest in him, and if she could finagle a way to spend most of a day with him, it would be a perfect gift.

A mischievous smile gradually broadened her face as she recalled her parents planning another shopping trip. "Well be gone all day Saturday," her mother said, informing her of their plans.

The sky dawned bright and clear. Sunlight flicked through the curtains in Marianne's bedroom, gradually brightening it until it was flooded with golden hues which gently woke her from her pleasant dreams.

By midmorning she was alone on the farm in the barn and saddling up her pony. "This is just like I promised," she commented to herself and pulled the saddle's cinch strap up tight. Her parents had left only a few minutes earlier with Jonathan and Leon in the back seat and didn't expect them back until late in the afternoon. Immediately afterwards, Ethan had left for Warren's house in his father's farm truck.

Marianne led Rocky out into a beautiful day of bright sun, warm temperatures and a soothing soft breeze blowing up from the south. She put her foot in the left stirrup and swung up lithely into the saddle. "We'll ride over to the Isaac Walden Cabin this morning, come home and then go into town and see Barb," she said and gave him a nudge with her heels to set him in motion. "I told Barb I'd have the day all to myself and that we'd ride in there later after I have lunch and you've had more oats."

Riding home across the stubble field around eleven-thirty, Marianne noticed a familiar car parked in front of the house. As she got closer, she noticed that it looked like Richard's, although he hardly drove it anymore because of the gas shortage. Someone waved out of the passenger window and on looking closer, she recognized Barb.

Marianne waved back. Two minutes later, she hopped down off Rocky. "Hi," she shouted and motioned for them to come to the barn. The black sedan lurched and slowly moved down the short, graveled driveway towards her.

"Give me a second!" Marianne shouted and led Rocky into his stall, gave him some oats and went back outside.

Barb bounced out of the front passenger side door to greet her. "Surprise," she said gleefully and giggled.

Marianne forced a smile, disappointed that her plans might be ruined. "What're you doing out here?" she asked. "I thought our plan was for me to come into town so we could hang out together!"

A guilty look edged Barb's face. "Ooops," she answered without apologizing or attempting to explain why she changed plans; however, Marianne reasoned that the answer was sitting behind the steering wheel.

"Hi, Richard," she said and gave him an emotionless glance and a limp wave. He nodded and waved back weakly. She suspected that Richard realized that she was disappointed in more than just Barb and their plans.

Barb smiled. "I've got someone I'd like you to meet," she said, ignoring the tension and gestured towards the car.

"What's going on?" Marianne whispered without moving.

"Richard came over with a friend that I'd like to introduce you to," she answered. "I explained that we had plans and told them where you lived and that you had horses, he said he wanted to meet you. That's why we came out," she answered. "Let me introduce you," Barb added.

Marianne found him to be nice looking with blond hair and an infectious, dimpled smile. His name was Tim and he was very personable.

After the introduction and several minutes of light banter Marianne, seeing that riding her pony was going to be interrupted for the time being, said, "Why don't I go turn Rocky out into the pasture? It'll only take a few minutes."

"Why don't we all go?" Barb offered.

The four of them walked into the barn. Marianne went into Rocky's stall, led him out and started unsaddling him.

"Would you mind if I take a short ride on him before you do that?" Tim asked.

Marianne thought for a few seconds and then somewhat enthralled that he was interested in riding a horse, she answered, "Instead of that, why don't I saddle up Buddy, our other saddle horse and you can ride him instead and I'll go along with you on Rocky?"

"Buddy?" he asked. "You have other horses?"

Many farmers had sold off their horses in recent years and made their farms entirely mechanized. Her father had an old 10-20

McCormick Deering tractor and a fairly new International Harvester H. "Yep," she chirped. "We've still got three horses and he's our other saddle horse."

His eyes brightened. "Hey, you know, that sounds like fun!" he said and her mood imptoved with the opportunity to still go riding, and also ride with an attractive guy.

Tim looked at her, looked at Rocky and said, "Where is he?"

"I'll go get him and be right back," she answered and ran out through the stall into the farmyard with Buddy's bridle.

"Richard doesn't want to drive around and waste gas, so we'll wait here until you get back and then go into town and have a coke," Barb proposed.

"Sounds good to me," Tim said. "What do you think, Marianne?"

"I suppose so," she concurred, hardly having a choice without appearing miffed that her original plans had not materialized. None of this was actually how she pictured spending her sixteenth birthday. "We'll be back in about an hour," Marianne announced.

"That's okay. Just take your time," Barb said and flashed Richard a warm smile.

"You can go sit on the lawn chairs up by the house instead of sitting out here in the car!" Marianne informed them.

"We're okay here," Richard answered. "Right, Barb?" he said, winked and she giggled devilishly.

Marianne took Tim riding along the familiar route around the woods and down the old dirt lane, always so familiar, yet always interesting for one reason or another. As they rode and talked, she discovered that he had only known Richard since his freshman year in high school. Before that, he said he had attended a one-room grade school by the Kaskaskia River near Ficklin, a small spot in the road, between Garrett and Tuscola.

"Do you two hang out together?" Marianne asked.

"Not really, but yeah...sometimes," he answered, chopping up his thoughts. "I suppose we did a lot more when I first met him than we do now after Barb came along."

"The same goes for me and Barb," Marianne commented. The topic always disturbed her and she quickly changed the subject, feeling she'd start gossiping if she didn't. Not knowing what else to say she offered, "Look, those low shrubs back in the woods are starting to bud and turn green already."

"They're the first green I've seen this spring!" he stated, seeing that she wanted to keep her opinions private. They rode along silently for another minute. "I'm really enjoying the ride, but I think maybe we should turn back!"

"You think so?" she asked. They had been gone only twenty-five minutes more or less and she would have liked to have ridden on a bit longer.

"Yeah!" he answered and adjusted himself in the saddle. "It'd probably be a good idea!"

Suddenly it dawned on her that Tim hadn't been on a horse in some time and might've become chaffed and was feeling uncomfortable. "We'll turn around and take a shorter way back, if you don't mind," she suggested.

He grinned sheepishly. "I'd like that!"

The car doors stood open when they returned. Richard and Barb sat on the grass, leaning against the sun-warmed, concrete foundation of the barn with a sleeping cat curled up by their feet. Barb was snuggling under Richard's left arm. He had a straw in his mouth and his shirt tail was pulled out on one side of his rumpled pants. Several stray straws were stuck in Barb's hair and the two top buttons of her blouse were undone.

"Did you have a good time?" Barb asked.

"Yeah...we did," Tim said, answering for both of them. "How about you two?"

"We did too," Barb tittered and gave Richard a clever look. "We had a big straw fight up in the hayloft and Richard won!" she added with a sheepish smile.

CHAPTER FORTY ONE

Early May, 1944

Marianne, thinking that Barb was looking unusually sad and tired, walked with her down the second floor hallway toward their English class.

Between them, things weren't quite the same as they had been two years earlier. Nevertheless, their differences had narrowed recently and they were enjoying each other's company again and had even started to share some secrets once more. Their new-found friendship had been a gradual process after Barb had visited her with Richard and Tim on the farm. Marianne's concern about what she thought was Barb's nearly total infatuation with Richard hadn't changed, but she had grown to accept it.

She dated Tim twice after that. On her first date with him, the two couples doubled; on their second one she and Tim went by themselves to see a movie. From the start the second date had been pleasurable, although they debated which theater to attend. He wanted to see "Life Boat" by Alfred Hitchcock in Arthur and she wanted to see "National Velvet" starring Elizabeth Taylor and Mickey Rooney in Tuscola. They flipped a coin and she won. He groaned playfully about losing but didn't resist.

"Are you okay?" Marianne asked, ambling slowly along as another student dashed past them for the door. Before Barb could answer, Marianne cried, "Oh no," and the two of them hustled toward the door also, realizing they were nearly tardy. They flew through the door, walked as lightly and quickly as possible to their seats and sat down just as the bell rang. Mrs. White had a rule that students had to be in their seat before the bell. Being tardy three times meant a detention. Their teacher, who seemed to have eyes in the back of her head, was writing on the blackboard. "You two girls should try to be a little earlier," she said without looking around.

Several students looked at them and smiled weakly. Sitting by the windows, Stella Mae mouthed, "I'll see you at lunch."

Marianne tried concentrating on the class's continuing analysis of the short story by Mark Twain titled, "The Celebrated Jumping Frog of Calaveras County," without success. During the preceding days they covered the story by Washington Irving titled "The Legend of Sleepy Hollow" and Edward Everett Hale's "A Man without a Country," without her losing her concentration; however, now Barb worried her to the point of distraction.

Two-thirds of the way through the class period, Marianne saw Barb put her head down on her desk. While in the process of answering a question that a student had just asked, Mrs. White looked at Barb with a concerned look on her face and walked toward her desk. All eyes in the classroom followed her. She was one of those instructors who hardly strayed from the space between the teacher's desk and the blackboard. Not knowing what to expect, the students in front swiveled around to follow her movements. Her students didn't put their heads on their desks in her classroom without a very good reason, and they didn't know what to expect Mrs. White to do or say to Barb. "Are you sick?" she asked in a concerned manner.

"I don't feel very well," Barb answered softly.

Mrs. White turned to two boys in adjacent seats. "Will you two boys help Barb down to the principal's office?"

After class, Marianne and Stella Mae carried Barb's English book, folder and notebook down the steps to the office and knocked. They found Barb, pale and lying on the cot used for such emergencies.

"I'm going home!" she told them. "The secretary called my mom and she's coming to pick me up!"

"What's wrong?" Stella Mae asked.

"I don't know, but I haven't been feeling well for a couple of days now."

"It's probably just a touch of the flu," Marianne said to comfort her. "You'll probably feel better in a couple of days!"

Pale and curled into the fetal position, Barb said, "I hope so!" and moaned.

"I gotta run to study hall," Stella Mae exclaimed.

"And I've got to get to my next class," Marianne said and patted Barb's arm sympathetically. "I'll check on you again after my next class!"

"Mom'll probably pick me up before then."

"I'll see you in about forty-five minutes if you're still here?"

"Maybe this weekend at the drug store would be better," Barb answered.

"I hope you're up and around by Friday, and if you're not, I'll see you around seven on Saturday!"

Saturday afternoon after doing her chores and helping her mother around the house, Marianne led Rocky out of the barn and groomed him. While using the curry comb to remove the last patches and strands of long winter hair from his coat, she hummed "Mairzy Doatz," to herself in rhythm to the short swipes of her arm. The unusual song she'd heard on the radio that morning had stuck in her head ever since; she sang just above a whisper, *"Marizy doats and dozy doats and liddle lamzy jivey. A kiddley divey too, wouldn't you?"*

She daydreamed and sang softly to herself, *"If the words sound queer and funny to your ear, a little bit jumbled and jivey."* Concentrating on her job, she didn't hear the car approach until it was only a few yards away. *"Mares eat oats and does eat oats and little lambs eat ivy,"* she whispered softy.

Richard's car crunched to a slow stop in the gravel much like the first time he and Barb had driven out.

"Hi, Marianne," Barb yelled through her open window.

Marianne patted Rocky on the neck and put the curry comb down on the ground. "Glad you're feeling better," she said and stepped over to the car. "What're you two up to?"

"Not much!" Barb replied with a look on her face that Marianne couldn't read. They talked about nothing very specific for a few minutes as people often do before getting into more serious topics. Suddenly, Barb's face flushed a deep pink and she said, "Why don't you get in the back seat and sit down…I need to talk to you!"

Marianne failed to pick up the urgency in Barb's voice to explain why she had come out and hinted that she needed to finish grooming Rocky.

"Please," Barb pleaded, "I really need someone I can trust to confide in and you're the first person I thought of!"

Marianne froze momentarily before continuing. "Did I hear you say that you need someone to confide in?" she asked and looked in through Barb's open, side window at Richard and saw that his face looked shallow and drawn.

"Yeah, I really do!"

It took a couple of seconds for her to contemplate, feeling that something wasn't right and she had a gut feeling that she was going to hear more than she wanted to know. Reluctantly, she opened the door and got into the back seat. "What's wrong?"

Barb looked at Richard and changed her position so that she could see Marianne's face and then began a rambling monolog about how close her family was to her, what school meant, and why she and Richard were so compatible. "We're like a pair of socks, aren't we, Richard?" she said and studied his face.

"Uh huh," he answered and stared straight ahead through the windshield.

A long silence followed. Marianne couldn't imagine what was going on as there didn't seem to be any point in what Barb had said so far, other than to have Richard confirm how close they were. There was something in Barb's tone of voice that made her feel uncomfortable about where Barb's discourse was leading. Not wanting to hear more, she attempted to excuse herself politely, "I need to finish grooming Rocky."

"No, no, wait, Marianne. Please don't leave! I really have something very important to tell you!"

Marianne got a very curious expression on her face. "Well, what is it?"

"I'm pregnant," Barb said without much emotion in her voice, although her facial expression told a different story.

Stunned, Marianne became unable to speak for several seconds and then blurted loudly, "No! Oh, no! You can't be!"

"No? No?" Barb said irritably. "Well, I am!"

Marianne leaned forward against the back of the tall seat. "How long have you known?"

"For at least a week or so!"

Marianne couldn't believe what she was hearing and fell back against her seat cushion.

"You're sure, really sure and you couldn't be wrong?"

"I'm positive I'm pregnant! I went to Mattoon and saw a doctor!"

There was another long silence. Barb slumped in her seat. Richard was still staring out through the car's windshield toward the barn. "What in the world are you going to do?" Marianne asked.

Richard looked at Marianne through his rearview mirror without turning around. "For the last few days we contemplated all the options we could think of and we've finally made up our minds about what we should do, haven't we, Barb?"

"Uh huh," Barb answered and pulled herself back upright.

"What have you decided to do?" Marianne asked and got a disquieting answer.

"We're thinking about eloping!"

"What?" Marianne exclaimed as if she hadn't heard correctly which surprised her almost as much as the announcement of her pregnancy had. "You're not really serious?"

"Yeah, we are!" Barb repeated.

"When?"

"We're gonna catch an Illinois Central train in Mattoon first thing Monday morning and take it down to Cairo. From there we're catching a bus to Mayfield Kentucky where Richard has some family."

Marianne gasped and was lost for words for several seconds. "I can hardly believe this is happening!"

"Well, it is!" Barb assured her.

"Barb and me, I think we've got it pretty much figured out," Richard interrupted. "Instead of going to school Monday we're going to cut and have a friend of mine drive us to the train station in my car after he buys it. Actually, it'll be his this afternoon after he gets the cash to pay me and it'll be enough to get us by for a few days."

Barb interjected, "Once to Kentucky Monday afternoon I'll call my parents to tell them I'm alright, but not where I am. I'm not gonna let them know until we're married and be too late for them to do anything about it," Barb explained. "I've already sneaked enough clothes out through my bedroom window this week to get me by."

Richard explained, "I have an uncle in Mayfield, Kentucky that has a small business. He's always told me if I ever needed a job, to just give him a call. I did last week and I've already got one and we're goin' to stay with one of my cousins for a few days. I think we'll be okay!" he added and Marianne couldn't tell whether he was trying to convince her, Barb or himself that everything would be fine.

Marianne assumed that they had thought out their future plans logically; however, passion and not logic had brought them to this point in their lives, although she wasn't sure she agreed with their decision to elope. What they were planning made her head swirl. "What about your mom?" Marianne asked Barb. "Isn't she going to be worried crazy?"

Barb shook her head in bewilderment. Tears welled up in her eyes. "I know, I know, she's going to be really upset, my dad maybe even more so. I guess they'll get over it in time!"

What Barb said sounded familiar. It took only a few seconds for Marianne to recall the day she nearly drowned at Stella Mae's and she and Barb were late starting for home. Barb had just repeated the same phrase and her statement shocked Marianne even more this time, particularly since this situation was more serious than just being late getting home in the afternoon.

A bit confused, Marianne asked, "Why are you telling me all of this?"

Barb looked her straight in the face. "Remember the pact we made that we'll always be friends and never divulge each other's secrets?"

"Of course I do," Marianne answered. "But why are you telling me this?" she asked again, feeling that she was becoming too immersed in their intrigue. Barb and Richard were making her uncomfortable by telling her so many details.

Barb answered, "Because I know there's going to be all kinds of ugly gossip floating around town when I leave and I think I can trust you more than anyone else to keep my secret until there's a better time...until we're gone for awhile to let people know the truth!"

"How long do you expect me to stay silent?" Marianne asked, already privy to their secret and then having an ominous responsibility thrust on her that she hadn't requested.

"At least until we've been gone for a few days and we're married!" she answered. "I'll drop you a letter and give you all the details so you can tell my friends the truth and stop any gossip that's floating around. Please, Marianne, I know you can do this for me?" she pleaded.

Marianne, for several long, tense, seconds didn't speak and then said reluctantly, "Okay. Sure!" She looked over at Richard, saw him staring at the barn and shake his head imperceptibly. It was at that moment that she recalled vividly how they had sat and leaned against the foundation of the barn over a month earlier, loose straws in Barb's hair, his shirt halfway out of his pants and how disheveled they both were. *Now I know why they came to me*, she realized.

Richard, looking agitated, hit the steering wheel with the palm of his hand and swore under his breath. "We've got to go!" he snapped. The girls looked at him. Barb's face flushed red and she gave him a hard look.

"I'm sorry," he said, "I didn't mean to sound so angry but I've got lots of things I need to take care of before Monday morning and it only gives me a day and a half to get everything done. I don't have the time to be sitting here any longer."

Marianne watched the car pull away, picked up her curry comb from the ground and made a swipe across Rocky's shoulder. *Enough of this*, she though. *What I really need to do is go for a long, long ride!*

CHAPTER FORTY TWO

Early July, 1944

Haggard and sunburned, Marianne walked into the kitchen at six o'clock in the afternoon. The oversized, sweat-stained denim shirt she borrowed that morning from her father to protect her from the sun were rolled up above the elbows and her black lunch box dangled limply from her right arm. The effects of detasseling corn for three days showed, and still there were a few more days to go. "Hi Mom, I'm going to get some fresh clothes and go take a shower," she said and walked straight to her bedroom.

"There's clean washrags and towels in the linen closet," her mother yelled after her.

Minutes later, Marianne turned on the water in the shower and let it run until it warmed up. The grey, bare, concrete walls in the basement and the cool temperature they retained felt refreshing after sweltering all day in the stifling heat between tall rows of corn. What a relief the cool water was as she stuck her face into the soft spray.

If *I were swimming under a cascading waterfall on a tropical island right now it couldn't feel any better than this,* she thought and let the water run over her body until she felt rejuvenated. Then she poured Halo shampoo in her hair, lathered it up and pushed it into a pile on top of her head like a white turban. After she rubbed, scrubbed and wiped the grime off her body, she rinsed her hair, toweled off, got dressed and went back upstairs to the kitchen. Ethan sat at the table. Leon was busy setting it and Jonathan was listening to an episode of "Captain Midnight," on the radio.

"Can I help you, Leon?" his sister asked.

"No, that's okay. I'm seven years old now!"

Slowly frying chicken in a deep iron skillet, her mother responded, "You can give me a little help, if you'd like to. I've got sour dock greens boiling on that back burner. Check to see if they're done."

Quartered, canned tomatoes also sat on a back burner ready to be dished up for the table. She preferred using canned to fresh tomatoes for the simple side dish she called stewed tomatoes, created by adding little pieces of hard bread and a few spices. When the chicken was done she would make white gravy using milk, flour, some of the grease and the crunchy leftovers from the bottom of the skillet.

"See if the potatoes are ready to be mashed, and get me down a platter for this chicken and three other bowls for the rest of this stuff."

"So how's detasseling going, Sis?" Ethan asked. He had decided not to join the DeKalb crew this summer and had instead found a job in town at the grain elevator.

"It's okay!"

"Are many of the same people back this year?" he asked.

"About half of them, plus two girls I like!" she replied.

Their mother interrupted. "Jonathan, run out and ask your father to quit working and come in for supper and be sure to tell him it's about ready for the table."

"Oh, Mom, gee whiz," he moaned. "Can't I listen to the rest of my program first? It'll be over in a couple of minutes!"

"Go get your dad!" She insisted, seeing her food was nearly ready for the table and knowing that it would take some time for Milburn to stop whatever he was doing, come in and get cleaned up.

Jonathan lifted himself heavily out of the chair. "Golly geeee, Mom," he complained further and then suddenly ran for the door when he heard a commercial start to interrupt the program, hoping to return and hear the end of it.

"Lord, we thank you for this food and we pray the war will be over soon!" Milburn prayed, paused and held his head down for several more seconds collecting his thoughts. "Please, God, look after our troops in France, Italy and the South Pacific and help us bring as many of them safely home as possible!" He paused briefly and added, "Amen!"

"Amen," his wife repeated and the kids followed her lead with Amen's around the table.

"Okay, I think you can start passing the food," Gloria suggested and watched eager hands reach for the chicken.

Once all their plates were full and they were all eating, Marianne commented, "I saw something that really surprised me today!"

"Come on, Marianne, you were detasseling corn, weren't you? How could you see anything interesting?" Ethan asked, trying to jest with his comment landing closer to sarcasm than to a joke. He had been giving her a hard time ever since he had decided he wasn't going to detassel. "All you could've seen was sky in the space between two rows of corn!"

"Well, that's where you're so wrong!" Marianne stated unequivocally. "I know I saw something that confirms what Dad's been saying about us winning the war," she stated and added, "Pass me the chicken, will you?" without enlightening them with any further details. The dramatic nature of her delivery had an instant effect on her father.

Her father looked up and tried to read her face. "What'd you see that would've made you think we're winning the war?" he asked.

"She's crazy, she didn't see nothing!" Ethan insisted, seeing he was losing an attempt to rattle her.

"Stop it, Ethan," his father orderd. "Let her finish!"

"It was something I thought I'd never see. This morning they drove us up several miles north past Champaign to detassel. The field across the road from us was planted with green beans for the Stokely Van Camp Canning Company and there must've been a hundred or more German POW's pulling weeds and working in it. One of their military guards patrolling the road told us they were from a prisoner-of-war camp in Hoopeston and he also told us that there's several more prison camps just like it scattered around!" Marianne's news suddenly got all of her family's undivided attention. "I figure, if there are that many prisoners around the country, then the war has to be about over, don't you agree, Dad?" she concluded.

"It's very good sign and other evidence in the news lately'," her father stated. "They've been reportin' that our troops and our other allies have been winnin' on every front. Just this month the Navy reported they sank several Jap aircraft carriers and damaged three more in the Philippine Sea. And the Russians, who've had it so rough for more than two years, just defeated one of Germany's largest armies," her father stated with conviction. "I agree that all them prisoners are a good sign," he added.

Jonathan, sitting and listening intently suddenly stirred and piped up. "The American's liberated Che...Cher...Cherburg...Cherbourg two days ago!" he stated to show he also kept up with the war news and very interested in what his sister had seen. "Did they have on German uniforms?"

"No!"

"They didn't?"

"No, they didn't!" his sister repeated emphatically. "They wore denim hats, pants and shirts with a big POW written in big, white, capital letters across their backs. Our supervisor said he'd heard that three of the prisoners had escaped right after the camp was opened. He told us two of them were caught in northern Indiana and the third one was later found in southern Indiana, just north of Louisville, Kentucky. "If he remembered right," he said, "he thought they were trying to get to Florida and somehow get back to Germany."

"Probably on a German submarine," Jonathan stated, remembering how they had been sinking ships along the Atlantic Coast and even in the Gulf of Mexico.

"I'll bet they're mean looking," Leon surmised from past stories and a vivid imagination.

"I didn't see any mean looking ones. Most of them were thin, young and bent over pulling weeds by hand because they weren't allowed to have hoes or anything sharp. If it hadn't been for the guards standing around with guns, they would've looked like about anyone I know if they hadn't been dressed alike in those dark-blue denims."

"Yeah, and a big POW painted in the middle of their backs!" Jonathan sneered.

What Marianne didn't want to divulge was that her crew actually got close enough that several of the girls flirted with some of the younger Germans about their age. A few of the girls yelled, waved, and acted cute. They weren't really surprised when a couple of the German prisoners stopped working and waved but were shocked when the Germans yelled back in perfect English. The guards ignored the whole thing but the other girls' actions upset her.

"Wouldn't it be neat to have some Germans working in our fields?" Leon said.

Extremely bitter about the German's starting the war, his father stated sharply, "I don't think so!" He had no desire to see the enemy up close.

"When I was in town today, I stopped past my mother's place to see how she and Anna Lee were gettin' along," Milburn remarked, bringing the POW topic to an abrupt close. "I think it was good they moved away from here and Mom seems not as upset about things anymore."

"Susan," Gloria said, never referring to her mother-in-law any other way, "will never get over you winning the lawsuit," his wife said, never failing to remind him of the old dispute.

Milburn, not a person to hold grudges, had often wished he had never contested the suit. It seemed the whole thing was over being right instead of over the small amount of money involved, although, he had been struggling financially at the time. After winning, he had often considered giving them the money they had sought, but after giving it considerable thought, he felt it would only cause more hard feelings. The money wouldn't have corrected much and his wife would never have forgiven him. He had learned a hard lesson.

"I miss her not being next door!" Marianne declared.

"I do too," her youngest brother added.

"Anyway, things are as they are!" their father remarked. "She shared a long letter with me which she had just gotten from Donald."

Sitting dully silent after being rebuffed by his father, Ethan, overwhelmed with curiosity about what his cousin had written, suddenly changed his demeanor. Perking up, he asked, "What'd he have to say?" and leaned toward his father, anticipating an interesting report on his cousin's military life.

"He wrote all the usual things," his father answered.

"Like what?" Ethan pried, anxious to hear about any new experiences Donald was having.

"Navy life, some of the people he's met and what the weather is like up there in Port Townsend, Washington."

Ethan squinted doubtfully. "Washington?" he asked, not believing what he heard. "I thought he was going to Hawaii and then out into the Pacific!"

"He was in Hawaii and now he's up at Puget Sound where the West Virginia is bein' repaired, and refitted. Donald said he got his orders to be transferred up there after she'd been overhauled and the Navy had started assembling a crew for a shakedown run."

"The West Virginia repaired?" Jonathan asked rhetorically, in awe of what his cousin was doing. He looked at it as a great adventure, "and Donald's gonna be a crew member!"

"That's right," his father replied proudly. "The Japs might've sunk her at Pearl Harbor but now she's goin' to go back out there and get some revenge not only for herself, but for all them other ships they've sunk or damaged and for all the men who died at Pearl Harbor and every place since!"

"I want to enlist in the Navy," Ethan stated, his eyes wide with enthusiastic desire.

Milburn found Ethan's unpleasant topic confronting him again and hoped to squelch it. He replied sharply, "Finish high school first and then you can join the United States Navy!" Ethan's persistence was becoming like a stubborn weed growing in a row of beans and if you didn't pull it out at the roots, in a few days it would irritate you with its presence again.

"Why can't I join? You know I don't like school and I don't do good either!"

"Let's strike a bargain right here and right now!" his father said sternly, his face turning serious and marked by a shade of light pink. "If you help me around here on the farm for the rest of this summer, come this fall, after school starts, and you're still determined to join, I'll think very seriously about signin' your papers. How does that sound to you?" he answered without making a firm commitment.

"You know I'll get drafted when I turn eighteen and I don't want to go into the Army!" he said, using the same argument Donald had used.

Milburn had high hopes that the war would be over before Ethan turned eighteen and he was starting to worry that his son could run off and join up by lying about his true age as some young men were doing. If he could prolong his son's enlistment a few months, there might be less of a chance of his seeing combat; it was a simple matter of calculating how soon the allies might win. There was little doubt in his mind that the war was winding down and the contested areas were shrinking at an accelerated clip. Lately, a fairly common belief was that the war would be over by Christmas.

Milburn had only finished sixth grade and he hoped all of his children would finish high school. He could see that the times were changing very fast and a high school diploma was becoming more necessary if one wanted to become successful. Several problems faced him. Ethan didn't like to study and was often an aggravation when working around the farm. "By the way, I'm sure you know you can stay out of the service with a deferment by workin' here on the farm even after you turn eighteen," his father reminded him and wasn't surprised with the answer he got.

"I know that, but I want to join up!" Ethan stated emphatically, ending a conversation that wouldn't be mentioned again for some time to come.

CHAPTER FORTY THREE

Wednesday, September Thirteenth, 1944

Milburn came to the house for lunch acting mildly upset and sat down at the table. No one asked why and he didn't say anything until after he filled his plate. "Marianne, that pony of yours is causin' me a serious problem!" he said.

"What kind of problems?" she asked, cautiously.

"He's been chasin' the young calves around and tormentin' them. I'm concerned he's goin' to injure or kill one of them! Sometime this afternoon, after you finish eatin' and helpin' your mother I want you to go out there and move him over to the small pasture out in front of the house. I don't need this problem right now and I think he can stay out there until the calves get bigger!"

"You should've sold him when you sold Buddy and Maude this spring," his wife replied. "No one rides him much anymore!"

Milburn looked at his daughter and saw she was trying not to become emotional. Rocky was a contentious issue from time to time and discussing his worth was a snake pit.

What Gloria said was true. Rocky wasn't being ridden as much. Ethan was interested in other things and Jonathan didn't like horses. Leon was old enough to ride Rocky by himself now if someone else would saddle him up, but he had asked only one time since June when he acquired a bicycle for his birthday.

In no mood for a confrontation, Marianne chose to stay silent and think. She knew it was probably her fault that the issue had even come up and that she would have to take the blame for the trouble Rocky was causing. Recently, she was spending more of her free time away from the farm, having acquired other interests, some with strings attached, especially the ones that tied her to her social life.

Rocky wasn't being totally ignored. She still cared deeply for him and fed him his oats and an occasional carrot and whispered in his ear. Granted, she didn't ride him as much. *Maybe he's acting up because he's lonesome,* she wondered and the thought made her feel guilty. Marianne knew her father's irritation was partly a product of his hard labor. As he often said, he didn't need the added worries or expenses of some animal that wasn't serving a purpose.

Farmers treated most of their animals like commodities that were intended to put money into their pockets. Marianne knew this and how the burden of harvesting the fall crops weighed on her father. He accepted Rocky as a positive expenditure as long as he served a function and didn't become a troublesome debit. Her pony's worth was in the balance and Marianne had just gotten the message.

"I'll go take care of it!" she said without looking up.

CHAPTER FORTY FOUR

October Twenty Fourth, 1944

As Marianne walked into the house with her flute in one hand and her homework in the other, she heard her mother yell up from the bottom of the basement stairs saying that a letter had come for her.

"Who from?" Marianne shouted back.

"It's got a return address from a Barb Shaw in Mayfield, Kentucky," her mother answered. "I left it up on the kitchen countertop."

Instead of yelling back, Marianne dashed up the short flight of stairs to the landing, took her coat off, threw her things on the kitchen table and grabbed the letter.

"That wouldn't happen to be from Mary Clark's daughter, would it?" her mother asked, following her into the kitchen.

As far as Marianne knew, her mother was just assuming who had written the letter since it had a Mayfield, Kentucky post mark. Marianne was positive that Barb's parents had never divulged where their daughter was or why she had left. "I'm not sure!" Marianne declared, not knowing what to say, given her pact of secrecy. She hoped this was the letter that Barb had promised to send giving her permission to tell her friends where she was and what her plans were. Once she read the letter, she might have an answer for her mother and also have a means to stop the speculation and gossip flying around school.

For a month after Barb left, her absence had been the main topic in town and around the school and Marianne was positive she was the only person privy to any facts pertaining to Barb's story and whereabouts. It had been a struggle not to reveal the truth and now she was proud she had kept her pledge.

"I'm going to go change my clothes," Marianne told her mother, picked up her books and hurried to her bedroom.

Mayfield, Kentucky

Oct. 18, 1944

Dear Marianne,

Sorry I've taken so long to write to you but things have kept getting in the way as you might expect under the circumstances. I think maybe I should start from the beginning and tell you what's happened in the order they took place.

I'll start by saying me and Richard are deeply in love and I really believe we made the right decision to keep the baby and move away from Atwood and get married. You can't begin to imagine how really furious my mom was when I called her late in the day we left and not until after we had made it down here to Kentucky. She pleaded with me to go back home and when that didn't work, she made all kinds of threats. When she found out that I was not only eloping but pregnant, it got even worse. About the only thing I managed to accomplish by calling her was to let her know where I was and to give her a little peace of mind that I was okay. Before she hung up, I told her that I loved her and Dad and that I was sorry for disappointing them.

Gradually things are working out between us and she told me when I'm about to have the baby she wants to come down and be here for me. She calls occasionally and we both write at least once a week to each other.

The first night here we found a cheap room and the next morning we got in touch with his uncle who Richard will be working for. The job he got will pay just enough for us to get by and start a life.

Richard has a couple of cousins here. One, Bobby Dale, is the son of the uncle he is working for. On the second night Bobby Dale and his wife took us in and asked us to stay with them until we could get on our feet. They're so nice. He and his wife Joyce were our best man and woman when we got married with the Justice-of-the-Peace on the fourth day here. We didn't tell anyone that I was pregnant and now, since I'm now starting to get a little tummy on me, we're going to announce in a couple of days that I'm expecting.

After a month we found a small place that we could afford to rent and we moved out of his cousin's place. The little two bedroom house we found is small and is partially furnished but we've scraped together some other pieces to make it comfortable enough.

I hated to leave his cousin's house because Joyce and I have a lot in common, we talked a lot and I stayed busy around their house helping with her chores. Joyce is loads of fun, with a great sense of humor and always smiling. Richard and Bobby Dale have become close friends as well. We see them often and Joyce is like a sister to me.

They have a baby girl that is five months old and as cute as any baby I've ever seen. I can't wait to have one of my own!

Bobby Dale picks Richard up on the way to work every morning, although we live within walking distance of Richard's job.

I don't know what people have been saying about me back there but I hope it's not all bad. I can only imagine. You can tell any of my friends anything which I've told you.

Your good friend,

Barb

P.S. I miss Atwood and my friends so much I get a little homesick at times. Please write and give Stella Mae, Alice, Donna my address and also to anyone else that wants it. It's P.O box 308, Mayfield, Kentucky

Marianne slowly refolded the letter and slid it back into the envelope and laid it down on top of her dresser. She changed her clothes and went back to the kitchen to tell her mother the news, expecting it to be an awkward moment at best.

"You were right, Mom, that was a letter from Barb."

"What did she have to say?" her mother asked.

"She wrote to tell me she got pregnant and that she had eloped with Richard and is living in Mayfield, Kentucky!" Marianne replied, relating the information as if she had no prior knowledge of her friend's actions, intending to sound surprised by the news in the letter.

"I told you once that apples don't fall far from their trees," her mother remarked. "She's just like her cousin from Minnesota. Things like that really do run in families!"

"Why do you always have to say things like that when you know they're not a fact?" Marianne snapped. "Sometimes I don't think you even believe those things yourself!" she chided sarcastically.

Her mother's face hardened up and flushed. Marianne saw that her reaction shocked her mother; however, couldn't tell whether it was because she was ashamed of her opinion or mad at Marianne's angry response. "Things like that do run in families and you know they do!" she said defensively.

"Maybe you're right and that's why she moved to Mayfield, Kentucky!" Marianne said, being blatantly sarcastic by emphasizing the name Mayfield, her mother's maiden name.

"What do you mean by that?" her mother quizzed.

"I just don't believe things like that run in families and every time we've had this conversation, I've disagreed with you," Marianne stated firmly. "If you thought about it and looked very hard at your own family's background I'd either be pregnant or about to but I'm not pregnant and not about to be!" Her mother's mouth gapped open; she took in a deep breath and turned away. "I'm going out to do my chores," Marianne stated sharply, turned on her heel, and grabbed her coat before her mother had time to argue more.

"Your dad's out at the barn and he has something he wants to talk to you about," her mother shouted after her.

Halfway to the barn, she saw her father kneeling on the ground in the barnyard driving nails into a board which had become loose. Leon stood next to him watching intently a short distance away and three curious milk cows stood shoulder to shoulder watching also.

It was necessary for Marianne to walk through the milking parlor to get into the barnyard. "Mom said you had something you wanted to see me about!"

"I do!" he replied. "We're havin' more problems with that pony of yours!" he added, sounding irritated without looking up and drove another nail into the bottom edge of the board. Leon looked at her with a long face and she could tell from his demeanor that her father was not in a good mood.

"What kind of a problem is he causing now?" she asked cautiously. "He isn't pestering some other animals again, is he? Surely he's not bothering the calves any longer now that they're so much bigger?" she rattled on nervously.

"No, he's not!" her father answered and drove another nail. "He's makin' a big nuisance out of himself in another way and it's causin' extra work that I don't have any time for!" he replied sharply. "You need to go into the barn, get a couple of buckets and a shovel and come back out here and clean up this pile of oats where that pony of yours kicked these boards loose!"

Not believing she had just heard that Rocky had kicked the barn's siding loose, Marianne, dumbfounded, stood looking down at her father for a few seconds. The news caused a knot to form in her throat, making it almost impossible for her to breathe or ask more questions. She slowly walked off toward the open outside door of the stall a few feet away. A thousand pound weight seemed to be riding on her shoulders while a feeling of gloom swirled around in her head.

Later, after having spent the better part of an hour cleaning up the pile of oats, she decided to reprimand and question her pony verbally. "You gotta stop makin' a big nuisance out of yourself!" she demanded. "Do you understand? And, why do you behave like that?" she asked sternly and, even though she felt reluctant to do so, she gave him a carrot. "Why?" she asked again, and scratched behind his left ear to show him the affection and the love she had in her heart for him. "I know I've paid less attention to you lately," she added. "I still love you just as much as I always have!" He tossed his muzzle up and down. Marianne knew he was only reacting to her affection and really hadn't understood a word she had said; however, she hoped that he might have read something in the tone of her voice that would encourage him to stop causing problems.

"You know, you're not only hurting yourself by causing trouble, you're also causing me to worry and have a lot of pain!" she explained. Rocky looked at her with his miss-matched eyes as if looking for sympathy. "I've got to go get a shovel and some buckets and go clean up that mess you made. When I finish, let's go for a short ride."

CHAPTER FORTY FIVE

Friday, October Twenty Seventh, 1944

In the early afternoon, while waiting for the final football game of the season to get underway on the cool, bright October day, Marianne, surrounded by a small clutch of her closet friends, Stella Mae, Alice, Donna, and Evelyn sat at the top of the bleachers behind the field house. They chatted about nothing in particular until Donna interjected, "Do you know that we're losing another one of our classmates?"

"Another one?" Alice said as if it were a daily occurrence. "Who's leaving this time?"

"Joanne Smith," Donna said. "She dropped out of school today."

"She did? Marianne asked, surprised by the announcement because she believed that she was always aware of what was happening in her small class.

"Why? She's not pregnant too, is she?" Alice responded.

Donna shook her head. "I don't think so! People drop out of school for other reasons, you know!" she stated and continued with what else she knew. "She told me that she hasn't been getting along with her parents and had decided to move out of the house. She even showed me a bruise on her arm where her dad had grabbed her."

"What's she going to do?" Evelyn asked.

"She said she's moving to Decatur and that she's already found a nice small apartment over there."

Because she had never had a hint of Joanne's problems, Marianne couldn't believe what she was hearing. "She has an apartment and is moving away from home?"

"Yeah, and she's accepted a job to work behind the lunch counter of Kreskes Five and Ten."

"That's two girls gone from our class," Alice said, paused, thought for a moment and brought up the topic of Barb. "I wonder how Barb's doing. Marianne, in the letter you got from her she didn't happen to say anything else other than what you've already told us?"

"Really Alice, what else could there be!" Marianne retorted.

"I thought maybe she might've confided other things before she left!"

"Believe me, she didn't and you know as much as I know" Marianne affirmed. "Just leave it alone, okay?" she said without sounding defensive. "Why don't you write her a letter? I'm sure she'd like to hear from you!"

"Maybe I will, if you give me her address," Alice said.

"I'll give it to you Monday," Marianne replied.

"I think I'll send her a post card," Evelyn interjected but got ignored when the girls became distracted by two military men walking up to the flag pole at the east end of the football field.

"Look at that," Stella Mae said excitedly and pointed. One was a Seabee who looked to have just graduated from high school and the other was Joe Wilson, an Army PFC, who had graduated from their school three years earlier. "That Navy Seabee guy is sure sharp looking," she observed.

Donna studied the Seabee more closely. "You really think so?"

"You don't need glasses, do you Donna?" Stella Mae asked and added, "He looks like a dream!"

"It's just the uniform," Donna argued, using a phrase coined after so many men had joined the military service.

"I agree with Stella Mae," Marianne replied and rolled her eyes teasingly, making the girls giggle.

A booming male voice struggled to come through the heavy static on the old public address system and the noisy clatter in the bleachers stopped momentarily. Once the static was brought under control, the announcer welcomed everyone to the last football game of the season and then announced, "We have two special guests from our armed forces with us today. They're here to help us honor our country's military personnel who are fighting for our liberty around the world. The man here on my right is United States Army PFC Joe Wilson from Atwood, whom many of you probably already may know. He's here to represent the Rajahs. The young man on my left is a Navy Seabee, Eddie Dotson from Monticello, supporting our rivals, the Owls. I don't need to stress how honored we are to have them both here with us today. Please give them a healthy round of applause!"

After the clapping and whistling died down, the high school band briefly played the Rajah's theme song. Only brief seconds after it ended, the poor speaker system came alive again. "Please stand," the big voice announced, eliciting the fans of Atwood High School Rajah and the smaller group of Monticello Owl spectators across the field slowly got to their feet. Every face turned towards the flag pole as the two uniformed men slowly raised the American flag to the top of its staff. The spectators put their hands to their hearts and a few former soldiers assumed the military style salute while the band played the National Anthem and everyone sang along enthusiastically, while the flag fluttered lightly in the bright autumn air. After the music ended and before anyone could sit down, the speaker made an added request. "I'd like everyone to remain standing and honor all our troops with a moment of silence!" Someone rang a small bell to mark the passing of time. A deep silence fell over the field and individuals could almost hear the heartbeats of the people standing next to them. A surge of air stiffened the flag. After a long minute, the bell rang a second time, cueing the end of silent meditation. Instantly the spectators clapped and whistled as the starting players of the teams streamed out to the middle of the field.

"I wish this war would end," Stella Mae remarked.

Sitting on the next lower level of the bleachers at Marianne's feet, Donna shifted around. "Marianne, is Ethan still trying to get your dad to let him enlist in the Navy?"

"Yes he is!" she answered. "He's very persistent about it and I don't believe he'll give up 'til he gets his way." What she omitted to say was how anxiously he wanted to enlist. Two days before, he and Warren had accomplished a feat that was on the verge of getting them into very serious trouble. In years past, Mr. Glidden, the owner and editor of the Atwood Herald, always had his very nice outhouse overturned as a prank during the week before Halloween. It was something he hated, but he knew that it was an expected adolescent behavior. This year he decided to put a stop to the mischief by sinking wooden posts deep into the ground on each corner and fasten them together securely with eye-bolts and small chains. The mistake he made, intentional or not, was to let it be known what he had done without realizing it would be taken as a challenge for some young rascals of the community to turn it over.

The small community had several adolescent risk takers like Ethan and his friends who obliged Mr. Glidden.

Somehow, totally unobserved, around two in the morning three days earlier, someone put a chain around the outhouse and gave it a mighty pull, uprooting the posts and inadvertently destroying the sturdy structure. To say the least, Mr. Glidden was humbled, embarrassed and put in a tough spot. Wanting revenge and aiming to regain his dignity, he went on the hunt. Snooping around here and there looking for the culprits of the deed, he swore to have them prosecuted; it was the only way he could have his pride mended and justice served.

The night it happened Marianne remembered waking up and hearing her brother sneaking out of the house around one o'clock in the morning and not slink back in until after four. His late night venture gave her good cause to believe that Ethan, Warren and a couple of their friends were the ones who did the deed and she surmised that was why Ethan started pestering his father constantly to join the Navy; he wanted to vanish before he got identified.

The morning after the outhouse was overturned, Rocky had kicked the boards loose on the barn again and their father was in no mood for more problems. He had experienced enough difficulties over the last several months. Spring had been wet and cold, delaying the planting of his crops and now the harvest season was starting off late and slow. When he wasn't in the fields, he was tending his livestock, mending fences, repairing equipment or taking care of other basic problems. The whole family sensed he was worn down and tired from the hard work, long hours, fighting the weather and coping with the physical wear and tear on his body. His mind had become affected from the labor and tension, altering his pleasant nature, and making him short tempered.

Marianne figured Ethan might scheme to manipulate his father under these circumstances and escape the jaws of justice by confiding the outhouse episode to his father in the hopes that it might be enough as an irritation to tip the scales in his favor and be allowed to join the service. She believed that her father would, under the circumstances, concur with his son's wishes and sign his papers just to get him out of his hair.

"Are any of you going to the after-game dance tonight?" Alice asked and found that everyone was planning to go except Evelyn, who said she hadn't gotten a date and would feel awkward hanging around without one.

Donna tried to encourage her into going. "Why don't you go anyway?" she questioned. "A few single guys always show up and I'm sure you could find one or two to dance with. Tonight shouldn't be any different, you'll see!"

"Maybe I will, since I live only a couple of blocks from here and I can leave any time," she answered without much enthusiasm.

"Come on and go!" Alice pleaded.

"I've got to go home and get a couple of things done before I go to the dance," Marianne said at half-time, worried about her pony. Worrying was something she had done a lot of since he had pawed the barn. At first she couldn't think of any logical reason Rocky had started acting up until she considered several possibilities and finally concluded that he was acting up because he needed more attention and missed Maude and Buddy, the other two horses that her dad sold awhile back.

"What time do you think you'll show up?" Stella Mae asked.

Marianne's date was due to pick her up around eight for the dance and didn't know if they would stop somewhere first. "Probably around eight thirty," she answered. This was only her second date with Fred Burns and, out of politeness she usually let her dates make most of the decisions unless they conflicted with her values. "See you guys later," she said, stepped down between the spectators in the rows below until she got to the ground, walked around the end of the football field and headed across the soybean stubble towards her house, having in mind to give Rocky as much attention as she could possibly spare in the short interval before her date showed up.

"There's that Navy Seabee guy again that you thought was so cute," Stella Mae whispered to Marianne as they stood along the edge of the gym floor in a small circle of their girlfriends and their dates. "I never suspected he'd come to our school dance!"

"Where?" Marianne whispered.

"There," Stella Mae said, nodding slightly.

Marianne glanced carefully around, not wanting her friends to notice her interest. Without having any success, she poked Stella Mae in the ribs with her thumb and slightly hunched her shoulders to let her friend know that she didn't see him.

Stella Mae darted her eyes and nodded toward the foyer of the field house. Following her cue, Marianne slowly shifted her position to sneak a peek; after locating him, she unthinkingly, she held her gaze for several seconds. It wasn't that unusual for a young, impressionable girl to notice a handsome young man in a dark blue Navy uniform and be mesmerized by him. Even after she turned her attention back to her friends and listened to their conversation, on impulse, she looked over in his direction again and watched the sailor briefly.

Fred noticed Marianne's detachment and then her wondering interest and was caught in an awkward situation. "Why don't we go get some punch," he suggested, and Marianne, her mind elsewhere, didn't immediately respond.

He looked at Stella Mae who gave him a weak smile while Marianne continued to stare across the open space at the sailor standing by a group of people. Stella Mae poked her sharply in the ribs with her elbow to gain her attention and said, "Marianne, Fred's talking to you!"

Deeply immersed in her thoughts, Marianne was slow to respond. "Huh?" she answered after an awkward pause and replied, "I'm sorry!" and blushed.

"If it is okay with you, I'd like to go over and get some punch!" he said irritably and gestured towards the faux café.

To break the obvious tension, Marianne attempted to stay unruffled and decided to step away momentarily. "Yeah, sure, it's okay with me but I need to go powder my nose first and then I'll be right over," she told him, looked at her friend and tilted her head towards the restrooms. "How about you, Stella Mae?"

The two girls walked along silently until they were about halfway to the restroom. "You were sure eyeing that guy in blue!" Stella Mae observed.

Marianne pretended to cringe. "It wasn't that obvious, was it?"

Stella Mae shook her head in disbelief. "Yeah, and I think everyone around us must've noticed!"

"Really!" she replied and made a pained expression.

"Don't worry about it," Stella Mae said, shook her head slightly and grinned. "I know you think he's cute or something. I do too, but what surprises me is seeing how you couldn't keep your eyes off that guy!"

"I don't think I was staring, though!" Marianne said, making a light defense of herself and then nonchalantly looked in the mirror to refresh her lipstick.

An hour later, after jitterbugging with her date, the man in blue stepped into her path so suddenly that she nearly walked right into him. "Sorry," he said and looked her straight in the eyes. "Could I have the next dance?"

Fred started to pull her away.

"I, I'm," she stuttered, caught off guard, unable to come up with a fast answer and stood awkwardly, unable to say yes or no.

Fred and the out-of-town Seabee sized each other up and Fred moved aside.

"I'll take that as a yes!" he said, and before she could react, he took her by the hand and led her back out onto the gym floor just as the band started to play its arrangement of, "You'll Never Know."

Remembering the introduction at the football game she asked, "So you're from Monticello?" in an attempt to sound as if her question was posed out of politeness rather than sound as if she desired to know more about him.

"Uh huh, and I suppose you're from Atwood!" he said jokingly and gave her a faint smile which caused her to giggle lightly. Half way through the dance, she found his confidence and the ease with which he led her across the floor appealing.

"What's your name?" he asked.

"Marianne!"

"Do you have a last name?" he inquired, leading her smoothly.

Marianne shifted her eyes away. "Yes, I do, but I'm not sure you need to know it!" she said coyly.

He studied her face admiringly. "I doubt that it's a well-kept secret around this place. I'm sure if I asked half the people in here they'd know what it is!" he said as a compliment.

"You probably did already," she said teasingly.

"I admit I thought about it earlier when I saw you looking me over. I just never got around to it. Maybe I should go ask the guy you've been hanging around with all evening?"

"He's my date and I don't find that very funny," Marianne said, suddenly pushing away from him in mid-step which nearly caused the two of them to trip over each other's feet.

"Hey, I'm sorry!" he said, catching his balance. "I apologize! I was only kidding!"

"You sure?"

"Yeah, I am!"

She studied his face until she felt he was really being honest. "Well, okay," she said, "my last name is Quinn."

They danced a few more steps. "Aren't you going to ask me what my name is?" he asked.

"I don't need to," she answered. "I already know it from the introduction you were given at the football game; it's Eddie Dotson."

They danced quietly for a few seconds more without speaking. "Have you been in the service very long?" she eventually asked.

"No, I haven't," he answered. "I enlisted over the summer and just now finished boot camp up at the Great Lakes."

"What were you doing before you enlisted?"

"After I graduated from high school last year I've worked with my dad on our farm."

"So, you're home on leave then?"

"Yeah, and I have about a week and a half left," he informed her.

"I suppose you've got lots of plans and things to do before you go back?"

"No! No! Not really! Leave has been a little bit boring actually."

"You mean to tell me that coming to a high school dance instead of hanging out in a bar is making the most out of your time?" she said when the music stopped.

A broad smile slowly crossed his face. "Probably not, but I'm enjoying myself right now!"

"So you'll be shipping out shortly?"

"Nope!"

The band began playing another popular song, "Paper Doll," and before Marianne could break away, Eddie snatched her hand and held it firmly. "One more dance?" he asked and when she didn't resist, he drew her close and slowly guided her out into the middle of the floor.

"I guessed wrong a moment ago. Can I try again?"

"Okay, give it another try!"

"So you won't be going overseas right away," she said.

"I will sometime. First, I've got to go back to the Great Lakes for a few days and wait until I get transferred out east to Camp Endicutt where I'll train for construction techniques," he stated.

"Where's Camp Endicutt?" she asked. It wasn't much of a surprise that she never heard of the camp; many new training facilities had sprung up across the country over the last four or five years.

"Camp Endicutt's a Seabee training camp at Davisville, Rhode Island," he answered.

During the remainder of the dance as they became better acquainted, she found out he was raised on a farm not too dissimilar from hers and instead of it being close to town, his was several miles out in the country east of Monticello.

"One more dance?" he asked after the music stopped.

Marianne took a step back and excused herself. "I can't! I should really get back to my date and my friends."

"How about a date then?" he asked and she quickly accepted a date from him for the following Sunday evening.

CHAPTER FORTY SIX

Saturday, October Twenty Eight, 1944

Marianne didn't come home from her date until well after midnight and even though she was tired, she was having a hard time falling asleep with so many thoughts rushing through her head. It was an hour before her head was heavy on her pillow and she was breathing in a regular soft rhythm with her eyes closed. A little after sunrise, she detected movement in the other end of the house. Something banged lightly in the kitchen and the faint smell of bacon frying reached her nose, something so familiar to her. Knowing it was a cold blustery Saturday and that she had duties waiting, she snuggled under her quilt feeling as if she could lie in bed for hours, secure and in total contentment.

By now, she figured her father was outside working as he had done for the last couple of days, tinkering and getting his corn picker ready for the field again. She appreciated him for starting his day without disturbing anyone until he came back inside and expected everyone to be up and dressed. Her two older brothers had probably been rousted out of bed and were in the kitchen eating before going out to haul wagonloads of eared corn in from the field to store in the crib.

Slowly Marianne extended her left leg out from under the covers, placed her foot on the cool floor and threw the covers off to the aside. She had her day planned as well. Right after breakfast, she would do house chores and then go gather the eggs. Later she'd help her mother with lunch. Maybe by two o'clock in the afternoon, but no later than three, she figured that she should be free, dressed warm and be able to tend to her own interests.

In the kitchen she was surprised to find only her mother. "Morning, Mom," she said sleepily.

"Morning," her mother replied, busily preparing a large hearty breakfast for her husband and two sons who would be working outside in the cold and wind during the blustery day. Bacon sizzled slowly in one skillet, home fries in another. Several fresh biscuits were stacked on a saucer in the middle of the table. Next to it was a lump of home-churned butter in a shallow bowl adjacent to a jar of homemade blackberry jam. Unbroken eggs waited on the counter next to a bowl of pancake batter. Her mother was just about ready to pour the first of the pancake batter into one of the hot empty skillets, leaving only the eggs to fry when everyone was ready.

"Before you set the table, Marianne, would you go check and see if the boys have finished getting dressed?" her mother asked. "I haven't heard any sounds out of their room after I told them to get up and your father's coming in here any minute."

"Marianne," her father said, taking one last sip of coffee, "as soon as you get finished helpin' your mom, I want you to go check the boards on the barn where Rocky pawed and kicked them loose the other day. As I was walkin' up to the house, I noticed him standin' there. Maybe he's startin' to work at them again and you need to see if any are loosened. If they are, you'll need to do somethin' before he gets oats runnin' out again!"

She had no idea how her father intended for her to proceed. "What do I need to do, if they are coming loose?" she asked.

"Maybe you should get one of those one-by-twelve's out of that stack on the south end of the milkin' parlor and nail it horizontally along the bottom sill of the bin on the outside of the barn to reinforce the siding."

"A one-by-twelve! What's that?" she asked, not totally sure of what he meant.

"That's a board one inch thick and twelve inches wide," he explained. "As I said, there's a stack of them along the south end of the milkin' parlor. You'll have to sort through them and find one that's about five or six feet long," he added, giving his instructions clearly. "You understand?"

"Yeah, I think so," she answered and took a moment to visualize what she needed to do. "And after I find the right board, you want me to nail it horizontal along the very bottom edge of the siding above the foundation, don't you?" she asked to make certain to do it right.

"That's right, along the bottom edge of the boards he kicked loose the last time" he answered dryly and paused momentarily. A pained look spread over his face. "You have to understand somethin', Marianne, if he keeps this up and gets into them oats again, I'm afraid he'll get foundered," he informed her. "If that happens, you know what it could mean, don't you?" he asked, not looking up from his plate, answering so unemotionally it was hard for her to read how concerned he was about this issue.

She felt that she couldn't breathe. "Yeah...yes! You're saying we might have to get rid of him," she answered, understanding he had more weighty problems to consider solving at the moment than those of her pestering pony. Her father worked from dawn to dusk nearly every day, sometimes even longer and she realized Rocky's existence was being left totally in her hands. The thought made her very anxious to go out and check on him and the pancake she was eating didn't taste quite as wonderful as it had seconds earlier.

"Let's get going, boys," their father said, pushed back from the table and got up to put on his heavy coat, winter hat and work gloves.

Gloria watched. "Marianne, before you go running off outside, I need you to do a couple of things in here first!"

Marianne felt panicky. "But I need to go check on those boards," she said frantically, hoping her mother would reconsider.

"I'm sure there's no need to rush or your father would have said so," her mother replied and started cleaning away the breakfast table. "It's not going to take us long to finish these chores in here if we hurry."

Instead of pleading further or making herself more frustrated, she rushed around picking up plates and stacking them by the sink. The only way she was going to leave the house without a confrontation and faster was to rush through the chores her mother had in mind. In bed an hour earlier she had estimated she'd be done helping around the house by one or two o'clock, which seemed fine then, but now, after what her father had said, she was on pins and needles, deeply concerned about the oat bin and the loose boards. If she worked hard and diligently, and with a little luck she might still find a little time to ride.

"I'll leave you to finish the kitchen while I go make up the beds and straighten the bedrooms. When you're done with the dishes, make sure to wipe off the top of the table and counter," her mother reminded her. "Oh, and by the way, I have a couple of pounds of hamburger thawed out. I meant to ask the men if they'd want chili or meatloaf for lunch. Which do you think they'd rather have?"

"Meatloaf sounds good to me!" Marianne answered without taking a second to consider. Food was the last thing on her mind at the moment.

Still sitting at the kitchen table, Leon exclaimed exuberantly, "chili!" The thought of having a large bowl of his mother's delicious chili, a pile of buttered soda crackers and a large glass of cold milk sounded a lot better to him.

Her little brother's instant response and his exuberance cheered her up a little. "I think since Leon is one of the guys, he has just made the decision for you, Mom!" Marianne exclaimed and flashed her little brother a wink and a smile.

Gloria was an excellent cook and never resented fixing whatever the family wanted, unless her desires outweighed them. "That's fine," she said. "I think they'd probably like chili better than meatloaf anyway," she agreed because it relieved her from the effort of having side dishes.

"While you're working in the kitchen, you can brown the ground beef in our large cast-iron kettle and turn off the stove. You'll need to get me two quarts of tomatoes juice from the basement, cut up two large onions, and four stalks of celery. Pour the two jars of tomato juice into the kettle, bring it to a boil, turn off the stove and leave the chili for me to finish."

After shaking the rag rugs out of the back door, Marianne spread them back down in the kitchen and looked at the clock. It registered exactly eleven o'clock. "Can I go out to check on the barn siding?" she asked.

Instead of answering her daughter's question, her mother said, "I hope you realize your father's under a lot of strain right now and he doesn't need to be worrying about problems that your blessed pony's causing!"

"I know!" *Please God, let the problems with Rocky go away*! she silently prayed.

While busily cutting up celery, onions and some green peppers for the chili, her mother said, "When you go out," she said, seemingly unaffected by her daughter's distress, "take the table scraps with you and throw them over into the chicken yard."

"Can I go out with you, Sis?" Leon asked.

"Sure you can, if you hurry!"

"Oh, my God," Marianne exclaimed, seeing Rocky standing up close to the barn next to a pile of oats that were steadily trickling out between the boards he had managed to knock loose again with his persistent tapping and pawing. He stood guarding his good fortune, munching and eyeing the other livestock in a threatening posture.

"Oh, noo! Oh, noooo!" Marianne moaned and hurriedly climbed the gate, ran over and tried to coax him away. She found him too stubborn to leave the mounded feast. All of her initial efforts failed. She tried to push him away and he planted his four legs on the ground so firmly that she couldn't even begin to budge him. "Stay here," she told her young brother, "I've got to go get his halter and I'll be right back!"

"Okay," he answered and waited until his sister was out of ear shot. Upset that Rocky was making his sister worry, he said fervently, "You're a bad horse! You really, really are a bad horse!"

After having several tense moments while struggling to force the bit into Rocky's resisting mouth and to get the halter over his head, Marianne was even more upset. Each time she tried slipping the bit into his mouth, he would toss his head and pull away. Finally her persistence finally paid off and she was able to guide him into his stall and close the door. "You've got to stop all this stupid nonsense!" she said.

Leon looked at his sister with a pained expression. Although he was only seven years old, he knew the situation was serious and that Rocky was the cause of it. "What're you gonna do now, Sis?" he asked.

"I've got to stop that grain from running out and pick up all those oats from the ground before Dad comes home and sees what a mess Rocky has made. Also, I've got to fix it so he can't do it again," she explained. What she didn't say was that she worried that her pony had already consumed so many oats that he might become fatally foundered.

Leon didn't know what they needed to do seeing his sister looking so troubled and desperate. "Can I help?"

"Sure, but first I need to get some five gallon buckets and a shovel to clean up that mess with," she told him. She hurriedly grabbed three buckets and a large, grain shovel, knowing they needed to work feverishly to remove the huge pile of oats before her father saw the extent of the damage.

"I can carry a bucket too," Leon suggested.

"Okay," Marianne said, and picked up another empty five-gallon bucket. "Leon, you can carry this bucket and the grain shovel."

Once back outside, Leon immediately started filling his bucket with oats.

"Wait Leon, we need to fix the leak first or more will keep running out," His sister told him. "I need you to run an errand for me instead of doing that!"

"To do what?" he asked.

"Do you know where our dad keeps the claw hammers and his nails in the garage?"

"Uh huh," he answered, because he liked to take a few nails and drive them into scraps of two-by-fours.

"Well then, go get me a claw hammer and a big bunch of nails. One's that are about this long," she said, demonstrating by holding her thumb and index fingers about three inches apart, "and hurry!"

She calculated carefully what she needed to do to avoid wasting time. Luckily, the oats had stopped running out. *Thank God for that,* she thought. It solved her biggest concern for the moment and she rushed to find a board from the pile that her father had described.

The most difficult task was to press each of the three loose, vertical boards tightly against the bottom sill of the barn and nail them in place. It took an hour before they could complete this task that had to be finished before the horizontal, short, two-by-twelves could be nailed across them. "You hold onto that end, Leon, and I'll get a couple of nails started," she said. Ten minutes later, they were finished. Once done, she surveyed their work and strongly believed it would make a stable patch to keep her pony from doing it again.

"Now, we've got to make that pile of oats disappear as fast as we can," she said, because she figured that the time was getting close to twelve when her father would be coming home for lunch.

"Disappear? How are we gonna do that?"

"With this shovel and those buckets, and we've got to hurry!" she fretted.

"Why?" he asked.

"Because Dad'll have a conniption fit if he sees that Rocky has knocked the boards loose again and has been eating oats!" she exclaimed and frantically shoveled oats into the first bucket. "I don't want him to know!"

"Why?" he asked again.

Concentrating hard on her shoveling it took a few seconds to respond? "Why what?" she asked.

As his sister was nearly finished filling up the first bucket, Leon moved another one over to her. "Why would he get mad if Rocky eats oats?" he asked. "You give them to him all the time!"

Under pressure and agitated, Marianne shoveled more oats off the ground while trying not to get angry at herself or upset over her young brother's questions. "Dad's tired and things haven't been going real good around here right now and with Rocky knocking the boards loose…well, I don't need to say anymore," she said. "Let's just leave the subject alone and don't say anything to Dad or our brothers about this, okay!"

Leon looked nervous and a little shaken by her request. "But what if Dad asks?" Leon wanted to know. "Would you lie to him?"

"I'd try not to," she answered, although she knew she would very definitely lie to him. However, she said to Leon, "I hope he doesn't, but if he does, I hope he only asks if I checked the side of the barn like he asked me to and nothing else," she explained, remembering what Ethan had told her about two years ago after being late coming home from Stella Mae's house and never had forgotten.

"And what will you tell him?"

Looking him in the face as she searched for some recognition that he understood her explanation. "I'll say I nailed the board along the edge just like he suggested and not mention that any oats had leaked out. You can see that's not lying. Right, Leon?"

"I think so, but what if Dad asks me what we did?" he continued, seeming to create more logical questions than her frustrated mind could cope with.

"Just tell him you helped me nail the boards up and don't say more, do you understand?" she asked, and then she spoke very slowly to make sure he got the point and plan right. "Say only what I just told you to say and say nothing else, okay?"

Leon shrugged his shoulders and nodded his head. "Okay," he agreed and while he didn't want to tarnish the bond he had with his sister, deep down inside he worried that his father might come straight out and ask if any oats had spilled out onto the ground. "I'll just tell Dad I helped you nail the boards on and nothin' else!" he repeated.

"That's good," she said and picked up two full buckets of oats to carry inside.

"Can I carry a bucket too?" he asked.

"Sure," she answered. "Let's fill one just half-full for you," she said.

Thankfully, and not until after they had finished picking every last grain of oats from the soil and were walking back up to the house, did she see their father's truck slowly make the last turn into the end of their driveway. Relieved and buoyant that they were finished before he returned, as she had prayed they would, she turned to her little brother and asked, "How would you like to go riding with me this afternoon after we eat a big bowl of Mom's chili?"

"Sure," he answered. "I'm hungry! Aren't you?" he asked.

"Sort of," she replied.

Leon's opinions about lying evaporated when he smelled the cornbread and chili, and his thoughts succumbed to his hunger.

Marianne rushed to ready the table while the men washed up. Her mother cut the warm cornbread into big squares, arranged them on a large platter and placed it in the middle of the table next to a plate of hard-to-find, rationed Colby cheese she had cut into thick wedges. Today Gloria didn't need to tell her family the meal was served to get them to sit down; everyone was famished and the appetizing smell of her food worked like magic to get them settled.

Luckily for Marianne her father never mentioned the barn, the oats or her pony. Instead, he talked about his harvest and how his corn crop was turning out to be somewhat better than he'd expected and the observation was putting him in a better mood. "I'm happy for the bushels per acre that I'm gettin'," he stated contentedly. "This may not be a best corn harvest we've ever had, but it's a long way from our worst. Before I got into the field, I estimated that it'd be well below average. All I can do now is pray that bad weather will hold off until I get most of it out of the field," he said and added,

"Maybe it's too much to wish for, but I'd sure like to get it all picked before we get rained on!"

His thoughts encouraged his wife to relate a weather report. "I hate to tell you what I heard on the twelve o'clock news before you came in."

Suddenly his mood changed. "What news was that," he asked.

"The weatherman reported that this section of Illinois could get heavy rain as early as this coming Tuesday evening," Gloria sadly informed him.

Milburn's face sagged and he shrugged his shoulders, having had accepted the ups and downs of a farmer's life several years earlier, but the stress sometimes got to him. He knew the obstacles nature could throw in his path and how God sometimes challenged his faith. "That's not good," he replied, "but if it's only a little shower, it won't make too much difference because the corn is good and dry right now and unless we get a good heavy soakin', I think we'll be okay if the weather clears afterwards," he said and considered some thoughts for a few seconds, and added, "I'd sure hate to see the fields get soaked though and then get cold and cloudy, because then I might need to wait for the ground to freeze to finish my pickin' like I did a couple of years ago. You remember how we had to haul the last load of the corn out of the frozen field in the middle of December?"

As a young man two years younger than Ethan was now, Milburn, on the old homestead he now owned and farmed six miles north of town had spent long days shucking corn by hand, one ear at a time, and tossing them over the high side of a steel wheeled wagon being pulled alongside him by a team of well trained horses that started and stopped by using verbal commands. Some years the corn shucking wouldn't get finished until January or later. One year he recalled working late into the night under a bright harvest moon.

"Maybe we'll only get a little shower," she said encouragingly.

"Well, no matter what happens, I just hope Mother Nature and the Lord will give me enough good, dry weather for a week or so more for me to finish my pickin'. That old two-row corn picker of mine can only pick so fast, you know!"

"Let's hope and pray!" she said.

"By the way, what do you think about me gettin' somebody out here to help haul the wagons out of the field instead me doin' it all by myself?" he asked.

"That's a good idea," she answered. "It might be hard finding someone right now with so much work available!" she added.

"Oh well, you may be right about that," he agreed. "Most men are either in the service or they've already got a decent paying job in Decatur, Champaign or some other place around here!"

"I could help!" she offered.

"You could haul the wagons in out of the fields but you can't do the heavier work that a man can!"

"What about me?" Ethan chimed in.

His father looked across the table at him and studied his face so closely someone would have thought he was trying to read it like a book. "You're in school, you know!"

"I know I am," Ethan answered, "but, you could still let me stay home and help since you really need someone?" Every eye at the table focused on him. They all suspected that he had waited for an excuse to drop out of school and at this moment his father had just presented him with an opportunity to wedge his foot in and keep the door open. Other than Leon's and Jonathan's spoons tinkling lightly against their chili bowls, there would've been a total silence of several seconds.

Ethan's father hadn't failed to notice his son's brooding or ill temper lately. He understood his own and thought the cause of Ethan's ill humor was either school or for not being allowed to enlist in the U. S. Navy. In reality, his son's foul moods were more than that; they originally had started with the outhouse incident and grew from there. Anyway, instead of flatly saying no, which everyone thought his father would do, they watched him hear his son out. "I suppose you have a plan in mind you'd like to share?" his father asked.

"Uh huh," Ethan said, "I do! You know I've been thinking about dropping out of school all fall, and now since you said you need some help with the harvest, why not use me?" he asked.

"And when the crops are all in, then what'll you do?" he asked, drawing Ethan's thoughts out for everyone to hear.

"Maybe I could enlist in the Navy!"

Milburn glanced over at his wife to see her reaction and watched as she dropped her shoulders slightly in resignation. "Why do that?" she asked with a worried look on her face.

"Well," Ethan said, "you remember last summer when Dad told me I could drop out of school if I lost interest in it? Well, I guess I have!" he answered bluntly. "If Dad will let me, I can help him 'til the crops are all in. I'll even do any other jobs around here 'til the end of November or later 'til the corn's all picked...and then, if he'll sign my papers, I'll join the Navy!" he argued. Ethan felt that he had found the perfect opportunity to manipulate his father to act in his favor.

Knowing this moment had been coming for some time, Milburn looked at Ethan for several seconds without saying a word. He had given considerable thought to this issue recently without revealing it to anyone. Weeks ago he realized that there would be a tipping point at some time or place where he wouldn't be able to keep his oldest son from dropping out of school and going into the armed services. Everyone sat and waited for his father to make a response. The extra-long silence made everyone rigid with tension. Ethan fidgeted uneasily in his chair. Finally, his father said, "I suppose I could use you," and surprised the whole family.

Ethan smiled. "So you're really saying I can drop out of school?"

"I am, but only if you agree to some of my conditions!"

"What are they?"

For bait, moments before, Milburn had used Ethan's eagerness to get some favorable concessions from his son. Milburn was shrewd and not easily manipulated and had maneuvered his son to delay his enlistment by at least two more months. "I'll tell you what," his father said. "I've been doin' some checkin' around about your plan to enlist in the Navy. You say you're goin' to agree to some conditions, if I'll let you drop out of school to help me," he said, reeling his son in like a fish on a hook.

"That's great," his son replied. "Yeah, I agree!"

"But," his father continued, "let me tell you right now, up front and good and clear, that I won't sign your papers until December," he stated emphatically, setting a boundary, "or for you to enlist for four years," he added, setting a second one.

"Why?' Ethan asked, looking disappointed.

"Because I need you to help me until all the corn is in," his father answered. "That has to be part of the bargain!"

"Yeah, I said I would," Ethan agreed. "What I'm asking is why you won't let me enlist for four years?"

"Listen to me carefully, Ethan; it's really a very simple matter! If the war happens to end shortly, like I expect it will, then you won't be stuck in no service for four years and you can come back home," he stated and went on to clarify. "Once you enlist, even if it's for two years, you're gonna be in for the duration of the war no matter what. If you can't agree to these terms, you'll have to wait until you're eighteen to join up!"

A broad smile gradually crept across Ethan's face from ear to ear. "Okay!" he said enthusiastically. "How soon do you think we can go to the recruiter's office and check to see what I'll need to do?"

"We might be able to go sometime this week, I suppose, if it rains and keeps us out of the field for a mornin'...then we can take some time off and go over there. Right now, we need to finish lunch and get back to work."

CHAPTER FORTY SEVEN

Sunday, October Twenty Nine, 1944

Even though Marianne already knew it was six o'clock, she sat on the edge of her bed looking reflexively for the umpteenth time at the ticking clock on her dressing table. Eddie told her that he would come to pick her up around seven-thirty and she had been anxious with anticipation all afternoon. Until a few minutes ago, she had been sitting with her father and her two younger brothers in the living room listening to radio shows, a favorite Sunday evening pastime for them since they had gotten electricity. She listened to "The Shadow," at five and then quietly got up and left. Her fellow listeners hardly noticed her leave as the mystery was ending and she left them to relish the programs of "Sherlock Holmes," "The Falcon," and their other favorite programs without her.

She couldn't get over the fact that she had accepted a date with a guy she had only talked to briefly and danced with twice. Her decision troubled her to the point that it caused a too often knot to form in the pit of her stomach. *Maybe it really was only the uniform*, she thought, trying to justify accepting the date, *or, oh my God, maybe I'm being drawn to him like a moth to a flame*. What bothered her most was that she became emotional and couldn't get rid of the warm feelings every time she thought of him. She had always pictured herself being very independent and beyond any romantic attachments. *What am I getting myself into?*

Marianne got a towel and went into the bathroom which years earlier had been installed in the large closet between two front bedrooms. The cozy space gave her privacy like a slim slice of paradise. She wrapped the towel around her head, poured some pink bubble bath into the small tub and ran warm water briskly in it to make a small mountain of aromatic suds. As the water continued filling the tub, she took off her robe and eased in, enjoying the luxuriating scented warmth.

Immersing herself in the steaming water up to her shoulders, she waited for the bubbles to come up under her chin before she turned the water off and leaned her head back against the enameled surface behind her. Closing her eyes, she soaked and let her mind wonder, daydreaming about her life. *Maybe things aren't prefect around here, although I must admit I think I've got it pretty good, considering. I've got lots of good friends, my own bedroom, and my pony!* The thought of her pony gave her a twinge of anxiety. A shiver ran up her spine even though she was warm. A stark image flashed through her mind of the pony standing against the barn in a hail storm working at the boards with his hooves. She still couldn't figure him out and questioned herself for about the thousandth time if in some way it was her fault for the way he had been acting. Guilt gnawed at her again! She pulled her knees up under her chin and shivered as steam rose around her.

I really suspect part of his problem is that he hasn't been getting the attention I used to give him...but I still give enough, don't I? Maybe it's because I got him spoiled and he does love oats. But maybe it's something else that's bothering him, she questioned and mulled the problem over in her mind. *Maybe he'll decide to behave,* she prayed. *Dad's really upset with him...that's for sure, and I know my dad's really upset with me too. The trouble I'm having with Rocky seems to make Mom happy. Leon and I rode him around yesterday.* She reflected back, picturing the three of them riding contentedly together for two hours. *We rode over to the field where Dad and my brothers were picking corn and afterwards over towards Mossberger's woods.* Marianne could still picture her and her little brother together and a little smile lit up her face. *When we came back, I curried Rocky and gave him a couple carrots and three lumps of sugar.*

A broader smile spread across her face as she recalled, *today I went out and rode him bareback for an hour to show him how much I care and love him.*

She soaked another fifteen minutes, picked up a handful of suds in the palm of her hand and blew them into the air. *God, I wish someone'd tell me why he's acting up the way he has been so I can make him stop,* she prayed and pulled the plug out of the bottom of the tub and waited for the water to drain out before rinsing off with fresh water.

At twenty minutes past seven, a nineteen-thirty-seven, black Chevrolet coupe pulled slowly up in front of the house and stopped at the end of the sidewalk.

Gloria was in the kitchen preparing a light supper of pancakes. "Someone just pulled up out in front," she announced. "I hope it's not company because I'm just an awful mess!"

From his position in front of the radio Jonathan looked around at his mother. "It's probably just Marianne's date," he said to her.

Shortly, there was a firm knock on the door. Leon jumped up before anyone else even made the simplest of moves to respond. "I'll get it," he said, able to be freed from the intrigue of the murder mystery as a commercial conveniently interrupted the program. When he opened the door, his eyes grew wide in disbelief on finding a Seabee in his uniform standing in front of him. His sister had told him yesterday that she had a date with a Seabee named Eddie, but Leon didn't expect her date to arrive looking so spiffy. "Hi!" he gulped and looked admiringly at the man standing there.

"Hi," Eddie said. "Is Marianne home?"

"Uh huh," he answered, unable to even blink.

"Would you tell her Eddie's here?"

"Sure," Leon replied and closed the door in Eddie's face with him standing outside and only a few inches away.

Leon took about two steps away before he realized what he had done and sheepishly reopened the door. "Sorry," he apologized. "You wanna come in?"

"Might as well," Eddie answered with an awkward grin.

Leon held the door open until Eddie stepped inside. "Marianne, your date's here," he yelled up into the house and waited. "Marianne," he repeated at the top of his lungs. When he didn't get a reply, he said, "I'll go get her!"

Left standing at the bottom of the steps, Eddie watched his Leon run up the steps of the landing and disappear into the house.

"Marianne, your date's here!" he yelled again and slid to a stop in front of the radio just as the last segment of "The Falcon" was resuming.

"Where is he?" his sister asked and looked around as she came out of her bedroom. "Leon, did he go back outside?"

"Naw, he's down at the bottom of the steps," he answered, sounding perturbed to have his concentration disrupted.

Eddie watched his date walk down the steps toward him with her soft, pink, coat over her arm. She hadn't taken the time to put it on in her rush to leave the house. "I'm sorry no one asked you to come up. Sometimes I just don't understand my brothers!" she added apologetically and started to put on her coat.

"He's just a kid...No offence taken!" Eddie replied and reached out his hands. "Here, let me help you with that."

The black coupe pulled up slowly in front of the house again at one-fifteen in the next morning. Eddie let the car run and turned off the lights, put his arm over Marianne's shoulder, leaned over and gave her a long kiss. "Could I see you again this week sometime?" he whispered in her ear.

"I suppose," she answered, thinking he meant Friday or so.

"How about if I come over and pick you up at school this afternoon?"

"Mmmm...I don't know," she said, feeling crowded. "I've got chores to do and things!"

"We'll just go have a Coke at the drug store and talk for a short time since you need to get home," he said, reading her reluctance.

"But I've..."

"Just a Coke!" he pleaded lightly. It sounded innocent and non-committal.

Marianne looked out the window without answering. It was a simple request. Seconds ticked by until finally she answered, "I might have that much time." At first she had wanted to say no for reasons that were not very clear to her. She seemed unable to think clearly, feeling emotions she had never felt before and having mixed thoughts about her decisions and questioning why she accepted his suggestions.

"Okay, I will, but you've got to promise me that you'll bring me home by four-thirty. I've got a couple of things I have to get done for my mom!" she lied, not wanting to explain herself, or to mention Rocky's behavior that was additionally clouding her thinking.

Eddie gave her another lingering kiss. "I really gotta go," she said two seconds later, pushed away and reached for the door handle. He watched her run all the way up to the house before he flipped on his headlights and drove up the lane to the highway.

CHAPTER FORTY EIGHT

The Next Morning

Marianne slowly opened her dry, scratchy eyes, rose up to a sitting position and studied her room's comforting familiarity. Two things she treasured as constants: her room that she could retreat into and the times she shared with her pony while riding across open fields with the wind in her hair and the sun on her face. Still exhausted from the previous night, she fell back against the bed and pushed her head down into her feather pillow, stared up at the ceiling and reflected in thought on the previous night. Several minutes she lay there dwelling on her life. Eventually she came to the conclusion that it was getting too complicated and she started searching for solutions to get it back in order. Two seconds later, it dawned on her that it was Monday, another school day. She threw the covers back, propelled herself out of bed and got partially dressed.

She tiptoed to the sink, washed her face and quietly went back to her room.

Once she brushed her hair and got fully clothed, she slipped on her carefully-tended saddle shoes and prayed that her parents weren't aware of the late hour she had sneaked quietly through the house in her stocking feet before crawling into bed like a shadow. Trying not to be discovered, she even used the old outhouse instead of the lone indoor bathroom next to her parents' bedroom and chose to wash her face and hands in cold water under the outside faucet by the back door.

Concerned that she might have a confrontation with her parents over her conduct, Marianne contemplated going into the main part of the house with trepidation. She cracked her door slightly, cocked her ear and strained to pick some part of the muffled conversation coming from the kitchen. Even with her best efforts, she wasn't able to detect anything other than her mother's muted voice and the dim sound of the radio. Thinking that her brothers' presence might somehow mask her entry at the table, she was very disappointment that she didn't hear their voices. She crossed her fingers and headed gingerly towards the kitchen.

What she initially saw didn't give her much encouragement. Her parents sat closely adjacent to each other talking in low voices at the back corner of the table, looking like a pair of judges ready to pass an unfavorable sentence on some hardened criminal. Neither of them looked up, which she saw as an ominous sign and made a chill crawl up her spine.

She expected the roof was ready to fall in, even though everything else appeared normal except her parents conversing in hushed tones. Coffee percolated on the stove and the morning news was being broadcast on the radio. Marianne strained to hear what her parents were whispering about to each other; instead, all she could hear was the news coming from the louder radio. The announcer was saying how difficult the conditions were for our troops fighting in a battle raging in the Hurtgen Forest. He stated that the combat taking place among the dense trees, and in the unusual snowy weather and cold conditions was slowing the Americans' advance. After a few seconds, Marianne heard just enough information to add to her anxiety and it weighed on her mind, expecting to have her own battle in only a few seconds.

"I'm goin' to try slowin' down Ethan's enlistment in every way I know how," she heard her father confide and immediately Marianne was relieved that their discussion was about something other than her.

Her father was so focused on what he was telling her mother that he didn't notice Marianne until she pulled out a chair to sit down. "Good morning," he said and ignored her as he continued speaking to his wife in whispers. Her mother leaned close to her father and only acknowledged Marianne with a glance without speaking, careful not to break the concentration she was maintaining with her husband.

Marianne detected high tension. "I hope so," she heard her mother say.

Marianne flashed a sleepy-eyed smile. "Hi," she said quietly and broke up her parents' very private discussion.

"You're sure up early!" her mother replied and watched her yawn.

"Oh...I just couldn't sleep." She answered, surprised neither one of them questioned how late she had gotten home the night before. Maybe they knew and were ignoring the late hour for some unknown reason.

"You do look a little tired," her mother observed. "Are you feeling okay?"

"Uh huh," she answered and rubbed her eyes. "Does anyone else want a piece of toast?" she asked, took two slices of bread, dropped them into the toaster and thought of Eddie. *He said he's going to pick me up after school and that we're going to go have a Coke at the drug store. I hope he doesn't think he can con me into not coming straight home after that!*

Every day that week while on leave, Eddie waited in front of the school patiently for Marianne to walk out through the front doors at the end of her classes. They spent about an hour each day together before she would request to be taken home for various reasons. The conflict of her responsibilities at home played against her desire to stay with him and it set her emotions on edge.

The last Friday night Eddie was on leave they made a date to go to a movie. "You don't mind if we go see 'The Fighting Seabees,' in Decatur, do you? It's supposed to be a very good movie starring John Wayne and Susan Hayward!" he told her. The movie was a highly fictionalized account of events that led to the creation of the Seabees and she could see that Eddie was very anxious to see it and she loved Susan Hayward anyway, feeling she and Susan were a lot alike.

Marianne would rather have gone to see "Since You Went Away," starring Claudette Colbert, Jennifer Jones and Shirley Temple, but she didn't put up an argument.

"That sounds good to me," she said, trying her best to sound interested.

"You're sure you don't mind seeing my movie instead of yours?"

Marianne knew it was a man's movie but consented, "Of course not!"

Eddie bought their tickets. "What would you like from the concession, some popcorn, candy and something to drink?" he asked.

"Popcorn and a Coke sounds good!" she answered.

Eddie handed their tickets over to the uniformed attendant standing in the gap between two red, velvet-covered rope barriers that partially blocked patron's passages into the ornate, cavernous auditorium that had a large chandelier hanging from the high, gilded ceiling.

"Where would you like to sit?" Eddie asked.

"How about the balcony," Marianne suggested.

They climbed the long, curved stairway and located two seats towards the middle front. Presently, the lights dimmed and they sat through the short trailers of upcoming movies. Following the trailers, Universal Pictures presented a movie short titled, "Blast Berlin by Daylight." The narrator of the film followed the crew of the huge B17 flying fortress on its bombing mission. Among the sequences in the film were shots of bomber groups streaking across the daylight sky on their way to attack Berlin. The entire audience sat spellbound as they witnessed long lines of vapor trails, crews on oxygen, flack exploding into grey puffs, and a bomber with one of its engines going dead. Towards the end of the film, bombs fell from various angles out of bomb bays and created fields of mushroom-like puffs on the ground thousands of beet below.

The feature movie was just as Marianne predicted. John Wayne played Wedge Donavan, a Seabee construction boss, who has differences with Dennis O'Keefe (Lieutenant Commander Yarrow) while building airstrips on Pacific islands. Both men have romantic interests in war correspondent Constance Chesley, played by Susan Hayward. Donavan saves an island from falling to the Japanese with his heavy construction equipment and wins the love of Constance Chesley.

A few minutes before mid-night, Marianne and Eddie sat in his car in front of her house. "I only have four more days left of my leave before I have to report back to the Great Lakes," he reminded her. "I'll have to catch the early train back to Chicago on Wednesday morning. Since I don't have much time left at home, my family has plans for me tomorrow and again on Sunday, so I won't be able to see you again until Sunday night…that's if it's alright with you."

"You mean is it alright if you don't see me tomorrow or Sunday or are you asking me for a date on Sunday night?"

"'For a date Sunday night!"

"I'm looking forward to it!" she said and giggled girlishly. She kissed him longingly one last time and hopped out of the car.

"How's seven-thirty sound?" he asked.

"See you then!" she said, and closed the door.

CHAPTER FORTY NINE

Early Saturday Afternoon, November Fourth

Milburn turned left on the last street corner before their destination and said, "I'll drop all of you off by the side door of Sears, and Ethan and I'll go on over to the Navy recruiters office. When we come back, I'll park in that lot over there across the street."

"That's fine," his wife remarked. "I don't suppose you'd have an idea how long it'll be before you get back here, do you?"

"No," he answered. "Why?"

"I'm just trying to determine how much time I'll have to do my shopping!"

"Shop as long as you like. After that heavy rain we had this mornin', I'm in no rush to get back home," he told her and looked out through the windshield at the leaden overcast sky. "The way this weather looks, we may not get back into the field for several days!"

"How does about four-thirty sound for us to meet you?" she asked.

"That's fine!

"Why don't we meet you in the waiting room here at the back door of Sears where you're letting us out?" Gloria said.

"That's fine!" he answered agreeably, pulled over to the curb and put the car in neutral. "Be careful," he cautioned, looking in his rearview mirror. "Don't get out on the left side, there's a lot of traffic!"

With Leon, Jonathan and Marianne tagging along, Gloria walked into Sears through the waiting room past a row of beige, vinyl-padded chairs. "We'll meet your father here at four thirty," she said as a reminder.

"At four thirty?" Jonathan asked, to reconfirm the time and place.

"Yes," his mother answered. "But why are you asking?"

"Because I want to go run around downtown and look at things!" he replied, hoping his mother wouldn't object.

"You can later. Now you need to go with me to look for some pants and a couple of new shirts for you...you're outgrowing the ones you have!"

He hated trailing around after his mother. "Aw shucks," he complained, even though new pants and a couple of shirts sounded good to him. His mother always took her own good sweet time shopping for the best deals. First she would look at everything available in Sears, check the prices of each item and then go around the block to look through all the clothes at Wards to compare prices between the two. Secondly, he knew from experience, that they would eventually come back to Sears and buy the first thing he had tried on. The process bored him to tears. "Doo I haave tooo?" he moaned.

"If you don't care what I pick out, then I reckon not, but you'll have to wear whatever I buy!"

Jonathan's face grew long as he struggled with the decision and reluctantly agreed to follow along. "Okay. I'll go help pick out my clothes."

"I'm going to run over to Kreske's to see if Joanne Smith is working today," Marianne told her mother. "I haven't seen her in a long time and I'd like to see how she's doing!" she added and took a step towards the door.

No one had expressed any logical reason why Joanne had dropped out of school and taken the job at Kreske's Five and Ten lunch counter. Marianne remembered someone saying, which she doubted, that Joanne wasn't getting along with her father. She wasn't very interested in middling to find out, but she wanted to see how Joanne was getting along now that she was living and working in Decatur by herself. Marianne had heard someone in her class had received a penny post card from Joanne with an open invitation for anyone to drop by the lunch counter and say hi.

The two girls had never been close friends. Joanne lived far out in the country and came into town to visit or shop with her parents only on Saturdays. It wasn't until Joanne started attending high school after having spent eight years at a single-room, country school that they became acquainted during their freshmen yea. What Marianne admired most about Joanne was her strong will, would stand up for herself and was independent, much like herself.

Joanne was the oldest of eight children in a family who always seemed to be tottering on the brink of poverty. She was reserved, close to five-feet-nine tall with thick auburn hair, penetrating grey eyes, and long shapely legs which she liked to show off by having them protrude down from under nicely tailored, handmade short skirts.

Marianne walked through the swivel glass doors and moved towards the counter a few feet away and found Joanne busily working, wearing a pink, pleated skirt, a white, short-sleeved blouse and a powder-blue apron; she looked appealing enough be a model in one of Coca Cola posters gracing the wall above the spigots and glasses of the fountain. About half of the sixteen stools at the counter were taken up by people having coffee, dessert or a late lunch. She took a stool close by the door, waited to be noticed and watched her former classmate get a heavy, white porcelain mug and a coffee pot and serve a customer at the far end of the counter.

After Joanne finished serving the customer, she turned around with the intent of putting the coffee pot back in its place, and as she did so, she glanced into the mirror behind the racks of glasses, cups and other serving items and noticed a familiar face. It took only a second for a big smile to light Joanne's face. She stifled a giggle. "Hi," she said at her friend's reflection and turned around. In the excitement of unexpectedly seeing a classmate, she started to giggle again before she caught herself and covered her mouth out of embarrassment. "What're you doing over here?" Joanne beamed.

"My parents came over to Decatur so I decided to ride along with them and say hi if you happened to be working!"

"Golly, Marianne, I'm really glad you did," she said, ignoring a customer.

"Me too!"

"Are you going to be around for a while today?" Joanne asked.

"Till four thirty!"

"Listen!" Joanne replied happily, continuing to ignore the customer, "I didn't take any time off for lunch today, so maybe we can go over to the Do Drop Inn and get a milk shake, some French fries and talk," she said and added carefully, "if you'd like to?"

"That'd be fun!" Marianne answered.

At the far end of the counter, an elderly woman that Joanne was ignoring glared down its length at the two girls. "Miss, do you think you could find time today to get me my check?" she asked gruffly.

"Sorry! I'll be right there!" Joanne apologized and rolled her eyes at Marianne. "Gotta go," she said. "Give me about ten minutes to take care of my last customers and I'll be free. Okay?"

The two girls walked into the classic, white Do Drop Inn restaurant with its black accented trimmings and took a table close to the front window where they could watch people walk by. They each ordered fries, hamburgers and drinks and chatted for some time about nothing in particular until Joanne wanted to know about school, her friends and if anyone had gossiped about her. "I hope people don't think I dropped out because I'm pregnant or something. I didn't believe I needed to explain to anyone why I left home!" she stated. "Once I got settled, I decided I wasn't going to write back home until I proved to myself that I could make it on my own. I admit that I weakened and sent a post card to Wendy Jones without leaving a forwarding address."

"School's still the same old thing," Marianne replied. "No one's been gossiping about you. Of course, I've heard people wonder why you dropped out of school, but I think that's normal.

"No one's accused me of being pregnant?"

"Not that I know of!"

"I miss school and my friends," Joanne admitted, suddenly turning sad.

"Then why did you drop out?" Marianne asked and quickly apologized for the indiscreet question. "Sorry! That's really none of my business!"

"That's okay!" Joanne replied and looked out of the window. She seemed to be trying to form a valid reason for what she hadn't yet totally resolved in her own mind. A moment later, she started to explain. "My father has always worked very hard to keep the whole batch of us kids clothed, safe and warm. I know he's never made much money, no matter how hard he's worked, it was never enough for my mother to put much food on the table. This year I finally concluded, after some careful consideration, that if I left home, my parents would have one less body to clothe and one less mouth to feed," she said with a pained expression. She looked back out of the window and continued, "Our house is also just too small for all ten of us kids. It finally got to the point where I couldn't study very easily and early this fall I guess I kinda lost interest in my lessons and my grades started going down. Everything was becoming a struggle around there so I decided to leave and live on my own. So here I am!"

Marianne remembered that it was Donna who reported seeing the bruises on Joanne's arm and she thought there might be more to the story than what Joanne was sharing with her, however, she wasn't going to pry. *Everyone has secrets that are better to be left hidden under the rug than haul them out and dust them off in public,* she believed.

"So here you are in Decatur!" Marianne said pragmatically.

"Yep!" her friend answered and seemed to brighten up.

"Do you think your decision has helped your family?" Marianne asked.

"Hope so!" Joanne replied with a thin smile of uncertainty.

Deciding to try and find an answer to a question that had been rattling around in her head for some time, Marianne inquired, "So, I suppose you're okay living on your own?"

"It's been much more fun than I thought it'd be. I'll confess that I was scared at first, then I found things to do and I've already made a couple of really nice friends. My mom and I exchange letters or post cards every few days to keep in touch."

"You sound so independent!"

"I still find myself feeling somewhat torn between wanting to live at home and being on my own," she said and Marianne watched as Joanne lost some of the sparkle from her face. "I feel good because in a short time I've discovered I can take care of myself pretty well. Maybe you should try it...and I could sure use a roommate."

Joanne's last couple of comments stirred up all sorts of unsettled thoughts in Marianne's mind, ones that she decided not to divulge to anyone. "Thanks for the offer. If I should ever need a roommate, and if your offer's still open, I might take you up on it!" she answered.

On the far wall was the restaurant's trademark red, neon ringed, white clock with black numbers. Joanne glanced at it. "I've gotta pay my check and run back to work," she announced. "Wouldn't it be fun if we lived together?" Joanne stated enthusiastically and hurriedly scribbled her name and address on the corner of her paper napkin. "Let's write each other," she proposed, tore the addressed corner off and handed it to Marianne.

Marianne read it. "Okay," she said, "I'd like that!"

CHAPTER FIFTY

Sunday, November Fifth

Milburn sat down and unfolded his Sunday newspaper. A good half hour eventually went by before he spoke. With self-assurance he said, "Everything I've been readin' in this here newspaper today is mostly about the presidential election that's comin' up the day after tomorrow and it only confirms what I've been sayin'. Now I'm thoroughly convinced the best thing for this country to do is to vote Roosevelt in for another term of office."

Gloria listened and tidied up her kitchen. She had some of her own thoughts about politics and they didn't vary far from her husband's most of the time. "And why's that?" she asked, believing whatever he was about to say probably wouldn't sway her thinking one way or the other.

"Well, as you know," he said, "I don't think Roosevelt's a perfect president. We've never really had one of them anyway and probably never will, but he got us out of the depression," he answered, "and I think he's been handling this war pretty darn good too. I don't believe anyone could give me a good reasonin' we should change administrations in the middle of all this fightin'," he added and paused to consider what else he might add. "I've said many times that I'm not very satisfied with some of his economic policies. Anyhow, what they're sayin isn't goin' to keep me from votin' for him this time, like I failed to do in the last election. I've been regrettin' that vote ever since!"

"How about Dewey?" she asked. "Didn't you just tell me the other day you liked the fact that he wants a smaller government with a less-regulated economy?"

"Yeah, I know I did and that's one of the things I really like about Dewey. Maybe if it was peacetime I might consider votin' for him, but like I said, I don't think we should be changin' horses in the middle of the stream! We can worry about them other things four years from now."

Marion listened to her parents' conversation for several minutes and then put on a heavy coat, a hat and gloves to go outside into the cold overcast Sunday afternoon. She walked to the barn through a landscape tinged with beige from the effects of the frosty weather over the last week. The muted colors and the coolness of the air reflected her mood. In the woods behind her house most of the leaves had fallen from the trees and were now blown into windrows by a strong wind days earlier. A swath of bean stubble bristled behind the barn while twenty acres of ripe corn between the farmstead and town was still needing to be picked. Off in the distance, wherever she looked, she witnessed much of the same. Late fall days like this were never her favorites. The beginning of November was the end of autumn's brighter seasonal cycle, a period of time that stretched over several weeks after all the leaves had fallen. The barren landscape before the first snows of winter whitened the ground always depressed her. Out of reflex, she tugged one of her knitted gloves a little higher up her wrist.

A ragged flock of redwing blackbirds flew over, migrating south against the leaden sky. For some time she stood and watched the undulating, black cloud fly toward warmer climes, and not until the last straggling bird flew over did she open the small, side door of the barn and enter into its familiar interior. Her pony stood in his stall out of the cold. "Hi Rocky," she said, picked up his bridle off a wooden peg, opened the stall door and stepped inside. He looked around at her. "I see you need to have that hide of yours curried," she told him and extended her hand out with a big carrot in it. "When you've finished chomping on that, I'm going to slip your bridle on and we're going over to the driveway of the barn and work on that hair of yours. After that," she whispered in his ear and tweaked it, "you and I are going to go for a ride just like I promised we would yesterday!"

She tied Rocky to a heavy sill in the driveway of the barn. "You didn't cause any trouble this week, did you?" Marianne asked, patted him on the side of his neck and gave him the second carrot. "I believe you're learning to be a good boy."

Once she was done with his grooming, she steered him away from the barn at a slow walk. They crossed the bean stubble on the way to Mossberger's woods. Marianne planned to ride along the back edge, come out on the other side, and then cross over a flat, wooden bridge used by farmers to move their implements over the dredge ditch. This roundabout way would put her onto the familiar old lane on the west end of the woods; from there she would use the old lane to loop back around towards home.

As she rode west across the soft earth of the bean stubble, patches of bright blue sky started to wink in and out between the clouds of the mostly overcast sky as occasional shafts of the sun's warm rays knifed down through those breaks in the clouds and lifted her spirits.

A short time after skirting the backside of the woods they came to the farmer's bridge. Marianne guided Rocky onto the loose wooden planks and instantly he balked. "That's okay," Marianne said soothingly and nudged him lightly with her heels to cross. "Don't worry," she commented, "the bridge is safe. We're not going to fall through!" Rocky tossed his head and only with Marianne's persistent coaxing, she got Rocky to reluctantly cross to the other side.

Several other times during their ride, he would stop walking whenever they came to any hard-packed-dirt surface and not move only until Marianne patted him on the neck and gave him encouragement. She became troubled by his behavior. "What's wrong?" she asked. "You're not mad at me, are you?" she questioned.

It wasn't until they reached the bean field again that his attitude improved, and then when they angled off across the field towards the barn, a quarter mile away, he suddenly seemed eager to close the distance.

Marianne was deeply troubled by the sudden change in Rocky's behavior. *For the last month he's been nothing but a pest and full of energy and now it seems like he doesn't even want me to ride him. I really thought I had him figured out. I guess I was wrong and I have no idea why in the world he's acting like this?*

CHAPTER FIFTY ONE

Monday, November Sixth

Every day at lunch, Marianne and her friend's chit chatted, and today she felt the subject of boys would gravitate to her involvement with Eddie. She was convinced that one of her close friends would broach the topic and the thought made her nervous because she wasn't sure how she might respond to questions.

She figured that her friends' curiosities had been building because she rarely mentioned Eddie other than after her first date with him when she had acted so giddy. At first she was only affected by his good looks and charm, but now things were considerably changed. She didn't want to share their relationship and she wasn't about to admit to anyone that she was becoming emotionally attached to him. One question would lead to another and then what?

It wasn't a secret that daily after school she would run to his car and the two of them would drive off together. After watching her leave for nearly two weeks, she was sure they were anxious to bombard her with a ton of questions. *My relationship with Eddie is entirely personal and it's absolutely no one else's business,* she thought and was determined to keep it that way.

Sitting in the seats of the nearly empty study hall, eating their lunch and talking, Stella Mae, Donna and Marianne slouched in three of the end seats by the windows and extended their feet into the aisle to face each other.

Donna removed the waxed paper folded around her peanut butter and jelly sandwich. "How's Ethan?" she asked.

"He's fine!" Marianne replied, and bit into a carrot stick.

"Does he know when he'll be leaving for the service yet?" Donna asked.

"He just found out," Marianne answered. "The Navy notified him Friday and it surprises me he didn't tell you."

"But I haven't seen him since last Thursday! So tell me...when he's leaving!" she said sadly, contemplating her life without him around.

"He has to report December the fourth."

"That's less than a month away!" Donna replied.

A few seconds later, just as Marianne feared, the discussion was turned to her. "So, is that cute Seabee of yours coming by after school to pick you up again today?" Stella Mae asked.

"Uh huh," she acknowledged with a sly smile.

Donna tittered, "Stella Mae's right!"

"Right about what?" Marianne asked.

"That he's really good looking and irresistible! I wouldn't mind if I had a guy who looks like that coming to pick me up!" Donna romanticized.

I don't think you're going to be waiting very long, if you're looking for someone in a Navy uniform," Stella Mae quipped, and she and Marianne chuckled. "You were so lucky to have found a guy like that to date for awhile!" Stella Mae added, sounding envious and supportive.

"Yeah, I guess so!" Marianne answered casually, without indicating her deeper feelings, doubts or concerns, after starting to feel tangled up in a big web, and she hoped she wasn't headed for a crisis of her own making.

Eddie had been parked and waiting for fifteen minutes before school was let out. Several students exited the front doors before he saw Marianne, Stella Mae, Donna, Evelyn and two other girls he didn't know emerge talking and laughing while holding their homework in their arms. Seconds later, five more girls flowed through the doors and joined them. The entire group of girls became a huddle of feminine maneuvering and they appeared to be very engrossed in whatever they were talking about. He expected Marianne to look his way, wave or give him some recognition, but she never did. After a few minutes, he became impatient and beeped his horn twice. Several girls looked towards his car briefly and as they turned their heads back around, Marianne stepped out of the group and walked in his direction.

Hours later, feeling overwhelmed and panicky, Marianne said, "no, no," and extricated herself out of Eddie's strong arms. "What time is it, anyway? I've really got to go home!" she rattled. "I told my parents you were picking me up after school and that I might be home a little late but if I'm any later than this, my mother's gonna kill me…she's probably already very upset by now!"

"Can't you stay just a little longer?"

"Please, Eddie, I have really gotta go!" she stated adamantly.

Eddie reached for her. "Please, Eddie, I need to get home!" she repeated and pushed his hand away.

"You know we won't see each other for a long time, don't you?" he said and grabbed her hand in an attempt to pull her towards him. "Today's the seventh and I'm leaving tomorrow."

She shook her head, pulled her hand away and slid over against the passenger's side door. "I'm going to get into trouble if don't take me home now!" she told him forcefully.

Eddie acquired an expression like that of a little boy that just had his bicycle stolen. "Okay," he said, sat up straight, started the car and backed slowly out of the inside driveway of the old dilapidated barn they had been parked in a mile from town. "You'll write to me, won't you?" he asked and turned on his headlights.

"Of course I will! I told you I would when you gave me your address. I will, I promise!" she answered, took her comb out, ran it through her hair a few times and straightened her dress.

It was well after ten o'clock by the time Marianne finally walked into the house. She stopped on the landing and used the mirror above the sink to check on her appearance and decided to run a comb through her hair twice more. She brushed her teeth and ran the comb through her hair once again before becoming satisfied with the image she saw being reflected. When she walked into the living room, all the family, except Ethan, was gathered around the radio. "Hi," she said. "What's everyone listening to?"

"Shhhh," her mother replied. "They're giving the first returns of the presidential election."

"And how's it going?"

"It's still awfully early to tell yet but it looks like Roosevelt's leaning towards another victory."

Even though Marianne didn't harbor an opinion one way or the other, she asked, "That's good, isn't it?"

Her father had cast his vote for the incumbent president. "I think the American people are making the right decision this time!" he said and turned his attention back to the radio.

"I haven't said anything to you about not being of much help around here for the last few days, have I?"

"No," Marianne replied.

"Well, it's got to stop!" her mother reminded her sternly.

"I know and I'm sorry about tonight. We just got talking and I forgot to watch the time," she explained even though she knew her reply wouldn't suffice as an excuse, and she really couldn't offer anything better after shirking her responsibilities over the last few days.

"I've never seen you acting like this before. Jonathan and Leon did your chores and fed your pony!" her mother said. "He is your pony, isn't he?"

"Yes he is!" Marianne answered somberly. She knew that she was wrong and had let all this happen right when Rocky needed her attention. How could she have ignored him? All of this came about because she had become preoccupied and infatuated with a Seabee in blue. Her behavior upset her. The guilt made her stomach hurt and now that Eddie was going away for an undetermined amount of time was upsetting to her also. She had a great yearning to run to her bedroom, bury her head in the pillow and have a long cry, although she knew it wouldn't straighten out the mess she had created.

"From now on I expect you to come home after school and help around here, and then, only after that can you to do whatever you please! You understand?" her mother queried.

Marianne stood, sober faced. "Yes!" she said with conviction.

"Well, I hope so!" her mother replied. "We got a letter from Donald today. If you'd like to read it, it's over there on top of those newspapers!" her mother added and pointed to the dining room table.

Donald's V-mail letter, raggedly torn open, lay near the newspaper's headline. "**Lexington aircraft carrier damaged by kamikazes**," she read and wondered if her cousin might have witnessed the attack. The story about the stricken aircraft carrier strongly beckoned her to read the article. Instead, after reading a few words, she found herself drawn more to his letter. She picked it up and hurried to her room.

Marianne kicked off her shoes, sat down on the edge of the bed and unfolded the V-mail letter. Donald's cursive handwriting was always nearly illegible but seeing that he had acquired the habit of printing, she was happy and started reading.

Wee Vee
October 24, 44

Hi Everyone,

Before I say anything else, I want to tell all of you how much I miss everyone and being home. How I wish this war could have been overwith yesterday. We've been at sea now for what seems like forever.

I've seen lots of action out here around lyete, in the philippines. The Japs weren't and still ain't happy with us for being here and this has caused us to be at our posts most of the time. Any time we're on alert I've had to sleep at my post in the gun turret which I did several nights in a row one time. Finally the Jap fleet tried coming up through the Surigao Strait after dark to attack us. That was on the night of the twenty first of October. We gave them our best and won the battle. I'm sure you heard about it by now!

My battle station is at a five-inch gun mount and as a crew member I get good views of everthing that's going on but the bad thing is I'm topside with only a gun shield for protection. There ain't any places to hide out there. Many times I wished I could've dug a fox hole in the deck. During the battle they're now calling the Battle Of The Surigao Straits we sank several Jap ships before they turned tail and ran. After that big battle I think things should be better for us because I'm sure they will think twice the next time they come looking for trouble!

We call the West Virginia the "Wee Vee". It has a very good reputation. She always puts up a very good fight and maybe that is why she's admiral ruddocks flag ship.

I heard some scuttlebutt aboard yesterday that we'll be going off the line and have our propellers overhauled. They were damaged some time ago when the wee vee ran aground and now she can't go as fast as she should.

Is Ethan still thinking about joining up? I haven't heard anything from him for sometime. Deloris, my fiancee, usually writes me twice a week and Granma and Anna lee write at least once every two weeks. Of course we don't get daily mail delivery as you can imagine.

Tell Uncle Milburn I think I made the right decision by joining the Navy. This war is hell out here, but the food in the Navy is good and I still believe being here is better than being in a foxhole.

Is everyone good?
How's the crops this fall, uncle?
How's your pony, Marianne?

Take care,

Donald

P.S. It's always good to get mail from home!

Please Write!

An hour later Marianne, contemplating, sad and feeling lonely, lay awake in her dark bedroom unable to fall asleep. After she lost all awareness of the hour, she finally closed her eyes and fell into a fitful asleep. It wasn't until daybreak, when the faint sound of a train whistle blowing its mournful voice several times into the crisp morning air as it transited the crossings in Atwood that she woke up and became conscious of the approximate time. The train's familiar low mournful whistle reminded her that Eddie would be catching a train at Monticello for his trip back to Chicago and would be increasing the distance between them.

"Good luck Eddie and take care of yourself," she whispered under her breath and fell back into a restless slumber that she didn't wake from until the sounds in the kitchen echoed and the smells of the family's breakfast finally woke her for the duration of a lonely day.

CHAPTER FIFTY TWO

November Tenth, Celebration of Armistice Day

Armistice Day was the day that had been set aside to celebrate the end of World War I which had taken place exactly at the eleventh hour of the eleventh day of the eleventh month and the date was set aside in honor of those soldiers who had served in the Great War which had taken an incalculable number of lives of the combatants. Even though Armistice Day was celebrated historically on the eleventh of November, this year it was observed on Friday the tenth, a day early.

During the Great War, the German and the allied forces fighting against them had each lost soldiers in the millions. The killing did not end until the very last minute of the eleventh hour and even then a few hundred soldiers managed to kill each other after the last shot was supposed to be fired. Now the world was busily doing the whole thing all over again in another great conflict, on an even wider scale, labeled as the Second World War, and people prayed for it to end.

In this new world war, America had two enemies left: the Germany axis across the Atlantic in Europe and The Japanese Empire that stretched across the pacific. The Italians had given up in nineteen-forty-three which made little difference because much of Italy was still occupied by German forces.

To show local support of our troops, flags were placed along the business section of Main Street in Atwood. At the Mackville cemetery, while The Veterans of Foreign Wars played taps and shot a volley over each of the two graves of World War I veterans, a former member of the conflict placed a flag by each of the headstones. Later that evening, the high school band gave a rousing concert featuring some of the most memorable renditions of World War I favorites.

In the middle of eating supper, Ethan expressed how much he wanted to go hunting at daylight on the opening morning of hunting season. "Warren and I want to hunt for a few hours in the morning," he stated forthrightly in the hopes of getting permission.

"I don't think I can afford for you to take the time off tomorrow," his father replied, holding Ethan to the contract they had made and nixing his wishes. "If the weather stays in our favor, I think we'll be able to finish with the pickin' by Tuesday and no later than Wednesday, and then you can go hunt all you want!"

"You mean on opening day I can't go hunting even for a couple of hours with Warren?" he asked disbelievingly.

"That's right," his father said. He took a long sip from his coffee mug and added, "But, you know, now that I'm thinkin' of it, I wouldn't mind if the two of us got up early tomorrow mornin' and drove up to the north place and walked the dredge ditch in the eighty where we saw all them birds last week while we were pickin' corn. If we get up before daylight and get movin', we'd be able to hunt when the sun comes up and still make it back and be out in the field by eight-thirty or so!"

"Can I ask Warren to come along? Ethan asked.

"Sure! Why not!" his father answered.

"I want to go," Jonathan said.

Leon looked at his father. "And me too!"

CHAPTER FIFTY THREE

Saturday, November Eleventh, 1944

Marianne worked around the house all morning helping to change the beds, clean the toilet and do other jobs required of women of the time. She and her mother hadn't spoken much to each other since the night of the seventh, after Eddie was so late getting her home. Taking the usual directions from her mother without a normal discourse made the task of working together seem more tedious and unpleasant. She felt guilty knowing the tension between them was her fault and that her behavior had driven another nail in the wall that was slowly separating them.

About ten o'clock her mother announced, "I want you to finish running the hand sweeper in the bedrooms while I go into the kitchen and get the pot-roast ready for the oven. Your father said he'd be in a little early for lunch. When you finish sweeping, you can come down to the basement had help me clean those five pheasants the men brought home this morning."

"Dang it," Milburn complained, walking into the kitchen for his lunch, "It's startin' to sleet."

"That doesn't surprise me. It's been looking like rain all morning and getting colder!" his wife answered.

"I know, but dang it to heck, I was hopin' it'd hold off until me and Ethan could finish that forty, and now it just don't look like I'll get it done like I planned!" he said, not only sounding, but looking very disappointed also.

"How much corn's left out there?" his wife asked.

"I'd say about ten or eleven acres, I suppose, but I don't wanna have to wait until the ground freezes up to bring the rest of it out of the field," he stated and pointed at the steaming roast sitting on the counter. "Save it for dinner. Ethan and I'll just grab a quick sandwich and go right back out."

Two hours later, the sporadic light, icy sprinkles gradually turned to a steady drizzle. Milburn shook his head and made one more determined pass through the field before giving up and stopping in the end rows. He turned his tractor off and got down to help Ethan unhook the wagon from his picker and attach it up again, in tandem, behind the empty one his son still had attached to his tractor's hitch. "Ethan, take them two wagons over to your grandma's old place and leave them in the runway of the crib. When you're finished doin' that, put the tractor in the barn over there," his father instructed. "Since it's rainin' I'm goin' to take the picker back up to the house so we can do some maintenance on it," he stated with a heavy taste of disappointment in his voice. With Ethan's help, they had almost finished getting the corn picked as he had planned, but the rest would probably stay in the field until much later and the thought brought his mood down. "Maybe it'll clear up in a couple of days and we'll be able to finish," he said without much conviction. "Dang it! Dang it to hell!" he agonized and got back up on the picker and drove it out of the field.

CHAPTER FIFTY FOUR

Sunday, November Twelve

The weather turned much colder overnight. A Canadian cold front drove strong, north winds and brought plummeting temperatures along with it. The farm family hadn't seen cold and wind like this since the February of the previous year, and after the mostly mild fall, the drop in temperature seemed to sink everybody's mood.

Gloria fixed thick slices of ham, scalloped potatoes, green beans and baked apples for dinner. Her husband, as was his usual custom on Sundays after church and before dinner, took to his easy chair and read the Decatur Herald. "The British think they've finally sunk that big German battleship the Tirpitz in the f j o r d," he said, spelling it out, at Tromso in Norway. "They've been trying to do that since the war started!" he related and went back reading to himself.

Eager to enjoy his last three weeks at home, Ethan, dressed in his warmest clothes, picked up his shotgun and left to go hunting with Warren.

Around two-thirty, Marianne threw on her heaviest coat, pulled a knitted cap down over her ears, slipped on her gloves, got two carrots from the refrigerator and went to the barn to see her pony. Yesterday, when the weather was somewhat more pleasant and she wasn't expecting the sudden change, she had planned a long ride for today. Now, with the cold wind blowing out of the north-west, she decided to just go check on him and keep him company.

Rocky, with his head low, ears down and standing on just three legs looked miserable. "You don't like this cold either, do you?" she asked, gave him a carrot, rubbed his ear and patted his shoulder. As she studied him, she got a terrible feeling that there was something wrong with him but she couldn't quite place it. She patted him again and walked around him twice and noticed that he seemed to favor one of his feet. She tweaked his ear again and gave him another carrot. Hoping that he was just trying to get some sympathy from her, she said, "I'm cold too and I've got some letters to write. I'm going to leave you alone for now. I'll be back out later this evening!"

She walked away thinking that she was by herself only to meet her father coming into the barn through the small side door of the milking parlor. "What're you up to, Dad?" she asked, surprised to see him out around the barn at this time of day on a Sunday.

"I came out to look after my livestock and do a couple of other things," he explained simply. "There's things I need to do before it gets any nastier outside and I'd like to get my chores done a little earlier today!"

She looked puzzled, and asked, "What do you mean?"

"The weather's changing for the worst about every minute!"

"It's not that bad, is it?"

"You must not have looked outside for the last half hour!" he stated. "It's getting' really messy!"

"I did hear the wind pick up," she said and started to walk away. "Do you want me to stay and give you a hand with anything?"

"I don't think so," he replied.

"You know I'd gladly stay!"

"No, that's okay. Go on and run up to the house and get warm," he said.

"Thanks, Dad," she answered. "You know, if you really need me, I'll stay!" she said one last time. Tonight, with no plans and lots of free time, it would be a good time to write Donald a letter and send Joanne a short note. "Mom might want me to help get dinner!"

she added, feeling guilty that she didn't just hang around and keep him company. "Oh, Dad, by the way, I was watching Rocky and I don't think he's feeling well!"

He studied his daughter's face. "What's wrong with him?"

"I don't know but he's just not himself. If you have a minute, could you take a look at him?"

"Of course I will, after I get my chores done!"

"Thanks, again!" she said, walked over and opened the small side door, stepped outside and found a bitterly cold wind laced with rain and icy pellets. Her father had told her rightly. She pulled her hat down over her ears, her coat tighter around her chest and made a dash for the house.

She didn't look up and peer out of the window in her bedroom until she had finished writing two letters. It was then that she noticed that the rain and icy mixture which she had run through to the house a while ago had turned into wind whipped snow.

Jonathan sat close to the speaker of the radio savoring a program. "Jonathan, run out to the barn and tell your dad supper's about ready. For the life of me I don't know what could be holding that man up from getting in here," she added sounding stressed.

"Aw, shucks," her son replied, always the one expected to fetch his father. "Do I really have to? You know Dad, he's always on time for meals!"

"Jonathan, you're like a tick stuck on a dog's back whenever you're around that danged radio. Now, you heard what I just said, didn't you?"

"Uh huh," he mumbled, "but you never let me wait to hear the end of my programs."

"Just hop up from there and shake a leg!" she demanded unsympathetically.

At the dining room table where he could look out of a big picture window, Leon sat drawing with a pencil. Enthralled by the first snowfall of the season, he said, "I'll do it!" and got down off his chair.

Two minutes later, he was dressed for the harsh elements. "Come here," his mother said, straightened his cap, buttoned his coat correctly and tightened his scarf snuggly. "That's better. Now make sure you let your dad know supper's almost done, you understand, and don't you linger!" she demanded pleasantly.

"Jonathan," she said, "since you didn't go outside to get your dad, you can get in here and help set the table!"

"Golly gee," he replied. "I wanted to hear the rest of that program!"

There was a moment of silence with no movement from her son. "Get up off the floor and come here and help out now!" his mother said sharply. "You can hear it just fine from in here!"

Buckwheat pancakes and small slices of leftover ham were on the menu for supper. Milburn pulled up his chair and sat down, "Pass them pancakes and your mother's homemade syrup down this way," he said brusquely. Because of his abruptness, everyone noticed that he didn't appear to be in a very good mood. He took what he wanted and passed the platter on to his wife. "When you've finished messin' with that ham, Jonathan, I hope you can find enough time to hand it on down this way," he grumbled.

Suddenly, the usual light banter at the table stopped and an uneasy air filled the room. Several very audible seconds ticked off on the kitchen clock before Milburn broke the heavy silence.

"How I wish we could've finished getting the corn out of the field yesterday!" he stated, returning to his dialog. It wasn't the first time he had complained about his corn crop and his demeanor illustrated the strain he had been feeling. "With this God-awful snow it might be January before I get back into the damn field," he said sharply. The turn of bad weather was a bitter pill for him to swallow. "I sure would've liked to have finished my pickin' and be puttin' my equipment away for the year before this came along!"

Because of his demeanor, everyone ate in silence without commenting. None of them could remember the last time he had used profane language. "If you don't mind, I'll take a couple more of them pancakes, and pass the syrup down this way again," he said without looking up.

Marianne started to speak and then bit her lip when she sensed that something else other than his crops was troubling her father, although, she had a small inkling, a premonition of sorts of what was transpiring and if it proved to be true, it would be dreadful. Finally she got up the nerve to ask, "Dad, you did check on Rocky didn't you?"

"Ummm, I did," he answered, paused as if he were reluctant to say more and looked squarely at his daughter. "He's foundered!" he announced without any nuances in his expression. His statement took her breath away, as if the air was being sucked out of her lungs. She gasped and swallowed.

"Is there anything we can do for him?" she struggled to ask. She had never seen a foundered horse. From the little she knew, it was a bad thing and was brought about mainly by overeating grain. She felt her face flush. Her pulse rose and her mouth went dry since she knew where and how her pony had gotten the grain.

"I'll need to call the vet tomorrow mornin' sometime and have him come out and take a look to see how bad he is," her father said unemotionally. "Maybe there's something that can be done. It's all a matter of how much he's been affected. Once the vet comes out and takes a look at him we'll know. Don't give him any grain tonight or tomorrow mornin' either!"

Marianne had tears in her eyes. "Carrots are okay, aren't they?"

CHAPTER FIFTY FIVE

Monday, November Thirteenth

In the middle of the afternoon, Milburn came in from outside wearing an expressionless face and with his jaws set. He took his shotgun out of the closet, checked it over carefully and took two birdshot shells out of the box on the high self above.

"What are you going to shoot, Dad?" Leon asked, home from school earlier than his two brothers and sister. This was only one or two times in his memory thathe had ever seen his father pick up either a rifle or his shotgun and rush outside. With their being in the country, albeit very close to town, with big woods behind the house and an even bigger, much thicker one across the field to the west, it was like inviting varmints of all kinds to come around to raid the hen house or create some other mischief that could prove costly for the farm.

His father didn't answer. With determination and a stern look on his face, Milburn headed for the door. Once outside, he broke the breach open and dropped a shell into the chamber of his gun.

"Wait up!" Leon yelled toward the already-closed door. He grabbed his coat without putting it on and rushed into the cold air, afraid that he was going to miss something being killed. "Where you goin' to?" he shouted after his father, who seemed to be very focused on solving some major problem with his firearm. Leon ran across the snow-covered yard while pulling his coat on. His father was standing by the barnyard fence about sixty yards away from the barn. "Stay behind me," he firmly stated and without looking around, swung the shotgun up to his shoulder.

Leon slipped his hands into his bibs to keep them warm and looked to see where his father was aiming, hoping he might see some wild animal bent on mayhem. Instead, he saw that his father's shotgun was aimed toward Rocky standing close to the side of the barn softly kicking at the section of the wall three feet away from where he and his sister had nailed the horizontal boards into place a month or so previously and where another small pile of oats were leaking out onto the ground.

He watched as his father tried to control his anger. "Dang it to hell," his father said and lowered the gun as Rocky continued to paw and bang lightly on the boards. "Dang it to hell," his father repeated, put the gun to his shoulder again, pointed, paused, gave up and lowered the shotgun again. Finally, after a second or two of thought, he threw the safety off, swung it back to his shoulder and pulled the trigger. There was a large report. Rocky flinched, kicked and stopped pawing.

"Maybe that'll teach him a lesson and keep him away from there!" he said gloomily, unaware that this was actually the third time he had gorged on oats. He knew the next action might be a very undesirable one, and he hardened himself to the inevitable. Although frayed with emotion, no one would have seen it on his face or in his demeanor because he was determined to harden himself against the consequences of the evolving situation.

Leon met his sister at the door as she was coming in from school. "Dad shot Rocky!" he announced pointedly without thinking. Marianne gasped, then screamed, "Noooooo! Oh noooo, my dad's killed Rocky?"

Shocked by his sister's response, Leon stepped back; his mouth gapped open and he became speechless momentarily. He saw his mistake and needed a few seconds to gain his composure enough to answer. "No, no," he stuttered, "Dad didn't kill him; he just stung him with some birdshot for knocking the boards loose again! Rocky's been put in the barn!"

Boiling in anger, red faced and becoming sick to her stomach, Marianne took a deep breath. "How bad is he hurt?" she mumbled, feeling weak in the knees.

"I, I don't th, think he's hurt very m, much!" he sputtered.

Quickly gaining her self-control, she turned around, flew back out the door and ran to the barn. A few minutes later, she tore back into the house and started going through the medicine cabinet, grabbing a pair of tweezers, a bottle of peroxide, some medicinal salve and a handful of cotton swabs.

"What are you doing, Sis?" Leon asked.

"I'm going out to the barn to treat Rocky. Pellets are stuck in his skin and I need to take them out so they don't get infected!" she explained and turned to leave again.

"Wait up! I'm coming with you," he said and put on his coat, hat and gloves. Before he could finish, his sister was halfway to the barn.

Marianne gently pulled the hair away from each of the red, scattered welts in Rocky's skin and plucked out small pellets from here and there. Most of them were just barely stuck in his skin and it made the process easy and fast. Rocky hardly flinched as she worked. Each pellet she tweezed away and dropped into her tin can made a faint plinking sound. Her little brother worked along with her, swabbing each small wound with peroxide and then putting salve on it after she finished.

Marianne was mad at herself for letting all this happen. *I know I could've made things different,* she thought blaming herself. She also faulted her pony for acting the way he had been, but most of all, with each pellet she plucked and dropped into the tin can, her anger raged higher at her father for what he had done. *This wasn't necessary,* crossed her mind more than once as she worked and thought that she might never speak to her father again.

"So, Dad, did you call the veterinarian?" Marianne cautiously asked her father from the other end of the supper table. She was without any inkling of how conflicted her father was over Rocky's condition. If someone were to ask her what her father felt, she wouldn't have been able to come very close. He was the one that had bought the pony at a time when he couldn't easily afford it and had done so against the advice of his wife. The pony had been for his children to love and to tend to in the hopes it would keep them occupied enough to prevent them from wandering. His first surprise had been that Marianne was the only one to take much interest in the pony and the second surprise was that Rocky didn't have the affect he had desired of keeping them grounded, close to the farm and their heads on straight. In his mind, the joy and contentment his daughter had found in the animal had more than made up for the miscalculations until now.

"I will tomorrow," he answered.

"Was Rocky hurt very much?" Jonathan asked, having lost almost all interest in him.

Marianne gave him a cold stare. "Go see for yourself!" she answered. Tears welled up in her eyes and she pushed her plate away and ran to her room.

CHAPTER FIFTY SIX

Wednesday, November Fifteenth

The veterinarian went into Rocky's stall, talked gently to him and patted him on the neck to keep him calm. He ran his hand down his side, carefully lifted his right leg and checked his hoof and joints. When he was finished, he put the leg down and moved over to the pony's left leg before checking his back legs. Minutes later, finished with the examination and ready to give his prognosis, he commented, "I don't think there's much we can do for this pony! I'm sure you're already aware that he's foundered. He's sore and nearly lame and he'll only get worse!"

Milburn had been about ninety-nine percent positive he knew what the veterinarian was going to say before he even asked. "You think there's any hope for him?" He didn't have to wait long for the final analysis.

"You might give him some ease from his discomfort for a couple of days, if you add a thick layer of straw down in his stall to keep him off the concrete. It would also help if you could get him to lie down part of the time; however, I don't see how he can be cured from the shape he's in. My professional opinion is that it would be hopeless to try; he's only going to get worse and I feel that he should be put down!"

Milburn needed only a few seconds to make the inevitable decision after hearing the Vet's prognoses. The night before, he had decided to get rid of the pony, if that was what the Vet suggested. He was in no mood to put Rocky down himself and he surely didn't want his daughter to witness the act and to watch his carcass being hauled away on the meat wagon unceremoniously. He saw no possible way to avoid the unpleasant consequences of his decision and furthermore, he couldn't foresee any events that were beyond what he had anticipated.

Marianne ran straight to the barn after school and saw her pony standing on a thick layer of new bedding. The sight gave her hope.

CHAPTER FIFTY SEVEN

Friday, November Seventeenth

Milburn picked Leon up from school and brought him home for lunch and he came running excitedly into the kitchen. "Mom, Mom, there's a truck coming down the lane and it's pulling a horse trailer," he exclaimed.

"I guess that'd be Jay Cartwright," she replied. "Your father wasn't expecting him to be out here until early this afternoon, not now!"

"He's bringing another pony?"

"No, no, he's not, he's picking up Rocky, Marianne's pony," she answered anxiously.

Leon couldn't believe what his mother said. "He's coming to get Rocky?"

"That's right!"

"Why?"

"You'll have to ask your father that question," she said, recalling that she hadn't wanted her husband to buy the pony and now she wanted to avoid being entwined in the web of emotional turmoil caused by the pony. It still made her a little angry at times to think about her husband's purchase and she still agonized over the act as a betrayal, and deep down, she hadn't totally forgiven him. And now that the consequence of the purchase was playing out in such a negative manner, she felt it was better to avoid making any comments and to stay away from the crisis that was unfolding. She wasn't one to openly hold a grudge or say, "I told you so," but it was registered in her mind now.

Leon watched the truck pull slowly on past the house, headed for the barn.

"I'm gonna go out there!" he exclaimed and ran to get his coat, hat and gloves.

"Stay right there," his mother said. "Your Dad brought you home from school for lunch and you need to eat!"

"But I want to go watch!"

"It doesn't matter; you're not going out there until you eat a sandwich and have some soup," she repeated more firmly.

"Gosh darn it," he replied, pouted and plopped down on a chair.

"Just stay there and I'll give you a bowl of this hot chicken soup and some soda crackers," she said to distract him. "It'll be good for that cold you're getting!"

"What about Dad?"

"Your father can eat a little later!"

"Can I have a glass of milk too?" he asked.

When Marianne came home, she hustled straight to the barn to see how her four-footed friend was doing and found his stall empty and the inside door standing open. She ran outside and looked over the fence into the barnyard. Not locating him anywhere, the realization of his absence quickly hit her. "Where's Rocky," she screamed. "Where's my pony?" she screamed again, even louder and ran toward the house. "Oh, no, Oh, no," she muttered over and over. She felt that she'd been blindsided. "At least I should've been given time to say some goodbyes to my pony!"

Gloria confirmed her daughter's worst fear.

"Rocky's gone? Dad got rid of him?" she wailed to her mother.

"Jay Cartwright came and picked him up just around lunch time," her mother answered without turning around to face her.

"It's not right what you've done!" she said.

"I had nothing to do with it!" her mother corrected.

"You could've stopped him, even if you wanted to!"

"All I know is your pony was foundered and the vet..." her mother said and stopped before she completed the sentence to tell her daughter that they were going to put him down.

"Dad didn't have to sell him and I'll never forgive him for this!" she said and ran to her room crying.

Over the next few days, whenever Marianne was around, the house was filled with troubled tension. She did her chores in silence, refused to talk to anyone and only left her room to eat, go to school or go out to see her friends.

CHAPTER FIFTY EIGHT

November Twenty Second, Leaving Home

On a cold brisk Wednesday, the day before Thanksgiving, Marianne, Stella Mae and Donna were lucky enough to catch a ride with one of the senior boys to the drug store after school, where, without her knowledge, two of her friends hoped to console her over the loss of her pony. They planned to draw Marianne out of her depression after observing the mood swings and sadness they witnessed after Rocky had been sold the previous Friday.

They found the drugstore nearly empty. A woman and a man sat at the counter talking and having coffee and to their surprise, they found Joanne sitting by herself all alone in the row of empty booths. "Hi," she said happily, seeing three of her former classmates walking towards her.

Marianne couldn't believe her eyes. "Hi!" she answered and flashed a warm smile, the first one in days.

"Wow," Stella Mae exclaimed a bit on the dramatic side. "It's sure good to see you Joanne!" The three girls, curious and anxious to hear about her new life and adventures in the big city, stood around the outside edge of the booth.

"Are you staying long?" Donna asked.

"Only for a couple of days," Joanne replied, jovially, "and then it's back to the wonderful world of work," she added. "Why don't you guys join me?" she said and gestured to the empty space in the booth around her. "We can talk until my dad comes by to pick me up, that's if he hasn't forgotten!"

Marianne slid in next to her and the other girls took the seat across the booth from them.

"You're home for Thanksgiving?" Donna asked.

"Uh huh! I'm a little homesick and want to see my family. This is the first time I've been able to get away from work and come home since I left," she answered. "Maybe I should also mention that I'm hungry for a little of my mom's home cooked turkey and stuffing also!"

"Why haven't you ever come home for a weekend?" Stella Mae asked. "Decatur isn't very far away!"

"Because I've been trying to put my little apartment together on my free time and get settled in," she explained. "This is really the first time since I started working that I've been able to have a couple of extra days off, and that's only because I was lucky enough to rearrange my work schedule with another girl. She usually works Saturdays, so we traded places. I'll have to catch the train back Saturday morning to work a couple of her shifts," she explained.

"You wouldn't happen to want some company going back, would you?" Marianne asked out of the blue, acting on impulse. Recently, she had been considering to leave home. The same unpleasant homesickness and possibly the same range of emotions Joanne had expressed faced her and it had given her pause. Her question to Joanne finally was setting a new course in life for her.

All three girls looked quizzically at her.

"You didn't tell me you were going to Decatur for a day!" Stella Mae replied.

"I plan to make it longer than that!" Marianne corrected. She hadn't even slightly hinted to anyone that she was thinking of dropping out of school and leaving home, although the idea had been stewing in her thoughts ever since her father sold Rocky so unexpectedly, sending him away without consulting her or having an opportunity to offer him any goodbyes. She felt bitter and deceived and had finally decided she couldn't live on the farm.

Stella Mae studied Marianne's bearing for a moment. "You mean for a couple of days?"

"Hopefully not! Much longer than that!"

"You mean you're going to stay over there for a long time?" Donna asked, having difficulty accepting what her friend was indicating.

"Yes, for a long time," she answered. "I'm leaving home!"

The other girls were stunned by what they were hearing, but Joanne grabbed Marianne's wrist excitedly and squeezed it. "Why don't you become my roommate like I offered?"

"You serious?" Marianne asked.

"Yeah, of course I am. Didn't I sound serious when we talked in Decatur?"

"I thought you might be. I wasn't sure. Anyway, things were different for me then than they are now!"

"You and I are going to have so much fun together!" Joanne exclaimed.

Marianne hesitated. "I think I need to warn you, if I do, I'm not going to have much money to help with the rent until I find a job!"

"We can work out those details later," Joanne replied. "Finding a job might not be much of a problem for you either because Kreske's just happens to be looking for someone to fill a vacancy at the lunch counter and I can't imagine you not getting it since you already have some experience."

Marianne's anxiety was eased, finding a place to live and with the possibility of getting a job. She couldn't believe her good luck.

Joanne's father came in and stopped a few feet away at the end of the counter. "Hi, Sweets," he said to Joanne. "Hi, Dad," she answered. "Hi girls," he said and asked the waitress for three packs of Lucky Strikes. "Your mother was about ready to start supper when I left so I suppose we should get cranking towards home, if we're planning on eating a hot meal tonight."

Marianne slipped out of the booth to let Joanne out. "Would you like a ride home?" Joanne asked as she brushed past. "We're going right past your house."

Later, at the dinner table, it didn't seem to be a great surprise to her parents and they didn't show a big reaction when Marianne explained her plans in detail. If only her father had been more forthcoming about his decisions in dealing with Rocky maybe things would have been different. He hadn't given her any excuses for his actions or offered an apology and she couldn't get past her emotions long enough to logically consider her father's rationality.

In reality, her father didn't need to make any excuses for putting down an animal that was in pain and saw no hope of a cure. It was the right thing to do. Furthermore, if he had told her that her pony was being sold, she would have pleaded and begged and the inevitable would still have happened. Her pleading would have made the issue even more heart wrenching for both of them. Marianne realized her father accepted that animals came and went on the farm as a natural process and he accepted that fact stoically. What she didn't realize was how this affair had pained him so deeply. In time she would accept his position; the subject would never be mentioned again, but now it was the catalyst for her leaving. She felt that she had to get away because of the injustices her young mind perceived.

"I can give you a little money to help you out!" he told her, "and don't forget where home is!" Many farmers, including her father, were land rich and cash poor.

Thanksgiving was a somber one.

Early Friday morning Marianne's suitcase was sitting by inside the back door. "Dad," she yelled up the steps, "We need to go or I'm going to miss my train!"

Leon stood and watched his sister carry her large suitcase out of the house and down the sidewalk towards the waiting car. Suddenly he swung the door open and yelled, "Wait up, I wanna come along too!"

Milburn parked the car up against the curb by the train depot. "I'll get your suitcase," he said, turned off the ignition as his daughter started to open her door. "Wait a minute, there's no need to hurry" he said, and pulled out his billfold, removed five crisp twenty-dollar bills and handed them to her. They looked at each other only as a daughter and father parting company could. "Take care of yourself and remember you're always on my mind!" he said, and heard his daughter say somberly, "Thanks, Dad!"

Standing inside the depot, Donna, Evelyn, and Stella Mae waited to see their friend while talking to Joanne.

Marianne, her father and Leon walked up onto the depot's platform. Off in the distance to the east a train whistle blew at some crossing. "I'll go get my ticket," Marianne said to her father and was happy to find that three of her closest friends had come to see her off and to find Joanne waiting. A minute later, the five girls came outside as the train's whistle blew again, this time much closer.

Leon stood by the station's large, utility wagon beside his father while the black, steam locomotive with several passenger cars in tow pulled up to the depot, clattered, screeched, stopped and released a big puff of white steam that enveloped Marianne and her four friends standing close to the tracks.

Already standing between two of the middle cars, the train's conductor swung off the train and placed a wide stool under the steps for the convenience of any passengers that would be either disembarking or boarding. A few seconds later, an Army private on crutches hobbled out, steadied himself, and carefully lowered himself off the train and down onto the platform.

Marianne started to board the train but hesitated, stepped back and waited until Joanne boarded first. She picked up her suitcase, handed it up to her friend, turned, smiled and waved a weak goodbye to her sad looking little brother and her stoic appearing father. They watched her grab the long, iron perpendicular handhold beside the iron steps, pause momentarily to get her balance and then follow Joanne into the passenger car. The conductor looked up and down the station's platform one last time to make sure everyone was out of the way and in a practiced dramatic fashion bellowed, "All aboard that's coming aboard." Once he determined that every passengers was aboard, he gave the engineer the all clear signal and shouted, "Next stop, Decatur!"

ABOUT THE AUTHOR

Larry D. Quick is an accomplished artist with a master's degree followed by post-graduate studies. Now retired from a career as a visual arts teacher, he enjoys writing poems and short stories; this is his first published novel. He lives in northern Illinois.